THE PUKUR

D.K. Powell

THE PUKUR

Addison & Highsmith

Addison & Highsmith Publishers

Las Vegas ◊ Chicago ◊ Palm Beach

Published in the United States of America by
Histria Books, a division of Histria LLC
7181 N. Hualapai Way, Ste. 130-86
Las Vegas, NV 89166 USA
HistriaBooks.com

Addison & Highsmith is an imprint of Histria Books. Titles published under the imprints of Histria Books are distributed worldwide.

Library of Congress Control Number: 2022938743

ISBN 978-1-59211-144-2 (hardcover)
ISBN 978-1-59211-223-4 (eBook)

TABLE OF CONTENTS

DEDICATION

To all those who lived, worked, and shared their lives with me at LAMB, Bangladesh from 2006 to 2014. There's not a day that goes by I don't think of you and miss you. You brought me the greatest moments of joy and I will always be thankful.

The traveller must knock at every foreign door to reach their own,

and meander through all the outer worlds,

to reach, at the end, their own innermost temple.

— *Gitanjali*, Rabindranath Tagore

CHAPTER ONE – A BEAUTIFUL MORNING

She quietly watches both of them as they die.

The girl doesn't get up from her seat. She doesn't say anything. She just watches. She doesn't lift a hand to do anything. The twelve-year-old doesn't even shed a tear.

She just gazes at them.

The man looks quite peaceful, really, almost sleeping like a baby, as they say. Only the sharp rasping coming from deep in his chest gives any indication something is amiss. He is, at least, breathing. There's that.

A humming rises.

The woman sits further away behind her, and the girl can't see if she is breathing or not. She notices red drops dripping from the woman's face and the growing dark pool spreading out from just below her belly. It goes through her mind that the burgundy stain clashes badly with the bold yellow fabric.

That beautiful dress, she thinks, *I've always loved it. She's so pretty when she wears it. It'll be ruined now.*

The sound of rasping stops, and the girl turns her head slowly to look at the man again. Movement from his chest has stopped; the colour has completely drained from his face.

No blood…

Sophie glances down at her own legs, realising her own unique stain spreading across them for the first time.

Oh…look at that…

She glances up at the man again and then closes her eyes. She doesn't want to look at him again. Not like this. To stop herself from thinking about him, she instead allows the warm sunlight coming through the window to shine down on her face. For the first time, she realises her cheeks are cold. The rays feel nice, but they aren't enough to take away the numbness of the freezing air.

The humming rises. Louder and louder, needles pressing on the ears.

She turns her head again to the woman. It's getting much harder to think now. The pain. *Sleep*, she thinks and closes her eyes. This little girl speaks just three words the entire time she is awake; softly, barely a whisper, and just before the humming takes over completely.

"I love you," she says simply, without emotion. It's a fact.

Such noise, such pain, needles piercing the brain.

Sophie rests her head as best she can and gives in to sleep. Something deep inside tells her not to do this, but she's tired. So very tired.

It's two hours before the police find the car, lying in a ditch, half covered in pure, untainted white snow, freshly lain.

It is a beautiful morning.

CHAPTER TWO – THE ACCIDENT

It really had been a beautiful, crisp winter morning when the Shepherd family decided to go for a picnic.

It had seemed like a great idea. Pack up a big hamper of delicious food, throw it in the back of the car, go for a drive to some deserted park and have a summer picnic in the middle of winter. After all, no one else would be out on the roads today, not with all the snow that fell that week. It was ludicrous but also thoroughly British.

It had been Stephen Shepherd's idea. He was always a crazy fool and as headstrong as they come. Elizabeth Shepherd was more sensible and worried about safety on the road, but Stephen wouldn't hear any of it. In the end, it was Sophie's pleading insistence that made her mother give in and allow it to happen. Who can resist their own daughter, after all? Secretly though, her mother was pleased and thought the whole idea a lovely surprise to take advantage of the bright sunshine that, for once, was shining down on the world. The weather forecast said it would be 'changeable' today, but it had been shining *all* morning; so clearly – like usual – the BBC weathergirl had it wrong again. That was also thoroughly British.

But her father was wrong, as it turned out. There *was* someone else on the road that day. A youth, newly passed his driving test, was 'giving the car a spin,' and he was the *best* driver in the world with *the greatest skills* and had the meanest sports car *ever* – so he believed. The reality was something else.

To be fair, that particular stretch of country road was known for being treacherous. Although only a couple of people had died along it over the decades, this was simply because hardly anyone ever used it. The road was full of twists and turns to avoid ditches and trees so that tractors from the local farms could still use it. It had been turned from a lane used by farmers and village locals into a 'solid modern and reliable road' by the local council who hoped to see it become the main route for distant villages. The scheme didn't work. There were many skid marks left by cars going too fast on the 1000-yard stretch of road where it left the main junction until it reached the first village hamlet. As the villagers often complained, the youth today were always in a hurry and usually overestimated their ability to handle corners; or underestimated the angle of the bends. Just as well not too many youths lived round here.

But even with that allowed, if this kid knew the road at all, he should have known better. Instead, it was a classic case of driving too fast, and when the other car came around the bend that day, the youth's car was already zigzagging across both sides of the road, having lost control seconds earlier.

Her father did his best to slow down and get out of the way, but it all happened too fast. The car careered into the driver's side, sending both cars off in opposite directions. The youth's vehicle went head-on through the hedge and into a huge oak tree which stopped the car swiftly and with great efficiency. The youth, of course, was too good a driver to need a seatbelt. He was killed instantly when he went through the windscreen and before he hit the tree.

The other car had no hedge to slow it down. Instead, it went down and was stopped by the solid earth at the bottom of the ditch even more effectively than the oak tree had stopped the youth's car. The car flipped over and would have ended upside down had it not struck a glancing blow on a large tree stump that caused it to twist. It ended more or less the right way up, albeit now facing the opposite way from whence it came.

Unlike the youth, everyone in this car had been wearing seatbelts which is why the girl wasn't killed by the fall. But it was an old model car, and there was no airbag in the steering wheel. When the father's chest hit it with full force, the metal had no give and crushed his chest, causing major internal bleeding. The mother, who had been sitting in the back, had cracked her head on the window and the low roof above several times after the other car hit her side. That first blow had knocked her out. She never woke up.

Because no one knew either driver was out and about that morning, no one called the police. It was, after all, wintertime, and the weathergirl had assured everyone it was changeable weather and people should avoid going out if they could or risk getting caught in a snowstorm.

The snow did come about half an hour after the crash and fell for about an hour after that, laying thickly, covering both cars before it stopped. Two vehicles went past that stretch of road at separate times, but the drivers didn't see either car. They had been too busy concentrating on keeping to the bendy road, now half-hidden by the snow, and avoid hitting the hidden kerb.

The third driver *had* noticed the youth's car and called the police immediately on his phone while he drove but didn't stop to check. It was cold and the clouds were turning a dark grey. More snow was coming and they had to get home. Perhaps they would have stayed had they seen the youth sprawled on the bonnet, but his body had been completely covered with snow and it just looked like a badly smashed and abandoned car. The driver only made the call to make absolutely sure and to do his duty.

Even when the police arrived and found the youth's body, they did not initially see the Shepherd's car, further up and low down in the ditch. The snow had hidden the skid marks of both vehicles, and the ditch was particularly deep. Several minutes passed, and just as the paramedic crew was in the last stages of getting the youth's body into the ambulance, one copper noticed what looked possibly like a car half-buried further down in the ditch on the opposite side. A great cry went up, back-up was called for, and two policemen raced down the steep and treacherous slope as fast as possible.

Initially, everyone thought that all three members of the Shepherd family inside were dead, but the lead paramedic felt the slightest hint of a pulse in the young girl's neck. She was a mess, no doubt of that, but she was alive.

Just.

CHAPTER THREE – THE SILENT BEAUTY

Even when she is doing the housework, she is a real beauty. She has never had to work at this; her entire appearance is as delightful as it is innocent. Perhaps this is what makes her so astonishing and makes men stare so; and perhaps that's what makes the other maids jealous of her too.

She stands in the kitchen, brushing away, occasionally throwing back her *orna*, which keeps slipping from her shoulders as she bends to swat at the occasional cockroach with the broom. Her bare feet pad softly on the concrete floor, which feels particularly cold this morning. Her soft, light-brown skin contrasts with the harsh white of the floor. It is not an unattractive combination.

If anyone had been in the house at that point, they wouldn't even have known she was there. She is as silent as the dawn rays and no less marvellous to look upon. But no one is in the house. No one is ever here except for the owner. No one would dare – apart from this young girl, and one other too, but that particular fearsome creature has no desire to enter here anyway.

The beauty finishes her sweeping, lays down her broom under the cooking stove, turns to the work surface, also made of concrete, and picks up the stacked tins of the *tiffin* box by the metal handle. Leaving the kitchen, she walks through the hallway – always with no trace of a sound no matter how easy it is for even the slightest noise to create an echo here – and enters the front room. Crossing the house's largest room, she nimbly wraps one length of her scarf loosely around her head with her free hand.

Reaching the other end, she takes her *chador* from the hanging rack next to the door and notices a small trail of ants marching in single file down the faded white concrete walls. She makes a note of their general direction for dealing with later, then, with the blanket wrapped tightly around her neck and shoulders, she opens the door and steps out onto the small veranda.

Her sandals are damp from the early morning fog which permeates everything before evaporating in the bright sun. Gripping the *tiffin* in her left hand, she leaves the veranda and heads out towards the centre of the village.

The sun is sharp and bright, and she feels the rays prickle her cold cheeks. It is a wonderful sensation, and she welcomes this companion, aware that it will be a friend no more but 'the enemy' in a few months' time. It is a good metaphor for so much here. That which feeds you and brings you life will also kill you and make you suffer. For now, though, this sun is longed for and blesses all.

Walking past trees and bushes, she keeps her head down as befits her status. There are no men around at this moment, so it doesn't matter. Nevertheless, out of habit, a natural urge for protection maybe, she tugs on her scarf under the *chador* to pull it a little tighter around her head. The winter fog may have lifted, but there is still a chill in the air. She knows that he likes it best at this time of the day.

Soon she arrives at the fencing. The wire mesh almost reaches the height of her head, but she can see through it anyway and indeed has done so while approaching to check where he has placed himself today. She spies him over in the far corner and turns to the left to walk over to the gate. She tramples dark and dry leaves as she goes, yet even these make barely a sound under her feet. This woman all but floats.

Passing through the gate, she pads slowly and gracefully along the path made up largely of disused bricks sunk into the silty mud. She doesn't walk too close to the edge where the steep drop of the bank leads to the water. The path is slippery at the best of times, and childhood experiences taught her long ago how easy it is to end up swimming for your life.

So, she keeps to the centre, stopping only for the occasional snake to scurry from some hiding place and slither quickly down the bank before disappearing into the green waters. She is not fearful of these creatures, although childhood experiences have also taught her that it hurts when they bite. She remembers once picking up what she thought was a fish from a pool just like this one and discovered to her dismay and pain that it was a water snake instead. She knows that they startle easily, but they will return the favour if you leave them alone.

Finally, she reaches the place where he sits, rod in hand, motionless and wearing his perpetual look of frowning at something displeasing him. A fly bothers around his grey-white beard, but he either doesn't notice it or has no desire to swat it away. His entire concentration is on the patch of water where the line from his rod has landed. It is as still as he is.

She says nothing as she reaches his bench and bends to place the *tiffin* quietly by his side. Rising, she looks at his face – or at least as much as she can see under his cream Panama hat, and wonders if he has more creases around his eyes now than he did when she first met him. His skin is barely white any longer. Has he been in this land so long that the sun has finally baked him brown?

For his part, he doesn't notice her at all or at least doesn't acknowledge her if he does. He does not look at her. He does not see how astonishingly beautiful her eyes are. He does not admire her almost perfect form. He does not consider how she makes even the working clothes of a maid seem more captivating than a princess in the most costly of gowns. He does not feel a heart full of love beating alone. He cares not about such things.

Hesitating for a moment, she opens her mouth to speak.

"Bugger off!" he shouts without moving his head even for a second. A little bit of expelled spit catches on his beard.

She closes her mouth again and turns to leave as silently as she came. Only when she is back at the gate on the other side does she turn around to look at him one more time before fixing her mind on dealing with that trail of ants she recalls in the front room.

He hasn't moved at all. It is not a good sign. Later, when she examines the contents of the *tiffin*, she'll know if this morning will be a good one or not. She prays she will see nothing inside, but a feeling tells her she will find the snacks untouched.

The sun is cutting through the last remnants of the morning fog, drying and warming everything it touches. But it cannot penetrate the cover of trees surrounding much of that area. There, the fog lingers, still and cold, and nothing inside can be warmed if it chooses to stay.

CHAPTER FOUR – THE DARKNESS AND THE LIGHT

The darkness...

...a screeching sound...screaming and then...

...light.

But not a clear, brilliant, beautiful light. A dirty, 'smelly' light. Like light through dirty water.

Water. Yes, that's it – water. That's what the darkness is like. Dirty, deep, dangerous.

She swims to the light, but it is not welcoming. She hears voices, but they are not ones she recognizes. They talk about her but don't beckon her to them. She moves towards the dirty light in curiosity, but she does not rush. She can't. The darkness is sticky and pushes against her. She moves, but it weighs her down. She hears strange sounds through the water's darkness. Beeping and high-pitched sounds. Movement of wheels. Metal against metal. The voices are frantic. They talk about her. They say her name. "Stay with me, Sophie," says one of them. Sophie. That was a name she knows. Whose is it? Hers? She wants to find out and moves a little faster towards the light – the lights. There are several, and they move and change and grow and fade. Then she feels a hand. A hand on her leg. It pulls her back with a sharp tug away from the light. The pain. The pain is excruciating. The hand pulls harder on her leg. She hears snapping as the hand twists and cracks bone. The pain is so, so much. Make it stop. Then the leg is wrenched free, and she sees the limb descend, deep into the darkness. A sense of urgent panic overwhelms her. She must get it back. She can't lose it. She abandons the light and swims down, deep down. She hears one last voice from the light. "We're losing her, Doctor..."

Darkness.

"That's it! Wake up, sweetheart..."

Sophie opened her eyes.

For a moment, she did nothing else. She just stared out into the glare of the room, painful though it was to do so. Her eyes hurt. Her throat felt uncomfortable, as though it was blocked. Her body felt numb.

And she was not alone. Someone was there. The room looked like a hospital room, but she wasn't sure. It had been a long time since she'd been in one. But the white walls and the equipment she could see told her that this was where she must be. She had expected the smiling face of a caring nurse or doctor but didn't get that. She *did* see a face, but it was neither smiling nor welcoming. And it certainly wasn't medical staff.

The scrawny old face stared at her as though she was an alien. It wasn't an unkind look. More one of being startled that Sophie was looking at her at all and perhaps discomfort with the fact. The face glanced shiftily to the side, as if to some person out of Sophie's view. Mental cogitations were written all over the wrinkles as the face decided that someone needed to say something.

"You look a bit chirpier today, love," it said, as she put down her mop beside a bucket and came closer to peer at her. Her breath smelt of cigarettes.

"But then you would, wouldn't you? You have yer eyes open for a start off." The face cackled, and Sophie could smell the strong odour of cigarettes from her mouth. Sophie tried to speak, but something was stopping her. Slowly, she became aware that the face had a body and the uniform of a cleaner.

"Where am I?" she rasped. Her throat was sore and felt really horrible. It hurt to speak.

"Don't yer know, love? Yer int St Luke's, ain't yer." The cleaner moved away from her bed and picked the mop back up. She bent over and started wiping the floor. "Best hospital in town, I always say, coz it's the only one, that's why." Again, she cackled away to herself and drew in a raspy breath before continuing with the floor. She spoke as she mopped, her voice slightly kinder.

"They've been at yer for some time. Yer nurse will be back in a moment, I think. She's been busying around yer all morning."

Sophie looked around her and could see she was in a private room about ten feet square. 'Private' was an odd concept. There were windows to her left, and she could see blue skies and clouds but not too much else from her bed. The opposite side, however, was a completely glass wall. She could see what looked like a TV set for some hospital drama. A desk with an array of monitors, various mysterious pieces of equipment on wheels, most with wires and tubes leading out of them, and nurses moving intermittently back and forth. It was clearly just part of a longer corridor. The tableau succeeded in being both busy and desolate at the same time.

There were tubes of all shapes and sizes leading from big and scary-looking monitors next to her. Most of them – to Sophie's alarm – were leading into her arms or under the bedsheets which pinned her down. She could feel that some of the tubes were taped to various parts of her body, and when she moved a little, she could tell there were needles under her skin.

What was she doing here?

She tried to think back.

Think back to what? Sophie could remember nothing. She could remember coming home from school on a Friday and being glad that the week was over. She was looking forward to snow coming, as the weather forecasts predicted, building snowmen and throwing snowballs at her dad in the back garden. She sensed the weekend must have happened but… *what happened?* Only a vague, blurry sense of the weekend taking place told her that it was not still a Friday. But what day was it? Monday? It felt like a Monday.

"Sorry," she said to the woman, who had gone back to cleaning the floor, "what day is it?"

"What day? Thursday, me lovey. All day." She cackled to herself again, unaware that she had thrown Sophie into great confusion.

Thursday? Had she been asleep a whole week? Before she had time to try and work this out, she heard a door open from the direction the cleaner had glanced at just a moment before, and a nurse walked in. She took one look at Sophie and smiled.

"Oh good, you've come around," she said, guilt written over her face. "We were wondering when you would finally wake up. We started bringing you round a while ago. Sorry I wasn't here – I just had to pop out to the front desk. Honestly, I've been glued to you all day, and you pick this one moment…."

She came up to Sophie. One hand stroked her hair lovingly, while the other took her wrist and started to take her pulse.

"You obviously like your sleep. You've stirred a couple of times, but each time went back to sleep. I thought you'd never wake up! God, don't tell anyone I missed you coming round. I only left to tell someone to get the doctor." She leant in and whispered, "We're not supposed to leave you alone," and grinned sheepishly.

Sophie looked up at her. She was a young nurse whose name was Sarah, according to her name badge. She seemed sweet and was obviously trying to keep things light and gentle for Sophie. She appreciated the attempt.

"Could I have some water, please?" Sophie asked, her voice still croaky.

"In a moment," Nurse Sarah said, "the doctor is just coming, and he will want to see you first."

"Why am I here? What happened?" Sophie asked. She could feel tears welling up and tried to choke them down. There was no reason for tears, she tried to tell herself. At least, no reason she knew. So why the tears?

Sarah didn't look at her and busied herself with timing Sophie's pulse. "The doctor is on his way, and he'll bring you up to speed with things."

She looked up at Sophie, and her hand stroked her hair again. "You've been in a nasty accident, sweetheart," she said tenderly, "but you will need him to tell you the details. I'm just the nurse and there's a lot he needs to go through with you."

***

That first day was the worst.

Everything the doctor said hit her like a brick. He did his best to bring things to her gently, but there was no getting around the fact that Sophie's life had been turned upside down. Half of what he told her she didn't believe – or at least she didn't *want* to believe. The pain she felt in her body, her inability to have enough strength even to sit up by herself, and all the medical equipment around her told her that he was not lying.

But he had to be.

It must be a cruel, horrible, practical joke; a conspiracy like in a movie. She could not have been in an accident. Not the way he said. She would remember it, wouldn't she?

The doctor had been almost a caricature of the kindly, middle-aged, white-coated doctor figure but his accent suggested that he was from some kind of Middle Eastern country, which dispelled the illusion. Sophie never found out his name. He didn't offer it or, if he did, she hadn't been listening. He had a gentle voice. That had helped, but it hadn't stopped Sophie from being angry with him or from screaming at him – half-silently, croaking really – to get out because she didn't want to hear any more lies.

She could not bear to hear it when he told her.

He told her she had been in a coma – not for days but for weeks. Nearly two months, in fact.

He told her that swelling in her brain had caused complications and meant they'd had to induce a coma to keep her alive.

He told her that she had received extensive injuries to her body inside and out – particularly her legs, which had been badly broken – and that there would be scarring that would not entirely fade.

He told her – though he was reluctant to say it – that her life would never be the same again.

He told her that her whole world had been shattered and everything she ever knew was gone.

He told her she was lucky to be alive, that the ambulance had got her to the hospital just in time to get her into theatre, and how a delay of thirty minutes would have meant she would not be here now.

He told her both her parents were dead.

He told her they died in the car crash that so nearly took her too. They had died quickly and without suffering, he said.

He told her all this, and all she could think was that she wished she were dead too.

He told her to rest now as she curled up into as much of a ball as tubes and unused muscles would allow and sobbed into the bedsheets.

***

The second day was like a waking coma for Sophie. Nothing seemed real.

She had been introduced to Amy, the physiotherapist, the day before and Amy had decided to let her rest that day. Apparently, Sophie had been receiving treatment from her while she was in the coma to keep her joints from seizing but now, said Amy, they needed to begin re-building strength in her legs. It was on this day that Amy and Sophie began their work together to get her 'back on her feet again.' It started slowly, though. There was no attempt to get Sophie up. Instead, they spent nearly an hour doing leg bends and stretches while she lay on the bed.

Amy wasn't the only visitor that day. It felt like the whole world wanted to see Sophie, yet she knew nobody, and she continually waited, against all hope, for just two people to walk through the door, however impossible that was. The nurses checked on her regularly; various doctors came to visit, some trying to be gentle and sensitive, others failing to be. One young doctor had tried to suggest she "must feel very lucky to have recovered so well."

Lucky?

Before the accident, that would have been enough for her to snap at him about not being an idiot. She might only be twelve, but Sophie suffered no fools in her life; even the odd teacher or two had been nervous of getting on the wrong side of her at times. But now the fight was gone. She just ignored him and carried on staring out of the large hospital windows that looked out onto hills and meadows. He eventually went away.

Then came the psychologist, Dr Alice Todd. She was nice, somewhere in her thirties and with black hair, which Sophie noted was the most beautiful she'd ever seen. However, Sophie felt uncomfortable with her questions which were all about "how are you feeling?", "what can you remember about the accident?" and, worst of all, "tell me about your parents." Sophie quickly used the excuse that she was tired and wanted to sleep to bring the session to a close. It was not far from the truth – she was pretty tired. She slept until her next visitor.

The social worker, whose name was Terry (but she never found out his surname), was a wiry and more serious man, even though he tried to be friendly enough. It was evident that he was busy and that there was a lot of paperwork to be done for Sophie while also trying to keep the conversation light for her benefit. He spent most of their session together talking about the future.

He told her that much of the preparations had been done, and she had a home to go to. Sophie only had one other relative, according to the records, at least in England. There was some vague mention of a relative living abroad, but otherwise, there was just her aunt who lived nearby. Aunty Hannah. Sophie knew her well. She lived locally, and their families were close – or at least they had been. Sophie had not seen her much over the last few years, but as a little girl, she went around to Hannah's home a lot.

With all her grandparents having passed away long ago and no other uncles or aunts, Hannah was the only one left in her family. Terry told her that Hannah had agreed to have Sophie live with her, Graham, her husband, and her daughter, Millie. Sophie's aunt had been to the house and taken all of Sophie's stuff and had been appointed sole executor of her parents' will, with sole charge of all their possessions to hold in a trust fund for Sophie for when she turned eighteen. The house had been in a prime location and was sold quickly. Terry assured Sophie that Hannah had gone through the house and kept all the personal items like photo albums, home DVDs, computer files, personal letters, and so on. Sophie could see them whenever she wanted to.

Sophie didn't know why but she didn't want to see anything. She was glad she wouldn't have to go back to the house. The thought turned her stomach. She needed to pretend right now that it had never existed. She needed to push away any thoughts of her parents just to survive the day. But images of her mum kept flashing into her mind like bullets fired from a rifle. Each one stung sharply with pain more real than that of the still-healing wounds to her body.

Terry had prattled on about various other things; how he had been to visit Hannah's house; the family seemed really nice; she would go there as soon as the doctors discharged her. But all of this meant nothing to her. She didn't care. Again, Sophie claimed she was tired and brought the session to a close. Again, she slept. She was *so* tired.

Again, she was woken by another visitor. This time it was Liz, who told her she was an Occupational Therapist. Sophie had no idea what that was, which made Liz laugh. She did that a lot, and her smile beamed out of her face all but permanently.

"I get that a lot," she had said about Sophie's ignorance, "even staff here sometimes haven't a clue."

Liz told Sophie her job was to get her able *to do* again. "Doctors patch you up," she said cheerily, "psychologists take care of the noggin," she tapped her head at that point, "physiotherapists get you on your feet again, *occupational* therapists make sure you can actually manage life once that lot leave you alone!"

She added that this meant helping Sophie to wash and clean herself and make sure her home would be safe for her to live in. She would help Sophie cope with any weaknesses she might have, figure out what she could do safely, and make sure she got back involved with others and her schooling as soon as possible.

"We help you to become *you* again," Liz said with a grin, then, in a conspiratorial tone, whispered, "but the physios get all the credit."

She laughed to herself, adding, "*that's* the problem with doing a job no one understands."

Liz helped her to wash using a bowl of hot water and soap that she brought to her bed. Sophie was quite surprised at how hard it was to do, especially without soaking everything around her. Liz spent most of the time giggling at her attempts. Had she really forgotten how to use her arms? Had things been different, Sophie would have found their time together fun. But then, had times been different, she wouldn't have been seeing Liz at all.

Amy returned soon after her session with Liz to do yet more leg stretches – this time also getting Sophie to sit up and dangle her legs over the side of the bed and lift them up against gravity. She couldn't believe how hard that was too. Her feet felt like they were made of bricks, and she quickly became exhausted. Amy beamed at her and told her she had done brilliantly. She was a cheery soul, but Sophie gave her no smile, not even a grin. She just stared at the walls until someone told her what to do, or slept. It had been a long day, and Sophie just felt numb in every way.

Sophie missed the one visitor she really wanted to see. Aunty Hannah had been both days, and both times Sophie had been fast asleep. The nurses told her later that her aunt had been to visit but hadn't wanted to wake her. They told Sophie that she had been excited to find that she was awake, and they had been requested to tell Sophie her aunt loved her very much. Her job was the only reason she had not been by Sophie's side when she was brought out of the coma, but she had been to see her every day since the accident.

Sophie's first smile came on the third day when she finally got to see her Aunty Hannah walk through the door and come into her room.

"Oh, my girl," her aunt said, rushing to her side and giving her as much of a hug as she could without pressing on Sophie's still tender wounds. "I've been so worried about you."

Hannah was a tall, slender woman who looked good in the fashionable clothes she wore but was not the type to dress flashy. She had the kind of a smile that made you warm to her instantly, and her long, straight blonde hair was light and gentle to the touch. Sophie hadn't realised just how much she had desperately wanted to see her until then.

"Oh, Aunty Hannah, I'm so glad you came," Sophie said. She instantly felt a flood of emotion, and tears welled up in her eyes. Hannah looked at her with her own tears flowing.

"My darling, oh my darling," she said, giving her another hug, "it must be so hard for you."

They held each other for a long time, both sobbing as Hannah gave Sophie the chance to let out pent-up grief more painful inside than any of her wounds.

"They're gone, Aunty Hannah, and I don't know why," Sophie said, "I can't remember the accident at all. I can't remember…," tears welled up again," …*me* in the car at all. The last thing I remember is the morning and thinking what a beautiful day it was." Sophie had begun to get little flashes of memories about the weekend but nothing about the picnic (the police had found the hamper full of food in the boot of the car) or the accident at all. She didn't add that both mornings as the sun came in through the thin curtains in her room, she had relived that time, waiting, expecting her mum to call up to her and tell her it was time for breakfast. Then, confusion, as she would open her eyes and *nothing* was right, followed by horrible fear and sorrow as she realised all over again that her mother was never going to call her name.

"Oh honey," Hannah said, looking at her and wiping tears from Sophie's face with her thumbs, "it doesn't matter. Take one day at a time. I'm here now, and I'll visit you every day. When you're well enough, we'll take you home with us. Millie is *really* looking forward to having her big cousin staying with us again!"

That was when Sophie smiled. The last time she had seen Millie, she was barely walking, and she was *such* a cutie. She would love to see her again. Hannah's daughter was so beautiful and, for Sophie, so free of any pain.

"Thanks, Aunty Hannah," she said, giving her a big grin, "I'm really glad you're here. You're all I have now. Please don't leave me." Tears poured down again. It was like opening a huge valve having her Aunty Hannah here, and Sophie could feel her tense body releasing the emotion she had locked inside. She did nothing to stop it.

"I'm not going anywhere, I promise you," Hannah replied, holding her tight. She grinned and added, "I'm not going to leave my favourite niece, you know."

Sophie laughed through the tears.

"I'm your *only* niece," she croaked.

Hannah gave her a squeeze and giggled.

"But you're still my favourite." They held each other for a long time after that. Not speaking much, just holding hands and hugging and crying. It was good for them both, and Sophie was sad when Aunty Hannah finally had to go.

"I'll be back tomorrow, I promise," Hannah said as she left, "and every day until we get you out of here and take you home with us."

Days turned into weeks as the same visitors came again and again. The physiotherapy progressed from simple leg exercises to standing with a frame and eventually to walking with sticks. The occupational therapy got Sophie bathing herself properly and making visits to the playroom on the children's ward where she had been placed to talk to the other two teenagers who happened to be staying at that time. Neither stayed long, though, and Sophie found their chatter irritating.

She put up with the counselling from Dr Todd but never enjoyed it. She knew that these sessions were important because, without Dr Todd's permission and approval, she was never going to get out and live with Aunty Hannah – the one thing she wanted more than anything else. Thankfully, Sophie was starting to get some of the fight back in her; enough at any rate for Dr Todd to be convinced it would be okay for her to leave the hospital and enter Hannah's care.

As she got stronger, so the talk of leaving came more often. Terry had appeared once or twice more just to check everything was alright. She would not go to a new school right away as the school year was close to finishing. Instead, she would start fresh in the September term. By now, it was close to June, and Sophie felt like she had been in that hospital forever. Liz had made sure she got plenty of books to read. Sophie was an avid reader and had missed the chance to wade through a good historical novel, her favourite, but Liz also made sure Sophie got some lessons with a private tutor who came to the hospital to give teaching sessions to children who were staying long-term. Sophie was the only one, and that suited her fine. She hadn't wanted to see any of her old friends and certainly wasn't interested in making new ones. The only relationship which mattered to her now was with Hannah.

One day, Liz had appeared and told her they were going to do a 'home visit.' It turned out to be a wonderful day for Sophie because this meant going home to Aunty Hannah's. Liz took her by wheelchair through the hospital and down to her car. Then she drove her to Hannah's house, and Hannah had taken time off work to be there when they arrived. The house was nothing special – a typical three-bedroomed semi-detached in a middle-class urban town – but to Sophie, it was a dream palace after staring at the uniformly identical off-white hospital walls for weeks.

Once inside, Hannah had made the three of them a cup of tea, and then they looked around the house. Liz watched carefully as Sophie used her walking sticks to help her around and manage the stairs. She was getting pretty strong now and, when she did use the sticks, she was skilful and agile.

Most importantly, Liz could see the determination in Sophie's eyes. She *wanted* to be better, and she *wanted* to be in this house. Liz couldn't have asked for more.

Finally, the day came when the doctors, psychologist, social worker, and both therapists all agreed in a 'team meeting' that Sophie could go home with Hannah. She would need to continue counselling with Dr Todd and have regular outpatient checks with them all, but otherwise, she was free. Sophie was told, and someone phoned and informed Hannah that Sophie could be discharged whenever they wanted.

Sophie had not expected the day of leaving itself to be such a problem. For the first time, her aunt wasn't being her normal, cheery self.

"Come on, Sophie. We'd better pack your things quickly." Hannah said. "I don't think we should keep Graham waiting."

Sophie looked up at her aunt's worried face. She had a shifty look in her eye, as though something was distracting her. Sophie didn't know what it was but figured it involved Graham somewhere along the way. She never called him Uncle Graham because he hadn't always been there from the beginning. He had married Hannah a couple of years previously and, whilst he was nice enough, he never seemed to be particularly involved with the family when she and her parents had visited. She knew he had a temper but then her dad had been a little like that too. Hannah had always worked hard to keep him happy, as if not wanting to risk displeasing him. Hannah was that kind of a person, always wanting to keep you happy.

They packed up her few belongings – a couple of books, some clothes, some chocolate snacks, and a couple of teddy bears – and then went to say goodbye to all the nurses who had helped Sophie. Most of them she was going to miss, but not the night staff, who generally had been a bit unpleasant and had woken her every couple of hours in the early days to check on her. She could do without them and was looking forward to a proper night's undisturbed sleep. Maybe then her thoughts would be more settled, and she'd have some real dreams again instead of lurching from deep sleep to deep sleep.

They did the goodbyes and the hugs, but Hannah rushed Sophie through the whole thing. She was clearly anxious to get out and into the car. If

Sophie hadn't been on walking sticks, she was sure her Aunty would have made her run. She had really wanted to say goodbye to Amy and Liz, but they were nowhere to be seen, and Aunty Hannah was clearly in no mood for wandering around the hospital trying to find either of them. That made Sophie sad, but she didn't argue.

As they approached the car, Sophie could see a man leaning against it. He was stocky and medium height with brown hair and a permanent frown etched into his face. She knew him. Graham began to open the driver's door when he saw them coming. He didn't say anything, but he kept looking at his watch as Sophie hobbled, slowly, to the car. He grunted some vague kind of greeting to Sophie as she passed but didn't open the door for her to get in. Instead, he just got into the driver's seat and left Hannah to sort Sophie into the car and put her bag into the boot.

He turned the keys in the ignition and started the engine. The girls got themselves sat down, seatbelts on, and they began the journey. Sophie was as nervous as she had been when Liz had driven her a few days earlier. She didn't trust cars any longer even though she couldn't remember the accident. Cars were responsible for her parent's death. The sooner she was out of this one, the better. But even the fear of being in a car could not dampen her excitement of finally leaving the hospital.

She closed her eyes for the journey but could feel the sunshine on her face. The darkness under her eyelids lightened briefly each time a gap between trees or buildings let the sunlight bear down fully onto her. But, to Sophie, the flashes under her eyelids felt like violent needles of light breaking into the darkness of her spirit. The only distraction was the uncomfortable burning of her legs, which was hardly any better.

Still, Sophie Shepherd was going home or, at least, she was going to the closest thing to one now. That would have to do.

CHAPTER FIVE – FATHER

Hannah opened the door on Sophie's side of the car and helped her get out. Again, Graham didn't bother to help, though he did, at least, take Sophie's bag from the boot and take it into the house.

"Here you go," Hannah said. "Mind how you step. Be careful. Don't forget to take it easy on those sticks, as the doctor said."

Sophie didn't mind the fussing. She quite liked it, really. It took her mind off the fact that Graham had said nothing during the entire journey from the hospital to the house – he just drove in a moody silence that seemed to quash any attempts by Hannah to start a conversation.

Sophie had seen his face in the rear-view mirror. It was sullen, perhaps even angry. From time to time, his eyes met hers, and it seemed to Sophie that he was looking at her with derision; as if looking at a piece of dirt. A deep foreboding came over her. Graham didn't want her here – that much was obvious – but why? She had no idea, but she also really didn't care. Nothing mattered much anymore. Everything was…numb.

She got into the house and was greeted by the little bundle of joy that was Millie. Sophie realised, as her niece grabbed her in a bear hug with a great cry of, "So-pee" that it had been some time – at least a year maybe? – since she had last seen little Millie and the seven-year-old was swiftly becoming not so little. Sophie winced a little as Millie clung to her, and Hannah, seeing the pain she was in, ordered Millie off Sophie with scolding 'don't-you-know-she-has-just-come-out-of-hospital' type of words.

Sophie grinned as Millie was led away. "I want to see all your dolls tomorrow, Millie," she shouted after her. "I've missed them!"

"O-kay So-pee," the little girl hollered back. She never could get Sophie's name right, and it had become something of a joke between them now.

Sophie had always been her favourite in the family. Of course, it helped that she *had* been the right age to enjoy still playing dolls with Millie. Being an only child herself, Sophie enjoyed her niece as the closest thing she had to a baby sister. The closest she would ever get to a sister now.

But that had been before Graham. Sophie had never met Millie's dad. He'd been long gone by the time Hannah had been six months pregnant – a foolish fling at the time. Graham appeared while Millie was still a toddler, and it had only been two years ago that Hannah had finally married him.

Sophie didn't really know him but had vague memories of coming around and things being a little tense whenever Graham had been there. In the end, her parents increasingly made excuses about being too busy to visit "*Your* Aunty Hannah," and they eventually stopped coming round at all. Sophie wasn't fooled, though. She knew her father didn't like Graham and once overheard him telling her mum that "Hannah don't 'alf pick 'em." And how he was "a rum 'un." Her dad had always been a plain speaker – speaking things how he found them – and more than one person had told Sophie she had inherited the same trait.

She sat down on the sofa in the living room and put her sticks to the side. She was going to have to stop using them, the doctor had said. Sophie rubbed the back of her knees. They ached badly. *I'll try tomorrow,* she thought, *too tired today.* Sitting back in the seat, Sophie looked around the room she'd sat in many times before without a thought. Everything was in its proper place; the modern-looking furniture, the ornaments on the shelves, even the remote control for the TV – which was massive, it seemed to Sophie. There wasn't a speck of dust. It was a far cry from life in the Shepherd family home. Their house was always a mess. Her dad used to complain that he'd married the messiest woman in the world and she'd spawned an evil copy of herself in the form of Sophie. But he was just as bad. The girls may have left shoes and clothes everywhere and the house cleaning was done only when desperately needed, but his desk in the study was covered in bills and work left undone – and he always put off doing the dishes. Sometimes, the state of their house caused real stress; but for most of the time, they lived in a bemused state, shifting mess only when in the way.

Or they used to. Now Sophie was going to have to get used to a very different kind of life. Hannah and Graham's place, in comparison, was a showroom. Not quite a guest and yet not quite one of the family, she would have to keep out of the way until she figured out how everything was expected to work here. To do so would be no hardship. Sophie had little desire to be with anyone. Millie, she could manage, and Hannah brought some comfort, but otherwise, she wanted no one around. The thought of seeing any of her friends from school made her feel physically sick. Hiding away here was just about the best she could hope for. Sophie still had little idea what was meant to happen now, and, to be honest, she really didn't care. She just wanted to hide away until the numbness she felt inside left. If it ever would.

The first few days passed by peacefully enough. Sophie spent most of her time in the back garden, small though it was, enjoying sitting in the sun. On days when it rained, she sat in a comfy chair Graham had brought up to the spare room where she slept. On wet days, her legs hurt much more and it was all she could do to walk to the chair. Thankfully, the window had a view looking over the town. It was not a pretty view, but it was enough for her.

Aunty Hannah had brought her some books, and Sophie read them from cover to cover over a couple of weeks, yet not quite as voraciously as she would have done before the accident. There was little joy in reading for her, but she read from habit as a book lover in the past and the repetitiveness was a comfort. She read Roman history, Napoleon Bonaparte, and *Wuthering Heights* because Hannah knew she loved history and period novels, but she couldn't concentrate on them. *Wuthering Heights*, which, not so long ago, Sophie would have adored, meant nothing to her. The drama in those pages seemed like nothing now.

Mealtimes were pleasant enough with Aunty Hannah trying to make conversation with Sophie. Graham was ok, but he seemed to tolerate Sophie rather than enjoy having her around. But then, to an extent, he seemed to tolerate everyone. Perhaps it was just his nature, Sophie thought. He was a little friendlier – or at least louder, jokier perhaps – in the evening after he'd had a beer or two, but that was usually after Millie had gone to bed, Sophie tended to retire to her room and sit in the comfy chair. She would still stare out of the window and look at the town lights, even though it was dark. What she thought about, Sophie wouldn't have been able to say, had anyone asked. Yet, she did think. Over and over again, a hundred things flashed through her mind, but nothing concrete. Several times Aunty Hannah had seen her just staring and had said "a penny for your thoughts," but Sophie could tell her nothing. Hannah, wisely, didn't press. The numbness wasn't disappearing, and Sophie knew it.

Worse than the numbness were the nightmares. She had never had a goodnight's sleep since waking up in the hospital, but, back then, they had been short blasts of images she didn't recognize and that she couldn't remember once she woke up. All she knew was that they made her panic and she'd wake up sweating. Her heart would be racing and Sophie would feel she had been on the point of drowning. Now, the images were beginning to recur and the events playing out in her mind became more real and memorable.

Each time she felt like she was being buried, going deep down into something that was choking her. She'd wake up just as she knew she could not hold her breath any longer. There were other images – she couldn't remember them clearly, but they disturbed her – and she no longer looked forward to sleeping. Instead, she would sit in the chair late into the morning until exhaustion finally got the better of her. On one of the nights, about a week after arriving at the house, she woke up the next morning to find she had never left the chair and was sat opposite her unused bed, covers perfectly in place as Hannah had prepared them the day before.

Most horrible of all, though, was the awakening from the dreams. It was always the same, Sophie waking, thinking her mother had called her to wake up. For one blissful second, she'd be back in her own bed at home, expecting her mum to be making breakfast. Then the awful sinking despair as she'd realise afresh that there was no mum, no breakfast, no life as she'd known it. That was the worst.

Everything seemed to be going fine over the next couple of weeks. Sophie was so quiet that Graham didn't really have any reason to grumble. Mealtimes were pleasant enough though she never hung around for long afterwards. Millie loved having her there, of course, and Aunty Hannah was grateful that Sophie would spend quite some time with her after Millie returned home from school. It gave Hannah the chance to get more work done around the house before Graham would come home from his office, change out of his suit and flop on the sofa with a beer, where he would stay for the evening except for eating and getting more beer from the kitchen.

Sophie couldn't say it was *nice*. But it was ok. Increasingly, the pains from her many scars were fading. Yes, there were days when they itched badly and sometimes her legs would be red raw from her being unable to resist scratching them. Sometimes she had to use the crutches, slowly, cautiously. Other times she flew around the house on them or didn't bother to use them at all. The numbness she felt hadn't gone, but it did begin to recede to the back of her mind for some of the time when she was doing things she could enjoy. Being with Millie was the best. She read to her, played with her dolls, played *Animal Snap* and other simple games, and sometimes even taught her about some of the things she'd learned in her history books. Sophie was a natural teacher and Millie adored her. Mealtimes were often spent with Millie telling her mum, with great authority, some fact about the Romans. Hannah would look appropriately amazed, winking at Sophie, while Graham just scowled and occasionally commented, "Don't believe everything you read in a book," while casting a suspicious glance at Sophie. Each time, Sophie bit her tongue.

Whether it was cats fighting next door, or the waste disposal men clanging bins, Sophie wasn't sure, but something woke her up pretty early one Monday morning. For once, she hadn't thought of her mum calling to wake her up, but she had been having a nightmare, as usual. She had woken from a disturbing dream where she had seen little Millie playing with dolls, someone standing behind her, but she couldn't see who. It was a man, but she never saw his face. Somehow, though, she knew he was bad. The dream was frightening, and Sophie was quite glad that, in a sense, she had woken up before it could become worse. As always, the last thing before waking up was the darkness and the sound of screeching tyres merging with the scream of a woman. Every morning now, that part was the same routine.

She sat up in bed and looked at the time. It was six in the morning and way too early to be getting up. She took her book on Egyptian history and started to read, but she was still too bleary-eyed to read properly. After about ten minutes of struggling to concentrate and follow the text, she gave up and decided that maybe she should just go downstairs to the kitchen and make herself a cup of tea. She got up, put on her dressing gown and padded, barefoot, out of her room.

She walked quietly past Millie's room. The door was open and she could see the little girl sprawled on her bed, sheets all over the place, fast asleep. Sophie smiled. Millie was clearly a wriggler, both asleep and awake. As Sophie crept down the stairs, she became aware of voices in the kitchen. They were Hannah's and Graham's. She had no idea they got up this early as she was never called until about 7:30 each morning. It explained why Graham was always dressed and ready for work, slurping a cup of tea when the rest of them were eating, Sophie thought, if they both got up much earlier than the two girls. Sophie could quickly tell now, as she got closer, that these voices were raised and some kind of heated discussion was going on.

"We can't do this forever," Graham's voice was saying. "We have bills to pay. *I* have bills to pay. We're not made of money, you know. You have no idea how hard it is to bring in a salary. The business isn't doing that well. You can't just go on spending my money. She needs to go where she can be properly looked after."

"Don't be silly," Hannah's voice responded. "She's our niece. She is welcome here, and it doesn't cost that much extra to keep her."

Sophie heard the scrape of a chair and then a little yelp from Hannah. She tiptoed along the hall leading to the kitchen.

"Graham, don't. That hurts."

"*Don't* call me silly. And she's *your* niece, not mine. I'm not picking up the tab for another one of your *hopeless* girls. One is bad enough."

Taking a deep breath and trying to control the rush of blood she could feel flushing her cheeks, Sophie came around the corner into the kitchen; for one moment, she could see Graham clutching Hannah's upper arm tightly as he stood over her. Hannah was sat at the breakfast table trying to peel his fingers off her arm with her other hand. The instant Graham saw Sophie, he released Hannah and turned his back on her to look out of the window while he took a mouthful of tea from his cup, his actions attempting to conceal what they all knew Sophie had seen, but the tightness of his body revealing the truth. Sophie looked at Hannah, who now attempted a sunny smile.

"Oh, hello you! You're up early."

Hannah busied herself clearing up her empty tea mug and tried not to make eye contact with Sophie. She kept her distance from Graham.

"Yes," began Sophie, uncertain what to do or say, "I couldn't sleep. Some noise must have disturbed me, so I got up."

Still in his boxer shorts and T-shirt, Sophie noted, Graham finished a final mouthful from his mug and banged the cup down on the kitchen work surface.

"I have to get ready for work," he muttered and pushed past Sophie as he left, not even glancing at her once. His face was sullen, but that was nothing new.

"Everything alright?" Sophie asked when he had gone upstairs.

"Oh yes, yes. Just a little argument. Nothing to worry about," said Hannah, but Sophie could see that she was holding back tears and continually rubbing her arm, now red and blotchy from where Graham had held her. *He must have really dug in*, Sophie thought. Hannah, aware of where Sophie was staring, tried to pull the short sleeves of her nightshirt down to cover it a little. It was a hopeless gesture, but she did it almost instinctively.

"Would you like a cup of tea?" she asked, trying to change the subject, and turned to fill the kettle up.

"Yes," said Sophie, equally anxious to alleviate the tension, and took a seat at the table. "That would be lovely. Thank you."

"Graham was just talking about problems at work, and he gets a little grumpy in the mornings." Sophie could tell Hannah was lying, but she smiled and nodded back. She knew better than to say anything. "He'll be chirpier later, you'll see."

Yes, after a beer, Sophie thought, but she said nothing.

Aunty Hannah made them both some tea and sat back down at the table.

"Aunty Hannah, can I ask you a question?"

"Of course you can, darling! What's on your mind?"

"Would you prefer it if I lived somewhere else? Terry, in hospital, did say that I could possibly live with some foster parents if it didn't work out here." Sophie looked up at her aunt to see how she reacted.

Hannah paused, then looked up from her cup. "Of course not, Sophie. You're welcome here; you know that. And Millie would be devastated if you left. We want you here. Honestly."

"Even Graham?"

"Yes, of course. He's just grumpy in the mornings."

"He's grumpy all the time."

"No, no," Hannah hesitated again, "work is just hard at the moment. He has all the pressure of running the company, and he's had to lay off one or two labourers recently. The building trade just isn't booming right now."

"I get the feeling he doesn't like me."

"Heavens, no!" Hannah got up from the table and came over to hug Sophie. "He does, honestly. He is just taking a little time to adjust to not having as much space and privacy. He'll come round; you'll see."

Sophie was far from convinced, but she left it at that. It was always hard to get the truth out of Aunty Hannah if it wasn't nice – she just wanted to please everyone all the time.

But what do you do to please someone who is nasty? Sophie pondered. She sometimes wondered why Hannah was with Graham at all.

Was he the only guy who had ever taken an interest in her or something? It felt to Sophie that Aunty Hannah was more liked a caged animal than a wife.

"Can I play with you, So-pee?"

Millie was standing at her doorway with dolls in hand. Sophie smiled, put down her book and got up from her bed.

"Of course, honey," she said. "What would you like to play?"

Millie beamed at her and trotted into the room. She sat down with the dolls and started positioning them straightaway.

"Can we play 'Mummies and Daddies'?"

"Oh, that's my favourite game!" said Sophie, and she grabbed one of the dolls.

"I like playing 'Mummies and Daddies' because then I get to tell the Daddy what to do." The little girl giggled and squirmed her shoulders as she spoke. *You're just a bowl of sweetness,* Sophie thought, *I could just eat you all up.*

"Ah, wouldn't that be great if we could do that in real life?" Sophie looked at Millie as she said that, trying to read her expression. The little seven-year-old didn't look up as she spoke.

"Yes, it would. Daddies never listen in real life. They come home tired and just sit in front of the TV and eat crisps and drink beer." Sophie had to admit that some of that had been a bit like her own father. For a second, the thought of her own dad, and her loss, made her flinch. She fought the urge to think about how much he used to hug her and how she hated it because she didn't like to be thought of as a kid anymore and how, so, so much, she'd give anything for one of those hugs right now. She fought it because she couldn't cry in front of Millie. It wasn't fair to this gorgeous bundle of joy. *You should never know any pain ever,* Millie willed the thought to the girl, *you deserve to grow up happy and complete.*

"Yes, they do, Millie, you're right," she laughed, swallowing back her thoughts. "My dad would come home and sit in front of the TV to catch the news. My mum always brought him a cup of tea, sometimes even had it made *before* he got home, and sometimes she would *actually* rub his shoulders while he watched. Can you imagine that? If he wasn't too tired, I would sit on his lap and we'd have a cuddle. He would turn the news off and find some children's TV for us to watch. We'd watch for ages, and then, most times anyway, I'd turn around to say something to him and see that he'd fallen asleep." She paused for a moment, feeling a sudden wave of emotion as she remembered what it was like being Millie's age. She surprised herself by just how much she missed her father, a man she used to complain was 'hardly ever there.'

She shook herself out of her daydream and said: "Anyway, he must have been so lazy. Mum *never* had the chance to watch TV and have a sleep."

"Do you miss your daddy now that he's in heaven, or are you glad he's gone?" Millie said, oblivious to the insensitivity of such a question. Sophie felt her saliva congeal in her throat and choked back tears that threatened to gush. *I'll save them for later,* she thought to herself.

"Yes, of course I do. I miss Mum *and* Dad. I hope they *are* both in heaven and having a great time. I hope Dad is giving Mum a neck massage right now and that *she* is getting the chance for a rest!" Sophie laughed to herself at the image of her parents sat on sofas on top of fluffy white clouds watching a TV set with an angel behind the desk, reading the news.

"I wish my daddy was in Heaven." Sophie was a little shocked by this, even though she knew Millie tended to be blunt like that sometimes. She also knew Millie meant Graham. Aunty Hannah had brought her up to think of him as her dad.

"Oh no, Millie, that's not a good thing at all. Why do you wish that?"

"Because you miss your daddy because he's in heaven, and I would like to miss my daddy too. Besides…," she faltered over her words for a moment, as if weighing up whether to speak her thoughts or not, "besides, that way, he couldn't be mean to Mummy or me any longer. We could love him again."

Sophie stopped in her tracks as what Millie had just said sank in. Her heart pounded and the scars on her legs all ached simultaneously.

"Does he hurt your mummy?" she asked cautiously. Millie carried on playing, absent-mindedly clashing two dolls together, and didn't look up, but she nodded her head.

"Badly?"

"No, but mainly he just is really mean to her when he gets angry." She pushed two dolls together and made little aggressive-like noises under her breath as she smacked them together repeatedly. "Or if he drinks too much."

"Does he ever hurt *you*, Millie?" Sophie never took her eyes off the girl as she spoke. Millie stopped playing and looked up at Sophie. For a moment, she said nothing but just stared at her.

"It's okay, Millie," Sophie reassured her, stroking her arm with her hand. "You can tell me. I won't tell anyone." Millie looked down again and started twirling the hair of one of the dolls.

"Sometimes. He says he's sorry the next day and once he hurt my arm so badly that Mummy phoned up school the next day and said I was ill and couldn't come in, but I wasn't; so she told a lie, didn't she? Why did she do that?"

"I don't know, Millie, but I know that your mummy loves you very much."

"I know," said Millie. "I don't wish *she* was in Heaven. That would make me very sad." She went back to staring at her dolls and then added, "does it...? Does it make you sad that your mummy is in heaven?"

"Yes, Millie. It makes me very sad indeed. I miss her loads and I'd do anything if I could get her back." Sophie struggled to keep the tears back. She wasn't going to cry in front of Millie. It wouldn't help her to see her older cousin sobbing away. She gave herself a few seconds to compose herself before speaking again.

"Anyway, we're not getting much playing done, are we?" She tried to give a huge smile for Millie. "Let's play, shall we?" She picked up one of the dolls nearest to her. "Who's this one going to be?"

"Mummy," said Millie decisively, "because she is the most beautiful doll I have."

"For god's sake, can't you get one of your girlfriends to do it?" Hannah sighed.

"No, I've told you, it's my friends I'm going out with. You knew this was going to happen, Graham, weeks ago." Hannah pleaded. Graham's face was red, but he was just cross. He hadn't got really angry yet, and Hannah was scared of what would happen if he did.

"I wanted to watch the game tonight. Why can't you go out a different night?"

"Because this has been booked for ages, that's why. It was on the calendar. You know it's Andrea's fortieth tonight. She's my oldest friend and would be horribly upset if I didn't come." Hannah wasn't shouting like Graham, but Sophie could hear every word nevertheless. She was glad Millie was out playing with the neighbours next door. She would have been scared to hear Graham's voice. Sophie herself was nervous. She had concluded long ago now that she really didn't like Graham – ever since the time Millie had told her just what kind of a father and husband he was. She wasn't scared of him herself, but she knew that Hannah and Millie were. She knew that Graham knew they were too and was making use of that fact. The only thing Sophie was scared of was the power he had over his wife and daughter – and therefore, Sophie herself.

"But that was before that bloody girl was here. How am I supposed to look after that…" he hesitated for a moment, "that *cripple* and still watch the match? The words stung Sophie as she listened. *Cripple?* She looked down at her legs. They were still badly scarred and she had to wear skirts or shorts because fabric still irritated and hurt them. She was just about off her sticks now and only used them if she was really exhausted after going for a long walk. She couldn't believe he still thought of her as disabled somehow and less of a human being as a result. *I wish I could show you how much of a cripple I am on your shins,* she thought, grinning at her own evil intentions.

"Oh darling, don't say that," Hannah was trying to use her soothing voice. "She's not a cripple and barely uses the sticks now. She's no bother, and I'll make sure Millie is all washed and ready for bed. You can get her down before the match begins and Sophie will probably just stay in her room out of the way. There's beer in the fridge, all chilled and ready. You'll have a great time.

"Huh – a great time without my wife with me and with *her* brood to look after," Graham snapped back. There was silence for a moment; then he said: "You can go, but I bloody well want you back by 10:30. You understand? Don't you dare be late."

"Yes, yes, of course," Hannah sounded disappointed but also glad that it meant that, for now at least, she had won and could leave.

"Leave your mobile on. If either one of them causes any trouble, I expect you to come home straight away."

"Ok. It'll be alright, Graham, honestly."

Sophie heard Hannah shut the front door behind her soon after seven that evening. Almost instinctively, she felt her scars tingle and her joints ache; something which always seemed to happen if she was anxious or tired. She rubbed her legs and stretched out her limbs two or three times. Millie was washed and in her pyjamas and was sat on the sofa next to Graham. They didn't touch. As soon as the door shut and Graham heard her get into the car one of her girlfriends had driven to pick her up, he turned to Millie.

"Go on," he barked, "get to bed."

Millie hadn't argued. She clearly knew the drill. Graham had already had several beers and had another can in his hand now but the match had not even begun. She took herself straight off to bed. Sophie, feeling sorry for her, went and tucked her in. Millie hadn't cried or anything; she just lay there in the bed, staring and saying nothing. Sophie could tell that this was not the first time Graham had 'babysat' her and sent her straight to bed earlier than usual. She felt so sad for Millie.

After an hour or so, and the match well and truly started, Sophie decided it would be ok for her to go quietly downstairs and make herself a cup of tea. Her muscles still ached and she felt tired. A cuppa would be just the trick to wake her up. The kitchen was right next to the living room, so she would have to be quiet. She didn't want to alert Graham and give him an excuse to spoil Hannah's evening by making her come home. Hopefully, he would be too absorbed in the game to hear her.

She went into the kitchen and boiled the kettle. She made a cup of tea with the tea bag still in the cup and got ready to leave. She just had to add milk. She got the milk from the fridge and poured some into the cup before turning to put the milk back. She felt a sudden sharp twinge in her leg, causing her to bend a little as she winced and caught the mug with the milk jug, sending it flying off the work surface and crashing onto the floor. She held her breath.

"What the *hell* was that?" She heard Graham bellow drunkenly from the sofa. He appeared a few seconds later in the kitchen doorway, swaying uncertainly with beer can in hand.

"Sorry," she said quickly, "I just caught the mug. I'll clean it up. Go back to your match."

"You *stupid* girl!" he shouted with a vicious sneer on his face. "You stupid, clumsy little girl. Did you get your clumsiness from your dad or what? I bet you did. No wonder he couldn't drive a car properly."

Sophie felt blood rush to her cheeks, and she bit her lip to stop herself from shouting back at him. She *wasn't* going to spoil Hannah's evening, not after she'd helped her so much all this time. She couldn't do that to Hannah. Choking back the anger, she grabbed the dustpan and brush and swept up the broken crockery as fast as she could. Graham watched her, and she could hear him noisily take another swig from the can.

"Just make sure you pick up every bit of it," he said. "God help yer if Millie stands on a piece and cuts her foot. I'll give yer a damned good hiding, I'm telling you now."

Sophie's blood was boiling. "Don't even think about it, *Graham*." She snapped before she could stop herself. Despite how hard it was for her to bend down, she had picked up the last of the pieces and put them in the bin. She didn't try to make another cup. She just needed to get out. Graham had said nothing but instead took a final big gulp of beer and drained the can. Sophie took the opportunity to get out of the kitchen as fast as she could and get upstairs to her room. But as she was halfway up, she saw him come to the bottom. Sophie knew he was going to follow her up, and this wasn't over yet.

"Don't talk to me like that, girl," he shouted drunkenly as he staggered up the stairs after her. "I'll show you who makes the rules in this house."

"Get lost," she yelled back at him, fury now rising fast inside her, and slammed her door shut once she got into her room. Her heart was beating so wildly it felt like it was going to burst. There was no point trying to contain her anger now. He had pushed too many buttons. How *dare* he say those things about her father? A second later, Graham flung the door open and grabbed her viciously by the arms. She cried out, but he ignored her. He shoved Sophie across the room, and she crashed into a corner with a scream.

"You little...you little..." He hesitated as he swayed without something to prop him up. Concentration was etched on his face as he was evidently struggling to remember words. "*Bitch,*" he hissed.

"Leave me alone," Sophie cried, tears falling down her face but still standing defiantly. Her legs cried out with pain, but she wasn't going to let this drunk get the upper hand on her. "You're a mess. You should be ashamed of yourself, drinking so much you can't even stand up properly. You're supposed to be babysitting Millie and me! You couldn't babysit a rock in your state!"

Graham took an aggressive step towards her, and Sophie shrank further into the corner, arms raised, anticipating a punch like she was sure he must have done to Hannah. Like she was certain he was doing to Millie.

"Oh, you don't need a babysitter," sneered Graham, his voice dropping, "not a pretty thing like you. Yer a woman if you can talk back to me, Sophie." He stopped for a moment. The silence was worse than his rants.

"Pretty Sophie."

His voice had changed from sneer to whispered leer, and she could see an evil-looking grin fixing on his lips. He quickly sidled up close to her, his body almost pushing hers against the wall.

"And I'm completely in control, I can assure you. *Pretty girl.*" He breathed alcoholic fumes at Sophie that made her want to retch. She hated the smell of alcohol. She watched him move closer, his mouth opening and getting closer to hers. She saw his eyes tracing her body, and she realised she had never felt so exposed and vulnerable in her life. His hands stroked her shoulders and down both arms. She knew just what he was going to do.

She knew too that she wasn't going to let him.

She brought her knee up hard between his legs. The pain of the action shocked her as all the muscles in her leg spasmed, but satisfyingly, she heard him gasp before feeling a blast of his stinking breath on her face as he doubled over. Sophie tried to push past him to escape, but just as she struggled free from his body pressing against hers, he grabbed her hair and tugged her backwards.

"*You evil bitsh!*" He screamed, slurring at the same time, and brought his right hand down hard on her cheek. His aim was bad, but still, Sophie caught much of the blow and landed in a heap on the floor, stunned and in agony.

For a moment, he stood over her, hand raised, ready to strike again, body swaying as he struggled for control of his balance over the alcohol and the pain. Sophie looked aghast at Graham's twisted face as he contemplated what to do next. She could see he wanted to beat her senseless and, despite his inebriated state, could probably do it too. But she also saw the mental torment running chaotically through his mind. Why he was stopping himself, she couldn't tell. Perhaps, even his drunken brain could tell he would bring considerable trouble on himself if Sophie were to reappear in hospital with unexplained bruises when Social Services would still be keeping a keen eye on her.

Graham turned and staggered to the door, clutching his groin and moaning.

"To hell with *you*. You can go live in the street for all I care. You should have died with ya mammy and yer daddy." He staggered down the stairs, and Sophie heard the fridge door opening and rattling as Graham looked for another beer. He'd drunk them all.

"Sod you, you don't need a babysitter, so I'll go to the pub then, eh? *You* can do the babysitting."

He staggered out of the door, muttering "She's a bloody animal" to himself, slamming the door behind him and leaving Sophie sobbing on her bedroom floor. She'd blown it. Things were never going to be the same now, and she had probably just made things much worse for Aunty Hannah and Millie. For the first time since she'd been told about the death of her parents, Sophie cried out for her mum and her dad, begging them to come home, say this was all a joke. She pleaded to the air that she was sorry for every bad thing she'd ever done or said to them, and if they'd only come back, she would be the best daughter ever; she had learned her lesson. In the end, the sobs quietened, and she lay mutely where Graham's smack had sent her.

You should have died with them, she thought. *He's right.*

CHAPTER SIX — THE HOLIDAY

"Sophie! Sophie, get up! We're going on holiday!"

"Coming, Mum."

Sophie opened her eyes blearily. *What was that?* Had she heard correctly, or was she dreaming?

She opened her eyes widely. Her heart skipped a beat.

It had all been a dream. A bad dream.

Hope filled her heart. It was just like out of a story. Her parents weren't dead; they were alive and waiting for her downstairs. She lay in her bed, grinning to herself. How she was going to give her mum a big hug today! It was like *A Christmas Carol* all over again. Now she could truly appreciate both her parents and how wonderful they were. Now she knew what life could have been like if they were gone. She lay there, basking in these thoughts, holding off going downstairs as long as she could bear it before she would bounce out of bed and run – at full speed – down the stairs to her loving parents. She was going to give her mother the biggest hug ever.

"Come on, Sophie. Millie – you too, please!"

The words pierced Sophie like a knife. She could feel her face change from joy to confusion and then, slowly, to disappointment. No, it wasn't a dream. It was reality, grim and horrid though it was. Of course, it wasn't a dream; Sophie didn't have those anymore, not since the accident. There was nothing but confused nightmares now.

As if to reinforce the horrible reality of it all, the sun shone through the curtains and burned her scars uncomfortably. They were beginning to fade but were still very tender. They seemed to be telling Sophie that even nature was out to get her, and she half wondered to herself what terrible wrong she had done to result in cosmic judgement being dished out onto her again and again. Hadn't she suffered enough?

A wave of depression hit her. She'd said 'Mum' automatically. Just for one small moment, Sophie had been transported back to happiness, back to before, back to when it was just Sophie and her parents. It was a terrible, cruel trick. Realising where she was and who she was with, nausea came rushing back to her. She was back with Hannah. She was back with *him*. It had been three days since they had fought, and Sophie hadn't really seen Graham at all in that time. He had been going to work early, and when he returned, Sophie had been in her room and remained there, reading. He had not eaten with the rest of them at mealtimes, but then that was nothing unusual. He often didn't in the evenings. If the sport was on (which it usually was), he wouldn't budge from the TV. They all ate at the table in the kitchen. She hadn't told Hannah what had happened that night, but she could tell from her attitude that she knew something was going on. Hannah had been a little distant from Sophie since the day after Graham's attempted grope.

"Sophie! Come on – get up!" Hannah sounded stressed. *What was going on?* Sophie got up, padded along to her cupboard, pulled out a T-shirt, and swapped it for her nightie before finding some shorts and putting those on. She hated seeing her legs. The scars were ugly and kept reminding her that even her body was not normal, let alone anything else, but the scars also hurt too much to bear jeans or loose light trousers yet. Even skirts were a bit uncomfortable when they rubbed. The doctors said this would fade. Just give it time, they said.

Sophie came down the stairs and was surprised to see Graham positively beaming.

"Good morning, sexy," he said, winking at her as if enjoying some big joke. Sophie almost shuddered. "You're just in time for a good old cooked breakfast."

He was dishing out sausages from a frying pan to join the eggs and beans that were already on everyone's plate – including Sophie's. Hannah sat in her usual place next to Millie but didn't make eye contact with her – deliberately, it felt to Sophie. She just sat quietly, eating her breakfast. Something was wrong.

"So…," said Sophie, thinking of something to say to break the odd atmosphere in the room, "…everyone seems cheery this morning. What's going on?"

"It's a bright and wonderful day, that's why!" said Graham as he bounced around the kitchen with the frying pan in his hand. "Don't you just love this kind of weather?"

Sophie decided she couldn't bear him in this mock happy state any more than she could in his usual sullen one. The man needed bringing down a peg or two as far as she was concerned.

"I'm glad you think so, *Graham*," she said, thinking of how she had defended herself that evening. "Good to see you're obviously not tender any longer."

Graham threw the empty frying pan into the sink. All three girls jumped when it crashed into the other dirty pans. Anger flashed on his face as he turned around to face Sophie. He hesitated for a moment and then, after what seemed a kind of internal struggle, he brightened and said:

"Ha! *Whatever*. Today is a wonderful day. The sun is bright, the sky is clear." He looked out of the window as if to confirm his opinion. "It's a perfect day to go *on holiday*." He finished and then looked back at Sophie with an odd look on his face. It almost looked like *triumph*.

Sophie looked at Hannah for an explanation. "Holiday?"

"Yes," Hannah replied quietly, "we're... going to go away. All of us, you know. We've all been getting a bit stressed recently, so this would be a good chance to get away and relax for a bit." Here she looked at Graham nervously as she spoke. It was very bizarre to Sophie. Hannah's face seemed etched with guilt.

"Yes," said Graham, putting his hand on Hannah's shoulder. Sophie could see her body tense. "We are going to go on a little adventure. We're going to get all mystical, open our minds and experience the exotic charm of the East." He sounded like he could have been reading out of a travel guide.

"Where?" Sophie asked simply.

"India. Or rather, next door to India – Bangladesh. Same thing. They're all Asians. They're all shopkeepers, and they all smell of curry." He laughed at his own joke, and he reminded Sophie of the cleaner she had awoken to after the coma. She'd been the only one to think herself hilarious too. Her comments were positively genius in comparison to Graham's backward thinking, though. *Racist pig*.

The idea of Asia did not lack appeal for her however, Sophie admitted to herself. She loved travelling, and her love of history gave her the wild desire to explore all the lands she had read so much about. She had never been anywhere like India before. Or Bangladesh – wherever it was he said they were going. Maybe it would be good for them all to go. Sophie now really disliked Graham, but she didn't want to see her Aunty Hannah's life turned upside down.

"When do we go?"

"Today," Graham said.

"*What?*" Sophie couldn't believe it. Holidays take days of preparation. You *can't* just go halfway around the world on a whim.

"I got the tickets two days ago," Graham continued, "and I went to the embassy yesterday and got the tourist visas for all our passports. They were slow, of course, but what do you expect from *Pakis?*"

Sophie clenched her fists. *Don't do it,* she told herself, feeling the anger build up inside. Up until the accident, she had been a typical white, middle-class girl. She didn't know many non-white kids, though there had been a few at school. The odd Chinese girl, a boy from Nigeria, came one year, went the next. One or two Asians. Yet she had never been able to cope with racism when she heard it from the bullies in the playground. They tended to avoid her anyway because she had never been intimidated by them, but they *did* go for the Asian kids, and Sophie had rescued more than a few from being beaten up over time. Although she had never particularly thought of any of the Asian girls as friends, she couldn't bear seeing anyone attacked just because of their skin colour. She had never been scared of racist bullies, and she wasn't about to start now.

But, *right now*, Sophie knew she needed to get out of this house and go somewhere new, somewhere where they might get a bit of space away from Graham. Hannah, despite whatever she was hiding and feeling guilty about, was right – it would be good for them to get away. She choked back what she wanted to say to Graham and bit her lip.

"Okay," she said eventually, relaxing her fist. Rather than challenge Graham's racism, she would let it lie. She got on with eating her breakfast and pretended her eggs were his head as she mashed them up with her fork.

Sophie figured it would probably annoy him more if she kept him guessing what she was thinking and why she was grinning as she attacked her plate. When she occasionally looked up to see his face, she was pretty certain the plan was succeeding.

They spent the morning packing cases. Apparently, it had all been arranged secretly. Graham had searched online and found cheap tickets, and Millie's school had agreed to let her off school. Sophie thought this a bit odd because *her* old school used to be a nightmare for friends trying to get holiday time off. She thought that was normal for most schools but, no, Hannah had assured her the school had agreed over the phone. She did seem shifty, though, when she told Sophie, and she got the impression Hannah was not telling her everything.

It was around lunchtime, when all the bags were packed, that everyone seemed to disappear. Sophie was just finishing putting books and her MP3 player into her rucksack. She had tussled for hours about whether or not to bring *Wuthering Heights* with her. It had taken a long time, but she had slowly got into the book and found the sense of isolation from the book strangely comforting. She decided, in the end, not to take it. India, Bangladesh – whatever – didn't seem to be the ideal place to read about the desolate Yorkshire moors. She had packed her final things when she suddenly realised how quiet it all was. She came out of her room and looked in Millie's. She'd hardly seen her cousin all day, and nothing looked packed at all. She went downstairs to the kitchen and then the living room. No sign of anyone. Several packed bags sat on the floor near the front door, but not many. Not enough for the three of them, surely? Sophie's bags were still upstairs, but even though she didn't have much to put in them, she seemed to have as much as the rest of the family put together.

While she stood there, the front door opened and Hannah and Graham walked in. Hannah had been crying, and there was no little girl alongside her.

"Where's Millie?" Sophie asked immediately. Hannah said nothing but moved quickly to the kitchen, out of sight. Sophie thought she heard her stifle a sob. Graham looked a little sorrowful for just a moment, but then his face hardened as if he was stepping back into a role he was playing.

"She's come down with summat," he said sharply, "she's ill, so she can't go. We're not cancelling this holiday, so we've given her to April, Hannah's best friend."

"What?! How can you do that? We have to cancel. A friend can't look after a sick girl. It's not fair on either of them."

She looked to Hannah for confirmation that this was the wrong thing to do, but her aunt just looked at the floor and wouldn't look up. Graham took an aggressive step towards her, and Sophie unconsciously took a step back.

"Do you have *any* idea how expensive it is to get to Bangladesh?" he raged. "We can't get our money back on the tickets now. We fly in five hours!"

"You can't just leave a child without her mum when she's ill. She'll be beside herself."

Graham moved to grab Sophie's arm, fury on his face, but he thought twice about it and stopped himself when he saw the steely look on hers.

"Look," he said, lowering his voice, "April is a nurse. She knows how to look after a sick child. Millie's not that bad, but we don't want to risk taking a child with a small fever to a country with God knows what kind of diseases there. You don't want her to be *really* sick, do you? Do you want her to pick up malaria or dysentery, eh? She could die from them at her age. Do you want that?"

Sophie met his gaze for a moment but then looked away and shook her head.

"Then that settles it. Millie loves April anyway. She practically lives there half the time, and April has a little girl, Anna, about the same age who dotes on her." He smiled at Sophie, trying to look reassuring, but he just looked creepy. "She'll be fine."

Sophie was not taken in by his change of approach. "Well, I'm not. I think you've bullied Aunty Hannah into this, and I don't believe she wants this at all."

"Look, you *little...*" Graham clenched his fists, his teeth, and his eyes at the same time. He took a deep breath and then opened his eyes. "It's done, right? We're going. Hannah *is* ok with it. April is fine with it. Just leave it.

Get yer bags. We're gonna have lunch and then leave for the airport." His fists were still clenched, and Sophie knew she had pushed the conversation as far as she would get away with.

Graham wasn't going to budge.

Sophie tried her best to get Aunty Hannah alone before they left for the airport. She was desperate to find out what was really going on and to find out what her aunt was truly thinking. But Graham seemed to sense this and stayed glued to Hannah's side all the time. Even while he went in and out to the car to pack the bags, he insisted that Hannah had to come with him to "open the doors" and "hold the boot open." She had to give up in the end. Graham was not going to let the girls be alone together.

She wondered if she should just make a total fuss and refuse to leave, but, deep down, she was quite keen to go. It was just the disgust she felt that they were all playing by Graham's rules, and she didn't trust him. *Something* was up; she just knew it. Sophie also really hated the fact that Millie wasn't with them. It was so unlike Hannah, who doted on her daughter. She was clearly still upset that Millie was not coming. Had she screamed and cried and begged to come with them? Sophie thought Millie would have done that. At the same time, there seemed to be almost a kind of relief on Hannah's face too. It was just not adding up.

They reached Heathrow airport after a couple of hours driving and went through a procedure Sophie knew well. Her parents had taken her on holiday every year for as long as she could remember. Spain, France, Italy, Florida – she'd done all the usual tourist destinations – but never Asia. They checked their bags, went through passport control without a blip, idled away two or three hours shopping in the duty-free shops (though Sophie didn't buy anything herself – she had no money and probably wouldn't have bought something if she had) and eating in the cafes. Graham had already helped himself to several beers along the way and increasingly grinned inanely to himself.

Finally, it came time to go to the departure lounge and, once checked in to the waiting area, they then sat and waited for another hour before the plane and crew were eventually ready to board passengers. The plane was nice enough with plenty of films to watch, but Sophie was disappointed there was no "Learn Bengali" section on the Study menu of the screen in front of her. She could learn Arabic but figured, from all the Arabic announcements she heard on the plane that it might be a bit much to expect to be fluent by the time they reached Abu Dhabi.

They arrived in Abu Dhabi after about seven hours. It felt, to Sophie, like much longer. Thankfully, they only had a short stay at the airport there before then doing the whole waiting-to-board thing again for the plane that would eventually take them to Bangladesh. Maybe it was because they had done the whole thing before at Heathrow, but Sophie felt everything went by much faster on the second flight. They were up in the air very quickly, and she settled back into watching films again. She didn't even bother with trying to look for a language to learn this time. She was too sleepy.

Sophie did look at the people on board this second time, though. She noticed how, on the first flight, most of the people had been white-skinned, but, this time, they were almost all Asians. She also noticed how Graham was quietly uncomfortable with this fact and permanently looked like there was a bad smell up his nose. He grunted responses if an Asian asked him the time or wanted to get past him when they were queuing, and he tutted away at everything they did. So Sophie thought it to be real justice when it turned out their seats on the second flight were not together, and Graham had been seated next to a rather plump Asian man who fell asleep almost as soon as they took off. He half lay on Graham's shoulder, snoring and dribbling slightly, and nothing Graham could do would wake him or move him.

Sophie, by contrast, was sat in the aisle seat across the way from a young Asian man who, she had to admit, was rather gorgeous. She was desperate to talk to him and strike up a conversation, but she was too shy and decided against trying. Besides, what would she talk about?

Hi, how are you? I'm Sophie, and I'm twelve, and my parents were both killed in a tragic accident, so now I live with my aunt who is married to an evil man. Do you like ice cream? Not a brilliant conversation starter.

After another five hours or so, they touched down in Bangladesh at Dhaka airport. The place was not what Sophie was expecting. After the gleaming wonder that was Abu Dhabi, this airport felt dirty and lacked any of the technological marvels the other airports displayed. It was easily, so Sophie thought, the *worst* airport she'd ever been in. She had plenty of time to be sure of this fact; the queue at Immigration was *huge,* and it seemed to take the uniformed and armed officer at each desk an age to process each passport.

The three of them had coped with 'lining' up at the desk. There was no 'line,' really, of course. About two hundred Bangladeshis crushed around four or five desks wafting their passports in front of the officers. Despite being one of the first people off the plane (their seats had been at the front of the standard accommodation and not many had flown first class), Sophie, Hannah and Graham had found themselves at the back of a long queue which was about fifteen people deep and roughly three people wide.

"Bloody Asians," Graham had muttered, "didn't they learn how to queue from us when we ran the show? They can't learn a thing. No wonder they can only run shops, and it takes twelve of them to do even that."

Sophie tutted quietly to herself while Hannah shushed him, nervous of being arrested for his remarks. The guards, carrying large rifles, posted all around the airport area made her nervous, and reading online the night before about violent riots in Dhaka had done nothing to help. The capital city was clearly not going to be the same as London. Sophie had never seen her so edgy.

Graham was visibly keeping a check on his rising anger and was beginning to lose the battle. He was tired and had drunk quite a lot of alcohol on both planes and in the waiting lounge bars. His disgust for the Bangladeshi men was evident as he tapped impatiently on the desk in front of the immigration officer.

Eventually, they were cleared and were able to collect their luggage from the turnstile nearby but even then, Graham had nearly ended up in a fight with a Bangladeshi who had wanted to help carry the luggage. Sophie had to admit that the man seemed overly familiar with them all and stood far too close; nevertheless, aggressively squaring up to the man and telling him to "push off before I make you, *coolie*" was not a clever move, Sophie thought. It brought even more attention to them – everyone just stared at them – especially from the guards who came a little closer to where they were collecting their luggage, stroking their weapons as they did so – or so it seemed to her. Sophie just wanted to get out of the airport and get to their hotel before anything happened with Graham.

They collected their luggage and headed to the sliding doors indicated as the way out, all the time Hannah and Sophie being guided by Graham. He had been in touch with a tourist operator via email and arranged for a driver to take them to their destination. He would be standing outside and take them, Sophie presumed, to their hotel. At first, she wondered how they were going to find him, but quickly it dawned on her that the driver would be finding *them*. That was easy because they were the only white people in the whole airport. He would have no problem working out who they were. They walked towards the exit doors, which slid apart as they stepped out into the Bangla air.

And immediately, Sophie thought she was going to drown.

CHAPTER SEVEN – MY GOLDEN BANGLA

Amar shonar bangla
Ami tomaye bhalobashi
Chirodin amar akash, tomar batash
O ma, amar prane bajaye bashi

My Golden Bangla
How I love thee
Forever your skies, your wind
Oh my motherland, how they play my heart like a flute

– Rabindranath Tagore

It is said, by those that know these things, that every visitor to this land has exactly the same first experience. This is certainly true if they come by plane.

It is true if you don't count the airport itself as being Bangladesh but, instead, consider it to be 'international neutral territory.'

It is true, as long as the air-conditioning in the airport is working, which is not always the case.

It is true as long as you define your 'first experience' of the country to be stepping through the airport doors and out into that Bengali air.

It is possibly even true for Asians, used to their own hot countries; it is certainly true for westerners.

After hours and hours of flying time and, if you are unlucky, nearly as long waiting around in airport terminals, you will have become so accustomed to the air-conditioning that you might not even notice how cool and refreshing it feels any longer. But when you pass through those terminal doors, you notice it is no longer there. It is like entering through the gates of Hell itself. A wet hell that is, for it is not just the heat that attacks you – it brings along its brother-in-arms: humidity. The moisture in the air is so thick it is like trying to breathe water – like trying to breathe with your mouth over a pan of hot boiling water except turning away doesn't help – the thick, moist air is everywhere. It soaks into your lungs and permeates your blood.

There is no escape from it.

Oh god, where have I come? Sophie thought, trying not to choke as, simultaneous with gasping for breath, her ears were buffeted by the hellish noise of a million voices all screaming at once. Not only did the airport doors keep out the humidity, but they also held back the noise of Dhaka itself too. In front of them was a special 'drop-off' point for cars, lined and defined by fencing all around. Guards, holding their rifles tightly, patrolled the gates at either end; one for cars to enter and one for them to exit.

Clinging to the fences were hundreds of Bangladeshi men shouting for attention of some sort and behind them, even more trying to make their way to the railings. They filled every inch of the fence, almost completely blocking the daylight which glared angrily in the few spaces it could find. Sophie couldn't tell what these men were saying or even what language they used, but she found them terrifying. Some were obviously taxi drivers, but most of the rest… it was impossible to say. The noise was deafening and chaotic and, after nearly twenty-four hours of travelling with little or no sleep, Sophie had no energy left to handle any of it.

She stood, sweating from head to toe in just seconds of exposure to the outside, wishing she was back in the airport with its air-conditioning.

"God," spat Graham, "it's like a bloody sauna out here!"

Hannah swayed a little and steadied herself with the luggage trolley. "How can they live in this heat?" she said to no one in particular.

It was hot for Sophie too, but she accepted that. She had checked out Bangladesh on the internet with her little laptop while waiting for the flight and couldn't see why either Graham or Hannah would want to come here. It was an Islamic country for a start: you couldn't drink alcohol freely, and Bengali women were expected to cover up – just about as unlike Graham and Hannah as you could get. There was only one real beach – the longest in the world, so it was claimed – but they weren't going to Cox's Bazaar, apparently. That beach was southeast, and they were going to travel northwest to…nowhere, as far as Sophie had been able to see from the map. Bangladesh was a hot, humid country with a population made up mainly of farmers and had very little going for it, according to what little Sophie could find about it. She remembered her geography teachers at school talking about the place a lot – stuff about it being the world's biggest delta and things like that. It seemed Bangladesh was a good country to use as an example for a lot in geography, but that was about it – and none of it was very positive.

This was nothing that Graham would be interested in. Something was wrong, very wrong, and it bugged Sophie that she couldn't figure it out. She had given up trying to engage in anything but the most superficial conversation with Hannah, who had withdrawn into herself and had begun to wonder instead, on the journey, if Graham was involved in some kind of illegal drug trade. His business (he either owned or ran a company that built offices, she wasn't sure of the details) wasn't going too well, this Sophie knew, so maybe he thought a little 'international' money was a quick answer. She had determined that she would watch him closely to see if he would suddenly dodge into shady alleyways for a few moments at any time and catch him picking up dodgy packages.

Sophie watched Graham looking among the noisy crowd with purpose. What was he doing? He seemed to be looking out for someone specific. His drug dealer, maybe? Then, suddenly he raised his hand and waved specifically at someone. A small, round, middle-aged Bangladeshi came waddling towards him with a big grin on his face, and Sophie remembered that they were supposed to be met by the driver. *The driver could be the drug dealer*, thought Sophie, but she dismissed it quickly. This man looked nothing like how a dealer should look, she decided. In a way, she was quite disappointed.

"You Mr Graham, yes?" the man said in broken English.

"Yeah, that's me," Graham said with a sudden smile. "You're…uh…Okib, yeah?"

"No, no," said the man, waving his hand, "Akul. Please, *Bhai*, come this way. The guard not let me park long time. Maybe we have *beeg* problem." He held up his hands as if to indicate the size of this '*beeg* problem' and then turned around, grabbed one of Graham's bags, and started off. He clearly expected the girls to carry their own bags and to keep up with him. Various dirty and unkempt men tried to offer to take the bags for them, but Graham shooed them away each time. He didn't, however, offer to take their bags himself, so Hannah and Sophie waddled after him as best they could, clutching their cases which now felt twice as heavy as though the humidity was pushing down on them.

Quickly, they followed this funny little man who shot through people as though they weren't there. The same crowd, though it separated when the three of them got near, also became more jammed as more and more people milled around trying to see these strange foreigners, and it took longer for people to get out of their way. In the end, Graham had to push his way through them. Everyone in the crowd stared. Some smiled; others pointed and laughed. Some just stared with blank expressions on their faces as though they were from the armies of the undead awaiting orders from some evil mastermind. Most of them, it seemed to Sophie, were looking at her or Hannah. Graham had no patience for any of this and just charged his way through. It was the first, and probably the only, time in her life that Sophie was grateful he was around. For once, the man was useful. Gradually, the crowd lessened as they pushed their way through. Eventually, they came out of it and saw Akul waiting for them.

"Oh, good! You long time!" he said, still grinning from ear to ear. "No time waste. Long journey we do." He led them through to a car park which seemed even hotter inside under a thick concrete roof. Sophie could feel the sweat dripping down her back and her chest. Things got better once they put their luggage in the massive boot of the car and got in. Akul sat in the driver's seat (which Sophie was surprised to note was in the same place as with British cars – she was used to going abroad and seeing drivers on the opposite side), started the engine, and the air-conditioning kicked in. Both Sophie and Hannah let out an audible sigh as they stretched out in the cool air blowing across their faces. Graham sat in the front, and Sophie could see that he had crumpled in a heap, exhausted by the heat. Secretly, Sophie was pleased he was suffering the most.

The first hour of the journey was relatively okay. Sophie was still nervous about cars and rarely went in one if she could avoid it; not being able to remember the crash was a blessing for her in this one small way. She hated not knowing what really took place before the accident, and deep inside, she had a horrible gnawing guilt about it. Her psychologist, Dr Todd, had told her this was just 'survivor's guilt' but still…she wanted to know. She felt like there was something really important she'd forgotten, and things wouldn't be right until she could remember what it was and sort it.

But Sophie was also fairly certain that, had she remembered the crash, she would never have been able to set foot in a car again. She remembered a friend at school, who had been in a road accident which had been nasty – the cars had both been written off – but, amazingly, no one had been hurt. Her friend was petrified of vehicles for months afterwards, and still, whenever she travelled anywhere, she did so with her eyes shut the whole way. How could Sophie have ever gone back in a car again if she knew what the crash had been like? Sometimes, ignorance was, if not actual bliss, something close to it.

Nervous though she was of cars even without being able to remember the accident, somehow this journey was fine. The traffic was so intense that Akul could hardly move the car for much of the time as they tried to get out of Dhaka. It was totally chaotic, with cars, buses, and lorries seemingly trying to occupy all parts of the road simultaneously. In between the gaps were men on *rickshaws* and strange little green three-wheeled taxis with the letters CNG written on their backs. They looked like cages on wheels built for two, yet behind each driver, there were often four or five pairs of eyes peering out at them. There was very little in the sense of a right side and a left side. Vehicles looked for a gap and took it. All of this was accompanied by a constant beeping and tooting of horns. In England, this would have indicated many irate drivers on the verge of exploding into road rage, but here Akul was tooting his horn merrily away and singing some kind of Bangla song to himself while he did it.

Once they got out of Dhaka, things began to get a little too dangerous for Sophie's liking. Hannah, sitting next to her, saw Sophie flinch so often that the girl could tell from her face that she was worried Sophie was fitting. The problem was that, with the roads clearer now, Akul was able to go faster. Yet, the Bangladeshi drivers seemed no more inclined to follow any road rules than they had in the busy Dhaka streets. As a result, lorries overtook buses on bends; buses pushed through gaps barely larger than their width; the sides of the roads were littered with the wrecks of buses, lorries, and cars, which had clearly been in some horrible accidents. Most of the wrecked lorries, their loads piled impossibly high, were lying on their sides like beached whales. The other ones generally were held up by trees that happened to be by the side where they had tipped or by some poor unfortunate's car which had the misfortune of trying to pass by as the lorry tilted uncontrollably and then fell on to them.

There were still hundreds of *rickshaw* cyclists throughout the journey, and Sophie watched as, again and again, they – and the passengers carried on seats behind them – were forced off the road and into ditches as buses hooted their horns with great ferocity and sped past without slowing down in the slightest. For Hannah, it was alarming and scary. For Sophie, it was utterly terrifying.

But time heals – or so they say – and Sophie certainly had lots of time. For hours they travelled under the same conditions, and not once did they get hit or see any accidents happen in front of them. Somehow, everyone managed to avoid each other – even if only just and at high speed. Akul would sometimes slam on his brakes, which would alarm everyone (Graham just tensed and hissed through his teeth), but mostly this was to avoid hitting cows, goats, or chickens which wandered everywhere. It was quite funny to Sophie to see that drivers would swerve and brake for a small animal yet not even take their foot off the accelerator for a human being. Eventually, though she never relaxed, Sophie began to feel calmer and stopped looking at the traffic in front. Instead, she started to take more notice of the scenery they were passing through. While Hannah read a book in the back and Graham dozed off and on in the front (regularly smacking his head against the pane with a loud crack, Sophie noted with pleasure), she looked at the world going by her window.

And what a different kind of world it was. Sophie had spent so long being more or less alone – by choice as much as situation. Ever since leaving hospital, she'd made no attempt to contact any friend, finding her solace in books. She'd never been with more than three people in a room at any point, and then, they had all been family – Hannah, Millie, and Graham. The contrast with Bangladesh was stark. She thought how she would hate to live here for any length of time with so many people seemingly everywhere, all the time. And that wasn't the only contrast.

The whole land seemed to be completely flat, and everywhere was nothing but green fields and rivers. There were no mountains, no hills, not so much as even a steep incline. The only things stopping you from seeing forever up to the horizon were forests, jungle areas, or villages. The villages were usually half-hidden in the forest and jungle areas and almost seemed to grow out of them. Most of the homes were made out of the clay ground they sat on, and the roofs were mostly straw or thin metal sheeting tied down onto bamboo poles forced deep into the mud.

Sophie saw endless women either sweeping the areas around their homes or crouched in what looked a most uncomfortable and impossible position and peeling vegetables or slicing meat using a strange kind of knife that pointed upright from a base they held down with their feet. All of the women walked barefoot in the villages, though on the roads a few, but not all, wore sandals.

The men she saw did a variety of tasks. In the rivers, they waded up to their waists or further, with nets – some on bamboo poles – half-naked and pulling hard on the nets full of fish. Others were paddling small boats, often with nets over the side. In the fields, many men were up to their waists again, for these green fields seemed to be constantly water-logged and much deeper than they appeared. Sophie guessed these were rice paddies she had heard about and seen in school and on TV but always associated with China – not a former part of India as Bangladesh was. Others were on strange machines that looked like a cross between a small tractor and a large lawnmower you could sit on.

They went back and forth through the mud and water of their fields, ploughing up the watery dirt. These men were covered in the spray thrown out by these machines, and Sophie was glad they were not too near the road, or all the cars would be covered in the muck that was flying out. Still other men were crouching, just like the women, drinking small cups of tea or – to Sophie's disgust – urinating beside the road. Many of them didn't wear trousers or even shorts like Sophie and Hannah were wearing. They wore a wrap-around skirt-like material, tied in a knot around the waist like a cross between a sarong and a tablecloth. Most wore it long, but those in the muddy fields hooked the bulk of the material up between their legs and tucked it into the waist part, making a kind of really short pants. They looked, to Sophie, like they were wearing giant nappies, and the thought made her giggle quietly to herself.

Whatever the Bangladeshis were doing, they were all working hard under a horribly hot sun. Sophie was still warm even with the car's AC on, and she dreaded to think how awful the conditions were for these people. It was not even as though they appeared to be used to working in the heat. Instead, they all looked to be sweating terribly and suffering just as much as Sophie. She wondered why they did it. Why didn't they just work later in the day when it would be cooler? She knew there had to be a reason but couldn't think of what it could be.

This was a strange country.

Akul stopped at a service station about four hours into the journey, despite Graham trying to tell him that they had packed lunches and would rather keep going. Akul had very little English and made it evident that he was stopping for a break, even if they weren't. What they did for half an hour was up to them.

"Oh well," said Hannah, who secretly wanted a break anyway, "I guess we can use the time to freshen up. It is so hot in here."

Despite the AC being on, the car was still warm, but when they opened the side door, they all gasped as the humid air hit them again like a wall, just as it had when they left the airport. The girls peeled themselves off the hot leather seats and asked Akul where the toilets were. After a little miscommunication (he seemed convinced they needed food), he eventually grasped what they needed, and, accompanied by lots of "sorry, sorry" and enthusiastic noddings, he guided them towards a door. They went in and were grateful that the service station had AC inside too. But other than that, similarities with English ones were non-existent. The floor was dirty; the place reeked of curry spices, and despite a seating and dining area for about one hundred people, there were, maybe, fifteen men inside. No women. Just men, all of them looking at Sophie and Hannah.

More specifically, all the men were looking at their legs. Hannah almost instinctively tried to pull down her shorts, as if somehow that would make a difference to what they could see. Sophie could do nothing about her shorts, but her scars seemed to burn fiercely under the gaze of these strange, rude men. Their stares made her skin crawl. The girls made use of the toilets, which were filthy and reeked of urine, and then stepped back out into the restaurant area, where they waited for Graham to come out of the men's toilets. Within seconds, men started gathering around them. Not aggressively or threatening – just inquisitively, as if momentarily distracted by the girls as they were passing by but then forgetting to move on and, instead, staying put, quietly watching them – but it was disquieting all the same. They came too close for comfort and stared at the two of them. No one tried to talk to them, though one or two whispered to each other. They just looked, silently. Hannah and Sophie whispered amongst themselves in an attempt to look occupied and tried to ignore the growing crowd. There were now about a dozen men standing around them between a foot and two metres away. When Graham stepped out of the toilet, the girls rushed to grab him and get back in their car. As soon as the Bangladeshi men saw him, they quickly dispersed but only to a few metres away, where they took up their positions again.

They went back to the car and waited for Akul to come out of another part of the restaurant, still wiping curry from his mouth and with a big grin on his face as always. He seemed to find the whole world mildly amusing. He also appeared to have no sense of urgency as he chatted to guards standing outside or the odd passer-by who stopped him and pointed towards his passengers in the car. They must have been asking him questions about who these strange foreigners were, but he didn't seem to mind. In fact, he held an in-depth conversation with each of them, and it took him ten minutes to cross just fifty yards. By the time he got in the car, Graham was spitting blood and cursing away, absolutely furious, but Akul just raised his hands, saying, "No problem, sir, no problem," and smiled even more. Graham gave up trying to make his point about how they needed to 'get there' quickly – wherever that was – and sat silently fuming for the rest of the journey. Akul started the engine and began humming to himself without a care in the world. As they left, Sophie saw man after man, standing by windows or outside, just continuing to stare silently. *I've changed my mind,* she thought, *this is not a nice country, and I don't think I'm going to enjoy these few days here.*

She thanked God she didn't live here and wondered how anyone managed it at all.

"We're here, I think," Hannah said as the car passed through yet another set of mud huts after what felt to Sophie like endless hours. The light was fading, and she guessed they must have been on the road for at least eight hours. She looked up, bleary-eyed. She would have tried to sleep, but the car seemed to have no suspension at all, and the countless number of potholes meant that sleep was impossible unless you liked being shaken violently. Instead, she grabbed rest for seconds at a time and now felt like death. *Please let us be here,* she thought. *Please.*

The village area itself was nothing special – it looked the same as thousands they'd passed on the long journey here. There was a long, dusty road with no sign of habitation until they came to a large river that meandered its way through fields until it ran alongside them. Then it shot off abruptly as if no longer interested as the first set of huts and houses appeared. As they got deeper into the village area, Sophie could see that there were maybe a hundred homes and different sized buildings in the central area with, perhaps, a dozen or so more spaced out around the edges. The dwellings mainly were the mud and straw types which seemed the norm in this land, but some had corrugated iron roofs, while others appeared to be made of concrete and painted in a garish turquoise colour.

As they continued along the road, she suddenly became aware of a large clearing with a huge pool or small lake (she couldn't decide which) to one side. The fencing all around made it look like a pool, and it seemed to Sophie to be the focal point of the village area with the largest and best-looking houses surrounding it. It was the grandest of these that their car approached. The pool was green with algae and vegetation and looked disgusting, yet she could see several boys swimming and playing in it, some leaping from the bank, which was a good seven or eight feet higher and disappearing deep down into the water for a long time before whooshing up with a great cry of joy.

The car slowed down as it approached the house, which, in truth, was not as grand as it appeared from further away. It was actually quite run-down with paint peeling off the walls and wooden bannisters on the second storey veranda, which stretched across the front. The building looked like an abandoned prop straight out of a movie about the British Raj.

That figures, thought Sophie. She knew Bangladesh had been part of India, thus part of the Empire days from a hundred years ago.

But other than that, the house failed to impress. It was no mansion – being maybe only a little over twice the size of Sophie's two-bedroom house where she had grown up. It looked like it had been rather grand once, but not any longer. Nevertheless, compared to the other buildings surrounding it, the house was a palace.

The car pulled up to the path leading to the door. The garden area to either side was disorganised and untended. There were more weeds than flowers.

Who would live here? Sophie wondered.

"Get out," Graham ordered to Hannah. "Go get him. I'll get her bags."

Sophie froze. Graham's voice told her 'danger,' but she said nothing. She could feel her pulse racing. She stayed in the car and watched Hannah walk up to the door – which was more of a metal gate the size and shape of a door – and ring a little metal bell at the side. When there was no answer, Sophie saw her try to push the gate open. It didn't give. Graham, along with Akul, was getting something out of the back of the car. She could hear their conversation as they pulled and shoved bags around.

"No *Bhai*, it not possible today," Akul was saying. "We long journey do. Tomorrow we go back."

"No," replied Graham, keeping his voice down, "we agreed by email that we would make the journey up and back down again in a day. I told you we had to keep moving when you wanted to stop for lunch. We're paying you to do the whole trip in a day."

For the first time, Akul wasn't smiling. Instead, he looked very displeased and a little worried.

"Oh. I think some mistake, Mr Graham," he said, taking a handkerchief from his pocket and mopping the sweat from his brow. "I no can do another ten-hour drive tonight." He held the fingers of both hands up as if accentuating the number ten would help Graham to understand.

"You can and you will," demanded Graham. "It's what your boss agreed to by email, and it is what we need. We fly back to England tomorrow night."

What? Panic was now rising fast in Sophie's mind. *What was going on?*

She turned back to Hannah, who still waited at the gate. She heard an inner door open and could see the blurry outline of a large man through the netting covering the bars in the gate. He stood there for a second.

"Hannah? Is that you?"

It was a British voice, and a large, bearded man stepped forward to open the gate. Sophie could see him more clearly now. He was white and looked to be in his fifties, with thick-rimmed spectacles that looked even older. He was quite fat, and his beard was bushy and unkempt, but somehow, he looked muscular and powerful. He would have looked like Santa Claus if he hadn't had such a stern expression on his face which commanded respect.

"Hello Joshua," Hannah replied, giving him a light hug, "it's good to see you again. I wish it were with better news, though."

"What's wrong?" asked the man, Joshua, as he opened the gate wide. "Come in, please. I'm afraid you picked a bad day to come. My *ayah* is not here today, it's her day off, and I'm not so good at hospitality…" he added, "…as you know."

"Can you manage a cup of tea, Joshua?"

"Yes, I would think so."

"Then that'll be fine. I have someone I want you to meet."

Hannah turned towards the car.

"If you mean that husband of yours, I'm not sure I particularly want to," Joshua replied, "not after your last letter."

"No," said Hannah, beckoning to Sophie to get out of the car, "not him. Someone who is much more like you, I think."

Sophie got out of the car and walked nervously towards the house. Graham was now standing next to Akul as he spoke on the phone in Bangla, presumably to Akul's boss, to try and sort out their argument. By the look on his face, Akul was losing, his shoulders drooping pathetically. Sophie saw Joshua's face change from a reserved smile to a frown as he looked at her.

"Hannah, what's going on?" he asked quietly, turning to her. Sophie looked at her, too, her face asking the same question.

"Let's get inside, Joshua and sit down with a cuppa. You're going to need one."

It came as a shock to Sophie to find out her father had an elder brother. It came as more of a shock that this man, sitting in front of her with his bulk squashed a little in the chair, was that brother. This Joshua was nothing like her father who was – had been – slim, pale, always clean-shaven, and never stopped joking – at least when she was around. This man was the very opposite of these things and looked like his wrinkled and slightly scarred face would crack if he ever did more than a slight smile. He frowned throughout the introductions.

The room in which they now sat, sipping strong tea from thin cups – the smallest Sophie had ever seen – also looked like a set from a movie about British India. The chairs were made of bamboo but were comfortably padded and huge. Books lined the walls, and all looked more than 100 years old. A couple of paintings depicting scenes similar to what Sophie had seen on the way – paddy fields with beautiful, brown-skinned women bent over picking at them – hung on the occasional space between bookshelves. One final wall area was reserved for a hanging pendulum clock, the long brass weight swinging in perfect silence, but a deep *click* emanated from the box when it reached the end of each swing.

When Hannah told him that his brother – Sophie's father – was dead, his eyes flickered downward a little, but otherwise, he showed no sign of emotion. Sophie decided then that she didn't like him. This wasn't just his brother they were talking about – it was her father he obviously didn't care about. Then Hannah explained to him that Sophie's mother had also died in the accident, and Sophie saw a real flicker of shock and sadness, just for a moment.

"I'm sorry to tell you all this, Joshua," Hannah said unduly tenderly, Sophie thought.

"I can't believe it," Joshua said, taking his glasses off and wiping his eyes with his handkerchief. "Mary? Dead?"

He wasn't crying, but it was clear that Joshua was holding back how he really felt. Finally, he turned to Sophie after a few moments of silence.

"Young lady," he began, looking straight into her eyes, "I am truly very sorry for your loss. My brother – your father – and I had not spoken for many years. We did not part on good terms, and I came to Bangladesh many years ago – before you were born, in fact. He was a good man, though, and I'm sure you must miss him deeply. Your mother...well..." he hesitated for another moment, "she was a good woman too. You must miss them very much."

Despite not liking this man, Sophie felt emotions run through her, and she choked back the urge to cry.

"Yes, I do," she said as calmly as she could. "Thank you very much. I am sorry for you too." This last bit was a lie, if Sophie was honest with herself. He really didn't seem to care enough and was clearly uncomfortable with any of them being here. But Sophie knew how to be polite. She just wanted to get back in the car and get out of there.

There was a moment of silence then Joshua turned his gaze back to Hannah. "Well, it is good of you taking on their child, Hannah. That's very good of you indeed. It can't be easy."

"Well, that's just the thing, Joshua," said Hannah, now hiding her face from Sophie with her hand. "She's not just 'their child.' She's your niece, and we can't look after her any longer. We already have a child and not enough money to spare. Graham's business is not doing well and…."

Joshua cut her off. "Hannah, don't go where I think you are trying to go with this. The answer is no."

Sophie was feeling sick. Totally confused and feeling faint in the heat, she tried to concentrate on what they were saying. Was Aunty Hannah trying to ask him for money to look after her? Was she that much of a burden?

"But Joshua, you are her uncle, and a father figure would do her good."

"She's just as much your niece. You were her mother's younger sister, and you live in England. I don't!"

"Nevertheless," Hannah's voice was beginning to rise, in panic as much as in anger, "we can't keep her. So we've brought her here for you to take her as her appropriate guardian."

"What?!" cried Sophie, now realising just what was going on. *They were going to leave her here with this man. Alone.*

"The fact is that Graham has decided…."

"Oh, I figured he would come into this somewhere," said Joshua, his voice rising now too, "you always did fall for the idiots who would boss you around."

"Not always, Joshua," Hannah looked at Joshua with fire in her eyes, "not always. I'm doing what I feel is best for my family. I have my own daughter too."

At that point, Graham stepped through the door clutching one of Sophie's bags.

"We're all set," he said to Hannah. "You got everything sorted here then? We need to go now before 'curry-man' starts griping again."

Sophie stood up fast, her face flushed with anger.

"Just wait a minute. When was I going to be told? What the hell is going on here?"

She turned to Hannah with a pleading look. "Aunty Hannah, please, don't do this. You can't do this to me."

Hannah wouldn't make eye contact with her, but tears filled her eyes. "I'm sorry, Sophie, but it is for the best. You can start a new life here – get away from the horrors of the old. We hear your moans at night and know that you have haunted dreams. You're beginning to disturb Millie actually and…and…Graham can't sleep because of it. You're not happy with us. We're thinking of you, really we are."

"No, you're not!" Sophie shouted and pointed at Graham. "You're thinking of him. It's always him. Are you always going to let him bully you around?"

"Hannah, you're being unreasonable!" shouted Joshua. "This is no place for a girl to grow up. I'm a bachelor! I'm not set up for a girl. I'm not going to take her."

"I can see your house, Joshua." Hannah looked him squarely in the eye. "You have plenty of rooms here, and a maid. No doubt we can send you a little money…."

She shot a glance at Graham, checking his reaction, and added, "…probably."

"I don't want your damned money!" said Joshua, his face now completely flushed. "I want you to leave me alone! I haven't had anything to do with this family in over fifteen years, and I certainly don't want to start now!" He shot a look over at Graham, who had stepped back out through the door and left it open. He had put Sophie's bags just outside the door and now started putting them inside. His and Hannah's bags were nowhere to be seen.

"Don't you dare put that in my *bari*," Joshua barked at him, but Graham ignored him until he came level with Joshua. Then he put down the bag he was carrying and stood close to Joshua in an attempt to intimidate him. The older man didn't move.

"Now listen here, old man," hissed Graham, ignoring the fact that his aggressive move had not achieved the hoped-for reaction, "she's not my flesh and blood, right? I already have a girl who's not mine, and she's a handful enough without taking on some other mixed-up little cow."

Joshua's face hardened. "That's my family you're talking about. Have some respect."

"That's the point. *They're not mine.*" Graham pointed to Sophie. "She's somebody else's bitch."

"Don't you call her…"

"Don't *you* dare tell me what to do or to say," Graham shouted back, spitting into his face as he said it. "I'm no Indian nigger you can push around all day in your 'palace,' playing emperor. Oh yes, I know your sort, fancying yourself as king of the natives. You don't get to tell *me* what to do. You're the next of kin, and you have to take responsibility for her. We have just two tickets for the flight back, and she…" he pointed disdainfully in Sophie's direction, "is not coming back with us. You have all her medical records and everything you need. They're in her bag. I put them in. She's your niece. She'll never be mine."

He moved closer to Joshua until their heads were just inches away and hissed, "And, for as long as Hannah is my wife, I guarantee she'll be no niece of hers either. She'll do exactly what I say. Don't you even dream it will be otherwise."

Hannah had stepped outside, and Sophie followed her out.

"Please, Aunty Hannah, I'll be good. I'm sorry for whatever I did wrong, but please don't leave me here." Sophie was sobbing now, hanging on to Hannah's arm, desperately hoping she could make her change her mind.

Hannah was choking back tears too but shaking her head as though to send them away.

"Oh please, Sophie, don't make this any harder. I'm sorry I couldn't tell you before. He thought we'd never get you here. It…" She looked behind her to check that Graham was not there. Then she whispered, "…it was Graham's idea. You know what he's like, Sophie. It's hard enough keeping him happy as it is. I can't lose my husband. I can't be on my own again. You don't know how hard it is to bring up a child on your own. He's threatened awful things, and I can't take the risk; I just can't. I thought I could be there for you, but I'm sorry, I know I'm letting you down."

She took hold of Sophie and looked into her eyes. "I lost a sister too, Sophie. I'm grieving too. But I have my own little girl to think about, and I can't do that and have you around. Not with how Graham feels about it. He's..." she lowered her eyes, "...he's threatened divorce, and that's not the worst of it."

"Oh, but please, Aunty Hannah. I can't stay here. He's a horrible, fat, old man, and this is a stupid, smelly, *awful* country. How can I stay here? What does he know about looking after me? I didn't even know I had an uncle until now!"

"How can you stay with me?" snapped Hannah. "Are you going to stop Graham from getting angry? Are you going to bring in the money we need to pay the bills when he leaves? Are you going to let him beat you every night instead of..." She started to sob.

"Can't you see, Sophie?" she continued, "It's just not possible. Give Uncle Joshua a chance. He's alright. He's really very likeable if you get to know him. You'd be..." Hannah brought her hand up to Sophie's cheek and brushed it tenderly, "...you'd be *safer* here, girl."

"Just let me talk to Graham. I can persuade him – I'll even call him 'uncle' to make him feel like he's family."

Hannah shook her head. She held Sophie by the shoulders and, for the first time, looked at her fully.

"Sophie, Graham threatened to talk to Social Services – to talk to Terry – do you remember him?"

Sophie nodded.

"He wanted us to tell Terry that it wasn't working out and to put you into foster care. You know what that would have meant. Don't you?"

Sophie shook her head. "No."

"It would have meant we would have stopped being family. You would spend the rest of your growing up with strangers and never have seen us again. I couldn't bear to lose you completely. I just can't keep you now."

"But Aunty Hannah, you're leaving me with a complete stranger now!"

"But he's family, Sophie," Hannah shook her hard, "that's the difference. It means one day, when I've smoothed things over with Graham, I can see you again. We can still be family."

Hannah persuaded Sophie to step back into the house and took her to a room up the stairs where Graham had put her bags. It smelled funny, and though there was a bed in the room, it clearly wasn't ready for someone to stay. Instead, there were boxes and piles of books all over the place. Hannah tried to say goodbye there, but Sophie collapsed against a wall and cried.

Her aunt, now sobbing away herself, just put her hand on Sophie's shoulder and said, "I'm so sorry, Sophie. Please forgive me. Be safe," and with that, she left the room. As she stepped out of the door, she added, "I love you," but Sophie paid her no heed. She wailed as she heard Hannah and Graham getting into the car and wailed again as she heard the fat man try again to shout at them and demand that they 'do not leave without the girl.' She continued to wail as she heard the car drive off. Her crying didn't stop until long after any sound of an engine had ended.

After a few minutes, she heard footsteps coming up the stairs and knew that someone else was now in the room.

"Well," bellowed Joshua, "what the hell are we supposed to do now?"

Rage welled up with Sophie and exploded out of her mouth.

"*Get out!*" she screamed, "Get out and stay out. I hate you. I don't ever want to have anything to do with you!"

"Oh, whatever, you miserable child! This is my house that you've invaded. Don't ever forget that. I didn't invite you. You should never have come." And with that, he stomped back down the stairs. Sophie didn't hear him again, even after the sun went down and evening came. She stayed huddled in the corner, clutching her knees.

She was on her own. Her aunt, whom she loved and trusted, had betrayed her. Her parents were dead; the only other person she'd ever called family didn't want her, and she was five thousand miles away from home, stuck with a man she had been told was her 'uncle' but who didn't want her any more than she wanted him. If Graham could have been so horrible to her, what would this man do? He was uncaring, so unfeeling, so…repulsive. It was only a matter of time before he would try to hurt her; she was sure of it. There was no one now who could stop that; no one to protect her.

And Sophie knew, at that moment, right there, right in the corner of a damp, smelly house in the middle of a dreadful country where she now crouched and sobbed, that what little remained of her life which had survived the crash was now over. She was dead inside.

CHAPTER EIGHT — THE LAND

It is truly an enigma; a mystery so wrapped up in itself that it is impossible to unravel. It is a land so full of contradictions that outsiders often wonder why the *deshis* don't wander around in a permanent daze. Which, of course, is exactly what some of them do – or at least look like they do, to the outsider anyway. But most seem to intuitively understand this land, its impossible possibilities, its customs, its quirks. Somehow, they get it; they get that they can't get it.

One of the strangest things we can see right now – not far from the village, there is nothing but fields, green fields as far as the eye can see. Only a single railway line, raised up on stones and sand to rise above the waterlogged lands. It is the highest point in the area apart from trees and occasional *paka bari,* and they are all some fields away. What makes this strange? In one of the most densely populated countries in the world, there is almost no one around; the occasional labourer in the paddy fields tending his growing crops, waiting for harvest time, praying that the coming monsoon rains won't destroy everything again this year; a woman or two, walking the tightrope edge of mud piled up between the half-drowned fields with a large basket of food, clothes or even bricks – if she's helping the building labourers, balanced on her head. Perhaps a group of three or four toddlers, some barely dressed or completely naked, playing blissfully near the train tracks without a parent in sight. Otherwise…no one. No one in this overcrowded country. Impossible.

The silence is serene but equally as impossible. No wonder the original 'Indian lands,' which this small cuticle, cut off more than sixty years before from the shoulder of India, was a part of for thousands of years, were so highly favoured by foreigners. From Alexander the Great, who gave up after years of fierce conquest to extend his kingdom any further, to the great Mughal and Afghan invaders, to the British themselves who didn't so much invade the land as surreptitiously 'wheeled and dealed' their way into ownership before the inhabitants had much of a chance to figure out what was going on. They all came here looking for adventure, fame, fortune…but most of all, they came for peace. They came for silence.

With the sun beating down, with no major roads anywhere in sight, the only noises are the sounds of crickets (always heard, never seen) chirping away in their millions yet doing so with such quiet consistency that your brain filters the sound out and blocks it as though it were never there. Occasionally there is the noise of a disgruntled or lonely cow or the baaing of a kid goat that has momentarily lost its mother. But if you stand there on the tracks, you know you are in the middle of peaceful silence, and it is a healing sensation. It is only there that you realise just how tired, worn out, run down you are, as the heat and wind beat upon you in equal measure and massage your body and soul.

So where are all these people then? Is it a myth that there are too many people in this country?

Not at all. After a while, you start to notice that they were there all along. Almost blending in with the forests dotted around on the horizon, you begin to notice dozens of homesteads; little huts made of mud, bamboo, wood, straw, and tin. Ramshackle dwellings, some of which look about to collapse. Others are exquisitely ornate, with carefully handcrafted designs formed into the mud walls. There's pride in this work. Even the poor are house-proud and keep their homes clean and beautiful.

Inside every dwelling are women and children at least. They will be cooking, cleaning, sweeping, washing as the menfolk toil in the fields, at the construction sites or labour in the impossibly hot *it khana* – the brick factories which are little more than furnaces hotter than the gates of Hell with large oven chimneys reaching high into the skies. Under an already fierce and unforgiving sun, such places are reserved only for the very foolish and desperate; so, they never struggle to find people to work.

We keep moving along the train track. There's something quite exhilarating in doing so, stepping carefully on the concrete sleepers rather than the loose stone chippings in between. The track runs straight on as far as the eye can see and, behind you, straight on even further. Both ways are desolate and empty. There is nothing coming, so you carry on goose-stepping along the smooth white slabs.

The sun is delightful, beating down on your hands, feet, and face. Too much of this, and you will swoon from exhaustion; you can almost feel the water in your body being sucked out by the magical rays. But for now, for this short period of time before you beat a hasty retreat to your nice fan or AC-cooled abode, the sun is a delight, a friend, someone you know and trust, which is why you keep walking though it half blinds you as you stumble among the tracks.

You focus on the children playing up ahead of you on the other side of the bridge you're coming to. The tracks are straight, but deep beneath runs the river which lies in the bottom of a valley. From either side you can see the water snaking its way through fields, feeding into some, ignoring others. The drop is perhaps about twenty feet. Enough to be nervous about, and it makes you think twice before walking across the bridge where there is nothing between the beams unevenly spread along the passage. One slip, and you'll at least lose a sandal off your foot, but there's room for an unwary grown man to pass completely through the gaps and take the chance that the river is full and will take his weight before his legs can touch the bed.

The children, though, have no fear at all. They play on and around the tracks, sometimes next to the bridge, sometimes on it. One of them can barely stand; he's that young, yet he seems to understand the rules of survival. They play with sticks and stones from between the sleepers, often curiously prodding the piles seemingly to search for treasures. How cute they look, you ponder, how innocent and sweet. This is childhood as it should be; naive and at peace with the world.

As you begin your tentative steps across the bridge, carefully placing the firmest part of your foot onto the middle of each sleeper, so there's no danger of losing shoe nor life and trying to ignore the sight of the river far below, you realise the children have noticed you. You're a stranger, so it's no surprise to see the look of concern and worry on their faces. You must appear quite menacing. One of the older children makes a grab for the toddler, gripping his arm and hoisting him into the air like a bag of groceries. The toddler makes no complaint but continues to stare at you while flying to the side of the track. They all seem over-animated, though. Are you really that scary?

Too late, halfway across the bridge, you realise the true source of their concern and scampering. A horn blast from behind you tells you everything: a train is coming – fast!

Your feet need no command from the brain. They are already picking up the pace and stepping as fast as they can to get to the other side. A quick glance behind you, and you can see the monstrous engine is already huge. How did you not hear it before? Where did it come from? You checked just seconds ago, and nothing was there. What demonic magic is this? The blare of the horns obliterates the serenity to such an extent that you can't think straight. Panic now seizing your mind, you start to half skip, half run the remainder of the distance, wondering just how bad the fall into the river would be if you had to. Your chances of survival if that train reaches the bridge before you clear it are surely zero. Would the river bed merely break your legs? Shatter your hips? Would you drown?

No matter, with no seconds to spare, you make it to the last girder and fling yourself to the side bank as the train reaches the edge of the bridge. It does not slow down; it does not care that you are there; it continues relentlessly. You look up in time to see the children on the other side of the tracks are looking at you with a curious mixture of fascination and mild disgust before all you're aware of is the monster passing between you.

The noise is awesome in every way. The engine is a huge beast, but each of the carriages is no smaller. The roar from the machine is only just louder than the blast of hot, dirty air which piles into you, filling every orifice, every pore of your body. Almost as loud are the sounds from the carriages. The train is packed solidly, and like a wartime concentration camp transport, with people. Every carriage, every corridor, the steps leading up to each doorway, and, most of all, the roof. There must be thirty, forty people on top of every single sloped dome, and it feels like all of them are looking straight at you. A few people hang their bicycles outside of the carriage windows, literally holding onto the frames with their bare hands, presumably for the entire journey. All of the faces are turned towards you, staring, like some eerie portrayal of hell. You notice, just before the train gets too far away, that there are even people sitting around the skirt of the engine. Sitting with ankles crossed as though they were in some quiet suburban park drinking tea. It's all so surreal.

Then suddenly, as soon as the nightmare vision comes, so it is gone. The roar of a thousand demons vanishes, leaving only the tortured echo of souls damned for all eternity.

The cow-like ass of the last carriage is already just a pinprick in the distance. The fury of the gods, no sooner was it unleashed, now is barely a rumble in the far distance. The children, separated from you by this beast, are now back on the tracks, picking up stones and rummaging with sticks for objects of interest. They were never interested in you. Only the train piqued their attention, and then only for a few seconds. They have their own worlds to conquer, fantasies to play. The real world cannot compete. In this, they are the same as children all over the globe.

The crickets begin to chirp again. The farmers still toil, the women still walk. There is again a cool breeze, and the sun beats down, still faithful, still pretending to be your friend. This is the impossibility of this world, where bliss and fear, love and hatred, life and death all stand shoulder to shoulder as brothers, never to be separated.

CHAPTER NINE – DIDI

With great heartbreak I've abandoned my wishes
Enduring burning pain I've forgotten my desires
I've cried a lot, I can cry no more
My heart rends, Mother.

– Ramprasad Sen

Nothing can beat the sight of the Bengal Sun as it rises in the morning. It is mysterious, magical, and eerily beautiful as the huge red disk lights up the sky just above the fields and trees and cuts a path through the blackness of night. The Bangladesh flag is a simple green background with a red disk slightly off the centre, summing up the life of this former Bengal region perfectly. The red sun rises on a green land as if the two need each other for both to survive. The sun gives the land its life, and the land gives the sun its purpose. There can be no doubting this when you see such a dawn.

But the sun is an uncaring, callous friend. It cares not that its rays will beat down upon you and dry you out as you sweat and toil over your crops. The same power that gives your land its life will drain you of yours without sympathy and without mercy. There is no escape from the effects of the sun from April through to September, no possibility of finding relief. You can stay inside, but your crops will die, and the sweltering heat will drown you as millions of gallons of water, washed down from the vast Himalayan mountain range into the Bangla rivers, evaporate around you and begin their ethereal journey back to their mountainous home.

Yet the Bengal sun is life. It beats death every day because night time is death. The blackness that falls when the sun disappears behind the horizon is every bit as dark as the sun has been bright, and it hides all the dangers that Bengal keeps so jealously to itself. There are monsters out there in the night. Creatures that will kill you, eat you, possess you, and control you. The spirits come out at night, and everyone knows that you must 'stick to the path' or risk never being seen again. The 'Rakkosh' are everywhere, and they are hideous to behold. Many, who consider themselves enlightened and educated, have stopped believing in these kinds of horror stories and know that such creatures cannot exist. Yet every day, another child who has foolishly slipped out of the house for an adventure, or a young woman who found herself returning home later than expected from a dinner invitation, will never see the beautiful sun rise again.

But for the rest, it does rise and will, again, bring warmth and life back to the land. The sun is your friend, but this friendship does not come freely. There is always a price to pay, and, in this land, no one forgets it.

The first thing Sophie felt as she awoke was the warmth of the sun's rays on her face. She hadn't moved from the corner all night. She barely slept, huddled up and shaking from both emotion and lack of food, but dozed a little just before the sun began to rise on the horizon. Despite the warmth flooding through the window, the feeling of utter wretchedness, exacerbated by aching joints and burning scars, hadn't left her at all, and her mind quickly started again to worry and grapple with what had happened.

Why had Hannah done this to her?

Sophie had thought her aunt would be the one to help her get through everything. To get through the gut-wrenching pain she felt every single day. Be there for her when she needed a shoulder to cry on. Love her when she felt so unlovable. Even the threatening advances of Graham would have been worth it just to know she had Hannah there to turn to. Maybe even, eventually, Hannah would have realised what was going on and done something about Graham. Stand up to him. Protect Sophie from him.

Instead, she had betrayed her. She had abandoned Sophie thousands of miles away from her home and all her memories of her life, painful though they were. Hannah had no right to do that. Sophie hated her. She would never forgive Hannah for this. Not even if she came back through the door right now, in tears, and begged forgiveness, saying she had got it all wrong. If she offered to take Sophie back right now, she would refuse to go.

No, she wouldn't.

She would go back with her in an instant and never let go of her again. But, at the same time, she hated her. Hated her for being weak, weak against *him*. She knew that, in the end, Graham was responsible for this. It was all making sense – how quiet and ashamed Hannah had looked. How she had looked angry and upset when she returned from taking Millie to her neighbours but was holding it in.

I bet Millie wasn't suddenly ill at all, Sophie thought, *it was just a trick. Millie was never going to be coming with us.*

Anger flashed over her again.

How could they have used a holiday as an excuse? That was such a cruel thing to do.

They must have thought – and rightly, Sophie conceded – that they would never have got her on the plane if they had told her the plan. If they had let on that they were going to dump her with some fat old man, claiming he was some long-lost uncle or something. She was pretty sure that what they had done was illegal.

What if he's actually some kind of weird child killer? thought Sophie, now starting to scare herself rather than be angry. *Why else would he be living here? What if they are really giving me to one of those people I've heard about who sell children into slavery, and I'll end up in China as someone's servant having to wash floors and clean cutlery like some kind of Cinderella, except there'll be no Prince Charming because this is real life and it doesn't happen that way – or it could be even worse, I might be tortured, abused and…*Sophie's imagination was racing…*and I don't want to think what else.* Nausea came as panic welled up inside her. She *had* to get away from here. Get away from this man before he could sell her on the internet or whatever perverts like him did.

She scrambled to her feet, wincing as she uncurled herself, grabbed her rucksack – it was lighter than the other bags and had all her really important stuff – and went to the door to get out of her room and out of the house as quick as possible. It was not later than mid-morning and, if she ran now, she could make a good distance before nightfall. It was hot enough to sleep under a tree or something without any covers, and she could be back in Dhaka by the end of tomorrow. Of course, she had to concede, she was only *guessing* where Dhaka was, but it couldn't be *that* difficult. It was the capital city of the country, and surely *someone* would know enough English to help her get there?

But then Sophie remembered the men at the service station the day before. How they had leered at her, tried to stand close to her. How they had looked at her *legs*. Her horrible, scarred legs. Yet, she hadn't seen disgust in their eyes. She wished she had. *What if they're all like that?* She thought to herself, and a shudder ran through her. *What if there is nowhere that's safe? Nowhere safe until I reach the airport?* This thought stopped her at the door before she could open it. *What to do?*

No matter. She wasn't going to stay here and wait to be sold or killed. Her life might be dead, but she was not going to let someone use or abuse her. At least, if she was outside, she could run. She had to go. She had to go *now*.

She opened the bedroom door, stopped in her tracks, and gasped. There before her was an angel. The most beautiful creature she'd ever seen.

Joshua sat down on the bench and did his best to breathe deeply. He was not a man to accept change with ease. One of the many things he liked about Bangladesh was that *nothing* had changed much in hundreds of years even though, of course, change was ongoing all the time. It was a unique enigma of the land and people, and he appreciated its magic. This sudden intrusion in his life, though, was unforgivable. He had left England so many years ago, quite deliberately to get *away* from family and the stupidity of relationships. He did not expect them to suddenly appear on his doorstep. He wished now that he had not sent his forwarding address all those years ago when he left home with nothing but a single suitcase, all other possessions sold or given away, and cursed his younger self for that moment of weakness, that moment of faint hope that someone might actually worry about him.

He stared at the still waters in front of him. The murky green shade looking particularly unappealing in the morning light after the fog mists had cleared. He hadn't brought his fishing rod; he wasn't in the mood for fishing anyway, he admitted, and it felt odd to be sitting there by the pool without something in his hand. Thoughts were uncharacteristically whirling through his head. *Those eyes. Those blasted eyes.*

Joshua Shepherd was, by his own admission, an old fool. He had allowed people he despised to invade his house and behave outrageously. He should never have even begun to think of letting them in. Damn the English sense of hospitality. Damn them all, quite frankly. If it hadn't been for noticing her eyes....

He gave himself a shake. Whatever, he was stuck with an unwanted beast in his home, and he was going to have to make do until he could get things sorted out. He was pretty confident that they hadn't left the wretched creature with a passport, so the first thing he'd have to do would be to contact the British Embassy and arrange for a new passport and visa extension. That would undoubtedly take time, effort in endless visits to Dhaka to meet with officials and, in all probability, *ghush*. In all his years in this country, he still couldn't abide the collectively-accepted, ghastly, expensive bribes which everyone in any position of power, from lowly clerk to senior politician, was at liberty to extract from anyone needing their help. His British sense of 'fair play' was too ingrained even though Joshua could think of a hundred ways the British were just as bad; or worse. *God, what a damned mess.*

One thing was for sure: he was going to have to play host to this creature for quite some time – probably months.

"Well, if she's going to stay here for a while," he murmured to half-imagined fish beneath the waters' surface, "she'll have to bloody well follow my rules, or my god, she'll get what's coming to her."

It had been a while since he had felt this angry about something, and he didn't like it. He didn't like his calm, peaceful world being disrupted. But most of all, he didn't want to look into those eyes.

They both stood there for quite some time. One, open-jawed and tear-stained, the other beaming with a smile which came from her eyes as much as her lips. Even in her bewilderment, Sophie could reason that everything about this young beauty was perfect, from her skin which was smooth and dark as chocolate, to her hair which was jet black, long, and shone in the light of the veranda. Her clothes were clean and exotic, and her simple jewellery hung perfectly off her ears, from around her neck, and from her wrists and ankles.

From the moment this dark angel saw Sophie, she smiled widely, revealing perfect white teeth. Sophie could feel her heart sinking as her resolve began to leak away. There was something about this *goddess* that told her something good was here. The woman hadn't said a word, and yet she made Sophie want to stay.

"Good morning *Sho-fee*," the angel spoke in strained English, still beaming. "You sleep well last night?"

Sophie couldn't find the words; she simply stood, mute, mouth still open. The angel didn't seem to mind. She gently touched Sophie's shoulder with her right hand and turned the mesmerised girl around back into the room with a little giggle that sounded as sweet as raindrops to the twelve-year-old.

Didi (for that was the name, she told *Sho-fee*, that everyone around here knew her as) assured Sophie that she was safe, even if she was not in a place where she wanted to be. She looked to be in her twenties, and now that they were talking together, Sophie had the opportunity to look at her in detail. *Didi* had soft, dark-brown skin that didn't seem to have any blemishes at all. Her eyes sparkled with life, energy, and excitement all the time as she sat with Sophie on the mats she had laid on the concrete floor, and they talked together.

"I sorry that I no here when you yesterday arrive," *Didi* said. "Yesterday my *chuti*, my..." she searched for the English word, "...my day off, and I not know you coming. When I heard this morning, I come here straight. Now I help you settle here, and I hope be happy."

Her English was far from perfect, but Sophie, who didn't even have any real French after years of lessons at school, was impressed *Didi* had another language at all. They were obviously in a small village in the middle of nowhere, and the scenes of poverty Sophie had seen on the way were of the kind she'd only seen in school books and on TV news reports. Something told her that education in English was not something that would be a priority here – and why would it? How could English benefit a farmer in the fields? Yet *Didi* understood her, at least most of the time, as she babbled away about how she had to get out of there and find her aunt to persuade her to let her come home and that *this is all wrong!* She shouldn't be here.

Then *Didi*, smiling sweetly, had taken Sophie's hands in hers, put her thumbs gently on top, and stroked the backs of them. It was a simple action, but the love and care Sophie felt from this young woman was startling and comforting at the same time. This simple act of kindness was the most soothing and healing touch Sophie had experienced since waking up in the hospital months before. Tears welled up in her again, and she felt the drops land on her hands which *Didi* wiped away, making gentle *shushing* sounds as she let Sophie weep. Sophie barely flinched from her touch.

"I shouldn't be here, *Didi*," Sophie said through her tears. "This is not right. It's not fair. Why would my only family do this to me? What did I do wrong?" She turned her head in shame as she said this. But, deep down, she had a feeling she knew what she had done wrong and why she was being punished. Sophie couldn't quite put it into words – but it was there. *Something* she was forgetting.

Didi drew her close and hugged her. "I can see you very troubled heart. I help. I promise. I work for uncle and I here almost every day. I will cook for you, clean your clothes, you can ask any question, and I answer for you. We will be great friend – I promise. Anytime. No problem."

"Thank you, *Didi*," Sophie sobbed, "but I just want to go home. I don't want to be here."

"I know," said *Didi*, her hands gesticulating all the time in a way which Sophie found both comical and endearing, "this is all very difficult for uncle and you. He tell me all about it this morning. You are both have to live with each other until your uncle sort it all out. He will try to get you home. Soon. You see." Her face darkened for a moment, and, in a quieter, conspiratorial, voice she added, "Uncle not easy man. Very easy to upset. Big anger. But he good man. You see. *I* will make sure he treat you well."

Sophie laid her head on *Didi's* lap and gave a little sob. "I just want to go home," she whimpered. *Didi* said nothing but, instead, stroked her hair gently and made soft shushing sounds again. She stayed there until, finally, exhaustion overtook Sophie and she fell asleep – properly and completely – for the first time in days.

Her first conversation with 'Uncle Joshua' did not go well. As much as Sophie's time with *Didi* had been warm, welcoming, and long, the conversation with her supposed uncle was horrible, brash and short. He had tried to keep out of her way for as long as possible, but *Didi* knew the two of them were going to have to sort things out sooner or later. She prepared Sophie some breakfast that morning – something vaguely close to sliced bread with a jar of a substance which might have been jam but glowed with a bright red colour which seemed more at home in a sci-fi movie, Sophie had thought, but this did not have the desired effect of calming her. Instead, she seemed more annoyed.

Sophie felt better after a short sleep of a few hours and now was in a fighting mood. Why had this man, who was meant to be her long-lost uncle, not even tried to offer her so much as a snack last night or tried to see how she was or have any kind of conversation with her this morning? *What kind of an uncle doesn't even check on his newly-found niece?* she wondered.

It was *Didi* who brought them together. She came up to the room where Sophie's bags were still dumped after Graham had thrown them in and where Sophie now tried to hide away. There were no curtains, no carpet, just a few boxes of dusty books and the odd bit of broken furniture. Still unused by the girl, the bed was little more than basic wood, a foam mattress, and old sheets yellowed with age. Still, it was out of the way and had a door, so Sophie could just sit on the floor, watch the innumerable ants that milled around the edges of the walls and avoid her new enemy. She was rapidly coming to the conclusion that all men were, at best, idiots and, at worst…well, if not evil, certainly very, very bad. She hadn't decided which this supposed 'uncle' was yet and wasn't eager to find out. She wanted nothing to do with him. But *Didi* insisted Sophie came downstairs and meet him properly, so she dragged her feet all the way and slumped, sulkily, into the chair *Didi* pointed to in the front room.

He was already there, big, fat, and slightly wheezing in the far corner, looking equally sulky. His arms were folded, and he stared at her over his thin-framed spectacles. He looked a mess as far as Sophie could tell, and she didn't believe that this man was her uncle at all. In the past, she had seen the family resemblance between her mum, her only sister, Aunty Hannah, and Sophie herself, but this man looked nothing like her dad, whose brother he was supposed to be. Surely, this was a mistake?

They glared at each other for several seconds, both refusing to speak first. One of them had to break first, and Sophie was determined it would not be her. Eventually, the fat man gave in.

"I am not happy about this; you should know," he huffed, "not happy *at all*. This is not a playground, and it's not bloody Disneyland either. It's no place for a girl who knows nothing about the country. Do you have *any* idea at all how hard this will be for you? Do you even know what country this is? Or anything about the people, the culture? Anything?"

"Well, I'm not exactly here because I want to be, okay?" Sophie retorted. *What a horrible man,* she thought. She pondered, half fantasizing about his hideous ways. She recalled a lesson at school she'd had once on 'International Anti-slavery Day.' Guest speakers had come to teach the children all about modern-day enslavement. *I bet he is cruel to Didi and she only stays working for him because he has some secret grip on her. I've been taught about this kind of thing in school. 'Debt slavery' or something. I bet she was sold into slavery because he conned her family into taking a big loan they couldn't afford. She'll have to work for this ugly monster for the rest of her life.* Satisfied that she now had this 'monster' summed up, she relaxed a bit and kept a deliberate look of distaste on her face so that he would know *exactly* what she was thinking of him.

He leaned forward in his chair. "Well, that is something we both agree on then, isn't it? Neither of us wants you here. Hannah was quite wrong to do this. It isn't right, and the sooner we get rid of you, the better."

"Are you always so horrible? Or do you save it up to use on young girls and servants who deserve better?" Sophie got up and started to leave the room.

"Good God, girl – *I'm* horrible? You're the one throwing around accusations! Who's done nothing but scream and rant and make demands since the moment you arrived *without my invitation,* I might add!" The man stood to his feet in anger. He looked more imposing and frightening when he stood. "You know nothing about me and probably never will. Oh! What's the use? You won't listen to a word I say anyway."

"Well, that's another thing we agree on then, isn't it?" said Sophie whirling round in a fury. "I don't want to spend a minute longer in this horrible wreck of a house than I need to. This is a horrible country with horrible people, and you seem to be well-matched with them."

The Joshua-man's face flushed with anger. Suddenly Sophie was scared. Graham, like this, would be ready to lash out with his hands. This strange Joshua-man, though, stood there, furious but clearly in control.

"You will not talk about Bangladesh and her people like that again, do you hear?" He spoke quietly, but every word was laced with menace. "I've spent fifteen years of my life living with these people who have not had even a tenth of what you've had your entire life. You may have lost your parents, but for many here, that is a common-place event. They lose parents, brothers, sisters, and children all the time here. *Didi,*" he pointed at the Bangladeshi standing in the corner of the room, "has *no* family."

Sophie's face flushed at the thought. She had not considered that *Didi* might be an orphan like her.

"They have precious little food and work god knows how many hours every day just to bring something home for their families to eat. Each Bangladeshi works harder in a day than you have probably ever done in your life, so, no matter how much you might be angry or hate me, *show some respect to these people.* They deserve better from you."

Sophie stood there, stunned by his rebuke, feeling annoyed with herself for her meanness and annoyed with him for speaking words that rang with truth. She shouldn't have lashed out at Bangladesh; she knew that. *Didi* was one of these people, if nothing else, and she definitely liked her. How could you not? Nevertheless, he seemed to care more about this country than his own flesh and blood, and she wasn't going to forgive that.

"Whatever," she said as she left the room, "just get me out of here so I can go back to my own life."

"Oh, I will," the Joshua-man shouted after her. But then, after she had gone up the stairs to her room, on the verge of shouting again, he added instead in a quieter voice and with a slight shake of his head, "but just what kind of a life is that, hey? Just what do you have there, I wonder?"

Sophie finally went to bed late that night. It was the first time in three nights that she had a bed to get into. *Didi* had made it up beautifully with fresh sheets, and, she had to admit, it was comfy without being too hot, thanks to the ceiling fan turned on this time. *Didi* had made her some wonderful food that day. They had both had eaten a curry for lunch after the Joshua-man had eaten his and gone out. It was the most delicious meal Sophie had ever eaten. Not too spicy, but just enough to make her taste buds tingle and her belly feel alive. Then, in the evening, *Didi* had made her *nasta*. This food was like a combination of bread and cake, which was fried in sugar and oil. Again, it was delicious, and Sophie ate plenty. She had been starving, having not eaten properly since she left the UK, and she now went to bed with a full stomach. Her whole body was aching from all the crying she had done and from squatting in the corner of the room the previous night, and she readily snuggled down to sleep.

As she lay there, in the darkness listening to the endless chirruping of crickets outside, she thought about the things she had talked about with *Didi*. The woman was amazing, Sophie had decided. When the horrible Joshua-man had not been around, Sophie had spent time with her in the kitchen and watched as she endlessly chopped and peeled vegetables and skinned meat using the same kind of knife she had seen other Bangladeshis using on the drive up. It stood on a little metal base with the sharp edge pointed upwards – *Didi* called it a *boti*. She held part of the base down with her foot as she sat and pushed vegetables at the knife with alarming speed. The blade was clearly very sharp, as the skins came flying off and vegetables were sliced into small chunks, yet *Didi* never caught her fingers. When she didn't cook, she washed and wiped floors on her knees or tidied the house. She never stopped but was obviously very happy to have Sophie there to talk with.

Didi talked like she worked – nonstop! She told Sophie about the kinds of people here, how the village was hundreds of years old, how this house had been built, as Sophie had guessed, in the days of the Raj when Bangladesh had been part of India and ruled by the British. She told Sophie how the white owners of the house had been killed by mutinying Indian soldiers in a famous battle from long ago and how the wife's ghost was still said to haunt the area. Sophie was thrilled to hear stories like that, and *Didi* had many to tell. The day passed by quickly for Sophie, but it seemed impossibly long hours to her for *Didi* to work. It was dark outside and long after Sophie finished eating the *nasta* before *Didi* finally left for her own home.

One thing *Didi* had told Sophie she didn't like – the Joshua-man had to be called 'Uncle Joshua.' Sophie felt like it was a betrayal to do so. He was not, as far as she was concerned, any member of her family. She still believed there was some mix-up and that they weren't related at all. *Didi* had just smiled as Sophie repeated this throughout the day. She said nothing, but Sophie felt that *Didi* thought there was no mistake at all. In the end, Sophie was talked into agreeing to it, partly because *Didi* explained that it was a custom in the village for all older men to be called 'uncle' in Bangla as well as in English, but mostly because it was going to please *Didi*, and Sophie wanted to do this more than anything else in the world at the moment. The young woman was a ministering angel from God, as far as Sophie was concerned, her only friend at a time when she really needed one. So, 'Uncle Joshua' it would be…albeit through gritted teeth.

And with that, Sophie drifted off to sleep, exhausted, confused, and angry with life, but no longer distressed or scared. At least, not while *Didi* was around.

Noise. Lots of it. Like the sound of a hundred foghorns blasting over water. Icy freezing water. She is lying on it, the cold water freezing her hair. But she isn't sinking into it. Why not? She looks up and tries to move, but something is stopping her. A sheet, tightly wrapped around her body and tied down. She pushes out and upwards with her hands, but it doesn't move much. Instead, it seems to grow and comes over her head. She pushes up, but now it is more solid, more like a roof. The sirens are still blasting, but now they sound different. She hears screeching. The screeching of wheels and the metal ceiling above now has covered her and pinned her down. Down, back into the ice. A hand reaches in from the window beside her. It is a rough hand, torn and bleeding. It comes to her face and strokes it. She feels comfort from the warmth but then the fingers move from her cheek to her mouth. They push their way in. They hurt. She struggles, but the ice has frozen her hair. She can't move. Panic grips her. She looks through the window and follows the arm, bloody, muscular, threatening, all the way to HIM! She struggles, fear and anger rising. The noises are deafening and then suddenly stop, to be replaced with one single voice. A voice she knows.

"Sophie."

Sophie sat upright in the bed, fear choking her. She gasped in pain, desperately trying to catch her breath.

Where was she?

She looked around in the darkness, groping for something familiar, nausea rising within her. Sophie got out of bed and moved towards the faint outline of a doorway. It was coming back to her now – just where she was. Nausea overcame her, and she knew she was going to vomit. She remembered now. This door led to the adjoining bathroom, and she rushed through it.

Sophie made it to the toilet bowl just in time as she threw up everything she had eaten that day. Several retches later, she sat on the floor, shaking and sobbing between the heaving spasms as they gradually eased. The voice in her dream came into her thoughts, but it made her want to vomit again. She knew the voice but could not bear the pain of thinking about her.

She stayed by the toilet until *Didi* found her in the morning and took her, weak and exhausted, back to bed. The birds had taken over from the chirruping crickets as *Didi* got Sophie back under the sheets. The sun was just rising, but Sophie paid it no attention.

CHAPTER TEN - GHOSTS

Joshua placed his tackle box down by the side of his little fold-up chair and sat himself down in it, landing heavily. The little chair creaked under the strain of his weight but held. Before him stretched the body of water – too large to be called a pool, too small for a lake; for him, it was simply the place where he knew peace. He went to pick up his fishing rod and begin preparing the line but stopped before his hand could grab the rod from the ground. He sat back, looked at the water, and sighed.

What was he going to do? Nothing in his life had prepared him for this. He had decided a long time ago that family life was not for him and suddenly, he found himself with a beast from hell cunningly disguised as a small girl.

And not just any girl. *Her* girl.

That much was obvious, he thought with a sliver of a grin. The beastly child had all of her mother's stubbornness but without any of her wit or charm. She had obviously been spoiled all her life (undoubtedly his brother's fault) and had no respect for elders.

She won't last two minutes in Bangladesh if she doesn't know how to respect others. That's why she has to go, of course. And good riddance – horrible child.

Then Joshua felt just a tiny twinge of guilt creeping in. He *hadn't* been particularly nice either; he knew that. But, if he thought about it, the girl had yet to see him *not* shouting at someone. He was quite cross with himself, really. He was a teacher and yet had forgotten all his basic teacher training from all those years ago. *"The Teacher should be in control of his students at all times,"* the books and lecturers had said, *"never the other way around. Don't blame the child if you lose control of yourself."*

It was true. Joshua had been so confused by what was suddenly happening to him (it was so out of the blue after all) that he had allowed his judgement to be clouded by emotion. This would never have happened in his classroom. No child would have got away with talking to him like that, but then, he wouldn't have got angry with any student like that either.

He didn't usually need to. Mutual respect was the way he ran his classes. He didn't mistreat the kids, and they didn't take him for a fool. It was a good system, and it worked. Mostly.

Maybe he was being a bit harsh on Sophie. Maybe he hadn't spoken to her yesterday quite the way he should have. Maybe he should have given some consideration to the fact that she was just as much a victim of that pair of turds as he. He did feel sorry for her situation, but well, who was going to feel sorry for *his* situation, eh? No one – that's who. She was just too bossy, too spiteful, and just…too much like her mother. Joshua threw that thought off. He wasn't going to go there.

He didn't even know how old Sophie was. *Twelve? Thirteen? Older?* It must be early teens, he decided. She certainly *stropped* like a teenager. He'd left England before she'd been born – before her parents had even married – just. In the early days, Hannah had written occasional notes to him to let him know how the family was getting on, and he remembered her writing that Elizabeth was pregnant. But he had never responded – he just couldn't – and Hannah had then met Graham, and *all* communication ceased soon after. Graham had not been happy with the idea of Hannah writing to the former love of her life – unrequited though it had been on Joshua's part.

He sighed again at the thought of the past. What a damned mess it had all been. No wonder he had wanted to get away from it all. Joshua had never understood people and never particularly liked being around them. It was much worse when emotions got involved. He hated being a teenager, back when he and his brother, so cocky and so sure of themselves, had met two pretty sisters at a spectacularly dreadful party. He'd carried his brother home, if he recalled correctly, stopping only to let him vomit from time to time. Joshua had never been keen on drinking alcohol and, after seeing his brother retching like that, never really went near the stuff again. Still, looking responsible for his younger brother did no harm to his reputation with the two girls, and phone numbers and promises to go out to the movies had been exchanged. He had no idea that it would eventually lead to him falling out with his brother, the marriage of the wrong man to the wrong girl, and, when he could take it no longer, Joshua himself leaving England and never returning. Even now, years later, the memories were too painful for him. And he had certainly never, ever expected his brother's daughter to land on his doorstep.

His *niece*! He realised he was going to have to get used to the word. How the hell had that happened? The thought of it made him feel tired and old. Older. *She* used to joke he was born an old man. He hated that. Stephen, by contrast, was always the big kid, the joker. He could make her laugh.

So, what was he going to do? Obviously, the girl couldn't stay. That was quite out of the question. Trouble was – where *was* she going to go? It would take time to get things arranged for her to return to Britain. Visas were not easy to sort out in Bangladesh and even worse when there was no passport. He could report this all to the authorities, but that would almost certainly lead to a minor diplomatic incident which could see Graham and Hannah jailed in all likeliness, and then Sophie would be completely homeless. He could find himself under pressure to look after her all over again if both of them were jailed. Or she could end up in care. Joshua shuddered. His years of teaching in the UK had taught him that kids taken into care by Social Services did not usually come out bright-eyed and bushy-tailed. The lucky ones managed a life. The unlucky ones…no. Causing trouble for 'Dastardly and Muttley' was not an option. He'd have to lie to the embassy and say there was a mix-up and the passport got destroyed.

How was he going to afford a plane ticket to get her home? He had no idea how much a ticket was these days, having not left Bangladesh in nearly ten years. Flights were never cheap, and England was far away. What could he do? He had precious little savings, and though he received a nominal sum of money from a charity fund set up long ago that still gave a little support, most of his money came from investments in various projects and a few fields he helped to buy. It had taken years for him to do this with very little money and finally become more or less self-supporting. Some return on his investments came in the form of meat, vegetables, and other produce. Enough came in the form of *taka* to pay the bills for the house. The rest came in the form of *beton* from the school where he taught English and History. There was no way that would be enough to get a girl back to the country she should never have been made to leave.

Briefly, Joshua allowed himself to think about her plight rather than think of *her* as a problem. Just for a moment, Joshua allowed himself the luxury of sympathy for the girl. He wasn't going to do this for long, he told himself. Joshua knew just where sympathy led, and he was not going to let that happen. The girl *had* to go – that was that.

But to lose your parents and then be dumped 5000 miles away from your home by the only person left in your family who you *should* be able to trust? – that got him really annoyed.

Damn that Graham.

Hannah would *never* have done this had she got herself a decent husband instead of that overbearing and stupid thug. She should have had the strength to stand up to him and insist that Sophie stay with them. She was just weak – not like her sister at all. Elizabeth had been strong-willed, *too* strong-willed sometimes, but not Hannah. She had no sense of responsibility towards family. It made him angry just to think about it. By God, if *he* had a niece…then he stopped dead in the track of his thoughts.

She *was* his niece. He may not have liked her father – they hadn't spoken in fifteen years – but he *was* still his brother. He may know nothing about Sophie, but that didn't mean they didn't share common blood or that they weren't bonded to the same people – no matter how much Joshua wished that was not the case. And she was *so* young.

He shook his head to clear his thoughts.

Don't do this, old man, he told himself, *don't start allowing yourself to like that dratted creature.*

No, it was no good. She still had to go. This was not a place for a young *white* teenage girl with no idea how to behave or cope with this society. It wouldn't be fair on her. He would make arrangements.

"Next week," he said to himself out loud as he picked up his fishing rod with determination and set himself to actually *do* some fishing instead of winding himself up. "Give her a chance to settle in, recover, get herself together. It'll give me time to find some money, too. Pull a few favours and persuade that damned fool woman, Hannah, to take her back, if possible, too."

Yes, he thought, that will do nicely—no need to rush.

The clouds in the distance were beginning to darken as Joshua walked back to the house. It looked to him like a storm was brewing. As he reached the doorway, he reminded himself, again, of how he was going to do this.

No arguments. You're not going to get cross. You will be pleasant. You will remember that she is still grieving, and she needs space. She is just like a student. Being nice to her doesn't mean you have to like her. He stopped at the threshold for a moment, disturbed by that thought. *You are most certainly not to like her, in fact. She is not staying, and you will not get emotionally involved. She is a guest. One you didn't invite, to be sure, but one nevertheless and, if things go smoothly, she is only staying a short while…weeks at most. You can be nice. It won't kill you.*

He came in and saw Sophie sitting in a chair in the front room, reading a book. He was pleasantly surprised to see it was history. He fixed a big smile on his face, as best he could and only slightly fake. This was a subject he could share with her, bond with her over—a perfect opportunity to start again on neutral territory.

"History!" he said simply, but a little louder than he intended, not knowing what else to say, and just stood there trying to keep hold of his grin – something he was not used to doing. Sophie looked up at him, and her face turned to pure disgust at the sight of him. His heart sank.

"I'll read whatever I want! It has nothing to do with you," she snapped at him as she got up out of the chair and left the room to go upstairs.

For a moment, Joshua just stood there opening and closing his mouth like a goldfish, unable to find the words. He still hadn't even put down his tackle box and fishing rod yet. Just one word, *one word,* and she had stormed out.

What the hell was that? he thought to himself and despaired. He placed the box and rod down on a nearby shelf and went to the mirror hanging on the veranda wall. He looked at himself in the mirror for a moment, trying to remember what it was like to be young. What *he* looked like back when he was young. He put the smile back on his face, the one he had just used.

Joshua flinched. That wasn't a smile at all. It was, well, hideous, really. Like a cross between a snarl and an evil glare.

"Ah," he said out loud to no one in particular, "that explains it. You need to work on that, old boy."

He tried again with a smile. This time it seemed to work, but it hurt his cheeks to do it for long. Then he put the first expression, the one he thought was a smile, back on his face. It wasn't pleasant. Had it looked to Sophie like he was about to criticise her? He made a mental note not to try smiling again. He had never been very good at it even as a young man, and age and experience had not taught him how to be any better at it now. *It's not going to kill you,* he reminded himself again and repeated it continually like a mantra as he went to change his clothes.

Sophie came down later on for dinner. By now, it was dark outside as night had fallen. There were clear rumblings of thunder from a storm some distance away still. *Didi* had prepared curry and rice and, for the first time, her uncle and Sophie ate together. They sat at a moderately sized table made of bamboo, just big enough for about four people, in a room just off the downstairs veranda at the back of the house. They didn't speak. They just ate in the silence punctuated with gentle rumbles from far away. *Didi* stood watching in the corner. It made Sophie uncomfortable, but it seemed to be what *Didi* did. She never ate with either of them but always ate separately or, presumably, at home after she finished working. It seemed to be, from what Sophie could understand, what people did in Bangladesh. This time though, *Didi* seemed quite nervous. She was watching the pair of them like a hawk.

The light over the table flashed for a moment, then sputtered, then died completely. It took a while for Sophie to realise that the whole house had lost its electricity; it wasn't just a faulty bulb. At first, her uncle and *Didi* said nothing and continued as though nothing had happened. Then Joshua realised she had stopped eating.

"Don't worry," he said softly, "this is quite normal. During storms, the electricity generators often go down. When it gets really hot too, they sometimes deliberately turn off electricity to whole areas. There's not enough power, you see. But you get used to it. The power will come on eventually."

Just as he finished speaking, the lights came back on, and Sophie noticed, looking out of the window, that other dwellings in the distance had also been blacked out and were now shining again with various lights.

Joshua finished his meal first, looked up, and thanked *Didi* for her cooking.

"It was a wonderful curry as always, *Didi*," he said, wiping his mouth, "*dhonnobad.*"

Didi said nothing in response but wobbled her head in a way Sophie thought should mean *Didi* was really annoyed with her uncle's compliment but was restraining herself. Sophie was sure that couldn't be so but had no idea what that slight tilt of the head was meant to mean otherwise. She watched *Didi* clear up plates and cups and noticed how she and Joshua engaged in a bit of chatter in Bangla, but Sophie could understand none of it. She did spot furtive glances from both of them in her direction, though. Once Sophie had finished too and the table was clear, she sat staring at the table in front of her, not daring nor wishing to look at her uncle at all.

"Sophie," Joshua interrupted the silence, "can we, perhaps begin again? I think we maybe got off on the wrong foot yesterday. You are going to have to stay here a few days until we can get things sorted for you, and I don't want that to be unpleasant."

Sophie looked up at him. For once, his face seemed kind and genuine, and her heart softened slightly, only slightly. She shrugged her shoulders to indicate she was not bothered but was open to suggestions. Thunder rumbled again, a little nearer now.

"Come on," her uncle said, standing up and leading her to the front living room. As they walked along the long veranda, Sophie looked out at the lightning, which every second or so lit up the entire sky behind dark silhouettes of palm trees and mud huts. The whole of one side of the veranda was windows with netting on the inside to keep mosquitoes out and thick metal bars running down to keep thieves out too. The upstairs veranda was identical. In fact, all the windows in the house had the same netting and vertical bars, but the verandas had no glass sliding panels which kept out the wind and rain in all the rooms. The curtains, still pushed to one side of the windows, flapped wildly in the wind, which both cooled

Sophie from the heat and exhilarated her with its wildness. Uncle Joshua reached the front room first. He motioned to the sofa and padded chairs.

"Let's have a chat for a little while. Get to know each other."

"Ok," Sophie agreed, a little reluctantly, but moved from the indicated sofa to a huge, deep, round chair made of bamboo that virtually swallowed her whole when she sat in it. Sophie had discovered it early when reading her history book and had fallen in love with it. She could tuck her feet up inside it, and it felt like she was in her own womblike den.

But not now. Not when this man was present. This time, she didn't tuck her feet up but sat more upright and 'properly.'

Her uncle sat down on the sofa, and Sophie couldn't help but notice how it sagged with his weight. The sight amused her, but she kept it to herself. He seemed uncertain what to say next and was looking around as if to find inspiration over what to talk about.

"So…," he began nervously. Then his eyes alighted on a newspaper on the small coffee table in front of him. It was in Bangla, and there was a photograph of a large tiger on the front.

"Ah," he said, clearly now feeling on comfortable ground as he held up the picture for Sophie to see. "The Royal Bengal Tiger," he announced as though beginning a class with his students, "a most magnificent beast but unfortunately rather endangered these days. That's thanks to our fellow English countrymen and their excessive love of hunting during the Raj."

Sophie looked at him blankly, not really knowing what to say. He looked at her and then turned to examine the article.

"Alas, it would seem that one has escaped from a zoo in an *upozila* near ours and is on the prowl. It is always sad when these things happen."

"What's 'ooper zila'?"

He peered over the paper at her, not unkindly.

"*Upozila*. Bangladesh is split into several '*zilas*' or divisions. Each division is then split into several smaller districts called '*upozilas.*' It's an administrative thing, really. A bit like our counties and towns in England."

Curiosity got the better of Sophie. She wasn't warming to the man, she told herself, but at least he wasn't shouting.

"How did the tiger escape?" she asked.

"Oh," her uncle responded with a tired look in his eyes and crumpled the newspaper slightly in his large hands, "because zoos here are very poorly maintained, and staff rarely have much of an idea how to look after the cages. They don't have any better idea how to look after the animals either. Mostly, they're kept in dreadful conditions. And there just aren't enough trained tiger specialists in Bangladesh or India, which means that when one occasionally manages to break free, these shy but dangerous creatures can remain on the run for days or even months without being captured."

"That's good, isn't it?" Sophie asked. "I mean, I don't approve of animals being locked in a zoo. Surely, if it isn't doing any harm, it is good it remains free?"

"Well," said her uncle, folding the newspaper and putting it back on the table, "that's a nice thought, but it doesn't wash here, I'm afraid. That tiger, if no one catches it, will eventually eat anything it can get hold of – and that means humans, I'm afraid. When that happens, the villagers will want to have the animal killed, and no tiger ranchers will be able to save it if the people get to it first. Especially not when there is still a very high price for tiger teeth and hide on the black market. One tiger could feed a poor family for a year."

"Oh," said Sophie, not really sure how to respond to this. Talk of tigers as though commonplace was very new to her. She tried to imagine one wandering nonchalantly down a British road. She remembered once coming home late one evening with her dad from a treat out to the cinema. They had been driving along a deserted bypass and passed a cow wandering happily up the other side, in the right direction as though she was a vehicle. It had been a surreal moment which both Sophie and her dad found very funny at the time. Sophie smiled at the thought, and then pain tugged at her heart. She didn't want to think of her father.

Silence. Move on.

She looked at the shelves full of books around the room. In other circumstances, she would have loved this strange living room-cum-study with its musty books full of mystery and learning. Even with this horrid situation now, the thought of reading them made her tingle. Her eyes alighted on one particular book.

"Oh my God!" she said, standing and pointing at the book. "You have a copy of *Wuthering Heights* here."

"I do, yes," said Joshua, half grinning, half frowning. "Not a book I would have thought a twelve-year-old girl would want to read."

"I have a copy at…" She paused very briefly. *Home?* She didn't even know what that was anymore. "…Anyway, I didn't bring it. I was reading it. I found the way Emily Brontë describes the solitude of the characters strangely comforting."

"Do you indeed?" Joshua gave half a grin.

Sophie didn't add that half the reason she started reading the book was because she recalled it was one of those which sat on her father's small bookshelf of prized books Sophie hadn't been allowed to touch because they were old and precious. Not unlike this one. She had wanted to feel in some way closer to her father by reading something which was important to him. Right now, though, she realised, she needed to think of something else.

"You can borrow it, if you like, for the short time you're here?"

"No thanks," Sophie said and sat down again.

Silence again.

"Well," said her uncle, beginning the next conversation this time, "you'll be glad to know that I will do my best to be rid of you within about a week, I think, and then…."

"Get rid of me?!" Sophie went red in the face.

"Well, yes, obviously…it's what you want," he stammered.

"How would *you* know what I want? You don't know anything about me."

Now it was Joshua's turn to be red in the face. He sat forward on the sofa and looked even more serious – if that was possible.

"Now look," he said sternly, "you can't stay here. You know that. So, there's no point thinking you can. I'm letting you have a few days to recover from your ordeal. I know this isn't your fault."

"Oh well, thank you *very* much! How kind you are."

"For god's sake, can you not, for once, just be *civil?*"

"Don't shout at me!" said Sophie, herself now shouting.

"I'm not shouting!" her uncle shouted back.

"Yes, you are."

"No, I'm not," he stood up, enraged. *"This is shouting, you ungrateful wretch!"*

He stopped, horrified, seeing not anger in Sophie's face but fear. Her eyes watered. Quickly, he sat down again and tried to diffuse the situation.

"This is speaking normally. Not shouting at all." He winced at the inadequacy of his own words.

It was too late. Sophie got up from the chair and fled to her room upstairs. Joshua sat there for a moment, wondering just what had taken place. It had been going so well. Well, not so well, but good enough. They'd managed two conversations without shouting. She had even impressed him a little with her comments about *Wuthering Heights*. There was a spark of intelligence behind those young eyes, and he understood entirely what she meant about the comfort of the solitude, bleak though it was, described in the book. It was one of the reasons he was extremely fond of the book himself. But clearly, three conversations were too much.

Damn that girl, he thought. *She's absolutely impossible.*

Didi stood in the corner, having heard the shouting, looking anxious and sad. He looked at her, feeling cross with her, Sophie, the world, and...yes, alright...himself.

"Ki?" he snapped at her, "What? I tried, didn't I? But she's just impossible."

"Yes, uncle," *Didi* replied meekly and left the room to tidy the kitchen. The thunder was louder now and more ominous –it was going to be a big one tonight – but he ignored it. If it was trying to give him any kind of prophetic warning, it was lost on him. He didn't even notice the irony of the metaphor. It was the kind of thing he'd scowl at in a piece of fiction. Instead, Joshua sat there frowning and looked at the picture of the tiger in the newspaper again. For a moment, he allowed himself the fantasy of a tiger swallowing someone whole. The mouth was open, and two tiny legs were disappearing inside. They were a girl's legs. He shook the image away and felt guilty for being so cruel.

Suddenly, all the lights went out, and Joshua suspected that this time they would stay out for some time. This storm was a bad one, for sure. *This is insane,* he thought, and his thoughts went back to the uncouth creature now back in her room. This girl was going to be the death of him. He was not cut out for raising a child. Never was, never would be.

Thank goodness she wouldn't be here long.

The darkness again.

The sound of wheels screeching. A woman cries out and then…light. She rises out of the watery blackness and into light. But it is not white light. It is green and hazy. She feels hot and takes off her coat. Again and again, she takes it off, but each time she is wearing another one underneath. Suddenly she hears the sound of scratching. Like tree branches on windows. There is a strong wind, and everything is blowing around her. Leaves, trees, grass, jungle. She is outside and running. Running from the wind. Running from a sound. The sound of growling. THERE IS SOMETHING NEAR HER! She moves fast now, faster and faster, her coat coming off again and again. But still the monster is right behind her. She hears its claws and can feel its breath. She hears a growl, and the word "history" snarled. She knows who that beast is. "Sophie! This way!" she hears a woman's voice calling from a forest that is now in front of her. She knows that voice too. She trusts that voice. She runs into the forest and looks for her. Looks for her knowing she will keep her safe from that monster. Then she sees the woman in a clearing and tries to run, but now there are belt-like straps wrapping around her, holding her back, forcing her to sit down. She turns her head towards the voice and sees blood running down from the face to the stomach. The woman's dress is drenched in red. NO! The woman's face is a snarl. The eyes of a beast stare at her—red and angry. The beast opens her mouth, lets out a roar and leaps towards her. As she tries to back away, the belts around her tighten and squeeze the breath out of her as she tries to scream. She hears evil-sounding laughter and the sound of scraping on glass again and deep booming. Lights flash all around her; a car horn sounds, and then – the beast grabs her.

Sophie opened her eyes and sat bolt upright in bed. Lightning flashed repeatedly through her open windows, the curtains flapping wildly in the stormy winds which blew ferociously outside. The thunder boomed overhead as Sophie stared out of the window. She had never heard such noise or felt such chaos from nature. Again, she looked out of the windows.

There, in front of her and staring in, was the face of a monster. Red eyes glowed at her from beneath a mane of white hair trailing downwards.

Sophie let out a scream of utter terror.

Joshua all but broke the door down as he came rushing headlong into Sophie's room. The storm continued with no sign of abating, and the lightning lit up the veranda between their two rooms every few seconds as he hobbled along – the closest to running he was ever likely to get. He had assumed Sophie's door would be locked. It wasn't.

"God love us, child," he said as he crashed through and staggered into the room, trying to regain his balance, "what the hell can the matter be making that kind of racket? You're making more noise than the bloody storm!"

"There's a...a..." Sophie hesitated for a moment, still terrified out of her wits, but pointed to the window "...a monster, a ghost...something...outside." She cried and clutched her knees.

"What are you talking about, girl?" Uncle Joshua spat at her but turned to look at the window anyway. "Have you lost your mind? You're talking like an *oshikkhito* with superstitious nonsense like that! It's just the storm. No one is out there."

"I'm telling you," Sophie sobbed, "there was a woman out there, and she had huge..." she held her hands up to her eyes, "...*red eyes*. She was horrible. She must have been a ghost."

"There's no one there, I tell you. There are *no* ghosts. What's got into you?"

Just at that point, the electricity, at long last, came back on, and the room lit up brightly. Sophie squinted in the bright light, and instantly the fear began to drain away. She felt more than a little foolish.

"Never mind...I...I just had an awful dream, that's all," she said, half to herself. "I thought I saw my mum and she was bleeding, and I wanted to go to her but I couldn't because there were all these...," she held her hands up around her chest, "...straps wrapped around me and I couldn't talk either to warn her, and I heard this horrible laughing then I was certain I woke up and saw this...*thing*...at my window. It was so *real*."

She looked up at her uncle at that point and was surprised to see not anger or disdain on his face but concern.

"God love us, child," he said, grabbing a towel from the *alna* and sitting on the edge of her bed, "you are as pale as a sheet and shivering."

He put the towel around her shoulders to wrap her up and then, instinctively, put his arms around her to warm her up. It surprised them both. Sophie let it happen; she suddenly realised she was numbingly cold. Her uncle held her but froze as if he had done something terribly wrong that he couldn't undo now. His rubbing motions on her back became mechanical, as if patting some strange dog that you are a little wary of.

"It's ok," he said, desperately trying to think of something to say. "You just had a bad dream. The storms can do that when you first experience them. They are much worse than anything you get in England." Sophie could tell he was feeling very uncomfortable holding this girl who was invading his home, but she let him continue, grateful for the comfort he was giving her. She would never have thought he could do this, nor that it would actually feel ok.

"My first storm here gave me a nightmare too," he continued, desperately thinking of how he could get his arm away from her as soon as possible. It was a lie, of course, and he was fairly sure Sophie knew it too, but he couldn't think of anything else to say.

"Thank you," Sophie said eventually. "I feel better. I'm sorry I made such a scene."

He took his arm away from her and pulled away a little to look at her face, concern still in his eyes but less so.

"It's ok, Sophie. Just…" he patted her arms, "just try to get some sleep now without waking the whole village up again. The storm's passing. I don't think another is likely tonight. So, you should be able to sleep better." He got up from the bed and reached for the light switch.

"Try not to have another nightmare, ok?" he said as he turned the light out.

"I always have nightmares," Sophie replied, snuggling back into her bed. "Ever since I woke up in hospital, I've had them. They never leave me. I just wish I understood better what they are trying to tell me."

Joshua said nothing but just shut her door. He stood there, on the other side, for a few seconds and closed his eyes. The image of Sophie's mother flashed into his head.

"You and me both," he said quietly to himself as he returned, saddened, to his room.

CHAPTER ELEVEN – THE PUKUR

"Come!" Uncle Joshua barked at Sophie, "I'm taking you to the *Pukur.*"

The where? thought Sophie, but she said nothing. The grimace on her uncle's face was enough to tell her it wasn't worth it. Instead, she picked herself up off the ground where she was reading a book on Bangladesh history found on one of the many bookshelves in the house and followed him out.

As they reached the front door, she noticed his fishing kit all laid out and ready to pick up.

"Is the…buku…the pool I saw out there when I arrived?" she asked.

"Pukur, child, *pukur,*" Joshua shouted back, dropping his rod as he tried to pick up his folding chair. He huffed, "and yes, it is. We're going fishing."

"Er, I'd rather not. It sounds like the most boring thing in the world." *I'd rather die,* Sophie thought to herself but figured that speaking that out loud might push it, just a bit.

"Well, you won't know until you try it, and you *are* going to try it. Don't argue with me on this one girl – just pick up that tackle box there and make yourself useful."

So, the one moment of tenderness her uncle had shown last night was all forgotten in the light of a new day, it seemed. It was back to normal, whatever normal was (Sophie was yet to see any emerging pattern of 'normality' in this upside-down world in which she was now a reluctant partner), and they were going to continue fighting. Joshua finally succeeded in picking the chair and rod up and walked straight out of the door without even looking to see if Sophie was coming or for her reply. Obedience was assumed.

Didi touched her shoulder, and Sophie turned around.

"Sophie," she said in a hushed whisper, "you should know your uncle *never* allow anyone go with him to *pukur*. Is his special place and all village know that every Friday morning he go there fish by himself. He get *bery* angry if anyone disturb him."

She lovingly moved a wisp of Sophie's hair out of her eyes and added, almost with a hint of sadness, "in all my life I not know him ask anyone to come with him."

Sophie looked out of the wide-open door at her uncle's rapidly diminishing figure. Why was he asking her to come with her then?

"He is giving you a great honour he never do before." *Didi* continued. "But I think it make him *bery* uncomfortable. He has been angry all morning. Trying be nice for him. Please." Sophie stepped out into the morning sunlight. Trying to 'be nice' was something that would be easier said than done.

For several minutes, they sat on the bank in silence. Uncle Joshua busied himself with his fishing equipment, getting things out of his tackle box and threading the line on his rod. After a while, though, he had nothing left to prepare and couldn't avoid talking to this strange child any longer.

"Look," he began, "I think you should know that I'm not very good at this kind of thing."

Sophie looked at him surprised, again, by a sudden short burst of awkward tenderness. She said nothing but just kept looking.

"And normally," he continued, "I don't let *anyone* come here to the *pukur* – that's what they call this pool; it just means 'pond' or 'pool' in Bangla. This is my special time. The only time in the whole week when I can be properly alone."

He stopped fiddling with his rod for a moment and looked at Sophie.

"I need my space," he said. "It's nothing about you. I think…I think I could quite *like* you actually if I get to know you better. But I came here fifteen years ago to get away from people. I'm a loner. I was never the marrying type. *Never.*"

Sophie thought there seemed to be bitterness in his voice but was unsure where this conversation was going. *Where did marrying types come into it?* She was silent, so after a moment, her uncle spoke again.

"What I'm saying is, I'm not very good with people in my personal life. I like my own company – task-oriented introvert, and all that. So, I'm saying that we need to find boundaries with each other until we figure out what is going to happen in the long term. I know you don't want to be here and I don't…" he faltered for a moment as if thinking carefully about his choice of words, "…I *didn't* want you…to be here either. Regardless, I still don't want you to be unhappy, and I appreciate that my home is not a conducive environment for a girl. It's not likely to become one either, though. I'm not a family man, I'm afraid; I like my children to stay in the classroom – not in my home."

"Are you a teacher?" Sophie asked.

Joshua looked at her with a momentary expression of offence that she didn't know this about him, which gave way to acceptance that, yes, perhaps there was no reason why she should. He pointed vaguely into the distance as if somehow Sophie could see beyond the thick wall of trees surrounding the lake.

"Yes, yes, child – for my sins," he smiled. "I teach English and History at the school just over there. We probably need to get you enrolled, actually. How old are you?"

"Twelve. No, wait." A sudden realisation hit her. "*Thirteen*. My birthday's in March. *Was* in March. I missed it this year." She added, in case it needed stating, "I was in a coma at the time."

Sophie looked down at the water and was quiet. Joshua winced and felt a pang of sorrow for her again. This poor girl had been through so much, yet despite her temper and stubbornness (which he couldn't really complain about – not when he shared the same characteristics and was well known for those traits too), she was quite modest and unassuming in many ways. So far, at least, apart from their spats with each other, she hadn't been fussy or difficult or whingey; she hadn't made demands, and he had to admit he'd barely known she was there in the days she'd been his unwilling tenant.

"Funny," she said, at long last," I don't *feel* thirteen. But I guess I must be."

The old man next to her gave out a deep sigh which somehow sounded sympathetic and understanding.

"Time behaves strangely in this country," her uncle responded. "You can go years here and feel they were just months, or a week can seem like a quarter of a year."

Again, they were silent for a while. Then he cleared his throat.

"Ah well, thirteen then. I'm afraid that's bad news," he said, looking solemn again.

"Why?" Sophie asked.

"Because it means you might well get the grumpiest and meanest teacher at the school for some of your subjects when I enrol you.

"Great," said Sophie. That was all she needed. "Which subjects?"

"English and History," he said with a grin. "He's a rotter, I can tell you."

Sophie laughed out aloud. This bizarre, fat, gruff old man, allegedly her uncle, was full of surprises. One moment angry and scary, the next minute cracking jokes and being quite sweet. She didn't know whether to hate him or like him. For certain, though, she was going to have to get to know him better.

"I think it is going to take a while to get your return to England sorted."

"Ok," Sophie replied, "I think…How long?"

Joshua frowned to himself. "Well, that's the thing. I don't know. I don't have a lot of money. I live on savings from the work I used to do in the UK. I have investments here and there, earn a pittance from the school for the teaching I do, and receive most of my food from fields I have invested in. I don't know *how* I'm going to get in touch with Hannah nor how I will persuade her to take you back. That idiot Graham is a bloody nuisance, and he keeps her trapped in fear – *that* much is obvious. She looked so ashamed when they left – and so she should."

Sophie looked at the waters again. The *pukur* was a horrible, murky green colour that was thick and opaque. It was the most disgusting body of water she'd ever seen. She couldn't see how *anything* could be alive in those depths. Certainly not fish. She was kind of secretly pleased that Aunty Hannah had been ashamed. She hadn't seen her face when she got in the car and left. But Sophie also couldn't think how Joshua – *Uncle* Joshua, she decided she needed to start getting used to calling him – could get past the problem of Graham.

It took Sophie the best part of two hours to extricate herself from the *pukur* and her uncle. He attempted to show her the intricacies of fishing, and she tried to pretend to be interested. Her body, however, rebelled against her, and she couldn't help but start yawning with increasing rapidity as time went on. With every intake of breath, Joshua frowned a little bit more until he dismissed her, making an evident effort to do so politely and not in fury. Sophie, in her turn, did her best to look apologetic and not leap to her feet to fly like a cat released from a cage.

She returned to the house, which she noticed her uncle had called the *bari* and thought about how she should probably start to learn some Bangla words. If she was going to stay here for more than the hoped-for couple of days, then she might as well take it as a learning experience.

She stepped into the *bari* and took off her shoes. She'd realised that neither her uncle nor *Didi* wore their sandals in the house but always took them off at the door and walked around barefoot. It seemed incongruous to Sophie that her uncle, who spoke in such a pompous public-school-boy voice, should wander around with bare feet. She tried to think of university professors (Joshua seemed to her every bit the archetypal Oxford don type of teacher) wearing short-sleeved shirts, trousers made of thin fabric, and delivering their lectures in bare feet. The image seemed hilarious, yet somehow it didn't seem wrong that her uncle could be found reading in his study room, some great tome in his hands, with his hard, calloused, and bony white feet tucked up beside him on his couch with music playing softly in the background.

With *Didi*, barefoot was the natural and perfect state. It felt more wrong to Sophie when the girl had to go out and put sandals on. For Sophie, *Didi's* feet were perfect. All of *Didi* was perfect, of course, but watching her pad around softly in the kitchen or along the veranda seemed to Sophie like exquisite art in motion.

Why they took their sandals off, Sophie could quickly understand. Firstly, it was too damned hot. She'd come to Bangladesh wearing socks and trainers, and it had taken just one day to abandon the socks for fear her feet would actually melt away. Now she was aware of how badly her feet smelt when she removed her shoes and found herself washing them several times each day.

Doing so revealed the full extent of a second reason for shoes coming off: the floors were constantly filthy and took up the lion's share of *Didi's* work in the house cleaning. Sophie's feet, in just the time it took to come in, shed footwear and walk through the house, up the stairs to her room and stick one foot in the basin in one corner of her room, were black with dirt from the floors.

Each day, Sophie had seen *Didi*, as soon as breakfast was out of the way and her uncle had been given his second cup of tea, get down on her hands and knees on the harsh, unforgiving concrete floor and begin washing it by hand with a rag, a bucket of water and some kind of soap block. She spent an hour doing this each morning before then spending the rest of the morning chopping vegetables and meat on the kitchen floor itself and making lunch for her master. Then, after lunch, she again went back to the floors, sweeping them this time with a broom made from bamboo for the handle and what looked like long hair to Sophie for the cleaning fibres.

Today, Sophie decided she would try to help *Didi*. She might as well be useful. But as soon as she tried to put forward the idea to the girl, *Didi* threw up her hands in horror as though Sophie had just said the most outrageous thing and refused to let her touch anything in the kitchen. So, instead, Sophie decided she would keep the woman company and chat to her, and perhaps learn some things along the way. So she sat down on the hard floor in one corner of the kitchen while *Didi* chopped tomatoes, spices, and some chicken pieces. Somehow, the girl even seemed to make this look beautiful.

Didi's English was broken in terms of pronunciation and grammar, but her vocabulary was quite extensive. As the girls chatted, there was very little that Sophie said which *Didi* failed to understand. She spoke slowly and with a thick Asian accent but with surprising skill. Sophie felt quite ashamed that she couldn't speak any other language at all and felt she would definitely need to rectify this at some point soon.

"*Didi*," she said after a while, "am I allowed to go out and wander around the area? I've not seen anything here, and if Uncle Joshua is right and I'm going to have to be here a few weeks or maybe months," she cringed at the thought, "I should maybe get to know the place a little."

Didi said nothing but gave a little head wobble which seemed to indicate she was not convinced the idea was a good one yet didn't dismiss it either. It was most infuriating for Sophie. Eventually, *Didi* looked up from her chopping, fixed her eyes on Sophie's, and spoke.

"You should meet *Mashima*," she said simply before going back to her work.

"Why? Who is she?"

Didi grinned, flashing her startlingly white and perfectly straight teeth, but didn't look up as she ground what looked like a small fat piece of tree branch into a paste using a rectangular stone on a stone chopping board. The pungent smell of ginger filled the air.

"*Mashima* is bery wise, wise woman. She knows everything," and, with this, *Didi* put down the stone and flourished her hands in a big arc above her head to indicate the expansiveness of *Mashima's* knowledge. "She will help you learn things here. Teach you what to do, what not to do. You go listen to her. You learn."

"Is she nice? She sounds old and scary," Sophie laughed. *Didi* seemed to consider this thought for a moment and then said, "yes…she old. *Bery* old. She is…different. You must go to her and see."

"Ok, *Didi*, if you think I should see this *Mashima*, then I will definitely do so. But how do I meet her? Can I go out or not?"

Didi looked up at her and frowned as if Sophie had asked a stupid question.

"Of course, you can go! You are free to do as you please."

This confused Sophie. The head wobble clearly wasn't as certain an indication of displeasure as she had thought. But she had secured a result: she could go exploring.

After lunch – curry and rice, which Sophie had to admit was possibly the most delicious meal she had ever eaten – and Uncle Joshua had taken himself off to his study to read, Sophie decided to brave the outside world and find out what was there. She told *Didi*, and *Didi* responded by asking Sophie not to stray beyond the confines of the village. She would be safe around here, *Didi* said, because word gets around, and they all knew a strange white girl was living here now; but outside of the village was a different matter. Sophie promised.

She stepped out into the hot sun and moved forward in no particularly determined direction. Sophie had been here a few days now (though who knew how long? Time seemed to stretch out here with no sense of speed or urgency), and this was the first day she'd ventured out at all. This morning had been the *pukur* – boring though watching her uncle fishing was. At least they had got on reasonably okay. Now she was going exploring. It felt good to be getting air in her lungs instead of the sweaty, steamy air blown around by ceiling fans in every room of the *bari*.

She was also pleased with how well her legs felt. Although the soreness and itchiness hadn't gone away completely, they had faded into the background so much that she had to remind herself that the scars and muscles still hurt. Only when doing nothing or really concentrating on them did she feel discomfort. Even through the mosquito nets, the Bangla sun seemed to be a soothing balm and being out in the sun made her legs feel as though they were glowing with health.

She walked around the edge of the fencing behind the *pukur* just a hundred yards from the house. The ground was a strange dusty, sandy kind of soil. Solid yet yellow dust flew up as her feet scuffed the ground. Everything was different: the trees, birds, grasses, sounds – even the taste of the air. Nothing was what she was used to in England. The sun was glorious – no British person would dislike having some sun when it was the constant moan in the UK that the sun never came out. But the sun was also unbearably hot, and Sophie smiled to herself that such a complaint was also really rather British too.

Perhaps the oddest thing, though, was the constant chirping noise that she could hear – presumably from crickets – which didn't stop night or day. When Sophie concentrated on the noises, she realised the cacophony was all but deafening. Yet when she ignored it and thought of other things, it was as if the sound vanished altogether.

All around, in between coconut trees and dense shrubbery, were buildings and homes. She could tell which were which as the buildings, though small, were made of brick or concrete and were obviously office-style places while the houses were mostly made of mud and bamboo with corrugated tin roofs. Wherever she looked, she saw eyes staring back at her; Bangladeshi children, adults and elderly who stood perfectly still as she passed by and simply stared at her without saying a word. It didn't make her nervous, but it did intrigue Sophie. *Why were they doing that?*

After a while, both the trees and the dwellings petered out, and Sophie could see nothing much for miles around but lush green field after field with heaped up pathways, some as narrow as just a few inches across, which crisscrossed the landscape. The path she'd been walking along now came to a junction where it went left and right, both heading far into the distance. At this point, Sophie realised she didn't really know what *Didi* had meant by 'outside the village' but decided that as no one was near these paths and the central collection of village buildings was well in sight, she could go just a little further.

She turned left and wandered along the sandy yellow road but didn't go long before she realised one of the heaped paths led off to the left again, and if she went that way, then she could probably walk all the way around the village. *Didi* shouldn't object to that.

So, Sophie turned left again and carefully walked along the narrow, heaped path, noticing the fields on either side. They were water-logged with great clumps of long grass shooting out in semi-organised rows and columns. Sophie wondered what was being grown and vaguely recalled geography lessons (which for some reason often mentioned Bangladesh, if she remembered correctly). *Were these paddy fields?* she wondered. *Wasn't it just the Chinese that had rice paddies?* Geography wasn't her strong point, Sophie knew, and she wished now she'd paid more attention in class.

Once she had walked far enough to now be 'behind' the village (though there seemed neither 'front' nor 'back' to Sophie other than the path she had taken out of the place which she deemed the front), Sophie found the narrow path broadened and sloped up again to now cross over a double set of rail lines. These ran parallel to the dusty yellow road she'd turn off earlier and, like that road, stretched in both directions as far as the eye could see.

It seemed bizarre to Sophie that these tracks were simply laid bare like this. How come there were no fences erected to keep people away? Looking along the tracks, she could see random huts made from mud and bamboo again lying so ridiculously near the rails. Children, some barely able to walk, were milling around playing, carrying things, girls flapping wet clothes to lay them on the ground to dry. No one seemed to be even aware of the tracks.

She began to wander along the side of the track and, as before in the village, the children near these homes stopped in their tracks and simply stared at her in silence. They didn't move; they didn't talk. They just looked. Whether it was the heat of the sun or how uncomfortable Sophie felt with those cold, piercing white eyes scrutinising her like she was an alien, she suddenly felt intensely hot and felt sweat pouring down her back under her T-shirt.

At that moment, she heard a loud but distant honk from behind and turned to look. There, looking small but getting larger by the second, was a black square coming her way between the rails. Recognising the shape, Sophie stepped a little further away from the track, halfway down the sandy slope but stopped to watch the square grow and pass by.

It was remarkable that, apart from that one honk of the horn, the train had been impossibly quiet until just a few hundred yards away. Then, suddenly, it was loud and hot and terrifying as it thundered past, undeniably large and bulky yet moving with such speed that the hot wind whipped Sophie in the face and nearly made her stumble over. This was no train but a beast – an elephant on metal. No, *a hundred* elephants on metal. The horn sounded again, but this time the noise was deafening, and Sophie winced from the pain.

Barely able to look up, she glanced for half a second at a time and was able to make out the carriages, dark blue and looking ancient, filled with people, all of whom stared at her with those same haunted eyes. Some of the carriages weren't just filled: they were crammed like cattle with nothing but a sea of faces through the windows. Some people hung on the outside, onto doors and ledges between the carriages. About thirty people were running about on top of the roofs, jogging along as if the train wasn't moving at all. And one man held on to his bicycle through the window, his hand grasping the frame as it dangled from the side. For Sophie, the sheer size and speed of the train were utterly terrifying. As if to hammer home the point, the beast blasted its horn one last time before almost instantly vanishing in its own sound, the peace of the area restored even before the train was completely out of sight.

She stood there, rocking, eyes squeezed tight. In her head, horns blaring, wheels squealing, the sound of screaming. Distant memories she couldn't access yet somehow still there mingled with the sounds of the train, and she didn't know which was which. The scars on her legs throbbed with pain, her heart raced, and she felt the terrible urge to vomit.

She stood for what she felt was an eternity but eventually opened her eyes. The children, still in the distance a little, were staring at her again, the crickets were chirruping, women were laying out their blankets and clothes to dry in the sun. Just as the intense moist air was a blanket of water constantly pressing down, so the peace pressed out her fear and anxiety. She began to walk, her legs wobbling but holding, and continued on her way.

In the end, Sophie walked all the way around the village settlement before coming back in through the single road leading into the village itself. She turned to the right rather than use the left path again when she came to the *pukur* and found that on the opposite side was the school her uncle had mentioned that morning.

It was a concrete building like the *bari*, painted white and with a huge tin roof overhead. Two storeys high, it seemed to Sophie it could not hold more than a dozen classrooms. There was something quaint about it – possibly because the playing field contained nothing but badly rusted bars, slide, and swings that looked like they hadn't been used in decades.

The sun was beginning to cool and go down. Sophie realised that she had spent most of the afternoon walking; she was exhausted and desperately thirsty. She was also, perhaps for the first time, terribly hungry, and she looked forward to the food *Didi* would cook tonight. But though she was tired enough to fall asleep right there and then, she was not looking forward to sleeping. Sleep meant dreams, and dreams meant nightmares. With this thought in mind, she set off from the school and headed back to the *bari*.

"Mashima. Mashima, where are you?" She races through the trees and the jungle vines, looking, looking. Where can she be? She passes by the pukur and carries on towards the school field, but something is different about it. Hundreds and hundreds of cars, all bent and smashed, lie on top of each other, piled high like huge city buildings. She runs between

them. The sound of a horn in the distance increases her fear. Something is coming. "Oh Mashima, Mashima? Where are you? I have to find you. It's so important." "Try the pukur," says a voice from somewhere. Such a sweet voice. She knows it; she trusts it. Where from? What is that voice? "Try the pukur. It will save you, Sophie. She is there." She stands at the pukur, standing at the edge, looking, looking. Something is bubbling in the depths. She kneels and peers closer. What is it? What is that coming closer? A face? Yes, a face. Such a beautiful one, so lovely, coming closer and closer. She knows that face. From where? So beautiful. "I'm here, Sophie." The disembodied voice speaks so sweetly again. "I'm coming for you, Sophie." The face is clearer now; she is excited and no longer feels afraid. She sees the blood on the side of the face, running down swiftly. No! She remembers now; she knows this face. Too late, the hands reach up and grab her arms, pulling her into the water. She struggles, she fights to breathe, but the woman is too strong. The face still smiles sweetly but now she just wants to push upward, upward, away from the darkness of the depths. "Sophie, I'm here," the voice says from above as the arms continue dragging her down. "Come to me, my darling. I'm here for you." She wants to speak, but the slimy, green pustulant water enters her mouth, choking her. She is sucked into the water and tries to turn around and climb out. She climbs; she can see someone standing on the edge of the pukur. "Come to me, my lovely. Take my hand." She reaches out and grabs it and feels a strong pull, lifting her up, saving her. Out of the water she comes and sees her saviour. All of her. The red eyes, the horrible teeth grinning at her wildly. "I'll save you." The monster cackles and opens her mouth. Closer and closer she comes, the evil mouth growing bigger and bigger until, eventually, it swallows her and all is dark.

CHAPTER TWELVE – FRIENDS AND ENEMIES

Sophie had no idea how Mahfuza had ended up with her head under her arm, twisted awkwardly through Sophie pulling hard on the girl's hair. She had no idea how a crowd of the other children had formed so quickly around her to see the fight nor why she was so red-faced and angry as she squeezed her arm tightly around the girl's neck.

She did know, though, why she was screaming at her.

"Don't *ever* do that again to my friend. Do you understand?" she hissed in the girl's ear. The girl didn't respond – she could barely breathe. Some of the other girls watching were beginning to get nervous. Mahfuza was clearly in distress, and what had started out being very exciting – two girls fighting was *bound* to make a stir – was now getting out of hand, and they were afraid for Mahfuza, pinned under Sophie's arm.

"Sophie, *didi*, let her go!" one of the smaller girls said nervously. "You're hurting her."

"Not until she promises never to pick on Adhora or any other girl again," Sophie snapped back, releasing her grip on Mahfuza's neck just enough for her to be able to breathe again and speak.

"I promise, I promise," the girl gasped just as her knees gave way. She slipped out of Sophie's grip and collapsed on the ground, apparently out cold. Mahfuza's power was legendary in the school, so the sight of the fearsome, not-to-be-messed-with 13-year-old, seemingly dead, aroused mass hysteria from all, including Sophie, who had not quite expected things to go this far. However, some semblance of common sense was fast returning as shrieks and sobs erupted from the crowd.

"She's dead, she's dead!" wailed one of the girls, setting off a further wave of screams and sobbing from the smaller children who had been trying to watch from the outer edges. Sophie stared at them in horror. *What had she done?*

"She's not dead," she tried to reassure them, "just fainted. That's all." Even Sophie could tell she sounded far from convinced. Panic was rising in her throat.

"Sophie Shepherd, *what* is going on here?"

The sound of the headmaster's voice was unmistakable, and instantly the crowd hushed and parted, leaving Sophie and the prostrate Mahfuza in full view of the head of the school. Sophie could tell from the look on his face – which even with his dark skin she could see was turning deep red – that she was in very serious trouble.

Mahfuza, either awakened by the sound of the voice of authority or, more likely, as Sophie thought, was now 'miraculously' recovering at this coincidental moment, began wailing and thrashing on the ground with precise, well-rehearsed, histrionics.

"I can't breathe," she screamed, proving she was very clearly able to do just that. "I thought I was going to die."

"Oh, for heaven's sake, quit your moaning," Sophie snapped at her, "no one's believing you."

"Sophie!" the Head shouted at her, causing her to jump a little. "How dare you treat one of our *best* students this way. Explain this behaviour!"

Sophie stared at the man. He was small – though that meant average height for a Bangladeshi – and only slightly taller than she was. She had found him pretentious right from the start when she began classes a month earlier. She had no respect for him because she saw none for the students from him.

"She deserved it," was all she could spit out. The Head glared.

"Come here right now. It is about time you were taken down from your lofty position, Sophie Shepherd. Come here and take your punishment."

Sophie gulped. She knew what that meant and could see the teacher holding the ruler he always kept in his jacket pocket now in his hands. The ruler was one of two punishments of choice for the teachers in this village school. The lighter one was to be made to stand in the corner of the classroom with both hands pulling your ears for a specified length of time. It was humiliating – the class was encouraged to laugh at you – but relatively painless, unless you were too enthusiastic in tugging your lobes. But the ruler was preferred by certain teachers who took a degree of vindictive delight from inflicting pain. She had seen another teacher do this just yesterday to some unfortunate, terrified child but had so far avoided the dreaded instrument herself. This was only because she was white and therefore *boro lok*, the other children delighted in telling her. Now, those same children were relishing the idea that she would finally receive the punishment. Before she could do anything, they had crowded around her and pushed her towards the teacher – partly deliberately, but also partly by accident as they pushed and shoved to be able to see Sophie Shepherd 'take five' on her palms. She was still emotional from the fight and not thinking clearly. Normally she would have stood up to him and said no – no matter the cost – but instead, she instinctively held out her palms; she could feel her throat knotting with fear. Out of the corner of one eye, she spied Mahfuza looking up at her, the hint of a curl on her lips, whilst still trying to look as though she were tragically fighting for her life.

The Head looked at her palms.

"Not that way up," he said, "turn them over."

A gasp came from the children, and Sophie opened her mouth about to utter a complaint when he barked "*now*" at her. She flinched and meekly turned the backs of her hands upwards. She felt sick from her involuntary acquiescence yet powerless to stop. It was as though her body and mind were conspiring against her. The instant she turned her hands over, the ruler came down hard.

Thwack

He raised it again and brought it down again before the pain had fully registered through the shock. Sophie could see Mahfuza grinning openly now from the floor, and she determined she would not shed a tear in front of this toe-rag.

Thwack.

He raised it again.

"*Ahmed*, stop that at once. What the *hell* do you think you are doing, man?"

The sound of Uncle Joshua's voice had never been so welcome, and Sophie was pleased, despite the intense burning pain shooting across her hands, to notice the Head had himself flinched at the sound of her uncle's voice. *Justice,* she thought with venom in her heart. The *deshi* regained his composure very quickly and said:

"I know that this girl is your niece, but she has attacked Mahfuza, and this cannot be allowed. She must be punished with the greatest severity."

"I agree…" Joshua had now pushed his way through the children and stood next to the Head. His face was a grim purple, and Sophie could see he was struggling to regain his composure. "…but not through corporal punishment you don't, Uncle Ahmed."

It was the custom at the school for all the male teachers to be referred to as 'Uncle' and the females were 'Aunty' but Sophie still found it funny to hear her gruff relative use such terms with his colleagues and, especially, his boss. Usually funny, that is, but not today. There was nothing to laugh about with her current predicament. Her uncle turned to look at her, and she could tell that though he was defending her, he was just as furious, even before he knew the facts.

"And not with *my* niece," he said, still looking at her before turning again to the Head. "Who did she attack?"

The children, wide-eyed with delight at this verbal sparring between two equal giants, in their minds, immediately separated and revealed Mahfuza still on the floor who, on cue, began to gush with tears all over again and threw herself to the ground wailing about how she was sure she was going to have been killed and praising Allah that the Head had intervened when he did or she would surely now be stone-cold dead. Joshua took one look at her, rolled his eyes, and groaned.

"Of all the children to pick on, Sophie Shepherd," he muttered at her and then, said louder: "Stop your caterwauling, Mahfuza, and get up, girl. You should be on the stage with your talents."

Though Mahfuza wasn't entirely clear on what 'caterwauling' meant, she got up anyway and looked up at him defiantly. Uncle Joshua scared everyone else, including, to an extent, the Head, but Sophie could see that Mahfuza wasn't affected in quite the same way. She did what she was told because she liked to present the image that she was a model schoolgirl, but Sophie knew the truth – this was how she had come to be in this mess in the first place. For sure, the girl did not obey out of respect for any of the uncles, and she had not one ounce of fear in her.

Sophie knew that look on her face – she had often used it herself in the past. *I do not fear you,* the face said, *because I know that I am more powerful than you.* This seemed a provocative and unrealistic position for Mahfuza to hold, Sophie felt, but she did wonder why her uncle was not reacting more violently. He normally took no nonsense from anyone.

Uncle Joshua turned to the Head.

"Punish her you may do," he said in a subdued voice, "but you will not strike her again."

For a teacher to speak this way to the Head was the stuff of legend – or at least good gossip for the village for a while, and Sophie could see that her uncle was uncomfortable with undermining the Head so publicly. Ahmed said nothing, but his eyes spoke volumes: *You cannot talk to me this way.*

The two locked eyes and stared in silence for a few seconds. The crowd of children held their breath to see who would win. The Head was the first to speak. He turned to Sophie.

"Go. You have received your punishment," he said as though it had been his idea all along and Uncle Joshua had merely agreed with him. "You will clean the toilets after school for a week, and you will write a full apology to Mahfuza exonerating her from any wrongdoing. You should pray *that* will pacify her father when he hears of this."

Sophie's face creased into anger on hearing this. She'd have rather taken the lashings. She had expected detentions, loss of break times, or something like that. Both these punishments were designed to humiliate her. She started to protest, but her uncle cut her off with his hand. He spoke quietly but with ferocity below the surface.

"Sophie – don't make things worse. Just go home. *Now.* I'll speak to you later."

With anger and tears in her eyes, she stormed off the field, picked up her school bag lying untouched where she had thrown it just before the fight, and ran home before the tears leaked out of her burning eyes.

It had all started so well. Sophie's first day at school a month earlier had been almost perfect. Although school itself had begun in August around the time Sophie had arrived in Bangladesh, it had taken nearly a month for her uncle to get her enrolled, pay fees and generally get her settled enough to be ready for school. Sophie knew she was behind, having not had a day of schooling since before, well, since before things changed forever. She was bright and had always done well at school but was far from the top of her class in many subjects and knew she needed to work diligently to keep pace. She knew it would be hard for her to catch up with the work that she had missed. On top of that, she had a whole new curriculum to deal with and a very different school routine.

Thankfully, the local school was, as it proudly displayed on all banners and hoardings, an 'English Medium School.' Sophie was told there were many such schools in Bangladesh as English was highly valued, and this one followed the British National Curriculum, so it was especially highly sought after. It amused her that here 'British' was synonymous with 'best.' Her whole life had been spent in a lower-income state school, and she had never conceived of the idea she was lucky or in any way privileged in some way. Still, the strange infatuation with an English system meant that Sophie could get the same education in Bangladesh that she would have received at home, and so – when she *finally* returned – she would not miss anything she might need for upcoming exams. There would be differences and things done in different ways, but on the whole, she would pretty much keep up with her peers five thousand miles away.

In part, a throw-over from the days of the British Empire, the whole Indian sub-continent had inherited many things from the British when they left in 1947; their legal system, for instance, and a strong commitment to the British idea of education. Though the Government had created its own National curriculum in Bangla, many schools throughout the country still believed that the British system itself was the best. The reality was that this was quite true, not because the British education system was better than others – in some ways it was in an awful mess – but because English was, arguably, the true international language of the world and both the language and the qualifications from a western country like Britain opened doors to every area of business globally. To a developing country desperately clawing its way out of poverty, this was a very sensible approach to take. Uncle Joshua enjoyed explaining all this to Sophie in quite some detail. Despite herself, Sophie quite enjoyed learning from him too. It was a surprise to realise he was quite a good teacher and his reputation among staff, students and parents was second to none. He explained well and had the gift so few of her teachers in her old school in England possessed of making her interested in whatever he was talking about. Except fishing, she reminded herself with a smile. And he was still a crotchety old bag of wind at home.

She was treated like a queen on her first day. Presented in front of the whole 150 or so students and roughly twenty staff at the school assembly, they had all been excited to meet her, and at break times she had quickly been surrounded by children. Most of them fired questions at her about her life and background in everything from fractured, barely intelligible English from the little ones to very good quality English (albeit with an odd American twang to it) of the older. She was guarded about what she said and avoided saying too much about her parents, the accident, why she had missed so much school, and so on, but the children didn't seem to notice. The oddest thing for Sophie was that several of the small children would just come up to her and touch her skin before running off. Later she found out that this superstition persisted among many in Bangladesh that if you touched a white person's skin, some of their 'luck' would rub off on you. It amused Sophie. *If only you knew what my luck was like*, she had thought, *you wouldn't come within miles of me.*

The classes were basic. No computers, no interactive whiteboards. No targets on the walls or regular assessments as she was used to almost daily in her school back in England. Just the teacher, old-style desks like Sophie had seen in movies about schools a hundred years ago which even had flip-up lids so you could put books and stationery in them, a blackboard and chalk, and a small selection of textbooks and *khatas*. It was just like being in some Victorian novel, except the teachers were mostly Asian, though there were one or two white-skinned teachers like Uncle Joshua who taught at the school too, and (the biggest difference) was that every classroom had several huge ceiling fans which spun furiously. They hardly cooled the hot rooms at all, but at least they gave a breeze, giving the illusion of coolness, and took some of the perspiration from every moist body in the room as they all sat sweating heavily in the saturated monsoon-season air.

None of this was off-putting for Sophie. In England, she had never been one of the children who didn't like school. She was popular with students and teachers alike without being obnoxious about it; she was smart but not so smart that she received unwanted attention from the school bullies who could smell 'nerds and geeks' from forty paces. When she had, occasionally, crossed paths with some of the well-known 'mafia' in her last school, she had been strong-willed and could think on her feet; so, she never got the sharp end of their ways. She was also quite strong for her age, and bullies tended to think twice about tackling her. There were easier targets in the school. Sophie's school life had been relatively free of too many troubles, and she *loved* learning. Her parents had been life-long learners and, for as long as she could remember, there had been many evenings every week spent with all three of them heads down in their own book. Sometimes, they would be heads down in the *same* book; memories of those times were extra special to Sophie now, yet she couldn't let herself have more than the briefest moment of thinking about them before her chest felt so heavy she thought she'd suffocate.

The village school here, odd and perhaps slightly frightening as all new places are, was full of charm for Sophie, and she was desperately keen to catch up with her studies. Under better circumstances, she might almost have looked forward to learning from here. All around the school were trees and fields, which could be seen from every window of every classroom. It was a far contrast from the concrete metropolis she saw out of her British school with nothing but crumbling school buildings in the foreground and behind them in the distance obscenely dismal council estate obelisks.

Everything had been fine until she met Mahfuza. Sophie didn't need to be told that she was the school bully. Sophie knew the sort. She didn't walk – she strutted. She never asked for anything – she just took. When a teacher asked her a question in class, she had a sneer on her face that told everyone she considered the teacher a fool and that it was *almost* beneath her to answer. It must have been obvious to the teachers, and yet they did absolutely nothing about it. How could they? She always did, eventually, deign to answer – sometimes even the right one. Mahfuza didn't play *by* the rules; she played *with* them. She knew where to draw the line and how not to get caught. She never, for instance, gave 'the look' to Uncle Joshua. She knew she had no power over him. How she had that power over Uncle Ahmed, the Head of the school, Sophie could only guess.

Over the coming days, Sophie kept out of her way, not out of fear but out of common sense. She was quite sure she could handle herself with this irritant but didn't want to get into a difficult situation – not until she had settled in, at least. Mahfuza, it seemed, was taking a similar position, both sizing each other up like cats, wary and watchful of each other's presence and both 'choosing' to be somewhere else, neither challenging the other's place. It felt, to Sophie, like prey and predator stalking each other, but she was not sure which of them would turn out to be the prey.

"Sometimes, you are unbelievably *stupid!*" Uncle Joshua shouted at her as soon as he got home.

Sophie stood before him, having been 'summoned' by him, fuming as she listened to his tirade.

"Of all the girls to pick on at the school, you had to pick on *that* one. What in God's name possessed you?"

"You don't understand," she spat back at him, openly defiant, "I wasn't picking on her. *She* was picking on others. Everyone knows she is the school bully."

"So, you avoid her then!" he snapped back. "Not put her head in a lock and nearly twist the damned thing off!"

"I had no choice. She was going to hurt Adhora, and I couldn't allow that."

Joshua threw his hands up in the air, enraged all over again. "And there's *another* thing. Of all the girls to choose to be friends with. You don't want to hang around with Adhora. The girl is nice enough and all that, but she'll bring you nothing but trouble."

Sophie couldn't believe what she was hearing. Adhora had to be one of the sweetest, loveliest girls she'd ever known. It was in meeting her that Sophie had finally found someone, apart from *Didi*, who made living in this awful country worthwhile.

They had been placed together on the first day. Adhora Haque had been assigned to Sophie as her *shonggi*, her helper, and sit with her in each lesson as the class moved from room to room for different subjects. As she had moved to sit next to the slim girl, spectacles half dropping off her nose and jet-black eyes the size of saucers, Sophie instinctively felt that she was about to meet a soul friend. She'd felt it with *Didi*, and now she knew that they were both going to be good friends.

While that turned out to be true, it wasn't entirely instantaneous. Where Sophie was strong-willed, confident and defiant, Adhora was quiet, shy and almost irritatingly submissive. It took almost the first week for Sophie to soften her up enough to start speaking more freely. When Adhora did so, her voice was gentle and felt almost like a lullaby. Despite this, teachers either had no problem hearing her, or they just pretended to hear her; Sophie couldn't tell at first.

With the heat so intense (from what she was told, this was the situation for most of the year) during August, the monsoon season, all fans were turned to full speed from the first second of the day to the last. As a result, teachers had to raise their voices, if not actually to shout, in order to be heard, and children giving answers in class had to do much the same. But not Adhora. She whispered, yet the teachers seemed to hear. Even Sophie sitting next to the girl couldn't tell what she was saying, yet every teacher could.

In short, there was nothing in Adhora that was anything other than sweet and adorable. She exuded peace and calm, and there was no offensiveness in her whatsoever. Yet here was Uncle Joshua treating her like she was some kind of troublemaker. It made no sense. How could he justify saying something like that? Sophie's anger was bubbling uncontrollably.

"She's my friend, and you have no right to be mean to her like that," she raised her voice at him, not quite instantly regretting doing so, but with a sense of foreboding straight after the words left her lips. Her uncle's face was like stone, and suddenly all six feet of him seemed at least a foot taller and wider. He lifted a finger like it was an axe.

"Don't. Don't *ever* think you can talk to me like that, you *silly* girl," he said, face purple. "You pretty much put the daughter of the biggest *boro lok*, the most important politician in the area, into hospital, and I have to *defend* you against the Head – my boss, I'll remind you – showing him up in public which is just about the *worst* thing you can do to stop you from being lashed on the hands so much you wouldn't stop feeling intense pain for a week. I risk my work here at the school and my life here in the village by making enemies of these two men, and for what? For what? For the daughter of a stubborn fool who makes nothing but trouble and can't tell right from wrong."

"Better than being the niece of cold-hearted one," she hissed in return, no longer caring what happened.

He stood there, open-mouthed for one moment, then his composure changed, and the room temperature, impossibly, seemed to drop.

"Go to your room, Sophie," he said quietly but with menace. "Stay there until I decide what to do with you. Be assured: it won't be pleasant."

She turned around and fled up the stairs, slamming the door of her room as hard as she could. *Didi*, who had listened to the whole thing from the kitchen, could hear, muffled with a pillow though it was, a scream of rage followed by huge sobs. *Didi* moved into the front room where the argument had just happened and looked at Joshua but said nothing. He looked back at her and could read her face as well as she could read his. They had known each other a long time and hardly needed words.

"What?" he complained. "What was I supposed to do? Tell me that?"

Didi said nothing, picked up a teacup from a small table and went back into the kitchen. Joshua slumped into a chair and stared into space.

"I'm not cut out for raising devil spawn," he muttered to no one in particular.

Adhora had looked after Sophie that first week at school and spent her snack breaks with her – sharing her food with Sophie, who had brought nothing. Uncle Joshua hadn't thought about that. He'd made sure she'd got pens, pencils, rulers, books, and so on but gave no thought to her nutritional needs.

The two girls got on brilliantly, which had surprised Sophie immensely. The deshi girl was literally her first and only real friend, and Sophie hadn't expected even that. She still had no wish to get close to anyone. But Adhora was different, and Sophie enjoyed her company.

It helped that Adhora's English was good, albeit far from perfect. It was better than most of the students and a good number of the Bangladeshi teachers too. Sophie felt able to talk naturally to the girl. And Adhora seemed to, well, *adore* Sophie, and nothing was too much trouble. Sophie had to admit she quite liked that. The only fire within her new friend, it seemed, was reserved for P.E. class, specifically, playing 'Dodgeball.' This American game Sophie had never played before, much to the amusement of the whole class and the particular delight of the boys.

When they got out onto the field and split into two groups, which now faced each other in two rows, Sophie had no idea what was going on. The instructions by the P.E. teacher had all been given in Bangla, and the kids knew what to do so well that they got straight on with it. On the whistle blow, the boy opposite her shot to the centre of the pitch, where a row of balls had been lined up. Sophie hadn't moved, despite the rest of her group diving for balls at the same time. Her boy went back to his place and aimed the ball at Sophie. She held out her hands to catch it.

Suddenly Adhora smacked her hands away. "No, Sophie – don't try to catch it. If you miss, you will be out. You have to *duck!*" Just at that point, Adhora twitched her head to the side as a ball came whistling past her at high speed. Sophie realised that this was a game that could potentially hurt. She turned back to the boy opposite her *just* as he threw the ball as hard as he could. Thankfully, his aim was a little wild, and she moved out of its path with alarmed but relative ease. It quickly became transparent that those who were hit were out, and those who weren't had to pick up the balls and return fire. Some though had caught the ball, which meant the one who had thrown it was now out.

Sophie threw the ball back with relish but, alas, missed her assailant. On his return throw, she thought she would try to catch it. It couldn't be *that* hard. His aim was sure; Sophie's attempt to catch it wasn't. The ball shot through her hands like they were made of butter.

The ball crunched into Sophie's face, and she collapsed to the ground, her face stinging and ringing in her ears. She could hear some of the boys whooping with joy over their 'kill,' and the cries reminded her of the boys at junior school in England Sophie had seen playing at being 'Red Indians.'

She felt as sick as a dog. That ball had *really hurt*. From that time on, when Adhora told her something, she never doubted her word again.

But Adhora was a fiend at the game. Like a demon possessed, she dodged balls at speed and thrust them back like bullets, never staying long in one place. Before long, the boys were knocked out, and Adhora's team were the winners. Sophie could tell from the looks of resigned disgust on the losers' faces that this was a fairly normal occurrence.

Over the first week, the two girls became best friends. Their opposite natures seemed to complement each other, and it felt to both girls that they had known each other their whole lives. It soon became known around school that the girls were 'besties.' Their relationship began to be watched. Mahfuza may have been wise enough not to tackle Sophie directly, but now she had a weakness to exploit. Adhora was an easy target.

After a month or so, Adhora had invited Sophie to her house after school for *nasta* and some *cha*. *Cha* was a very adult thing to do. Every adult drank the thick sickly-sweet and heavily brewed tea which was consumed several times a day. *Chawallahs* had stalls everywhere and they were the centre of community news and gossip – for the men, at least, who would gather around them throughout the day, even taking *cha* before going home to eat long after the sun had gone down after a hard day labouring in the fields. The girls felt very grown-up to be taking *cha* at Adhora's *bari*. The home itself was surprisingly isolated, standing in the middle of a field not far from the *Satya nodi*, the main river which ran through that area, providing freshwater fish as the staple diet locally. Most *baris* huddled together in groups of four to thirty or forty or more. Adhora's home was a new build, a *paka bari*, an actual brick and concrete structure instead of the usual mud, tin, and bamboo *baris* which most people had. Adhora's father was obviously well off. The home wasn't as large or grand as Uncle Joshua's, built in the days of the British Raj as it was, but it was in far better condition with beautifully ornate tiles and brick work, brilliant white paint on the outside walls, and shiny silver gates and doors.

Sophie barely saw anything of Adhora's parents themselves. Her mother briefly entered the front room where the girls had sat themselves after kicking off their sandals at the doorstep, and she greeted Sophie cordially enough but with great reserve. She clutched Adhora's baby sister, Tahira. Adhora's father also came to say hello but never smiled. Instead, he seemed almost to be checking Sophie out, examining her to make sure she was suitable.

"You are Joshua Shepherd's niece, no?" was his first question.

"Yes." It felt strange to hear her surname used in connection with the man she called 'Uncle' but felt no family connection. Adhora's father frowned as though this was a bad thing.

"You like here, no?" Sophie wasn't sure if he meant Bangladesh, the village area, or his home. She played safe.

"Yes, yes, very beautiful."

She looked around the room. It was, oddly, more fascinating than beautiful. The walls were painted in a garish, almost luminescent green with strip lighting that made the whole room dim. Cupboards made from bamboo filled one wall. Through the glass panels stared eerie porcelain dolls in Victorian clothing. On another wall were several faded photos of family members, certificates and awards of various kinds, and a calendar. On top of one cupboard was an open book resting on a wooden book stand. Sophie knew this was a copy of the Qu'ran and was placed in the highest place in the room as a sign of honour and respect to the holy book. The room was slightly musty, and a smell of spices pervaded the air. This, Sophie guessed, was what wealth looked like in villages in Bangladesh. It was very different from Uncle Joshua's *bari*. There, books were the only thing proudly displayed. There were no ornaments, no cupboards on show and, oddly, now that she came to think of it, no family photos or pictures of any kind whatsoever.

Before she could process the thought, Adhora's father spoke again.

"Welcome to my home," he said, making it sound more like a threat than a heartfelt kindness. "Welcome to our country. We are happy you here. We hope you like our custom, our golden land. You learn from Adhora, she teach you *all* our ways. You will like, no?"

Again, she reiterated that she liked Mr Haque very much, thank you, and found herself looking shyly at her bare feet rather than meeting his harsh gaze. It felt like he was admonishing her and commanding her to learn from Adhora. Sophie wouldn't have minded this at all — she already hoped to learn lots from her quiet friend anyway. She looked up when she saw him rise to his feet and spread out his hands.

"Enjoy, please," he said simply as their *ayah*, their own *Didi*, came through from another room silently carrying a tray of *nasta* and *cha*; he left with a scowling nod to them both.

"I don't think he likes me very much," Sophie whispered to her friend as they munched on the snacks and blew at their cups of hot drink.

"Oh, no, no," Adhora replied in her soft voice, which rarely rose louder than a whisper away from the dodge ball games, "it's not that. He doesn't like your uncle very much. That's all. He thinks you must be like him and doesn't know you yet." She shrugged her shoulders and added, "he doesn't know if you can be trusted or if you will be a bad influence on me."

Gradually, over the next hour or so the girls had together before Sophie had to find her way home, she found out from Adhora that the two men had had a falling out. They had never got on particularly well: Hasan Haque, Adhora's father, was quite a conservative man who believed in tradition and had earned his good income through wise investing in various shops and garment-making workshops, which meant he spent his day touring around various places he owned making sure his staff and tenants were working hard and collecting his rent and royalties. He was a proud man who was used to telling others what to do and didn't like, nor expect, anyone to boss him around. He and Joshua had managed to dance around each other at various important meetings in the community, both recognising the stubbornness and pride in the other until Hasan had started building the house Sophie was now sat in. Joshua had tried to persuade Hasan not to build so close to the *Satya*.

"Your uncle thinks that if the river floods very badly, then we will be in grave danger."

"Is it likely?" Sophie found it hard to imagine how flooding could be that bad anyway. In England, flooding meant, at worst, wading up to your knees in water and maybe a few unfortunate homes ruining their carpets. She had seen the rains come down in Bangladesh and groundwater rise alarmingly fast and quickly understood why *baris* were built as they were. Rain could do minimal damage, and once a shower stopped, the sun seemingly would leap out again and dry everything with an almost personal ferocity.

"Oh, it is true the *Satya* floods every year," Adhora said, "but only enough to overflow the banks and fill up the rice fields along the sides. It is good. The river is our friend. We are far enough away not to worry, father says. We have been here three years now, and there has been no problem."

The thought came to Sophie, not for the first time, that life in Bangladesh was very different to England. She didn't know if she could ever get used to this way of living, but she was glad she wouldn't have to. It was just a matter of time for Uncle Joshua to sort out her passport issues and make arrangements to get her back home. She knew he had written to Aunty Hannah and had assured her he would 'sort things out between them' but exactly what that would mean, Sophie didn't know. She couldn't imagine living with her aunt again. She didn't know if she could ever trust her or believe her again. For certain, she never wanted to see Graham again. She hated him with every fibre in her body. But where would she go? Would she be put into care? Or were there yet more relatives she'd never been told about hiding away somewhere that she'd be dumped on?

Sophie supped her *cha,* for the first time grateful for being where she was. There was Adhora, and there was *Didi,* and both made her feel safe. On the other hand, Uncle Joshua was still an unknown and dangerous figure. For most of the time, he seemed a gruff and dislikeable man who resented the presence of Sophie interrupting his fishing and contented bachelor life. But Sophie was also seeing hints of a gentler side to him. That day at the *pukur* had actually been quite nice, despite the boring fishing, and she wondered if they would have more. The *pukur* itself was just as mysterious. On the one hand, the murky waters featured so often in her dreams that she shuddered whenever she went near the water, as she did every day. But then there was something so peaceful, so serene about the place. It drew you in.

The girls finished their little 'grown up' time together and Adhora accompanied Sophie back along the route they had walked, crossing the river and reaching the path which encircled the village and that Sophie knew well. They parted, firmer friends than ever, and for the first time, Sophie knew that when she left Bangladesh, she would be missing someone deeply.

It was a confusing feeling, and she shelved it away. There was already too much confusing her at the moment.

While the girls never actively tried to be anywhere near Mahfuza outside of lesson times, she increasingly sought them out. As the weeks passed, the bully figured out their routines and would often be in the area around the school or in the playground where they tended to eat their *nasta* at break, or have lunch out of their *tiffins* during the midday hour before classes reconvened. It was always Adhora she struck at. A banana skin tossed at her hair 'by accident' with a nonchalant 'sorry' thrown ingenuously on leaving; tripping her up with a foot randomly stretched out 'coincidentally' as she walked past in the corridor; an elbow in the face in reaching for a pot of glue kept on a side table close to where the girls sat for art classes.

As the days passed, the attacks became more frequent and vicious, but as Sophie's anger rose, Adhora's nature remained as calm and accepting as ever. Despite Sophie's best efforts to stand up and challenge Mahfuza, her young friend simply lowered her head in response and shook her head. She would not say anything to the bully.

This time it seemed Mahfuza had decided it was time to up the game. At break, she had simply walked straight up to the pair of them, ignoring Sophie, and gave a huge shove to Adhora's body with both hands. Adhora, arms clutching books at the time, had sprawled flat on the ground, pages scattering around her.

Sophie hadn't realised it before that moment, but she had absolutely reached her limit of doing nothing against the irritating little piece of trash. What happened next was something of a blur in her memory, but she recalled dropping everything – her books in her hand and the school bag off her shoulders – and launching herself at her nemesis. This girl was going to learn a lesson even if Sophie had to knock it into her thick head. The roaring crowd of excited Bangladeshi schoolchildren only increased the pounding of blood to her temples; reason and caution scattered far away.

Later in the day, *Didi* came to see her, tenderly pulling back the bed covers Sophie had buried herself in to block out the world and gently stroking her hair as she spoke soothing words.

"I hate this place, *Didi*," Sophie had told her, "I wish I were anywhere but here. That man is the most horrible man in the world."

"The headmaster?"

"No. Uncle Joshua!"

Didi sighed. "Oh…" she said, resting her hand tenderly on the back of Sophie's head for a moment. "You uncle, he a good man actually. He seem a little…" she searched for the word in English, "…angry, sometime, but he care about you."

At this, Sophie sat up and faced *Didi*, looking at her with determined eyes.

"How can you say that? How can you say he cares about me? He only cares about himself! He humiliated me in front of the headmaster; he said Adhora is a bad influence; he said I had done a bad thing for defending my friend. He doesn't care about me. He doesn't care for anyone!"

Didi shook her head fiercely as Sophie said this.

"No, no Sophie. You don't know him yet. I know him many, many year. He like Adhora but he no like her baba. They fight. Too much same. Men are stubborn, actually. But you uncle, he good and he care. He hide it. All the time, hiding, hiding his heart. It come out in big anger." She paused for another moment, her face betraying uncertainty that she should say something more. She decided she would. "He hurt long ago," she spoke softly as if fearing Joshua might be outside the door and listening in, "I think he never heal this hurt. It like a big cut in him, always."

Didi persuaded Sophie to get out of her bed and come into the kitchen downstairs to help prepare the dinner *Didi* was making. Strangely, the simple act of peeling and slicing potatoes, onions, and carrots had a calming effect, and Sophie felt a degree of tension release as she worked and chatted to *Didi* about nothing in particular. She even began to grin to herself, picturing holding Mahfuza's head in a lock in front of most of the school. She still didn't quite understand what this girl had over everyone, but she felt sure the girl would keep a wide berth from both Sophie and Adhora now. She had been shamed in front of the school, and Sophie understood enough to know that this was enough. What the repercussions would be for Sophie, though, she didn't know. But she felt she would find out sooner or later.

Sophie was grounded, for how long was yet to be determined, but she was allowed that first evening to pop out as the sun began to go down around six o'clock for a brief trot around the village grounds. The conditions were that she was not to stop and talk to any children she saw but to keep walking, get some air in her lungs, and then return home. She dutifully, if not happily, obliged and did as she was told. She walked out past the *pukur*, around the edge of the village where many of the *baris* were, past the school building, and back around to the *pukur*, where she allowed herself a brief moment to stop and stare over the fencing at the deep waters. Many of her dreams now featured water or some sense of swimming or drowning, and she wondered why that was so. But she knew from putting her feet into the *pukur* sometimes that the water was deliciously warm; in her nightmares, though it was always icy cold.

She moved on. As Sophie got nearer to her *bari*, she stopped dead. She had seen movement in the undergrowth next to her home in the small *bagan*, the garden area of trees, bushes, and exotic foliage found everywhere in the village and nowhere in England. She looked closer. *Was that someone there? A child playing a prank, perhaps?* She could not see clearly but was sure the shadows within seemed to have a vaguely human-like shape. She took a couple of steps closer, never taking her eyes off the clumps of bushes where she had seen the movement.

Then she froze.

Just for one moment, she thought she saw the hint of two red circles. *The eyes.* Her heart beat loudly, blood rushed to her head, and a hundred nightmarish images all flashed through her mind at once. *This can't be happening. I must be seeing things.* She clenched her fists and, with determination on her face, stepped closer to the bushes and peered in. If this dream monster of hers existed, it was time to face the creature and conquer this fear. At last.

But the sun had all but sunk now, and, as she got closer, the sunset shadows blurred; any sense of human shape disappeared. She peered in. For a moment, she thought she heard a single rasping breath, then suddenly, a movement. Something hissed and rose rapidly from the depths towards her. Sophie cried and shot backwards, losing her balance and landing hard on the half-muddy ground.

The *Moyna* bird shot past her and rose into the air, squawking and hissing as it went. Sophie looked at it in disbelief. She sat there for a moment, catching her breath, and then laughed to herself. What a fool! Sophie picked herself up, dusted off her bottom, turned around, and headed to the *bari* door. Just as she was about to go inside, she allowed herself one last quick but guilty glance at the bushes where she had disturbed the bird, but there seemed to be no menace there now. Whatever it had or had not been, it had flown away along with the bird.

CHAPTER THIRTEEN - RAKKOSH

Sophie looked down at her reflection in the *pukur*. A tired face stared back, but it wasn't an unhappy one, and that intrigued her.

Despite her total lack of interest in fishing, she had taken to sneaking through the gates from time to time. She realised she was taking a risk, as she wasn't clear whether this place was meant to be out of bounds for her or not. Uncle Joshua hadn't invited her again to join him on his Friday mornings, and, quite frankly, she hadn't wanted to be invited. Yet she could understand something of the appeal of the place. The enclosure of the trees almost all around the pool, along with the high fence on all sides, gave a sense of seclusion which couldn't be felt anywhere else.

Seclusion was something Sophie was valuing more and more. Yet, there was a strange contradiction with this rural life she was increasingly thinking of as 'normal.'

On the one hand, it was peaceful during the day except for the low hum of water irrigation pipes in nearby fields and the honking of horns from buses streaming past on the main road a few fields away; the occasional train blaring its own horn even further beyond yet louder than any other sound bar the *azaan*, calling faithful Muslims to prayer five times a day. The *azaan* and trains were infrequent, and all these sounds had a feeling of being far away. At night, there was the incessant sound of crickets and frogs which was so rhythmic that everyone was hypnotised by the tones, and it often surprised Sophie to remember that the crickets were there at all. When you concentrated on them, you realised the sound was almost deafening.

On the other hand, no matter how vast and peaceful the scenery seemed, it was also true that everywhere you looked, you would find someone. There was activity taking place in every direction. Slow activity, admittedly, at times while the sun beat down mercilessly, but activity nonetheless. This was almost always silent. The slow, stealthy footsteps of a woman, wrapped in a *sari* or wearing the baggy shirt-pants combination of *shalwa kameeze* usually worn by working or unmarried women, who might then rearrange the *orna* which had to be draped around the shoulders in some way for a woman to be considered decent. Such women would always be walking with purpose, perhaps carrying a large basket on their heads with sacks of grain, flour, sugar, or other commodity loaded within.

Men during the day were inevitably in the paddy fields, wading into ankle- or knee-depth waters depending on the rains at the time to tend their rice crops. Sophie had soon learned that rice was the staple diet in Bangladesh which everyone would eat for all three meals of the day. No one seemed bored of doing so – indeed, the idea of not eating rice appeared unthinkable – but Sophie was struggling with it. Having been used to a range of different accompaniments; pasta, bread, potatoes, and so on, she couldn't get used to boiled rice and curry mainly being the only meal. Still, it explained why men were always tending the vast numbers of paddy fields around the village which looked just the same as all the ones she'd seen in the car driving here from Dhaka, the only difference being that now the lush green which normally covered the whole country was giving way to a brown tinge as the crops came close to harvesting time.

Somehow, these silent, continuous movements of Bangladeshis were far more violent for Sophie than any of the myriad of sounds pervading the air. People were *everywhere,* and there was no escaping them, except at the *pukur.* Most of the pool was surrounded by leafy trees and bushes, which blocked out most of the view. You could just about imagine you were entirely on your own sitting there, and that's exactly what Sophie wanted.

The water itself scared her. Almost every night, the pool would feature in her dreams. Sometimes her monster was in there too with its red, glaring eyes. She had learned a Bangla word from *Didi* about this: *Rakkosh* – a hideous monster known to eat children, therefore, of course, much beloved to feature in fairy tales to scare little boys and girls into doing what they were told. The idea was comical, but Sophie's *rakkosh* was anything but, especially when she saw it coming for her from the depths of the *pukur.* Dreams about the pool were never nice, yet somehow it also beckoned her both at night and in the reality of day. Crouching on the soil of the bank now, she was peering in past her reflection and wondering how deep the water really was. How easy it would be just to lean forward a little more and allow gravity to topple her into the water. Would she find hands down there ready to welcome her? Or would she merely startle some of Uncle Joshua's precious fish?

Sophie heard scuttling in the long grass to her left and looked in that direction just in time to see a snake dart out from the reeds and splash into the water. It was instantly invisible. Light simply couldn't penetrate the *pukur*. She wondered if anything or anyone could penetrate her soul and make sense of the jumble of thoughts and visions which kept her company day and night. Perhaps, rather than wanting to escape the eternal busyness of Bangladesh, Sophie was coming here for respite from the chaos inside her? The pool seemed to quieten the noises. She wondered if this was what Uncle Joshua felt and why he came here too. Did he have his own demons to fight?

It was the beginning of November now, and Sophie had decided she needed to tackle Bangla, the language of Bangladesh. She'd picked up a few words, of course: *"Dhonnobad"* for "thank you"; *"Nomoshka"* for "hello"; *"Cha lagbe"* somehow meant "I would like a cup of tea" though Sophie had no idea how, and *"maf korun"* said to beggars she inevitably met on the roads somehow made them nod their heads and stop asking her for money – some of the time anyway.

But she didn't really understand what little she was saying, and she certainly couldn't read the writing. Nothing about it was familiar at all, and it made her realise how little she and her friends at school back home had appreciated how easy French was.

Sophie had not thought about learning the language properly before because, in her mind, she was never going to be *staying* here for long. But three months on, she knew that hope of returning to England was fading and that, for a while anyway, she was going to be stuck here. So, she might as well start learning how to talk to people properly, and Sophie knew exactly who to go to for lessons.

She knocked loudly on Adhora's door. The door opened after a few seconds, and Adhora's mother answered it.

"Nomoshka." Sophie gave the usual greeting. Adhora's mother, who had been smiling, gave a curt nod, but her lips became a little tighter.

"*Asalaam alaiakum*, Sophie," she said, stepping aside and ushering her into the house. "Please," she said, pointing to the seats in the front room, "*Bosho*."

Sophie did so and looked around the room while Adhora's mother left and went to summon her friend. Though Sophie had been here several times now over the last few weeks, she never could get over just how immaculate Adhora's mum kept this room. There was not a hint of dust anywhere – almost impossible to do in Bangladesh – and the room smelt of fresh, newly picked flowers, sitting in expensive-looking vases around the room. There were a few new additions. Several picture frames containing stylish Arabic letterings adorned the tops of the cupboards. Sophie had no idea what they meant or what they were for but thought they were incredibly beautiful.

Before she had a chance to investigate further, Adhora came in, beaming with delight at seeing Sophie.

"Hello," she grinned, "I didn't expect to see you. How are you?"

"I know!" said Sophie. "I had a sudden idea this morning and thought you were the perfect person to help. I want to learn to speak, read and write Bangla."

"Oh really! Good idea."

"And I want you to teach me."

Adhora's smile dropped from her face in a flash.

"What? Oh no, I couldn't. I wouldn't know how too."

"That's ok," Sophie assured her, "I do. I'll guide you. I just need you to give me the answers. I'll tell you what I want to learn and how, and you can give me the answers."

Her friend didn't look certain and shuffled her feet nervously.

"I don't know, Sophie," she said shyly. "I get awful shy. I don't know very good Bangla."

"I don't want very good Bangla," Sophie said, a little more seriously now. "I want the Bangla that's used around here. Everyday Bangla. What *you use*. Look, if you'll feel any better about it, I promise that if I think I need to learn things you can't help me with one day, I'll ask someone else to give me lessons. Okay? But I'd *really* like to learn with you. It'll be fun, Adhora! Oh, please say yes."

It took Sophie another five minutes to persuade Adhora to give it a go. Sophie knew exactly what she wanted and, by and large, she had the right idea. Sophie would say, "what do you call this?" or "how do you say that?" and then spend a few seconds committing the answer to memory. They went at it for over an hour, and it was Adhora who tired first. Sophie decided to go home purely to give her a chance to rest, but she made Adhora promise that they would have another lesson tomorrow.

Saturdays were always the most relaxed days for Sophie. While Fridays were technically the only day off in the week for most people, that *did* mean Uncle Joshua being invited to *dawats* and, as his 'ward,' she would have to go along too. It was okay doing this. There was food and *cha*, and she got to know many of the locals in the surrounding area. But she was tired out afterwards each time. Saturdays were a working day for most, though, and even her uncle seemed to spend most of his time at his desk scribbling away at something or other. Sometimes he'd be reading his paper, and this is how she found him when *Didi* called her to say he wanted to see her.

Uncle Joshua held the paper up high to catch the light from the window behind him as he peered through his circle-rimmed spectacles, frowning at some article inside which seemed to perturb him. On the front, Sophie could see a photo of a tiger.

"They've still not caught it then," she said, pointing at the photo. Her uncle looked up from his reading, looked confused for a moment, and then turned the paper to look at the photo.

"Oh, this? No, not yet. I wonder if this one was originally wild before being caught and ending up in a zoo? Tigers are very good at keeping out of the way of humans. I once spent a week on a boat in the *Sundarbans,* a beautiful place which I will perhaps take you to one day. The tigers live there. I'd hoped to catch a glimpse of one, but though we searched every day and I say plenty of fresh pawprints on the banks, they kept well away from us. This one seems to be doing the same except for brief forays into fields to snatch a goat or calf from time to time."

"I would have thought finding a tiger was pretty easy," said Sophie, "but this has been going on for weeks."

"Well, we're in an area with a large amount of forest and even remains of a jungle. Once upon a time, much of Bengal was a jungle, but the British destroyed a good deal of it. We live in the remains of some of it."

He put the paper down on his desk.

"Thankfully, its tracks are still very far from us, and our immediate area is mostly arable farming land, so I don't think we need to worry about it. It must be making farmers nearer to the forests a little nervous, though."

"Will they kill it?"

"Perhaps. But, so far, the beast hasn't harmed any humans, which means they are still likely to try to catch it first. Bengal Tigers are a protected species, and you only kill one if lives are endangered. As long as it keeps a taste for goat, it should just be a matter of time before the thing is back in a cage enjoying a la carte food every day."

He stood up and beckoned Sophie over to the sofa. She sat down, wondering what wrong thing she might have done now to need a summoning.

"So…" he began, slightly nervously, she thought, "how are you settling in now? Are you getting more used to life here?"

The question took Sophie by surprise.

"Erm…Yes, I'm…doing okay." She didn't want to admit she was almost enjoying it here. "I'm getting to know some Bangla now – Adhora is teaching me, and *Didi* helps me too. And school is ok. So, yeah," she stuck her thumbs up and smiled sheepishly, "…things are cool."

Uncle Joshua looked as uncomfortable as she felt with this exchange of pleasantries.

"That's good to hear." He paused. "How are the nightmares?"

Sophie froze for a moment. Could he hear her when she woke up from the dreams? She always assumed her screams were silent ones inside her head. He never came to her room at night, never made mention of the night terrors which still plagued her.

"They're…ok. Manageable, I guess. Getting a little less frequent." She laughed and added, "Fewer monsters."

"Good, good, I'm glad to hear it," her uncle said in a surprisingly compassionate tone. Then, as if to shake off the situation with which neither of them was comfortable, he changed the subject. "Anyway, I wanted to tell you that we've all been invited to a *gaye holud* tonight."

"What's that?"

"It is more or less the equivalent to an engagement party-cum-hen party," he replied. "It's a tradition in Bangladesh, though communities and religions do it in different ways to each other. The bride will be presented tonight, the night before her wedding, and the coming nuptials celebrated."

"Ok. Who's getting married?"

"No one you know," he chuckled and raised his hands in mock exasperation. "Not really anyone I know either! As often happens with these things. She's the daughter of someone's cousin's *ayah* or something. I tend to get invited to these things as the nearest thing to a *boro lok*," he saw the question in her eyes, "- rich, important person – they have around here, poor devils."

Sophie was relieved this appeared to be the subject Uncle Joshua wanted to discuss – yet another invite – and nothing more. She wondered how she would feel if he were to have said he'd arranged for her to go home already. She wanted to go, of course, but wasn't sure if she didn't want a little more time.

"You should also get to meet *Mashima* tonight too, at long last," her uncle's words broke through her thoughts.

"What? Oh, yes – the elusive *Mashima* I've heard people talk about so much." Sophie didn't feel like mentioning that her imaginations of an old woman had somehow become mixed up in her dreams, and the idea of meeting her scared her a little. "Is she...is she really a wise old woman?"

He looked her in the eyes and smiled gently.

"She's certainly no fool – she's had to learn things the hard way in her life, that's for sure. She's no spring chicken neither, and around here, the rumours go that she was alive in the time of the British Raj – which is nonsense, of course, but tells you she's old enough for no one to be able to guess her age. I doubt she knows herself. Villagers rarely record dates of birth properly even now, let alone back when she was born. She would have seen quite some things in her time, though. Terrible things..."

He went silent after this, and Sophie felt a shudder go down her spine. She didn't want to know about 'terrible things' in somebody else's life; her own were bad enough.

"Anyway," Uncle Joshua continued as if coming out of his own uncomfortable train of thought, "she's quite a character, and she gets everywhere. You won't be able to avoid meeting her, and it's probably best I introduce her to you."

"Why?"

"You'll see."

The *gaye holud* was one of the strangest things Sophie had ever been to. She walked with her uncle and *Didi* across a treacherous piece of land to get to the marquee standing off to the back of the village from the main road. It was treacherous, as most fields in Bangladesh are because the *mali* used to get around various parts of the water-logged rice paddy fields were so narrow. But during the rainy seasons, these became nothing but muddy slopes where you could easily slip and end up deep in the water, or worse, spread-eagled in mud. Their narrow nature meant that a twisted ankle was more than likely and a hurt pride certain if you did slip.

Despite his huge size, Uncle Joshua was adept at walking across these thin aisles – as was *Didi* – who kept having to stop and turn round to help an unsteady Sophie from falling into the water. There was much laughter from the two girls, though Uncle Joshua just scowled and told Sophie to be careful and both of them to hurry up.

When they finally reached the marquee, there were hundreds of people milling in and out of the various entrances dotted all around. Sophie could hear loud music from within that was highly percussive, but with a melody provided by an odd instrument she could not work out. As they got inside, she saw exactly how the music was being played.

Six men stood or sat around in a circle. Two of them played *dhols*, both hands free to beat the drumhead at either side. Two others played what looked like toy trumpets and made squeaky sounds like the plastic kazoos Sophie could remember getting out of cheap Christmas crackers. A fifth one sat down and played a tiny and cheap looking keyboard; wires twisted up from around the man's legs and up to a speaker with trails of bits of wire twisted together looping over branches of the tree poking in and out of the ceiling and looking ready to spark and set fire to the place. It was the keyboard making the odd sound Sophie couldn't place, often just sounding as though the man was merely flicking the fingers of his right hand up and down the keys randomly at speed. He did not play with his left hand. This hand, instead, held the keyboard steady on his lap while also grasping between thumb and forefinger a microphone close to one of the keyboard speakers.

The sixth man was responsible for making sure that the microphone carried a signal to a jury-rigged loudspeaker which was the device responsible for making sure the whole area for two miles or more in every direction could hear there was a *gaye holud* taking place. He busied around connecting and reconnecting wires. Sometimes he would get it wrong, and horrible feedback would erupt from the loudspeaker, causing Sophie to clutch her ears in pain. No one else seemed to be bothered by this, except the man himself, of course, who rushed around again trying to fix it. It was the most bizarre set-up Sophie had ever seen, and she was amazed the man never electrocuted himself considering the number of times he poked bare wires in and out of various electrical sockets dotted around.

The rest of the people in the marquee were split between guests and members of the family of the bride and groom or their neighbours. This second group ran around making sure there were enough chairs or benches for everyone, making repairs to the marquee, or standing talking with the guests. A small group of women, spotting Sophie and her uncle, marched straight to them and greeted them in English, Bangla, and another language Sophie didn't recognise. She was slowly realising that not every Bangladeshi was the same and that there seemed to be some communities that lived, worked, and looked different to others. Something told her these women weren't Muslims, but she didn't know why she thought that. Sophie was intrigued by their bright yellow *saris* and the fact that all the females were wearing them – even the girls. *Didi* had told her that it was most important to wear something old as she did not have anything yellow, and Sophie couldn't work out why. All these women were in yellow, yes, but they were clearly dressed smartly. Sophie felt underdressed in her scraggy T-shirt and jeans. For once, *Didi* wanted her to wear western clothes, yet this was a wedding party; surely, she should be in clothes which fit in? The only consolation was that Uncle Joshua was in a ridiculous yellow *Punjabi*-type long shirt which barely fitted – and that shade of yellow *really* didn't suit him. It didn't look good, and that made Sophie smile. Normally, her uncle always looked dignified.

The women told all three of them to sit down, and, as they did, Uncle Joshua turned to Sophie and thrust ten *taka* into her hand with a wink.

"For later," he whispered.

"What? Why?"

"You'll see."

Did her uncle actually just wink at her? The thought disconcerted Sophie completely, and she didn't notice the activity around her for a few seconds. The women had gone off but promptly returned, one carrying a large bowl, another a jug of water, and the third a towel and soap. The woman with the bowl suddenly sat down at Sophie's feet.

"Er...what's happening?" she asked as the woman slipped Sophie's sandals off her feet.

"You see," *Didi* replied with a big grin. "Don't worry."

Everyone now seemed to be watching Sophie and smiling, pointing, or laughing. She felt herself go red as the woman took her right foot and placed it in the bowl. The second woman now poured water from the jug over her foot. Its coolness made Sophie jump, and she squirmed as the first woman massaged her foot and washed it with the soap. Sophie's 'oohs' and 'ahs' were causing much hilarity around her. *Didi* found the whole thing hilarious, and even Uncle Joshua chuckled quietly as he watched.

The woman dried Sophie's foot and placed it back in her sandal. As Sophie began to put her freshly cleaned foot back down on the ground, the woman took her left foot and began again. Now that Sophie knew what to expect, she relaxed a little. Once over the shock and ignoring the fact a strange woman was messing with your foot – something that would never happen in England – it was actually quite pleasant. She still had no real idea why everyone found this so amusing. Perhaps because the water shocked her a little? She decided that this time she was going to enjoy it. She closed her eyes and smiled contentedly as the woman quickly massaged again and washed with water and soap, working her way up to her ankle and holding it firmly.

It was a few seconds before Sophie opened one eye to look at why the massaging and washing had stopped. The woman was *still* holding her ankle and seemed to be frozen there, looking at the ground. Sophie looked around for help or explanation. *Didi* was giggling away to herself, and her uncle just looked at her with a smirk on his face.

"*Didi*," she hissed, "*what is happening? Help!*"

Didi gave a little squeak of laughter and turned her back on Sophie, her shoulders heaving up and down. Sophie was drawing a crowd of interested Bangladeshis, all grinning, and she could feel her face going hotter and hotter.

"*Dhonnobad*," she said to the woman and tried to withdraw her ankle from her hands. The woman just held on tighter. Sophie tugged with her foot. The grip became tighter still, and the woman – who was much stronger than Sophie and had anticipated her reaction – planted her foot firmly back in the bowl so that Sophie could not move it again. She now began to panic. The woman continued to just stay there, eyes firmly fixed on the floor with her head bowed. Sophie looked at Uncle Joshua again, who was now clearly enjoying her public discomfort. He said nothing but made forward movements with his head towards the woman as if to say, '*go on then.*'

Suddenly, Sophie remembered the *taka*. She held up the note and heard a murmur of approving 'ahs' from the crowd around her. She looked at *Didi*, who had turned around again and half spoke, half pointed with the money indicating a question: *Should I give the woman the taka? Is that it?* Didi nodded her head in the usual Bangla way, which always seemed to say, '*Whatever you wish. If you like. Your choice.*'

Sophie leaned forward and gingerly put the *taka* note beside the woman. In an instant, her ankle was released, new water was poured on her foot, a quick clean was given again, and then it was dried and replaced in her sandal. The *taka* note had disappeared. Sophie never even saw it go. The crowd around evaporated with much discussion of what had taken place and lots of laughter.

"I'm sorry, Sophie," her uncle was wiping tears from his eyes with a hanky as he chuckled to himself, "we've all been through it, and we're all going to get it tonight. It's the custom."

As he spoke, the women had moved to him and went through the same ritual. When his ankle was gripped, Uncle Joshua waited a second, made a mock attempt to release the woman's grip, and bantered away with the women in Bangla at a speed that left Sophie's newly developing knowledge of the language behind. They were all laughing and joking but Uncle Joshua's ankle was still gripped. He reached down and popped a ten *taka* note by the woman.

"*Bang!*" she cried, shaking her head, obviously disapproving and not releasing her grip but still clearly playing the game. Her uncle's face scowled. The joke, it seemed, was now on him. Ten *taka* was no longer acceptable.

"What's going on, *Didi*?" Sophie asked.

"I think," *Didi* giggled, "that they are not accepting his money because he is *dhorni lok*."

"But he's not rich," Sophie protested but still grinned at her uncle's discomfort as he rummaged around in his pockets, looking for money. "You know that, *Didi*."

Didi indicated with her hands at all the people there.

"Look around Sophie. To all your uncle is very rich. They all *gourib*, very poor."

This was true, Sophie had to admit. Whilst she knew her uncle had limited finances and struggled to pay for Sophie's upkeep, he still employed *Didi* and a variety of part-time gardeners, milkmen, and others, and he lived in a *paka bari*, which very few in the area could afford to do. One or two lived in small brick houses, but most lived in straw or mud-clay huts. By comparison, Sophie and her uncle were very well off.

Finally, Uncle Joshua took out a fifty *taka* note – his twenty having already been rejected – and this finally saw him released. He muttered away about 'corruption being everywhere in this country' throughout all of the washing of *Didi's* feet. Sophie noted with interest that she only gave a two *taka* note. *Didi* didn't count as rich, then.

With *Didi* finished, the women moved on to other guests, carrying out the same ritual. Some just threw two *taka* notes without paying too much attention to the process. Others laughed and joked with the women, trying to pull their feet away or tickle the woman holding their ankles, who ignored all attempts to be cheated out of the payment, not even breaking out into a smile.

Sophie was intrigued by the whole ritual and asked *Didi* what it was all about. She assumed she would know the answer but all the more so because, for the first time, she noticed similarities between her friend and these women. There was a tinge to skin colour, a flatness of the face, and a common nose shape, which made her feel that *Didi* actually came from this community.

"When guest comes to our home for first time, they will always be greeted *very* careful and will also have foots washed," *Didi* told her. "At *gaye holud*, guest will pay some small change, as much or little as they can, and that *taka* is used to pay for wedding."

She indicated all the people milling around in the marquee.

"Most of these people are *gourib*," she said. "*Gaye holud* and weddings very much money."

Sophie understood. It was a fun way for guests to contribute to the cost of hiring a marquee, a band and feeding what was already over a hundred people sitting here. Sophie was sure that there would be more. As she had seen several times already, the villagers helped each other. Not just for special occasions like this but every day. No one saw it as unusual or strange. You helped your neighbour, and they helped you.

It was getting dark now, and someone had finally rigged up some lights which shone brightly into the marquee from various places. The party atmosphere seemed to be growing, and some women had started gathering near the musicians and held hands in a circle, swaying from one side to another. Eventually, one of them broke into song, and the others joined suit. There were only about a dozen of them, and Sophie thought how, in England, women would be embarrassed to do something like this in front of everyone – at least without several drinks beforehand – but not these women. They seemed lost in their own celebrating. *How marvellous,* she thought, *that people who live such hard lives could celebrate and enjoy life with equal joy.*

Then suddenly, it all stopped. The band stopped, the singing and swaying stopped. All attention was drawn to a small stage area that had been built on one side and adorned with all sorts of colourful, paper decorations. Sophie hadn't even noticed it until then, but now everyone started turning their seats around to make sure they had a good view of the staging. She soon found out why. From out of nowhere came the bride, surrounded by a troupe of other women and girls helping her in her beautiful yellow and red *sari*. The girl looked to Sophie like she could only be sixteen or seventeen and though she looked beautiful in her dress, jewellery and make-up, she had a solemn face perpetually looking on the verge of tears.

They watched as she was placed on the small stage, and two or three other girls sat around her, facing the guests.

"What's happening?" Sophie asked *Didi* but Uncle Joshua answered.

"This is the presentation of the bride," he whispered. "She is placed there with her handmaidens, and then she will be fed a little *mishti*, starting with the family and close friends, then *boro loks* – important people in the community – and then the rest of us plebs. At the same time, after feeding her a mouthful, we then apply the *holud* – which literally means 'yellow' and is just turmeric paste – to her face, arms or wherever we can see skin." He turned to her with a wry grin on his face. "It's messy," he confessed, "which is why everyone wears yellow or old clothes or, best of all, old yellow clothes! If the *holud* gets on your clothes, it will never come off. They stay yellow forever unless you bleach them."

Didi interrupted him. "No, no. I know way to clean."

"You do? Why have you never told me this answer to life's great mystery?"

Didi ignored or didn't notice his humour. "Why you think all your old clothes are still good after many years' weddings?" She turned to Sophie as if indicating that only another female would understand her apparent secret. "You put clothes in hot sun next day," she said playfully conspiratorially, "and then the *holud* will…puff…go away."

Sophie smiled at this, *Didi* beaming and revealing her gorgeous and perfect white teeth. She looked so beautiful it almost hurt Sophie to look at her. The woman made her heart ache. She mused at how many weddings *Didi* had seemingly washed her uncle's clothes for afterwards and how many years she had put up with his gruff acknowledgements of the hundreds of things she did around their home before leaving for her own. Why did she stay? She couldn't imagine he paid well.

She turned her gaze back to the stage and watched, fascinated as guest after guest came up, fed a mouthful of *mishti* to the bride and then took some yellow paste from the bowl placed beside the bride and smeared it on her face and hands. Some of the women burst into tears as they did it, clearly overcome with emotion. Sophie knew that this girl would, in all likelihood, live with her husband's family, probably far away and may never see much of her own family again. They were, in a very real sense, losing a daughter. This, she thought, might explain the solemn face of the bride herself.

Eventually, her uncle was invited up to take part and Sophie was encouraged to come up at the same time. She walked up with *Didi* and waited behind Uncle Joshua. He chatted a little in subdued tones to the bride, who gave tiny nods and grunts in answer as he spoke. He then smeared the *holud* on her face and sat back down in his seat. Sophie gave a respectful '*nomoshka*' to the girl and then followed what her uncle had done. She gave a small spoonful of the *mishti* to her, took some of the *holud,* which felt oily and slimy to her fingers and put a little patch on her left cheek. Then, not knowing what else to do, she looked at the bride and gave a little bow before sitting down.

After about half an hour, everyone who was going to go up had fed and pasted the girl, and the musicians began to play again while she remained sat with her handmaidens. But now, there was a different atmosphere. There was tension, excitement in the air and laughter and loud talking filled the tent. Sophie found it quite intoxicating.

"Sophie, *Bon.*" She heard *Didi's* voice next to her and turned her head. *Didi's* hand reached to her face, and Sophie saw too late that it contained a lump of *holud* on it. Unable to jerk her head away, she was smeared across her cheek, and *Didi* laughed at her.

"*Didi!*" she shouted at her with genuine shock at this uncharacteristic and sudden impishness.

"What's wrong, Sophie? Oh dear, let me look," said her uncle and Sophie turned to show him what *Didi* had done.

Before she knew what had happened, her uncle's hand had splattered and smeared a good lump of the paste on her forehead, and then he wiped his hand down her nose as if to add insult to injury. Completely stunned by what had just happened, she opened and closed her mouth several times, unable to find the words. At that moment, *Didi* lunged across her lap with a cry of "Uncle!" and caught Uncle Joshua square in the face with a lump of the oily paste.

"Why, you little…" he began with a grin, but *Didi* was up and running away before he could finish. With surprising speed, he was on his feet and chasing after her. Sophie couldn't believe what she was seeing. Were these the same two people she lived with each day? This behaviour was totally unlike anything she'd seen before, and it was, well, *childish*. She'd never seen them both so relaxed. Their normal boss-and-subservient-employee relationship seemed to have been replaced with one that suggested they had been close friends all their lives.

Then Sophie saw that they were in good company. Somehow, everyone seemed to have turmeric in their hands and were smearing – or trying to smear – anyone near them or chasing those that ran away. It was hilarious to watch, and after the third stranger came up to her and plastered some on her face or arms, Sophie realised she had to get up and either join in or try to run away.

She decided to join in.

By now, the musicians were playing feverishly. The little keyboard player's fingers were a blur, as were the high-pitched stream of notes. The drummers were swaying violently as they struck the *dhols* with greater and greater force—*boom boom boom.*

Sophie, unconsciously and without care or regard to what others thought, was leaping into the circle of women and out again, with no intention of following the lead of the others now though her steps were remarkably in time and mostly correct. She paid no attention to the others around, intoxicated, as she was, to the sound of the drums and the singing and the laughter and the chaos. Like the others, she was transported to another place, as though she were no longer in her body but whirling and twirling in space, looking down on someone else who looked like her still in the ring of women surrounding the men. She laughed from her belly for perhaps the first time in forever, and it felt *good.*

She kicked her feet out, she flung her body around, and she let the maddening melodies invade her head, filling every pore of her mind. *I am no longer here,* thoughts came into her mind; *I am everywhere and everywhere is me.* The women around her began to shriek with a strange warbling cry made by clicking the tongues over their top teeth.

"*Uula!*" they cried as one, sounding, to Sophie, like some kind of tribal war cry – and one that did not seem out of place here. Then she heard a new voice, different from the rest, joining in from behind her. There was a sense of something being different. The group seemed even more elated, even more ecstatic. Someone important had arrived and was joining in. Sophie turned her head and allowed herself to look to where she heard the new voice.

Staring at her, with a hellish grin, and standing at the main entrance to the marquee, was the ghost woman of Sophie's dreams. Her red eyes boring right into Sophie's brain, filling her whole vision. Sophie screamed and ran out of the circle. She took a stumbling step backwards, turned and fled out of the marquee, pushing through anyone in her way as she made it out into the night air. Her *rakkosh* was real, and it had come for her.

CHAPTER FOURTEEN — THE SUN AND THE DARK

Sophie stood there trembling in the dark. She had run to the end of the path and was now at the beginning of the fields between her village and this one. She had stopped just where the casting light from the *gaye holud* ended. The field was still and black as if brooding over some dark matter. It was menacing, daring her to move forward and face all the *rakkosh* that might be out there, buried in the shades.

The ghost of her dreams was real. How could this be? What kind of country was this where ghosts are real and, not just that, are *accepted* by everyone around? No one had panicked, no one had screamed, no one showed any sign of fear when the creature had appeared. Except Sophie.

Her heart was still pounding. *This made no sense.* In a world that was already a mess in her head, what had just happened brought a whole new level of insanity to it. *Maybe the ghost isn't real? Maybe I just thought I saw her,* thought Sophie. *Maybe I am just insane. I sure feel like I am right now.*

She had to get home. She needed to be in the safety of her bedroom with the doors locked and bolted. Ghosts and monsters there may be in this field, but she was going to have to brave it and run across. She knew that would not be easy; the *mali* were thin and difficult to walk on in the daylight without falling into the waterlogged paddy field. In the dark, without a torchlight, they would be damned near lethal. But she still had to do it. She took a deep breath, wiped the tears from her eyes and put out a foot to begin.

"Sophie! What's going on?"

She turned round to see who spoke from behind, but she already knew it was a less-than-pleased Uncle Joshua. She couldn't hold back her feelings. On seeing her uncle, she could feel the tears streaming out of her. She ran to him and gave him a huge hug that took him completely by surprise. His annoyance with her behaviour in the marquee instantly evaporated.

"I'm really sorry, but I just hate this place; it's got lots of monsters and what kind of place can have lots of monsters when they don't exist, but they do here, and I knew I'd seen it before. I knew I wasn't dreaming, and a ghost was really watching me, but you wouldn't believe me, and *now it's there*," she pointed in the direction of the noise coming from the marquee, "and everyone seems to think that's ok but *how* can it be ok it's a monster, for crying out loud…."

"Sophie, for heaven's sake, take a breath and calm down. You're babbling, girl!" Her uncle held her tight and stroked her hair. He could see the poor thing was half-scared out of her wits. "What are you on about? What monsters? What ghost?"

"In there! The ghost woman I've told you about. The glowing red eyes. She's the one I've seen in my nightmares trying to drown me, and she's the one who has been standing at my window when I wake up and hiding in bushes."

Uncle Joshua was silent for a moment and just held Sophie. Eventually, he spoke.

"Sophie, did she have long white hair?"

Sophie looked up at him. "Yes."

He let go of her, sighed and then began to laugh a little to himself.

"It's not *funny*," she said indignantly, "I'm really scared."

"I know. But I also know you don't need to be. There is no ghost, Sophie. No monster. Only *Mashima*."

Sophie felt the colour drain from her face. *Mashima*? How can that be? How can the wise woman of the village, the friend to all, so highly spoken of even by Uncle Joshua, be the evil creature of her dreams?

"I…I don't understand."

Uncle Joshua sighed again and took her hands in his. "Sophie, *Mashima* is very old and has seen some terrible things in her life. Her face is far from pretty, I guess. But more than that, *Mashima* is an *albino*."

"Albino? Aren't they people who have white hair? No hair pigment or something? But…she was worse than that. She looked more like a Western woman, and *her eyes*…." Sophie held her fingers up to her face to touch her own.

"Sophie, Bangladeshi albinos have little or no pigment at all. That means not just their hair, but their skin too is white. Or more accurately, pink because you, you know, they do still have blood like the rest of us – and *that* is still red, I can assure you. That means her eyes are a pinky-red kind of colour. There is no other colouring, only blood vessels. It can be very strange when you see one because they look almost like a white person who has been crying or something, and it takes a while to realise they are actually Asian."

She stood there, facing him, feeling a mix of emotions. She was still frightened, but now she was feeling foolish and angry.

"Why didn't you *tell* me this long ago then?" she snapped at him.

"I hadn't put it all together, Sophie," Uncle Joshua said, trying to be sympathetic. "You have nightmares every night. I hear you cry out every night. When you told me about the Ghost Woman, I had no idea you were talking about *Mashima*. I didn't know she was back in the area. She's a loner and goes where she wishes – one of the few women in this country who dares! She had been away many weeks when you first arrived, and she rarely tells people her business."

"But why was she standing at my window sometimes?" Sophie complained. "Was she trying to scare me?"

Her uncle shook his head. "Anyone who knows *Mashima* knows she does not need to try. She is a brilliant and brave woman when you get to know her, but you wouldn't want to cross her." He gave a laugh. "Even I would think twice." He thought for a moment and then added: "I don't know how she came to be at your window during the storms, but I guess she must have been if you saw her. I do know, though, that part of *Mashima's* wisdom comes from the fact that she *watches,* and she *listens.* She goes where she wills and when she wills and is probably the only woman in the whole division who can do that. She may well have heard, when she got back, that you had arrived in the village and went to look at the *bideshi* girl who had landed so dramatically."

Sophie kicked at the ground with her sandal. "Well, I don't like her and don't want to see her if she's like that. She sounds horrible."

Uncle Joshua grinned. "Let's leave it for tonight," he said. "We need to go home now anyway, but I think it is about time you two meet formally. I'll try to sort it for tomorrow."

They started to head back towards the marquee to pick up *Didi*. Sophie refused to go back inside, though. She had no interest in seeing that horrible woman.

"If you make me see her tomorrow, I won't like her," she said just before they got to the marquee entrance.

"To be honest, Sophie," her uncle replied, "I would be more worried about whether *Mashima* will like you." And with that, he went back in to find *Didi*.

In fact, it was *Didi* who took Sophie to *Mashima* in the end and did so the very next day. Sophie tried her best to refuse, but her older friend knew her too well and could push all the right buttons. No matter how scared of *Mashima* she might be, Sophie would always do what *Didi* insisted. They had argued and bartered over breakfast while *Didi* cooked up an omelette for her. It was a Friday, and Uncle Joshua had already left to go fishing in the *pukur*. *Didi* would take Sophie to *Mashima's bari* mid-morning on her way to take *nasta* to him at the pond.

The two girls left the home around ten in the morning. Sophie didn't go through the gates to the *pukur* while *Didi* took the *nasta* to her uncle but instead rested on a post, looked over the fencing and stared into the waters. She was brooding, and she knew it. She also knew that she was being silly. Whatever her dreams and whatever the reason *Mashima* had been peering in at her window from the balcony outside, she was a real, flesh-and-blood person and therefore not to be feared. However, this didn't release Sophie from the panic she felt and just made her feel more foolish and guilty than ever.

Didi came back to the gate, minus the *tiffin* box she had taken in and led Sophie on towards where *Mashima* lived. The journey took a while. Beyond where the *gaye holud* had been and further out than Sophie had gone before. They headed past all the fields and into the nearby forest. The trees were densely packed, and the sense of darkness intrigued Sophie. She felt like Little Red Riding Hood and amused herself with wondering if *Mashima* was the granny, or the wolf, or both. She did enjoy the coolness of the shade,

though. Even though it was November, it was still really hot. Sophie
wondered if Bangladesh ever cooled down.

Eventually, they came to a small hut surrounded by a particularly dense
clump of trees. Sophie laughed partly out loud, which made *Didi* turn to
look at her, but Sophie waved her hand to dismiss the question. It really
was Little Red Riding Hood meets Hansel and Gretel, she thought. The hut
was made of grey-brown clay, and the floor felt cool as Sophie and *Didi*
took off their sandals at the entrance. Considering the *bari* was made
effectively of mud, Sophie was surprised just how clean it looked and felt.
Carved and painted in white and red all over the walls, both inside and
outside, were many designs and shapes which were very beautiful and had
clearly taken some time to create. If the gingerbread house were made of
clay, she thought, this is what it would look like.

The hut smelled different from other homes she'd been to. She was
used to the smell of spices and freshly-cut fruit, which were the norm
wherever she went with *Didi* or Uncle Joshua, and there were hints of these
odours here too, of course. But much stronger here was the smell of
incense. It reminded Sophie of the joss sticks her mum used to burn when
having a bath. For a moment, that image flashed through her mind.
Remembering being a little girl, peering over the edge of the bath while her
mother lay submerged under suds and music was playing gently in the
background. Her mother smiling at Sophie while she pottered and played.
How old would she have been then? Four? Five? The tableau burned inside
her until she realised she felt nauseous and physically shook her head to get
rid of the sensation and the memory. She held on to the wall for a second
to recover herself and then continued inside. It was still too soon to allow
pleasant remembrances.

Mashima had made a kind of open veranda inside her small dwelling,
with a couple of chairs and a short table to one side. Light from the two
open window holes from the front lit the way, but still, the inside was quite
shadowy. A back wall contained two doorways – one on the right and one
on the left – leading into the two rooms that made up the remainder of the
house.

They passed through into the one on the left, and Sophie saw the
hideous *Mashima* on her knees, stirring some *cha*. It was as though she knew

exactly when they would arrive. The hot brown liquid was steaming. Sophie did her best to quell the rising panic filling her chest, and she told herself, yet again, that she was being silly.

The first thing to distract her was that there was no chair, just a mat on the floor. *Mashima* herself had not acknowledged their presence yet, but *Didi* seemed to already know this would be the case. She had walked in and sat herself on the mat in front of the woman and motioned to Sophie to do the same, as though this was completely normal. Sophie did so, and this was the first moment the old woman in front of her looked up and took notice. *Mashima's* face betrayed no emotion, but her huge staring eyes burned into the girl. Sophie wanted to look away but couldn't; she was compelled to return the gaze.

For the first time, Sophie could see that *Mashima's* eyes were not red. The fleshy surroundings of her skin and eyelids were a bright crimson, and the surrounding startling white skin and bright snowy hair exacerbated the redness. From a distance, all you saw were huge red eyes. Closer, her irises were clear grey.

Although her skin was white, the old woman had all the features of a Bangladeshi. It was like looking at a colouring book that hadn't been filled in. Sophie noticed there were many small blotches of a mild brown hue punctuated her face and neck. Like most old women, *Mashima* wore a *sari*. Hers looked faded and dirty yet, by some bizarre trick, she made it look dignified.

"You are the white girl then," *Mashima* said, betraying no hint of irony. She spoke in Bangla, and Sophie responded as best she could.

"Yes. Me."

"Are you frightened of me, little white girl?"

Sophie wasn't quite sure of this question and turned to *Didi* for help. Her friend gave the translation, and Sophie nodded, turning back to *Mashima*. The polite English thing would be to deny the accusation and fake being completely comfortable with the creature. But then, if *Mashima* had been polite, she wouldn't have asked the question in the first place. Sophie decided to be honest.

"Yes. Lots."

The woman broke out into laughter, rocked back and slapped her knees with bony hands.

"That is no wrong answer," she replied. "You *should* fear me. Everyone does. Everyone knows their *Mashima* knows all, sees all."

"Do you?" Sophie raised an eyebrow.

"Ha! No, of course not. But it does them all good to think it."

Sophie grinned at this. There was something about this strange woman…

"Everyone fears me because they know I suffer no fools. They can chase their *ghorar dim*, and I will happily crack them over their heads!" Sophie didn't quite understand her words, but *Mashima's* body language gave her the gist. "But why do *you* fear me, white girl? You have yet to cross me when I am in an angry mood, so you have no way yet to know you should be frightened. Yet you are."

"You my *Rakkosh*."

Didi let out a gasp, and her eyes widened in reproach at Sophie.

The albino in front of her cried with delight and laughed hard.

"Oh! White girl – you have given the best answer! I won't say I have never been called a monster before, but it has been a long time." She reached over and wagged a finger at Sophie. "You have courage inside you; I'll give you that. You don't really know it yet, but you have good spirit inside. I know these things. You'll see."

"Oh, you see the…" Sophie leaned over to ask *Didi* what the word for 'future' was. "…future then? You know what will happen to me?"

"No," the woman responded firmly, "anyone who tells you they can see the future is a liar and a fool in equal measure. No, white girl, I just see people. Clearly. I have no time for niceness and false faces. There is no colour in my skin, and I see no colour in others to disguise who they really are. I know people." She thumped her chest. "I know hearts."

Sophie smiled. *Mashima* seemed to her very intense, yes, but very sensible too. She was getting used to the wild, unkempt white hair and the strange looks this woman gave. She didn't seem so frightening. Not really.

"Why did you come to my balcony that night?" she asked, hoping that *Mashima* would remember back all those months and also hoping that she really had peered through her window and Sophie didn't now sound like a complete idiot.

Instead, *Mashima* looked at her and nodded. She had come that night.

"I go where I go," she began, "and I usually go at night." She pinched her skin. "This is no good in the sun. I burn. Lots. So, it is my habit to go out at night. It is better then. You see what is really happening when people think no one is watching. I go very far. Long time. Then I come back. It is what I do."

She pointed at Sophie again.

"I came back and heard the village talk – 'there is a strange foreign girl come to punish the teacher,' they said. I came to look and see what kind of creature you are."

Sophie felt rankled by the idea that people were talking about her or that they might have called her a 'creature.' She tried to check her anger by reminding herself that up until a few minutes ago, she had been calling *Mashima* a monster.

"And did you decide?" she said, assertively looking back, "what kind of creature I am? After all your observations of me, I mean."

Mashima leaned back on her feet, somehow defying gravity as she squatted. For the first time, the harshness in her face softened slightly, and Sophie thought she saw sadness. Not sadness from pitying something pathetic; sadness from someone who understood pain.

"What I know is that you have monsters," she pointed her finger back at herself, "but not this monster." She cackled and turned her finger to jab at Sophie's chest. "Your monsters are in there. They are living inside you and will eat you up, given time. I know." She turned her finger back and jabbed at her own chest. "I know."

Sophie felt a swell of sadness mixed with relief flood her chest. There was something about *Mashima* that told her she was a kindred spirit – just like *Didi*, but with an extra intensity. She knew this woman had suffered something awful – perhaps many things – but she didn't know what. Sophie glanced at *Didi* and could see she had her eyes closed and was rocking gently while nodding her head in agreement. Sophie realised she knew very little about *Didi* other than she had a home she went to in the village but where,

Sophie didn't know. Did the three of them all share the same pain? Had they lost family? Had *Didi* and *Mashima* lost their own parents through some awful tragedy? And if so, had…she struggled to admit these words into her mind…had they too been responsible for their deaths?

She pinched her leg hard to choke back the tears filling her eyes. She wouldn't cry. She wouldn't. For a few moments, they all sat there, looking at each other, kindness shared between them but with no words, no smiles, no outward show of emotion. Eventually, *Mashima* broke the silence.

"*Cha. Kao* – drink."

No different to the English, Sophie thought, laughing as she came out of her blackness. We drink tea to solve all problems.

She remained at *Mashima's* for much of the rest of the day. They ate a little rice and dhal with her and talked of many gossipy things happening in the village. *Mashima* gave as much as she took in this respect and was a mine of information about people. Yet she was never cruel or malicious. Always her words rested on facts and never strayed into making judgements about the motives or intentions of others.

There came a time where *Didi* said she needed to start making the curry for dinner for Uncle Joshua and Sophie, and they would need to leave soon. They said their goodbyes to *Mashima*. She grunted her goodbye back to the pair of them but did not step out of her room. She had dismissed them and now returned to her own world even as they were stepping out of the *bari*.

On the way back, Sophie said she had realised she had never been to *Didi's* home. They spoke in 'Banglish' now, using a mixture of both languages freely. Sophie had learned that nine times out of ten, if you didn't know a Bangla word, you could just substitute an English one and it would probably be understood.

"No, you have never been, that's true," *Didi* said. "You should come soon."

She turned and grabbed the girl's arm, her face suddenly alive with excitement.

"Wait! Why not you come tomorrow? Would you like to harvest?"

"To do what?" Sophie asked, puzzled.

"My village," the beautiful *Didi* smiled, "has some fields. Our rice crop is ready for harvesting. Tomorrow is my day off. You come and we will teach you to cut the crops."

Sophie loved the idea. "That sounds cool! Yes, ok, let's do that. But I don't know where you live."

"I will come for you. About 8 am. It is hard work, and you will want to do it before the sun rises too much. Very hot."

"Okay, sure. What fun!"

Uncle Joshua thought the idea was very silly, but he gave permission for his niece to go, nonetheless. And so, Sophie, wearing jeans, trainers and a T-shirt rather than *shalwa kameeze* headed off early the next day with *Didi* after she had eaten a banana for breakfast. At *Didi's* insistence, she brought a bottle of water with her.

Didi took her down the main road leading to their village and off to one of the villages Sophie hadn't been to yet. At first, the number of trees made her feel like they were heading to *Mashima's* again, but then the trees cleared, and she came to a few *baris* which were similar to *Mashima's* but generally a little larger.

She was greeted like a movie star. Barefoot children clamoured excitedly around her, laughing and speaking in such a village slang, Sophie assumed, that the words didn't sound like Bangla at all. Semi-dressed men came out of the huts, some re-tightening their *lunghis* as they came to see the *bideshi*, the foreigner, which the children were chanting at them frantically.

She didn't mind the attention. It was good-humoured, and Sophie was used to this now. Wherever she went, there were always stares, sometimes murmurs of *'bideshi,'* and sometimes little children would run up to her to timidly stroke her skin and then run back scared to their mums. The superstition was that if you touched a white person, some of their luck would rub off on you. *You really don't want any of my luck*, she would think, but outwardly just smile and move on.

There were six *baris* arranged in a rectangle around a shared flattened area. There was an earth *chula*, a mud-built cooking area where straw would be fed into the base and lit to provide the fire; whatever was being cooked would be in a pot placed on top. She could see they were boiling water, and various mugs and jars were surrounding the area, with some of the women pushing in straw to feed the flames. She knew they were making the obligatory *cha*, and they would sip and make polite conversation before beginning the work.

Didi introduced all the members of the village to Sophie one by one. She couldn't keep track of who was who, and *Didi* spoke so animatedly that even her English was hard to follow, let alone her Bangla. Everyone, it seemed, was related to everyone else, and the different names for various relatives abounded. Sophie had learned from her lessons with Adhora that relationships were much more important here than in England. It wasn't enough to know you had grandparents; you had different names for your father's parents and for your mother's. Uncles and aunts, older or younger, on either side of the family also had special names, as did their children. There were, quite literally, hundreds of names used to indicate the relative positions in the family and their importance. Sophie also learned that the names changed depending on whether you were Muslim, Hindu, Christian, Buddhist – and then again, there were various 'tribes' around the country that had their own names. She was quite convinced she would never learn even the most important ones; there were just too many.

Introductions conducted, numerous 'hellos' and 'thank you's' given, they all sat on the ground drinking the freshly brewed *cha*. Sophie knew there were different kinds of *cha;* she noticed she preferred *cha* made by some rather than others (and *Didi's* most of all, which was deliciously sweet), but this village was completely different. For a start, there was no milk of any sort in it. Sophie had drunk *cha* with cow's milk, condensed milk and even goat's milk. But this *cha* was black and quite bitter. *Didi* told her it was called *laal cha* and told her it was best with *muri* which she explained to Sophie was puffed rice.

As she spoke, one of the old women of the village brought out a plastic container full of this *muri*. Sophie would have expected this in her breakfast bowl had she still been in England. She was horrified, though, when the woman approached her, pulled out a large handful of the rice with her right hand and dumped it straight into Sophie's mug. She sat there staring at the heap quickly sinking into the tea; the *muri* soaked up the liquid while the woman continued round to all those with a cup and similarly deposited a handful in each drink.

Sophie looked at *Didi* and saw her eyes twinkling with amusement. *Didi* motioned to her that it was ok and to…what? Eat? Drink? Sophie wasn't even sure what it was she now had. But *Didi's* face always reassured her. There was no doubting she was safe when she looked at that most gorgeous of smiles.

Not for the first time, as Sophie supped from her cup and allowed rice and hot *cha* into her mouth, she wondered how special *Didi* was. It was one thing to be wonderful as the sole Bangladeshi working in the house of a strange Englishman and his chaotic, unwanted relative. It was another thing to be seen as just the same thing in your own home, yet it was obvious to Sophie that *Didi* was adored by the children here and respected by the elders. *What rock was this gem cut from?* she thought. And why did she work for her grouchy uncle, who barely tolerated her presence? Admittedly, *Didi* had a power over Uncle Joshua insofar as she could get away with far more than anyone else seemed to. He listened to her without dismissing her words instantly as he seemed to with all others. He allowed her to do her work without complaint even though, at times, Sophie noticed his immense displeasure of having to lift his feet while reading the paper when *Didi* was sweeping his study. Sometimes, Sophie thought *Didi* did it on purpose.

She surprised herself with how quickly the *cha* was finished and how delicious she found it. Once she had got used to the harshness of the taste, she realised the *cha* and *muri* worked perfectly together. She felt both refreshed and like she'd had a snack. She was ready to work, and that was just as well as, almost by intuition or telepathy, everyone stopped drinking and got up from the ground. The children, who had calmed while the drinking was going on, now became excited again. They swarmed around Sophie and began to lead her from the village out towards the adjoining fields.

In the village setting it had felt to Sophie like it was dominated by the women and the men sat almost like strangers on the periphery. But, in the field, it was the opposite way around. While the children, both boys and girls, young and old, went where they pleased, the women remained at the edge of the square field. Even *Didi* stayed back. It wasn't as though they were forbidden; every now and then, one would step into the field to admonish a child playing too roughly or pull a toddler back from approaching the array of sharp tools strewn on the ground waiting to be used. Instead, it seemed that they had no wish to enter this territory which was not their usual domain. Men controlled the fields and, Sophie suspected the women were thinking, they were welcome to them.

One of the younger men was either the leader of the group or had taken a shine to Sophie and was showing off. Either way, he had taken the responsibility to show her what to do, and he motioned her to come to the tools. Even though she responded with Bangla, he seemed to think she had no language and gave her instructions with grunts and hand signals. Perhaps he didn't understand her accent, she thought. Or perhaps his mind couldn't cope with the concept of a thirteen-year-old white *bideshi* girl speaking Bangla?

He picked up one of the blades from the ground. It was a small curved scythe about a foot long plus the wooden handle, which he now gripped and then bent down to the stalks before him. He cut two and twisted them into an intricate pattern before laying them on the ground beside him. Then he showed her she was to grab at a good handful of the grain with the left hand and cut sharply with the scythe towards herself. He indicated to be careful, patting his shin and demonstrating how the blade would slice into her leg if she did not judge the pressure for cutting correctly. He cut several more handfuls and laid them crosswise over the two stalks. When he judged enough had been cut, he then bound the bundle together with the stalks, picked up the whole lot and stacked them to the side. One of the other men then came and took it to add to some others which had already been done earlier.

Sophie thought she understood the principles and took the blade from him. Under his direction she bent down and began. Almost immediately, she was stopped when she attempted to twist her binding stalks together. No, no. That wasn't how to do it. She could see how much joy it was bringing him and the other men to correct her. It was all in good humour, but she was clearly just a dumb woman. She didn't mind; she was already beginning to realise the scale of the job. The field was filled with rice stalks, and even with all of them at it, this was obviously going to take hours. And it was just one field! All around, she could see dozens more. She had barely begun, but already she could feel new respect and admiration for these men growing in her. The sun was up and beating down on them all, but Sophie knew it was going to get much hotter yet. How did they survive this day in, day out?

She started cutting and, after about twenty minutes or so, got the hang of it and started moving with a rhythm and speed which pleased her. Her 'guardian' was still watching over her but was working alongside at the same time. She wasn't cutting or preparing bundles as fast as he, but she wasn't far off. At least, she convinced herself she was nearly as fast anyway. She was glad of his warning about the danger of the scythe: sometimes it was like cutting through rope with a butter knife; other times it was as if the stalks themselves were made of butter. What Sophie was sure of was that these blades were extremely sharp.

They bantered as they worked, about ten of them, Sophie mainly listening but, from time to time, responding to questions her companion would utter. Where are you from? How old are you? Is the *bideshi* teacher your father? Her answers would be repeated to the other men who all seemed equally fascinated with her. The women continued to loiter around the outskirts, occasionally joining in the chatter or sweeping paths with brooms made of bamboo and straw.

After an hour, Sophie realised the sun was really beating down now, and she was very hot. The work wasn't unpleasant, however, and she felt safe – partly because the men were all respectful of her, partly because *Didi* was nearby and Sophie knew she was under her protection. Even though the work was hard on the back and there was a seriousness to it all – this was their food they were harvesting after all – the whole village lost none of its fascination and amusement at a white girl working the field.

At some point, while Sophie particularly busied herself at the task, she became aware of a new commotion among the bystanders. She looked up and saw Uncle Joshua standing in the crowd. She felt her cheeks instantly flush. Horror was evidently etched on her face as everyone laughed when

they saw she had noticed him, and Sophie immediately looked down again
and worked with renewed vigour.

"How are you doing?" she heard her uncle shout to her from the side.
She looked up at him again.

"It's fun!" she said, surprising herself with how true that statement was.
"You should come over and give it a go."

Her uncle grimaced and shook his head. *Didi* laughed and then
explained to the others who didn't speak English, who were already
demanding to know what the white people had said. There was a ripple of
laughter, and several children beckoned the man to come over and pick up
a hand scythe. Now it was Sophie's uncle's moment to be embarrassed. He
refused with vigorous shakes of the head and scowled at his niece.

"I'll leave you to it," he said, starting to edge away. "I just came over to
check you hadn't sliced yourself to bits."

"No worries," she grinned back. "I have this licked!"

And with that, she turned back to her work, grabbed a handful of stalks
and slashed with enthusiasm, instantly cutting through so fast that she
couldn't stop the blade from going straight into her leg. Sophie cried out
and fell backwards. She held her left leg in the air for a moment, feeling
pain but hoping that she hadn't gone as far as cutting skin. After a second,
the tell-tale dripping of red told her she had – and deeply.

The clamour was instant. Her helper shouted urgently to the women on
the side. *Didi* leapt into the field and ran to Sophie. But Sophie instinctively
had turned her eyes to the departing back of her uncle. She saw him stop
and turn to check what the commotion was, and then the colour drain from
his face. She wouldn't exactly say he began running to her, but he certainly
rushed as he waddled back, and she could tell he was as scared as she felt.
The stinging pain from her leg made her panic all the worse.

Quickly there was a crowd around her, but *Didi* pushed through,
grabbed her leg to check how bad the cut was and then shouted for a *gamcha*
to be tossed to her. She tied the cloth around her leg just above the cut and
pulled it tight. With her *orna* she wiped around the cut to clear it of blood.

"My God, is she alright?" boomed a voice from behind the crowd.
Uncle Joshua pushed his way forward and spoke Bangla too fast to *Didi* to
pick up what they were saying, but Sophie saw him peering over the

crouching woman to see the wound for himself. He was calming down; *Didi* obviously said the cut wasn't that deep, and Sophie felt herself begin to relax too. *Didi* told her to come into the village to wash the cut, and she hobbled to her feet. Gravity brought fresh pressure to her leg, and she felt the sting intensify, but she was able to put a little pressure on her foot and limped back to the *baris*, wincing as she went.

"I'm so sorry," she said to *Didi* as the woman put her arm around her for support, "I was clumsy and careless. I'm so silly."

"No, no," her friend replied in English. "Everyone do it first time, Sometime two and three time too! It no problem. We clean. Bandage. All good."

Didi reassured Uncle Joshua again that the cut wasn't deep and packed him off to the house, promising she would bring Sophie back later. There was no need to worry. Sophie felt guilty at the fuss. At the same time, deep inside, she felt strangely touched and pleased that he had looked so concerned for her. The feeling was confusing but not unpleasant.

At the village, a bowl was filled from the deep well that stood in the centre of the courtyard. One of the older children was tasked to pump the long metal handle up and down, and a young one held the bowl underneath the pipe outlet as water gushed out. The handle squeaked with every thrust alternating with the sound of splashing water until the small child swiftly carried the bowl over. The women fussed around while *Didi* soaked a *gamcha* into the bowl and applied the rag to the cut to clean it. It was chillingly cold, but in the now fully risen sun, Sophie was grateful for the sensation.

It was rather a shock when she saw one old lady hand a box of plasters to *Didi*, who found the largest two or three and stuck them over the long gash above her ankle bone. The idea they would have plasters in a village made of mud, bamboo and straw seemed simply out of the question.

She ticked herself off. She knew full well that Bangladesh was neither as modern as England nor some backwards third-world country. Every village had electric wires running to the homes (sometimes worryingly dangerously so with loose cables draping from tree branches), and she was even aware that some villages had solar panels on their roofs. Many *dokans* on the roads appeared to do little trade in the snacks, drinks, and other household items for sale in the little shacks, but most had at least a black and white TV sat on the shelves so groups of men could stand around drinking *cha* and watching the cricket. Still, the plasters seemed strange, and it made more sense when *Didi* wound a bandage around her leg, which even Sophie knew made the plasters a bit pointless.

Leg sorted, she got up to head back to the field, much to the consternation of *Didi* and the others. Nevertheless, she headed back but was disappointed to see the men had continued on and finished the field. They had been so close to the end when she had cut herself, and Sophie was cross with herself again for the accident. She had really wanted to finish the field.

She said this to *Didi*, and her friend responded that she had done a good job; everyone was very impressed with her. Sophie knew her friend was being kind. She looked beyond the field to all those surrounding which were yet to be harvested. Did these belong to the village? Most of them, *Didi* answered. It had taken Sophie and the guys most of the morning to complete that one field, and the scale of the work involved began to dawn on her. She told herself that once she went back to England, she would never look down on a farmer again. *They should rule the world*, she thought; *why do we see farming as the worst kind of work? We literally can't eat without these people. Food I've eaten all my life has probably come from fields just like these, and I've never given it a single thought.* The longer Sophie spent in this country, the more she questioned everything she had thought she'd known back at home.

For now, though, the reaping was done, and as the men carried the bundles to the storehouses nearby, Sophie was led back into the village while the women finished making the lunch for everyone. It was, of course, rice – with *daal*, curried vegetables and chunks of goat meat. A bowl of sliced cucumber and fresh tomatoes was handed around. Everyone ate with their right hands, as was the custom in every home. The *daal* was exceptionally hot, though and Sophie, having learned through bitter experience in the past, used a slice of cucumber as a scoop for several mouthfuls until the food had cooled a little.

As she sat on the floor of one of the *baris*, finishing her food, watching the others eating and chattering away, occasionally politely refusing as someone offered her more rice, more *daal*, more meat, more vegetables, surely more rice, perhaps some more meat, she rubbed her stomach which felt pleasantly stuffed. She was undeniably happy. Happiest she'd ever been? Certainly more happy than she had been since the accident. A warm glow flowed through her body like someone pouring *cha* in through her head to fill every pore.

Sophie realised at that moment that she loved these people – most of whom she'd never met until today. She loved their life; she loved their simplicity; she loved their joy of living despite the obvious sheer hard work of maintaining such a life. She felt at home here, and she realised that it might even extend as far as affection for Uncle Joshua. He might be a grump, but his face had betrayed that he cared, and it surprised Sophie to think she might like that.

CHAPTER FIFTEEN – A SURPRISE FOR SOPHIE

Some things might be very different in Bangladesh, but other things were universal. For some reason, Christmas seemed to be one of the latter – with schools at any rate. Despite Islam being the majority religion in the country, with Hinduism as the next largest and Christians well in the minority, the Christian festival was acknowledged anyway and technically a public holiday. That meant schools broke up for term break, and for English Medium schools like Sophie's, some kind of seasonal celebration was needed.

The Christmas concert was obligatory even here, much to Sophie's disgust. She had hated them as a child and she still hated them now she was a teenager. It wasn't the religious side of things – state schools in England rarely paid much more than lip service to that – but the effort needed to develop a performance in front of the school and parents that wouldn't make you want to curl up and die from cringing.

Sophie had managed to persuade her class teacher to let her and Adhora do something together as a pair while most of the rest of the class worked on a group play in Bangla. Unfortunately, although her proficiency in the language had come on pretty well, Sophie still didn't have the fluency to be able to memorise huge streams of Bangla needed for a play. She did, however, have a trick up her sleeve.

"We don't tell anyone about this," she said when telling Adhora the plan. If there was one person on this earth she trusted to keep a secret, it was her best friend. "Not even any of the teachers. We just assure them we have it under control and will have a performance to show when it comes to our turn on the night."

This plan turned out to work, in part because when telling the teachers organising the end-of-term concert, they also asked for lots of fabric, thread and needles from the art cupboard to 'create' their act. During break times, the girls stayed inside working on their creation and that satisfied the teachers that they really were coming up with something.

During the weeks leading up to the concert, the girls increasingly kept their work hidden, using the locked store cupboard of one of the nicer female teachers to keep it safe from prying eyes. Most people semi-respected their privacy though they had come to learn that Mahfuza (who kept her distance from both of them but never stopped scowling and sneering when in sight) had been asking around both staff and students to try and find out what they were doing. This didn't surprise them, nor did it worry either girl. Mahfuza had lost her crown in the school since Sophie had put her in a headlock, and no one gave her too much attention now.

One break time, though, a teaching assistant wandered into the classroom where they were sewing and practising Bangla to collect some books from a back shelf. The girls paid her no attention – she was a small woman, even by Bangladeshi standards, barely spoke a word and moved as silently as a breeze – and they continued with their work. At one point, Sophie held up her fabric to look at it properly and let Adhora see. They had forgotten anyone else was in the room and nearly jumped when they heard a gasp behind them.

"Is that…?"

They turned and the assistant was less than a metre away, wide-eyed and pointing at what Sophie held.

"Shush, *Apa*!" Sophie said. "Shush Sister – say nothing to anyone. Please."

The woman giggled and nodded her consent. She left, and Sophie turned to Adhora.

"Do you think she'll say something?"

Adhora considered for a moment and then replied. "No. At least not in the short term. There are only a few days to go. It will be okay. *Apa* doesn't say much to anyone ever, so I think it will be fine."

Reassured, Sophie turned back to her sewing as both girls laughed and joked quietly about the assistant's reaction. Inside though, both were terrified. This could go so wrong, and they knew it.

Sophie looked at herself in the mirror. More accurately, she looked at her short denim skirt and her legs from several angles. It was the first time she had worn a skirt since before the accident. The scars on her legs had been too deep and too ugly even to consider it. They had also been irritated by light material like dresses and *shalwas*. Jeans had been the most comfortable for some reason, and she wore those most of all, even though during the hot months she regularly peeled them off and *Didi* was forever washing the few jeans she had.

It was no longer hot, however. Though the midday sun still beat down and made Sophie think of mild summer days in England, there was a chill to the air, especially in the evenings, and she was amused to see that Bangladeshis were now all wearing woolly hats, scarves or *kombols* around their shoulders as though they were treading through six inches of snow. Sophie had just about stopped wearing T-shirts and putting longer sleeved tops on instead. It was far from cold.

Nevertheless, despite considering it, she decided it was probably not a good time to try going outside with a short skirt. The scars had receded a little and no longer looked red and angry. They didn't throb and, though still tender, Sophie didn't notice them so much these days. In the mirror she could see them, but they were faint and she figured that no one would see them from a distance. It was something to consider then, perhaps in the new year when, she was told, it would soon get warm again.

The skirt was a bit shorter than Sophie would typically have gone for. It had been included in her case when she'd been dragged here, and it had been old even then. Sophie hadn't realised until putting it on that she had grown over the year. It only just fitted around her waist and she felt a little tarty with how far up her thighs the garment ended. But then, there were just the faint stirrings of feeling like that was okay. She'd never had any interest in boys in the days pre-accident. Since then, she hadn't even begun to think of them, even after a few at school had taken an interest in her. She had dismissed them as simply boys being curious about the *bideshi* girl and wanting to poke their noses in to find out all about her. But recently, she was just accepted as one of the students, and she was beginning to wonder what it would be like to have a boyfriend. Just a friend who happened to be a boy, of course. Nothing more. Never anything more.

The skirt would do for lounging around the house today, though. Adhora was coming over and they were going to do a final rehearsal of their performance. She was also considering trying to persuade her friend to try on some of her clothes. Coming from a conservative Muslim family,

Adhora always wore *shalwa kameeze*, but there would be a time before long that her family would consider her to be a woman rather than a girl and then she would wear a hijab. Yet Sophie knew her friend loved beautiful clothes and often confessed a certain jealousy for western-style clothes, which she knew she'd never be able to wear when she was grown up. She was happy with her life and there was no bitterness to this thought; it was just one of those things which wasn't an option in her life and culture. Sophie was determined that she could at least get Adhora to try on such clothes in the privacy of her bedroom.

Sophie bounced down the stairs, through the hall and into the front room. Her uncle was reading his newspaper as usual and she ignored him as she half-skipped over to the door. Adhora was due any minute, and she decided she would wait in the porch area and look for her.

"Just a minute, Sophie," her uncle said, lowering his paper and looking at her over his spectacles. She stopped, hand resting on the door handle. He waved his finger up and down at her, indicating her clothes. "You're not going out in that, are you?"

Sophie felt her face redden, half embarrassed, half rising anger that he felt he had the right to question what she wore.

"I'm just stepping into the porch. Adhora is coming and I'm waiting for her. I'm not going outside, not *properly* outside."

"Damned right you're not, young lady," he replied, "nor are you wearing that skimpy thing with a friend coming."

"What? Why not?" Sophie tightened her jaw and unconsciously clenched her fist.

"Because it's not appropriate. That should be obvious, girl!"

"But why? I see lots of girls running around in skirts and dresses in the village. What's wrong with me doing the same?"

Her uncle rolled his eyes.

"Yes, when they are like eight years old, that's fine. Even a bit older. But this is not a society that allows women to show off parts of their body considered more...private."

Sophie was now annoyed and couldn't hide it.

"Well, that's stupid and sexist. I should be allowed to say what I show and what I don't. And you are British too, just like me and you shouldn't accept such sexist ideas. You should be supporting me wearing a skirt."

"I get that, Sophie. Honestly. But the fact is, this is a conservative and isolated rural area with Muslims here definitely in the majority, and in Islam, a woman of traditional marriageable age – in other words, one who has clearly started puberty – is expected to cover up. If she doesn't, there is still the view that she is..." Uncle Joshua hesitated with his words, "...of questionable morality."

"So, you're basically saying I'm a slut. Thanks for that."

"Language, Sophie! I don't want to hear that word in my house, thank you. And no, I'm not saying that. But I don't want you to give a wrong impression about you. Especially as even I can see you're growing up. Boys will be taking an interest in you soon. You don't want to make yourself a target."

Sophie didn't relax the grip of her hands. Her uncle was condoning unacceptable ideas, and she wasn't going to let this go.

"How can you say that?" her voice trembled with emotion. "You aren't doing anything about the situation if that's true. Everyone should be free to wear what they like. And anyway, I'm not even going outside. Adhora is just coming here."

"Whether you like it or not, agree or not, you need to change your attire. Adhora comes from a particularly strict kind of family, though not the strictest for sure, and what you wear will get back to them. Trust me, Sophie – they wouldn't think twice about banning you two from seeing each other. You have to remember that, in the end, we are guests in this country. Every year I have to renew my visa to continue working here, and it is very easy as one of the few foreigners around these parts to accidentally cause a great deal of offence. You're not going to be here forever. You won't be here long at all, hopefully...." Sophie felt her face flush again at the last word, "...and it is important I keep both you and your reputation safe. That's all there is to it."

"But..."

"I said that's all there is to it. Go and change."

For a few seconds Sophie stood there, open-mouthed, filled with rage and incredulity. Her uncle was a sexist pig who cared more about his reputation than her and still couldn't wait to get rid of her. She knew, though, that there was nothing she could do about it. She would have to change. All her scars seemed to tingle, feeling her shame and embarrassment. A horrid dark cloud came over her mind, and she felt like crying.

She turned on her heels and marched back through the room to return to her bedroom. She stopped briefly at the door and said, without turning to look at him, "You have no idea how much courage it took to decide to wear this, have you? No idea at all." She toyed with the idea of adding 'I hate you,' mulled the thought for a second and then decided to leave. She walked silently back to her room instead, not waiting for a reply from a man who meant nothing to her.

Adhora came and went. By the time she arrived, Sophie had changed, but that acquiescence didn't stop her from telling Adhora about the argument. The girl agreed it was a shame she couldn't see Sophie in the skirt nor try on her clothes but also could see the point Uncle Joshua was making. "You don't know people yet," she told Sophie. "They talk and gossip and say bad things when given a chance. And boys, they are the worst."

Nevertheless, said Sophie, they *would* get Adhora in a dress sooner or later. She just had to find a time or a place where they could make sure no one would find them; then she would make sure they could try on clothes and maybe even try some make-up too. Adhora giggled, scandalised by the notion, but she didn't say no either.

After she left, *Didi* came up to see Sophie and have a chat. As always, she had heard the conversation between Sophie and Uncle Joshua. Sophie hadn't even realised she was in the house. *Didi* often moved in and out, taking rubbish bins out to the village tip, shopping or weeding the garden area where they grew a few vegetables. Somehow, she always seemed to hear the conversations in the house, though. It was uncanny especially given her fairly basic English.

Sophie complained to *Didi* that Uncle Joshua never seemed to like her having any fun or doing anything nice. "There's always a problem," she said. "Nothing I do is right or 'proper' or 'acceptable.'" She mimicked his voice and *Didi* smiled with both her mouth and her eyes as she always did.

Didi always had a way of calming her, especially after fights with her uncle. Yes, her uncle was a difficult man and, yes, he didn't always understand what it meant to be a girl or even just a teenager. But he did care about Sophie and wanted the best for her. *Didi* was certain of this. And Sophie had changed him.

This surprised the teenager. "Changed him? Me? How?" *Didi* looked at her as though it was impossible Sophie didn't know.

"You haven't seen how he change? He is softer now. More gentle. With me too. He smile more."

This revelation had shocked Sophie. She would hardly call her uncle 'gentle,' and she rarely saw him smile other than for the briefest of moments. Certainly, he was not the ogre she first took him for, and when they managed a conversation without arguing, he did treat her with respect and as an adult. But that was a far cry from being a gentle man. Still, it made her think.

"Why do you put up with him?" she asked *Didi*. "You've been working for him for many years, I know. You're young and pretty and really very clever. Why stay? I'm sure you could get work anywhere, *Didi*."

Didi wobbled her head in the way she did, quietly acknowledging that there may be some truth in what Sophie said, about getting a job, anyway. But the truth was more complicated.

"I will always work for him until he no longer want me to," she said with a seriousness Sophie had never seen before. "I owe your uncle much, much. I will never leave. He made me safe."

"How? Why? What is the story with you two?"

"You have to know my story first."

"Then tell me. Tell me now." Sophie was all ears. She knew she had hit on something potentially juicy, and she wanted to know. *Didi* just smiled.

"One day. Not today."

"Oh, come on! *Didi!*" Sophie implored.

"Ok, I promise you. When school term ends. You ask me again. I tell you then."

A deal was struck, and Sophie was satisfied with that. The school term was just a few days away, and then it was *Boro Din,* Christmas. Finally, Sophie would know the secret power that her uncle held over *Didi*. Maybe it would be useful.

The day had arrived. All lessons were cancelled and the entire day was spent in preparation for the school concert. A huge marquee tent had been erected overnight on the field, and the stage blocks kept in a storehouse next to the school had been dragged out and placed at one end to make the staging. Microphones, wires and speakers were being positioned, and the school kids were enlisted to put up decorations when not needed to rehearse their particular part of the concert. Everyone from the kindergarten children through to the older teens was equally involved.

The scale and size of the operation made Sophie terrified. The marquee was laid out to hold at least three hundred people, and the microphone setup was intimidating. She suddenly realised the magnitude of the disaster it would be if her performance with Adhora was a horrible mistake. She ate no lunch or any snacks during the day for fear she would throw up.

As time progressed and rehearsals were done (she and Adhora had insisted they needed nothing more than to just place their props on the stage and make sure everything looked right and for Adhora to test with the sound man that the recording she had would play properly over the sound system – which it did). Sophie wished the clocks to stop or slow down, but they relentlessly raced through the remaining hours. It was almost six o'clock, and then parents would start arriving.

The two girls snuck off to a quiet part of the school to quickly run through their actions one last time. They were pretty confident everything was just perfect, but when they returned to the marquee, they saw hundreds of parents turning up and taking seats. Their hearts sank. They clutched each other's hand while they waited and watched the stream of mothers in *saris* and fathers in business suits walking past to take their place in the tent.

Most of the teachers had now been home and returned, so they too were in *saris* and suits, greeting parents and chatting animatedly with them. Kids ran around freely, enjoying the opportunity to leap off the staging at the front and just run around between the chairs. No adult tried to stop them. It was noisy and, as Sophie noted, very un-British. *You're not in Kansas now,* she said to herself and smiled at the thought.

The headmaster, Uncle Ahmed (who had still never forgiven Sophie for the Mahfuza incident), opened the proceedings, welcoming everyone to the evening, praising the efforts of the staff and children for getting everything sorted for the night. He talked about numerous things that Sophie couldn't entirely catch the meaning of – the combination of fast-spoken Bangla and a poor sound system bellowing out crackly sounds didn't help – but the gist was that the children had worked extremely hard this term and parents should be proud of them. This was greeted with warm applause; then he handed over to one of the female teachers to act as the compere for the evening. She explained that the children would perform according to year grade, with the kindergarten class going first and Grade Ten teenagers going last. This pleased Sophie. She was in grade eight, which meant that if their performance was as ghastly as she now felt it would be, there was time for other performances to make everyone forget it, or at least numb the memory.

And so the show began. There were dances and plays, poetry recitals and songs, groups and solo efforts. Some, you had to love the children as your own to find merit. Others, especially the solo dancers performing traditional Bangla music, were astonishingly good. Just as with the preparations during the day, Sophie felt the concert was moving all too quickly towards her turn.

Then so it was. Another dancer was called on, and Sophie realised with horror that she and Adhora were now needed behind the stage to get ready to bring all their props on as soon as the dancer finished. The music came to an end and, finally, it was time.

The two girls quickly raced on stage with their props. They set up a table, attached some rope to bamboo posts on either side of the stage, stretched across and behind the table, then threw a large sheet over it to form a backdrop. Sophie and Adhora stood behind the cloth with the rest of the props and nodded to the sound man to start the music.

The audience (now comprising most of the school children who had joined their families after their own performances) experienced this: Bangla pop music blared out from the speakers and simultaneously, a puppet, about three feet tall, appeared from a slit in the backdrop. The puppet's mouth moved in sync with the singing, its legs danced, and its arms moved about amusingly and appropriately to the lyrics of the song.

In reality, Sophie only had a limited understanding of the lyrics, so the two of them had practised moves relentlessly to make sure everything fitted correctly. Sophie inserted her arms through the cloth and into the puppet's arms while Adhora used one hand through another slit to control the mouth while the other used crossed sticks to make the feet dance.

This would have been a perfectly fine and amusing puppet show for the audience, but over the course of the first minute or so, there were murmurs, then fingers pointing, then titters of laughter in addition to those who were laughing at the dancing. The doll, people began to realise, was Caucasian. It was wearing thick-rimmed spectacles. It was rather rotund. It had a thick white beard. It was, in short, reminiscent of the only white teacher the school had. More than reminiscent. It could only be Uncle Joshua.

The realisation was infectious. Some mothers raised their hands to their open mouths in shock, their eyes twinkling with barely concealed delight. Others just roared openly with laughter. Even the teachers, standing around the edges of the marquee, couldn't help but find amusing the sight of Uncle Joshua jiggling away to an upbeat Bangla pop song. When the song ended, the adults burst into applause, and the kids cheered and shouted as the two girls stepped from behind the sheet to take their bows.

As Sophie came to the front, she looked out, elated at the sea of faces, adrenaline still pumping, her heart racing. Her eyes locked on the back of the crowd. There was unmistakably the shape of Uncle Joshua standing, looking straight back at her. Next to him was *Didi*. Panic rose as she was too far away to gauge the expressions of either. She had no idea if he had taken it in good heart or if she had burned bridges forever. If she could just see *Didi* properly, she would know, but the woman was turned slightly, talking to another woman at the back. Sophie could glean no clues and knew she'd just have to face whatever was coming later.

For now, though, she was a hero. Kids congratulated her on the sketch. They all commented how they could see her uncle making those moves. She almost wished they would shut up about it in case her uncle came over and heard. Still, she loved the praise. It was the first time any of the kids had ever said she'd done anything well, and she felt her reputation had gone up finally after the Mahfuza incident. That said, she was now firmly in the box labelled 'rebel.' That was no big issue for her; not really.

While the last few acts performed, she hung around backstage. Adhora had gone to sit with her parents almost as soon as they had finished. Sophie wished her friend had stuck around. But, in the end, she decided it was time to make her way to the back and face up to her guardian.

Didi saw her first and came up to give her a big hug.

"Oh my god!" she whispered to Sophie, grinning, "I can't believe you did that. I thought uncle would go bang!"

"I didn't really think about him seeing it," she grinned back, "I just thought he'd hear about it later. I'm cringing that he saw us doing it." She looked earnestly at *Didi.* "Did he…? Did he like it?"

Didi looked back at her, said nothing but winked before turning around, holding Sophie's hand and dragging her towards Uncle Joshua.

He took one look at her and said, "Well, young lady. What do you have to say for yourself?"

Sophie grinned sheepishly, praying he wasn't going to make a scene and said, "If it's any consolation, the kids all thought you were a great dancer."

He frowned doubtfully, but there was the trace of a smile on his lips.

"I should bloody well think so," he said finally. "I'll have you know I was a good dancer in my time."

"Really? You?" Sophie replied, now sensing the danger was over.

"Well…" Her uncle leaned over towards her. "No. Not really," he whispered conspiratorially.

Sophie laughed. Perhaps it was the thrill of the school ending, the blood rush of the concert, or the emotion of succeeding with her sketch – whatever it was, as they watched the last seconds of the final performance on stage, Sophie lent her head against the arm of her uncle. For a brief, surreal moment, she imagined it was her father again she was leaning into, just as she would have whenever they went to any shows or musicals back in England. This marquee, with all its bright colours and strange sounds, was a million miles away from anything she might have gone to with her father; but still, for a second, it felt like she was with him again. She reminded herself that Uncle Joshua and her father were brothers. They shared some common genes, so, in a sense, there was a part of her dad in her uncle. Sometimes, like just now, she could see glimpses of that.

"Sophie," he said to her, breaking her thoughts, "when we get home, there's a present I want to give to you. I think now would be a good time. As soon as the final speeches are over, let's go, okay?"

"Sure, yes," she replied. A present? Her uncle had clearly said they wouldn't be doing Christmas presents as it was something he didn't believe in and, anyway, hadn't needed to do for many years. Yet, he had a gift for her now. Sophie was intrigued.

The concert over, speeches done, and the concert-goers quickly dispersing before too many people could be persuaded to get involved with clearing up, Sophie said her quick goodbyes to Adhora and left with *Didi* and Uncle Joshua. Although it was quite late, *Didi* returned to the house with them both (she would normally leave early evening for her own home) and made a cup of *cha* for the three of them while Sophie and her uncle sat and talked in the front room.

Joshua pulled open a drawer from his desk and produced a brown paper-wrapped slim package which he handed to Sophie.

"I guess this should have waited until Christmas Day, but, well, you know how I feel about all that nonsense. I decided that perhaps this was the perfect way to end the day for you."

Sophie fingered the slim present. It was too small and too thin for a book, yet it felt like some kind of booklet at least. She didn't know if she was meant to open it. She looked up at Uncle Joshua. For once, he seemed to be able to read her face.

"Go ahead – open it!" he smiled kindly.

She undid the wrapping, held together only by thin sticky tape. Inside was a burgundy-coloured card-bound booklet of some sort. She turned it over. The front was ornately patterned with gold ink.

"It's a passport," she said simply.

"Open it."

She did so. It was her passport. Fingers now trembling, she flicked through the pages logging the holidays she took with her parents, which were too painful to think of still. She came to the last page with anything on and saw the 'visa on arrival' stamp going back to the summer when she came to Bangladesh. Now, on the opposite page, was a large stamp that was new to her. She read the word 'visa' and knew what this meant.

"You're going home, Sophie," her uncle said gently. "We've made you legally entitled to be here, and that means now you can leave without any problems at the airport. So there's no rush, and I hope you'll want to stay

on a little longer. We've got used to you being here. But when you're ready
– maybe after one more term or so? — we can sort out a ticket and get you
back to where you want to be."

"But how…how did you get this?" She looked up at him. "This is my
original passport."

"A double miracle. Firstly, your hopeless aunt finally grew the inkling
of a spine and a smidgen of a conscience and sent me the passport in the
post."

He smiled ruefully at her, eyes rolling as he spoke.

"And secondly?"

"Secondly, the miracle that the bloody thing came at all. There is much
to love about Bangladesh, but the postal service isn't on that list. It took
three months to get here, and that, believe me, is doing pretty well. That it
arrived at all and in one piece is all but unprecedented."

Sophie said nothing but tears started to drip down her cheek. She didn't
know why. This was what she wanted. This was what she had been
desperately wishing for, for all these months. Now Uncle Joshua had made
the wish a reality, and she was going home. So why did it feel so bad?

"What's the matter?" he said worriedly. "I thought this would make you
happy. It's what you want, isn't it?"

"Yes. Yes, of course," she looked up at him, her eyes red now. "I'm
sorry. Of course, I'm happy. Thank you, Uncle Joshua. Thank you so much.
I know I've not been easy to live with, and you have had your home and
peace invaded by me. But I am grateful and, yes, this is the best gift I could
have. I think I'm just tired and overcome with the evening and everything.
I'll be okay."

She got up and started to cross the room. "I think I should go to bed,
actually. Goodnight, Uncle Joshua and, thank you again. Truly."

She didn't turn to look but rushed to her room. She sat herself down,
still clutching the passport open at the new visa page and stared at it. There
was a knock on the door after about ten minutes and *Didi* came in holding
two cups of *cha*. She sat herself on the floor with Sophie and pushed one
cup towards the girl before sipping her own.

Sophie looked at her and waved the passport.

"I'm going home, *Didi*. Look! It's finally time to start saying my
goodbyes. I was beginning to think I would never come."

Didi stroked Sophie's arm with her right hand.

"Don't go too quickly," she asked in Bangla. "I will miss you very much and I know your uncle will too. He doesn't show it, but he does like you. The house will seem very empty and very wrong without you."

Sophie nodded in agreement and laughed as fresh tears poured down her face. *Didi* shuffled closer and gave her a long and comforting hug which Sophie returned.

They sat there for a while, saying nothing but enjoying the closeness which women can always appreciate. Then Sophie looked at her and said, "Okay, *Didi*. It is time. I'm not going to be here much longer. It is time."

"Time for what?"

"Time to keep your promise and tell me your story. Term is over as of one hour ago, so you said you would tell me when I asked again. So, tell me about your life and how you came to be here."

The beautiful woman looked back at her, long and hard, as though weighing up the right thing today. She seemed to make a decision and took a deep breath.

"Okay, Sophie, I will tell you."

And she did.

CHAPTER SIXTEEN - DIDI'S STORY

I was given the name of Mridhu by my parents and was the only daughter out of four children. My brothers were all older than me, but still they always jokingly called me their older sister, 'didi.' I was born in a Hindu village a few miles away from here and near the Indian border. We were not strict Hindus, as far as I can recall, and we were neither poor nor rich. We did not live in a paka bari as fine as this, but our home was made from bricks and bamboo with a fine tin roof and ceiling fans in most rooms. We even had a TV set in my parents' room which would also be used when guests came for dinner.

They would sit and eat on my parents' bed, and the TV would be turned on. If we had been good, then my brothers and I might be permitted to watch the TV with the guests, at least for some of the time. It was the only time the TV went on. For the rest of the time, when we didn't have chores, we could roam where we chose. I recall it was a happy, peaceful time.

My mother was a hard-working woman who never ceased doing something – cooking, cleaning, sewing, washing, repairing. Ma was kind and respectful to all, but she had a firm hand if any of us tried to be cheeky or naughty. There were many times I saw her dragging one of my brothers into our courtyard, twisting his ear hard because he had been guilty of some misdemeanour or another. I received the occasional wrench on the ear too. But generally, I remember her being gentle with us all and she was always singing, quietly, contentedly, to herself. I would often fall asleep to the sound of her voice as she would sing sweet songs to me to help me sleep, and she was always able to pacify Baba when he came home angry or stressed, which was often.

Baba was not a bad father, but he owned a shop a few miles away, which gave him great stress. Every morning he would leave on his bicycle as the sun rose and he would rarely return home until the late hours of the evening. If business had been good, he was in a reasonable temper. However, if business had been bad or new supplies hadn't arrived, leading to loss of custom, he would be irritable, and one wrong move from any of us would see his hand applied in force. Only Ma would be able to soothe him and coax him out of his anger. On Fridays, he didn't work but sat around the village on his stool, reading a newspaper and chatting to anyone who walked by. He was a different Baba then. He would laugh and joke with us and play hard, swinging us around and lifting us onto his shoulders. He was a strong man, and he could lift even my oldest brother this way until he grew as tall as Baba himself in those last days. I lived for Fridays; they were pure joy.

All my brothers went to school and, when I turned eight, I was allowed to attend too, though Baba was not in favour. Ma convinced him that I should go, and eventually, he acquiesced. "Educating a daughter is like watering another man's field," he would say to her. I did not understand what that meant at the time, but now I know that my going to school meant extra work and stress for my father. Schools had fees, and there were always expenses for books and, in the end, I would marry some man and go live with his parents for the rest of my life. My husband's family might benefit from my education, but my father would pay for it and receive none. Such was, and is, the thinking in villages.

Nevertheless, Ma got her way eventually, and I started school. I was quite a good student, I think, and always worked hard, knowing how important it was to impress Baba. For four years I was a diligent model student, and though I never achieved the highest marks in the class, I always did well enough, and teachers were pleased with me.

That changed one day when I was twelve. Our mathematics teacher was not very good. He did not care for us and often cancelled classes without notice. He gave us very little tuition because he wanted, like many other teachers, to suggest to wealthy parents that their child was failing because they needed extra tuition – which, of course, he could provide after school for a fee. This was the way many teachers supplemented their meagre wages, but this teacher was especially dreadful, and no one wanted lessons with him. And so, he gave us all a test paper which was impossibly hard. The whole class failed.

The teacher dutifully, deliberately, informed the headmaster. I still recall the headmaster's face – full of rage – when he stepped into our classroom with his cane in his hand. He whipped every single one of us for disgracing the school with our results and dishonouring our maths teacher. He slashed at our backs and upper legs, telling each of us we were lazy and deserved to be beaten by our parents.

I barely made it home after that; the pain was so intense. Ma washed my wounds, but I could not walk or sit on a seat for many days. I lay on my bed, unable to go to school–- or even to swat away mosquitoes – until the scars healed. By that time, Baba had removed me from the school. I was thankful he did not beat me – he threatened he would – but he certainly sided with the headmaster and refused to believe me when I said all the children had been whipped. It was clearly my fault. I was the lazy one. I had disgraced the school and my family. This was the reason I should never have been allowed to go to school. My education was over, and I never went to school again. I was not even allowed to keep my books. Baba burned them all. A distance grew between us and I never really spoke to him again after that. I regret this now. Time makes us all wiser.

I don't know what day it was or whether I had turned thirteen or not when my life ended. All I know is that it was some months after Baba removed me from school and it must have been around monsoon season, for the thunderstorms had been particularly vicious that year. I know that one evening I went to bed content and, if not happy, at least at peace with the world. I woke up to my peace shattered.

I remember stirring from my sleep to the sounds of screaming and shouting, and the first thing I saw were hands reaching through the bars on my window trying to grab at me. There was a strange light in the room, and I felt I was choking. At first, I thought I was having a nightmare, and I tried to resettle myself and persuade myself to think better thoughts and go back to dreaming of nice things. Then I heard a wrenching sound, and one of the bars from my window landed on me.

I screamed and sat up, covering my blanket around me. I saw the arms were real and they were a man's. He was trying to crawl in through the window. I screamed again. "Shut up!" he shouted. "Wake up! You need to get out. Now!"

His cries finally lifted me from my sleepy stupor, and I realised that the strange light in my room was my door ablaze. I was coughing because smoke was filling the room and much of the noise I heard was that of the crackling of fire raging. The man was hacking away at the clay around my window, which held in the bars we used for protection. They were relatively easy to remove for a determined person and were meant only to deter would-be thieves. The window was barely large enough, though, for anyone to fit through.

"Climb out!" he said to me when he could see I was properly awake and knew the seriousness of the situation.

"My Ma! What about my brothers?" I called back. Don't worry about them right now, I was told. Save yourself first.

He was right, of course. Had I tried to save them, I would have perished in the flames. But still, I wish I hadn't listened to him and had tried anyway. But he was an older man, and I was well conditioned to obey when a command was barked at me.

I scurried up to the window, and he grabbed at my arms. Between us, I managed to get onto the ledge and squeeze through the space created by the removal of two out of the three bars he'd had time to claw out. It was tight, but I was still small, and I was very slim. I fell into the mud outside. It was raining hard. As I was handed over to one of the women in the village to be taken to safety, I looked back at my bari. I could not understand how the fire was leaping so high into the sky when the rain was so heavy. All around me was commotion as men and women attempted to put out the fire or at least stop it from spreading to other baris nearby. I never saw my family again. My beautiful Ma, my Baba, my brothers – they all perished that night. I never even saw their bodies.

I was in deep shock for several days and utterly inconsolable. The womenfolk kept vigil over me and wept with me as we mourned the dead. Gradually I found out what had happened: a lightning strike had hit the house and almost immediately torched one of our sleeping rooms before quickly spreading to a second. I was lucky in that my room was furthest from where the lightning had hit, and there had been at least minutes before the flames reached my room—enough time to rescue me. For a long time, I wished the lightning had come to the other end of our bari. At least then my beloved brothers would have lived.

There was no time to be allowed to grieve, however. Bad fortune is rarely followed by good, at least not immediately. The deaths of my Baba and brothers meant that I was now the heir of what could be saved from the house – which wasn't much. Worse, though, I inherited my Baba's shop and the fields he owned which were worked by tenants. I discovered no one likes a young girl to be so rich.

Relatives – or so-called relatives – crawled out from nowhere. These 'dudher machi' swarmed over me, hoping for access to money and land. I discovered aunts and uncles I never knew I had, claiming they had some right or other to this and that. Claims of money promised by my father. Eager desires to see I was looked after with a son just happening to be in need of a wife. I was a little young, but they would overlook this in my time of need. Of course, if I married, my husband would then become the owner of all I had possessed. Even I knew this.

My neighbours were kindly and shooed these people away, but over the next few days, the situation got worse. Some men became more aggressive, more demanding. They were owed, they threatened, and they would take what was due, and by implication, 'who' was due too. My village was protective of me but couldn't be there all the time.

I was cooking the rice on the shared chula outside one day when I became aware of one of the men, who had claimed to be a cousin from another village, approaching me with a knife in his hand. There was no one in any of the baris – the men were working the fields and the women out shopping for food. There was nothing I could do but scream in the hope that someone nearby would hear me. That, and throw the boiling hot rice at him, which I did.

I won't repeat the words he spat at me as he flung his hands at the hot rice sticking to his clothes. It was enough to make him back off for a moment, and by the time he had recovered enough to think of revenge, people had started running into the courtyard. This was enough to scare him away, but I know the look in his eyes said that he would be back. The plan to marry me off was now obviously just a plan to kill me instead.

They came close to succeeding when they tried to poison me. Not just me but all our homes which shared meals. They must have put something in the curry that night while we were all so busy in and out of baris and the courtyard. They did not know that my mashi with whom I was living had a habit of tasting a portion of meat from the pot to check it was ready and would throw what she didn't eat to the stray dog who lived around our houses. No one owned him, but he made a good guard dog at night.

The food was served up, and I was given a bowl of meat first. I took a mouthful and was about to take more, as others were, when my mashi cried, "Oh my god, look at the dog!" We all looked as the poor beast vomited out blood and collapsed, whining. Within seconds I vomited too, thank God, before anyone else had started their food. I shudder to think what would have happened to us if we'd all eaten. As it was, I'd had just a taste and was poorly all night but made a recovery. The poor dog died an agonising death after many hours of suffering.

After that, it was clear that something had to be done about me. I was putting everyone in danger, and there were too many enemies to be vigilant against them all. The common consensus was that I should be married off as soon as possible. A marriage-maker was called upon to begin finding a suitable boy for me despite my protestations that I did not want to marry. But how could I argue? They were all risking their lives for me for as long as others wanted me dead.

It was about a week after the poisoning that one of our family friends came to visit me. I only knew her as 'apa,' she being a Muslim woman and much older than I, but she had known my Ma since they were children and loved us.

She spoke first to the family looking after me. She had heard of the plans to marry me, and she had another suggestion. There was a bideshi man, newly come to the area to work as a teacher. He had trained in Dhaka in Bangla and had a good grasp of customs and ways of doing things even though he'd only been in the country a few months. Currently, he had no ayah to help him, and – obviously, as he was a man – he wouldn't be able to cook for himself or keep his fine bari clean.

She suggested that I work for him. No one would touch me if I worked for this foreigner. There would be too much risk. He lived sufficiently far enough away to be largely out of their reach anyway, and I could live in a nearby village with one of her cousins. I would have to learn Muslim ways, but they were a tolerant village, and there would be no pressure to convert.

The idea provoked much discussion among the villagers. Some did not like the idea of me working for a single white man. Others were more worried about me living with Muslims when I was a young Hindu girl. They had all heard stories. It is funny how men of different faiths can live and work side by side for all their lives and yet still blow up into fear and loathing over a crisis only to go back to living side by side the next day when it is all over.

Anyway, the options were weighed, and, as I belonged to no one and I had expressed no wish to marry, they decided that this bideshi could at least be given a try. This way, I would be earning an income and, as it often comes down to, money is a winning solution. So, Apa left to sort out the details and, a week later, she returned to take me to the bideshi.

Your uncle was a handsome man in those days, Sophie! He was already so commanding, so sure of himself, but, back then, he had a haunted look about him as if he was running away from something or wanted to forget the existence of some problem none of us but him could see.

He certainly didn't want me around. When Apa introduced me to him, he made no secret that he didn't want a girl messing around with his things. He liked being on his own, and that was that. Apa had to persuade him, in a voice that told me she had already had this conversation with him before, that he had no one to cook, no one to clean and no one to wash his clothes. He begrudgingly acknowledged that there was some truth in this, and he would take me on, but only on a trial basis of three months. I, on my part, thanked him profusely for giving me a chance; but this only seemed to make him even more uncomfortable. He told me 'enough of that nonsense' and bade me follow him into his home.

Oh, Sophie! Your uncle may have been a handsome young man back then, but even in the short few days he'd been in this house he'd made it a disaster. The house itself, I think, had not been lived in for many years and your uncle brought many boxes of books with him along with new furniture he had ordered and had made in Dhaka brought up with him. There had been no attempt to clean the place beforehand, and dust mingled with books, cockroaches and ants.

Perhaps that was what saved me in those days? I scrubbed and cleaned and tidied and bought as few things as possible on the allowance he gave me to make this place a good place to live in. I did my best to keep out of his way as he tutted every time I stepped into the same room as he, but I moved quickly and silently. Within a month, I could creep into a room and remove his plates or cups without him noticing I was there. Or maybe he just got used to me and pretended he didn't see me? Either way, he stopped tutting. I made this place as clean as it was possible to be. Still now I thank my Ma for all that she taught me and my Baba for teaching me that hard work and discipline will never let you down.

The three months trial went without ever being mentioned again. I don't know if I ever passed in that time – your uncle has never said! But I guess I am still here after all these years means I must have done well enough.

One day, he came to me and talked to me properly for the first time rather than just answer my questions about what he wanted to eat or taka to buy food for the week. He asked me to sit down at the table.

"Mridhu," he said – in those days he still called me by my proper name – "I think it is time we talked about your education. I know you have no money and cannot think of going to school. I also understand that you used to go and had potential."

Yes, I confirmed, this was true.

"I am not comfortable with the disparity between us," he told me, "and I want to correct that. As you look after me, so I will look after your education."

He told me that every day, if I agreed, he would spend an hour teaching me when he returned from school. He would teach me everything he could: English primarily, but also history, philosophy, maths. He was true to his word, and I enjoyed ten years of his teaching. He would often give me much more than an hour before I left. Sometimes it would be two hours or more. I was in heaven. The schooling I thought I would never have again I now had in abundance. He was generous with his books. If he saw I took an interest in one of his, he would tell me to take it and keep it.

I was only ever poor at speaking English. I could never work out the grammar. But I can read it and understand it much better than I speak. In all other areas I did my best to be a faithful student. The voice of my former headmaster accusing me of being lazy never left me.

We stopped lessons only when it finally dawned on him that I was no longer a child. He seemed to see it suddenly one evening as we discussed the history of the civil war in Bangladesh. He looked at me so strangely then.

"Didi," he said – having long since called me that title even though I was neither his sister nor older than him – "you have grown up. I don't think there is anything more I can teach you now. You are free to live your life. Be who you want to be."

But I already knew who I wanted to be, Sophie. I already knew who I was. I had never known such happiness as I had being a simple maid for him. He was my family, my only family, and there was nowhere else I'd rather have been. There is still nowhere I'd rather be.

Besides, I am in my twenties and getting too old for marriage. I am not Hindu enough and not Muslim enough for any man, and there will always be a whiff of suspicion about me having worked for a single white man for so many years. I have a good life in my village, as you have seen, and they are kind to me. They have become family, too, and I am content with the blessings in my life.

Only sometimes do I find myself stopping when I am walking home across the fields because, on the wind, I swear I can hear the quiet sound of a gentle voice singing a soothing lullaby. Just for a moment, and then it is gone.

CHAPTER SEVENTEEN – MANGSHO

To kiss in public is a crime in this country,
To take bribes is never so.

– Nochiketa

"Sophie, *bon*, I don't think you can wear that to the bazaar."

Didi was wearing her 'I don't approve' face, Sophie decided. It was funny because *Didi* was not very good at being stern, but also, annoyingly, recently, as she was doing it more often.

Ever since telling Sophie her story, it seemed that *Didi* now felt their bonding was complete and she could treat Sophie the way she treated her adopted family in the village, which, as the girl had seen for herself, was often with an iron hand – albeit a beautiful one. But, to be fair, Sophie had conceded, *Didi* was right: they had completely bonded, and if anyone were to boss Sophie around, it would have to be her *Didi*.

Sophie was still kicking herself that, despite learning Bangla for so long now, she had never even considered that *'Didi'* actually had a real name – Mridhu. Family names always left her bewildered – there were so many! — even Sophie knew that *'didi'* just meant 'older sister' in non-Muslim communities (and *bon* was the standard term for any younger sister, which *Didi* now used with Sophie all the time). The girl had been her first friend, the first Bangladeshi she'd met once they arrived at the village, and she knew no Bangla then. Perhaps this was why she had never questioned things? As it was, it seemed everyone used this name as a *dak nam* for *Didi* anyway. No one ever used 'Mridhu.' She had told Sophie to continue calling her *Didi* – so *Didi* it was.

More importantly, Sophie now knew that the one person in this world who understood how she felt was *Didi*. She had lost her entire family at around the same age as Sophie had. The young woman gave her hope that the nightmares might fade and Sophie might find reasons to enjoy life again one day. They were truly sisters, and she so hoped she might find her own 'Uncle Joshua' to depend on who wouldn't let them down.

It was still weird to think of him as such a person. She could see now why *Didi* cared so much for him. Unlike a husband or a father, he did not have expectations. For all his grumping, Sophie realized that her uncle had never chastised or complained about *Didi* – unlike the way she saw many of the wealthier Bangladeshis treat their own *ayahs*. Often, they were little more than paid slaves. Some lived with their employers in rooms no larger than the bed they slept on, which was itself only a thin mattress on the floor. Those *ayahs* were allowed to see family only occasionally. Some did treat their maids well, but it was undoubtedly pot luck if that was the only job you could do. *Didi* was not just treated respectfully by Sophie's uncle. He trusted her and, in his own, unspoken way, cared about her.

She had seen more of this during *Boro Din*. Perhaps it was knowing *Didi's* story, or perhaps it was just there being no school and Christmas celebrations among the few Christians who lived in the area that allowed for more relaxation and fun. *Whatever*, Sophie thought she saw how relaxed her uncle was around *Didi*. On the 25th December itself, they had gone out to visit Christian friends as a trio. *Didi* had worn a beautiful metallic blue *sari*, Uncle Joshua put on his best white shirt and Sophie, under *Didi's* instructions, wore a silky smooth *shalwa kameeze* which was a mix of green and red patterns. The fabric had felt good against her scars. Going out together was almost like being a family again. It felt disloyal to think it, but Sophie could almost have imagined they were her parents – if it were not for *Didi* being far too young to be her mother and the idea of Uncle Joshua being romantic with *anyone* was just too silly for words. Still, the experience had been uncomfortably nice.

Earlier in the year, Sophie had experienced the bigger festival of *Eid* which was the big Muslim celebration. She had nicknamed it *mangsho*, partly because she had just learned this word for 'meat' and really liked the way it sounded, but also because, for her, it felt like the whole time had been spent eating it. House after house had been visited with her uncle, and they had been repeatedly presented with mountains of beef or goat meat. The homes in the area had all been raising their cows or goats, fattening them up for weeks before killing them on the day and speedily cutting them up. She remembered the pools of blood on the roadsides with a shiver and had hoped *Boro Din* wouldn't be the same.

Afterwards, she decided that if *Eid* had been *mangsho*, then *Boro Din* was *nasta*. They munched their way through an assortment of deep-fried sugary snacks, which were absolutely delicious, but after the fifth household of the day, they started to make Sophie feel ill. Fun though it was to celebrate a very different kind of Christmas with friends, sitting in their front rooms and gossiping away, she came home swearing she'd never eat food ever again.

Of course, she did; but the feeling of nausea remained for a few days, and even now it was January, it still returned a little whenever she was offered anything deep-fried. Fortunately, this month offered little in the way of celebrations. This was the time where the winter was harshest.

'Harsh,' it turns out, is a relative term, as Sophie found to her surprise. She had been told how awful the winters were yet her teachers at school had said the temperature rarely dropped below four degrees *above* freezing, and it never snowed. She could remember winters in England where their town had been completely snowed in; daytime temperatures were well below freezing, and her parents often were nervous about what would happen if the central heating broke down. Bangladeshi winters sounded like a walk in the park by comparison.

She was shocked to find it was not so easy. For two weeks now, she had woken up in a cold, damp bed, dressed in cold, damp clothes and shivered her way to the breakfast table each morning before going to school. Sophie realized that with no thick jumpers and coats, no central heating and with windows and nets designed to keep heat out rather than in, a few degrees above freezing felt every bit as bad as several degrees below in another country. Worse, the *kuwasha* came every morning through the mosquito netting both in the veranda windows and through the nets over the beds. That's why beds and clothes were all damp each day.

Weirdly though, the sun was out as usual by mid-morning, and everything felt dry and warm again. Noon on a January day could easily be mistaken for a quite acceptable English summer day. This was a country, Sophie decided, which made no sense.

The cooler weather, though, did make excursions easier, and, for the first time ever, Sophie was going to go to the bazaar with Adhora. This involved getting a ride into the nearest town, Kholatipur, which would be the first time Sophie had gone anywhere using transport (something Adhora had called a *vangari*, but Sophie hadn't figured out what that was), and she was excited about the idea of going shopping. Her uncle had eventually allowed her a small allowance, but she had almost nowhere to spend it until now.

There was nothing to get in her way as her uncle had been squeezed by both *Didi* and Sophie to give a reluctant acceptance to the proposed trip. But now *Didi* was about to be a stumbling block. She stood there in the doorway, scowling.

Sophie sighed. It seemed that since beginning to learn Bangla and getting used to Bangla ways, more was expected of her. *Mashima*, of course, never approved of anything, but as she was like that with everyone Sophie didn't mind and looked forward to their semi-regular visits for *cha* at her *bari*. She was a tough old boot, but Sophie liked her. Her uncle, these days, tended just to frown over his newspaper at anything she said or did but otherwise pretty much kept out of the way. He was content to let *Didi* do the mothering.

Sophie held a flimsy but bright top to her body and looked at it in the mirror. "*Didi*, you worry too much."

Didi was definitely taking her role pretty seriously. Far more seriously than Sophie would have liked. From what jewellery she wore, if any, to make-up, to the pronunciation of her words – seriously, how can anyone tell the difference between d, dh, D and Dh? For English people, these were all the same.

Thankfully, *Didi* was pretty rubbish at backing up criticism with authority and discipline. The result was that Sophie won every time. Her uncle heard *Didi* telling her "don't do that" and "don't do this," and so was pacified. But Sophie would then do it anyway and *Didi* never stopped her. She just shook her head disapprovingly and grinned from ear to ear at the same time. It was very endearing, really.

But not today.

Didi took the top from Sophie, put it back on the *alna* and said in English, "I have worry. This not like normal day today. Today strangers see you."

Sophie's trip to the bazaar was long overdue. Even all the little children at the school went to town regularly – often every Saturday – but Sophie had never been because her uncle rarely, if ever, went at all. Instead, he always sent *Didi* to buy food or asked others who were going anyway to get extra meat for him. Today, *Didi* had suggested Sophie and Adhora came along with her and saw the place for themselves. Sophie was usually quite bored on a Saturday and so was eager to go, so it was annoying that *Didi* seemed to be having a more difficult time than usual with her clothes. For once, though, she wasn't backing down.

"All the more reason to wear what I like. No one will know who I am." She picked out the strappy top again.

Adhora had pointed out to Sophie several times recently that they were both showing more obvious signs of developing. Adhora's parents were looking at her more suspiciously these days, and she knew they were weighing up when it was time to think about wearing *shalwar kameezes* and *ornas* like all the unmarried women in the village. The girls did wear these for school – it was the school uniform for the older years – and Sophie would wear her nicest ones for festivals and invitations to go out. The *shalwas*, the loose trousers made of light cotton, she had to admit, were really quite comfortable on her still slightly tender scars. But the *kameezes* were all thicker material, and with the *ornas* worn around the neck too, it was all too hot for Sophie; even in *sheetkal*, the winter season they were now experiencing, which made Sophie laugh—once the sun was up, it was still summer as far as she was concerned, and it was still far too hot to cover up. So she had decided it had to be T-shirt and skirts still.

"No," said *Didi*, "not good time. Many boys go there. Bad boys. They not nice to girls. Make fun. We want no trouble."

Sophie had always thought it unfair that men could wear pretty much anything they want including western clothes like jeans and T-shirts, but girls suffered scrutiny. She would regularly see males from boys up to at least forty-year-olds wearing T-shirts with English slogans adorned on front and back. Even that day she did the harvesting at the village, the younger men in the fields had been in tees at least with only some wearing the traditional *lunghi*. In general, the older men often wore tees, too though they tended more to wear traditional *punjabis*. Older working men always wore the *lunghi*, which gave air and freedom for the legs to move. *If I were a boy, we would not be having this conversation right now*, Sophie thought.

Didi took the top from her again. "Please *bon*," she said, "wear a *kameeze* at least today."

Yet again, Sophie pondered how girls did not have the same luxury as boys in this world. Whatever you wore as a woman, you had to be covered up. Only little girls showed their legs in skirts and dresses. But Sophie was not quite ready to give that up yet. She had lost so much of her childhood over the last year, and she was clinging on to what little was left while she could.

"No, I can't," Sophie countered, thinking of an excuse. "The cloth still hurts my scars." To make her point, she rubbed her arms. She was telling a fib, but only a small one, she decided. It worked. A look of guilt passed over *Didi's* face.

"Oh yes, so sorry," she said, "yes, you must be comfortable." There was a pause, and *Didi* looked worried. "It will be okay."

Now it was Sophie's turn to feel guilty. She hated pulling that trick. It had the desired effect though – she knew she could now wear whatever she wanted and would meet no resistance from *Didi* now. She pulled out the strappy top but put away the knee-length skirt she had originally planned to wear. She pulled out jeans instead. It wasn't perfect, but they would do.

They went downstairs a few minutes later once Sophie had changed. Uncle Joshua was in the front room reading the newspaper in Bangla as usual. Sophie thanked her lucky stars. With luck, he wouldn't even look up and notice what she was wearing.

"We're off to the bazaar, Uncle," she said in her sweetest voice.

"Hmm?" Uncle Joshua mumbled without taking his eyes off the page.

"What are you reading?" she asked, just to be as nice as possible.

"Oh, just the latest on this tiger business."

"Have they still not caught it?"

Uncle Joshua held the paper up to show her the front picture but didn't look up at her.

"Amazingly, they have caught it, finally. It was a wily beast, and it took quite some effort from what I've read, but some villagers managed to trap it and sold it on to a zoo. There are pictures of them putting the poor thing into a box, ready to transport it to another part of the country. Probably all very illegal but at least they didn't kill it and sell the skin. Big market for tiger hides, teeth and bones in China."

"Why didn't they just release it back in the wild?"

"Because rumours are it killed a man. At least, one local man has disappeared, and the tiger is being blamed. If it is true, that does make the beast more dangerous. Once a tiger tastes human flesh it will want to taste it again. So they will need to keep it caged up rather than release it back in the *Sundarbans*. Something I don't approve of – it's a magnificent creature! Just so wrong to lock it up. The only reason these animals keep wandering out of the jungle is because there's so little of it left and men keep encroaching on the area. What would you do if you couldn't find food? You'd go searching, wouldn't you?"

Sophie stood at the door and opened it.

"I know how the tiger feels," she shot at him and quickly left before he could respond.

Joshua looked up as *Didi* reached the door behind Sophie.

"I get the feeling that was aimed at me," he said to *Didi*.

Didi grinned, shrugged her shoulders and ran out of the house after Sophie. Joshua shook his head and returned to the paper.

The first oddity of the day was the *vangari*. This, as Sophie found out after they had met with Adhora and the three of them walked up to the main road, was a type of three-wheeled bicycle used to transport people and produce from place to place. There was a well-known part of the road where *rikshaws* and *vangaris* were stationed. *Didi* motioned to the *vangari* driver nearest them, and he cycled over to them. *Didi* haggled with him over price to get to Kholatipur, but Sophie could see that he kept glancing at her as they talked and that her mere presence was raising the price. Eventually, he and *Didi* came to an agreement, and the girls got on to the flat board over the back two wheels. It was easily big enough for the three of them, and Sophie suspected even more Bangladeshis could crowd on. As she thought this, she noticed a family of eight go past on the back of one, and she chuckled to herself. The Bangladeshi sense of personal space was almost non-existent. She couldn't imagine eight British adults sitting on a board about the size of a small table.

The journey there from the village had been as strange as it was wonderful for Sophie. *Didi* sat on the side and near to the *wallah*, watching his every move critically to make sure he cycled carefully, while the pair of girls sat at the back, cross-legged and facing backwards. The old *vangari wallah* pushed off, literally standing on his pedals and using his slender body weight to turn the wheels until he had built up speed.

From the back, Sophie could see the whole panorama without the hindrance of the glass or metal you get with cars, buses or trains. The slow speed produced by the old man meant she had plenty of time to look around and take note of what was happening in the area. *Didi* or Adhora explained things when Sophie didn't understand what was going on or wanted to know the Bangla name for things. At the same time, the slight speed they managed meant a cool breeze to her back which was most welcome in the sun, though she pitied the poor man for having to cycle in it. *How do they manage this during the summer seasons?* she wondered.

Sophie amused herself using as many Bangla words as she knew to name the things they passed. They went by *mathi* and endless *khal*. She watched young men, *jubokra*, leaping off various *shetu* that line all of Bangladesh's roads, into the rivers and streams meandering underneath. She asked *Didi* about the larger ones and found out they were called *nodina*. Sophie supposed it should not surprise her how there were so many names for things to do with water. She had learned from Uncle Joshua that Bangladesh was the world's biggest delta. The whole land was built mainly on the silt washed down from the Himalayan mountains over thousands of years, and rivers, streams and estuaries ran through every part of its length and breadth. To Bangladeshis, the differences were important. It was as much a land of rivers and streams as it was a land of lush green fields.

Beautiful though Bangladesh was – and the people often just as lovely – Sophie had to admit that it was also probably the smelliest and dirtiest country she'd ever known out of the many her parents had taken her to since she was a little girl. With men at liberty to lift their *lunghis* and pee at the side of the road at any time, and all rubbish seemingly just dumped along the way as people went about their business, the odours were often overpowering. But though Sophie was used to this now, she was not prepared for the reek from the market town.

The pleasant part of the journey had ended all too soon, and they had come into the town. They headed towards the centre straight to the bazaar itself, and the smell was nauseating. As they slowly made their way down the roads, avoiding potholes, dogs and goats in equal measure, Sophie could not believe the number of *dokans* there were. Each one usually measuring a metre to two at most and not much deeper inside; these were more like little cubicles that stood side by side with no gap except for the odd road leading off here and there. Everything possible to buy was being sold. One shop for beds, being made on the street outside; another for bookshelves; yet another old and massive TV sets; many, many more selling sweets, crisps, toothbrushes and trinkets of every type. Sophie's eyes nearly popped out when she saw in one *dokan* a *napit*, who stood behind his client sat in a chair but looked over his shoulder, chatting to the men sat down by the side, not looking nor caring about the blade in his hand poised at the client's throat and moving up and down swiftly. Sophie hoped this man knew his trade so well that the man being shaved would come to no harm. She didn't know if women could get their hair cut in these *dokans,* but she made a mental note never to find out.

As soon as she saw the bazaar come into view, she knew this market wasn't going to be like the ones she used to go to with her mother in England; not because they sold very different things though; mostly it was meat, fish, vegetables and fruit along with various other assortments; just as you would expect...

Sophie realised she was hesitating to think 'back home.' The word was coming less easily to mind when she thought of England, and that fact surprised her. Giving herself a shake, she returned to her original train of thought. No, the difference was not in the things but the smell.

Discarded meat and fish parts were strewn everywhere, and huge flies swarmed over everything they could find until they were batted away by the stall-keepers with their blood-stained hands. Several huge chunks of meat and fully skinned goats hung on huge hooks above their heads; the flies finding them were left undisturbed for long periods. Even in winter, the sun's heat was powerful, and the meat started to go bad quickly. Skins of dead animals lay strewn on the floor, some piled up by the small boys working for the *dokaners* or even smaller boys trying to persuade them to give them a job or, at least, a few *poishas* from their pockets.

They dismounted from the *vangari*, and the *wallah* attempted to bargain a few more *taka* from *Didi*. The journey was hard, he claimed. The *bideshi* was heavy. *Didi* took no prisoners in dealing with him. As soft as she was with Sophie, the woman tore into the man, shaming him, demanding to know what kind of a man finds three small females hard to carry? She said it loudly and derisively, so the man took her proffered money and hastily left. The girls began the shopping trip.

Despite the smells, Sophie was excited. There were hundreds of people milling around, and it felt like everyone was talking at once. She could feel her heart pounding as she and Adhora followed *Didi* around the rabbit warren of stalls. *Didi* walked like a woman with a mission. She knew exactly where to go, which stalls they needed to go to and which ones, next door, to avoid. With the sight of Sophie trailing behind her, many of the *dokaners* urgently begged them into their shops. They were met with cries of *pliz, you come, you come, we have top quality, what you want? We have, come, pliz, pliz,* which *Didi* waved away with her hand without breaking her pace.

Everything had been fine for a while. Sophie got some looks, of course, but she expected that. Even in the village, if she went out and around, people would come out to stare – the ones who didn't know her personally but had heard about her. Most of the men were polite, though and not like the men she remembered at the roadside cafe when they had travelled up from Dhaka months ago. She still remembered the way the men there had stared at her legs like they were *mangsho*. At the market, the men looked but not for long, treated her kindly, offered her chairs or stools to sit on while *Didi* haggled and bartered over prices for the food she bought.

Then they moved on to some of the *dokans* down a side street. It was crowded with men but only a few women. Sophie didn't notice a group of six teenagers at the far end, but one of them noticed her and signalled to the others. Sophie was looking at *ornas* hanging up when she became aware of someone standing right behind her, looking over her shoulder.

"What you doing, Baby?" the boy's voice purred. Two of the gang had come round behind *Didi*. She scowled at them, and they kept a small distance, pretending to look at one of the many things to buy hanging from the *dokan* tin roof. Adhora looked terrified to Sophie. She stood still staring into the shop as if hypnotised, but Sophie could see her legs were trembling slightly.

"Shopping," Sophie mumbled, not looking around. She could hear his breathing in her ear.

An arm reached up from behind her and up to one of the *ornas*.

"You look good in this."

"I can choose for myself."

"Or this one, Baby?"

The hand moved to another *orna*, and, at the same time, Sophie felt the boy put his other hand against her bottom and squeeze hard. She leapt around and pushed the boy away with one hand while delivering a slap to his face with the other.

Then she noticed how tall he was. His face was ugly, but he was very muscular, and she knew he could hurt her if he wanted. His look of confidence told her he was the leader of this gang and the boys would do whatever he told them. He looked shocked for a moment, then laughed.

"Hey, what's big deal, Girl? I just being friendly, friendly. You want we be friends? Yeah?"

"Get lost," Sophie spat at him and grabbed Adhora's hand to leave. *Didi* by now had turned around, hearing the slap and the look on her face confirmed for Sophie that they were in a precarious state. The girls pushed through a gap and Sophie heard *Didi* say something angrily at the boys in Bangla. The boys responded with shouts and catcalls in English and Bangla. Sophie could tell without looking that they were following them.

The girls tried to move faster up the narrow paths between the *dokan* stalls to get away from the boys but to no avail. They kept up with her, asking questions, laughing, and when they could reach, touching her arm, stroking her hair. *Didi* tried to shoo them away each time, but they just laughed louder and pushed her away each time. It was clear they did not consider Sophie to be worthy of any respect at all. Older men standing around the *dokans* shook their heads disapprovingly, though whether it was the boys' behaviour or Sophie's skimpy top they disapproved of was hard to tell. Either way, they didn't interfere. Finally, *Didi* grabbed Sophie's and Adhora's hands, and they started to run. The boys ran too, their laughter revealing how they considered this to be even better sport.

They turned a corner and almost ran into *Mashima*. The boys soon followed and briefly, only briefly, stopped in their tracks at the sight of the strange, haggard albino.

"Come on, Honey," the larger one who had squeezed Sophie's bottom sidled up to her, "let's be friends. You want cuddle, Sexy!" The others laughed as he said this, and he winked at them. He put his arm around her shoulder. Sophie began shrugging it off when suddenly a stick whooshed past her head and cracked hard against the boy's arm.

He leapt away in pain.

"What you do that for, crazy woman?" he shouted at *Mashima*. She stepped closer to him, moving much faster than anyone would have guessed she could with her *lathi* in her hand and brought it down on him again and again. First the shoulder, then the head as he staggered downwards under the ferocity of the blows. Around them, the men roared with laughter and began pointing at the boys.

"Pick on a little girl, would you, heh? You *shukor bacha!*" *Mashima* screeched at the boy in Bangla, his friends staring in horror. A couple instinctively began to back off. The *dokaners* were watching the fun now.

"Makes you feel like a real man, does it?" she spat. "Makes you feel 'sexy'?" she imitated his voice. "Can't get a wife, heh? You too damned ugly, boy. No one for you to beat at night because you no good in bed! Can't impress any parent, I'd imagine." Her *lathi* continued to rain down blows as he knelt, hands raised, trying to deflect her blows. She didn't let him speak. "Who would want a pig for a son-in-law who prefers little children, heh?" The *dokaners* laughed more. The boy was now on his own;

his friends had vanished into the rapidly growing crowd before too many could recognise them. The whole area would know about this incident by the end of the night, and this youth's shame would be repeated around many *chawallah* stalls late into the evening. *Mashima's* words were more stinging than her blows – fierce though they were.

"Leave me alone, you crazy bitch," he half complained, half pleaded. "What's wrong with you, mad woman?"

"Oh, *pagol* am I?" she whacked him again with her stick. "I'll give you crazy, you silly *chagol*. A goat beaten by an old woman. Look at them all laughing at you." She pointed with her stick at the crowd that had rapidly drawn around. "They laugh at the little goat being tamed. And so they should!"

She said more things that Sophie couldn't follow but then gave a chance for the youth to stagger to his feet and back-pedal down one of the alleys as fast as he could. His final parting shot was just one word. "*Rakkosh!*"

"Yes, that's right," screeched the old woman, her face red with fury, "and don't you ever forget it!"

She turned back to look at the three girls.

"Oh, *Mashima* thank you!" said *Didi*.

"Yes, I've never been so thankful to see someone in all my life!" agreed Sophie, beaming at her strange elderly friend. She thought once again how she was glad she was not an enemy of this powerful woman.

"Are boys always like that here?" she asked.

"Not normally," *Didi* replied. "I think it is because you are a *bideshi* and new here."

"*Bapre!*" scoffed *Mashima*. "She would have been fine, you young fool, if you had dressed her right! Look at her – no wonder they treated her that way." She looked right at Sophie and said, "you dressed like animal to sell at market. You are *mangsho*."

Sophie felt her cheeks burn with embarrassment and turned to Didi for support. *Didi* stared intently at the ground.

"I should not have let you come out without an *orna*. They thought you had no shame. I am sorry."

Sophie felt tears well up in her eyes. She had upset and shamed *Didi*, and that was unbearable. It was Sophie who had insisted on coming out without the right clothes.

"No *Didi*, no. It is my fault. You tried to warn me and I ignored you."

"Nevertheless, I promise Uncle I look after you, and I let him down. I've…" she hesitated a moment, "I've never been with *bideshi* woman into town before. I no idea this would be so bad."

Mashima grabbed them both by the shoulders and marched them towards the *vangaris*.

"Let's get you both out of here before that little pest come back with even more. I may be a *rakkosh*, but even I can't stop whole army of pigs-who-would-be-princes with just my *lathi*."

They all took a *vangari* back, and Sophie noticed it was considerably cheaper than it had been in coming to town. *Mashima* did the haggling. The *wallah* took what he was told to take. Sophie got the impression that the *wallah* would have gone for nothing if *Mashima* insisted. Clearly, she could scare grown men as well as girls and teenage boys. Sophie was truly glad that this strange and ruthless woman was on her side even if her criticisms were harsh and unfeeling; they were trustworthy. Sophie would not forget that again.

When she got back to the house, Uncle Joshua was nowhere to be seen. The newspaper he read earlier was on the table open at the photos of the tiger being forced into a small wooden crate. It looked angry and scared at the same time. Her fingers reached out and touched the tiger's body.

"*Mangsho*," she said to herself thoughtfully. Then she turned and went to get changed.

CHAPTER EIGHTEEN - KUWASHA

It was just as well this strange and bewildered little English girl came to Bangladesh in the summer and not January. Though she found the first couple of weeks heading into winter unpleasant, she didn't experience the full force of the season until a couple of weeks after the ill-fated visit to the bazaar; for, in late January, *sheetkal* season begins in earnest and is heralded by the coming of the ghostly *kuwasha*.

The fog had been around already but only briefly for the first hour or two of daylight. Until mid-January, it had been something Sophie considered beautiful and serene to look at over the fields through her window when she got up. But by breakfast time, it was gone, like the memories of a pleasant dream, the sun having warmed it all away.

Now though, as if this had been some kind of war no one was aware of fighting, the *kuwasha* had conquered the sun's rays and banished them completely. The fog persisted from dawn to dusk.

Kuwasha is not just fog. It is a dense, impenetrable fog that glues itself to every tree, bush, building and person. The fog that writers of supernatural tales imagine when they begin their stories with "There was an eerie fog that night…." Had Sophie met *Mashima* in these circumstances, she may well have died of fright; or so she had been thinking these last few days since the fog had descended.

For the first couple of days, it had just been incredibly beautiful. The *kuwasha* also deadened sound, so the whole village had an eerie silence to it. Even the noise from the main road up the white lane, normally clearly audible at any time of the day, was all but gone. Now Sophie looked out of the windows and would see nothing but fog all day, not just out of the back fields from her room but through the *lichee bagan* and out over the *pukur* when she looked out of the front windows or stood in the porch. Walking to school and walking back meant pushing through the mist. To Sophie, it felt as if the entire outside world had been taken away and would never return.

When the *kuwasha* came down and decided it no longer needed the sun, the temperature rapidly dropped. By the first evening, everything was cold and Sophie, when looking out at the *pukur*, thought that now the *kuwasha* looked sinister. It was hiding something; she was sure of it.

Now she was going to sleep in a cold, damp bed and not just waking up in one. Clothes were permanently damp. The window nets, so good at keeping mosquitos out and letting any breeze in during the summer months, could do nothing to prevent the *kuwasha* from entering and impregnating everything. The concrete floors were slippery with condensation and felt icy cold to bare feet. There was simply no escaping the misery and gloom.

This is horrible, thought Sophie as she came down the stairs for breakfast. Uncle Joshua was already there, munching away on muesli and yoghurt, freshly made by *Didi*. Apart from a thick jumper, there was no sign that he was aware of any difference in the weather at all. Not that he would show it if he were. *Didi*, though, was wearing two layers of *kameeze* plus her *chador*. She was clearly feeling the cold. At least it is a Friday today, thought Sophie; I don't have to go outside and can just cuddle up with a thick blanket and read a book all day.

"I thought we'd go out to the *pukur* today," said Uncle Joshua, as though reading her mind and aiming to spite it. Sophie's heart sank. It was only the second time he had offered, and the last time it had been an order. He said this as a statement of fact rather than a barked command, but Sophie knew that this was an invitation of honour, and refusal was not an option; it certainly meant that he had something he wanted to say.

"Okay," she said simply and started to eat her breakfast. She could see, without looking up, that her uncle had raised his eyebrows. He had expected a fight, she guessed, and she had surprised him by not giving one. *You don't know everything about me*, she thought with a delighted sense of smugness.

By the time they got the fishing gear altogether and taken it all to the *pukur*, the sun was trying to break through the dense fog and warm up the area. Of course, it wouldn't succeed, and the *kuwasha* still hung all around, making the huge pool feel even more eerie than usual, but at least it was not so bone-chillingly cold any longer.

"We won't fish on the quayside today," Uncle Joshua told her. "We'll go on the boat and try to catch some of the larger fish that stay in the deeper waters."

The boat was a rowing type with two large oars and room for about four people in it. It was slender and long, fitting two people at a time on two seats. Sophie had never really been on a rowing boat before, discounting silly boating trips at theme parks with her parents when she was little and wobbled quite a bit as she got in and tried to sit down where her uncle told her. Just as she reached the right seat, she lost her balance and all but fell into the oily green waters. She knew this *pukur* was deep – even near the sides – and that no one under the age of sixteen was allowed within the fences without being accompanied by an adult. There was a good reason for that: you wouldn't want to fall into this and have no one around to see. The thought of doing so was a recurring feature of her nightmares each night.

With all the gear and rods on board, Uncle Joshua sat opposite her and grabbed both oars. Slowly, but clearly with expertise, he took them out into the centre of the waters. The *kuwasha* from here seemed to have eaten up most of the village. Sophie could see just the odd hint of a tree here or a building there; otherwise, it felt like they were completely alone. There was no one and nothing else beyond those misty walls.

Sophie stared into the dirty water of the *pukur*.

"My nightmares usually begin just like this." Too late, she realised she had said that out loud.

Uncle Joshua looked at her but said nothing.

Sophie stared deep into the water, trying to see if she could see anything beneath the surface. She couldn't.

"I dream I am in dark water and I can't reach the top. I'm drowning but seem to…not drown, somehow. All I know is that the water is dark and full of death."

Joshua looked over the boat into the water.

"Ah well," he said, "there you'd be wrong."

"Sorry?"

"This water is far from dead. This *pukur* is far from dead. Even though you can't see deep into it, there is life there right enough. Snakes and eels live in its depths, shrimp live higher up and tend to eat up the dead stuff. Fish live all over it. There may not be many here now, but their young are deep down there, becoming fishes, getting ready for the season next year."

"It smells dead enough. It really pongs at this part of the pool," she held her nose.

"I have no idea what you're talking about. You can't smell anything in this fog. It's too dense."

"There's definitely a pong. Anyway, carry on with your point. So, there is life down there, buried deep, right? Is that a metaphor you're reaching for, Uncle Joshua?"

He looked at Sophie again. "Maybe you're not drowning in your dream. Maybe the water is the best place to be and is trying to keep you safe? Sometimes, the darkness is the best place to be. No one can see you there."

"Is that why you came here all those years ago, Uncle Joshua?"

He was silent.

"Did you come here to be in the darkness where no one could find you, contact you?" Sophie thought she might be pushing her luck, but they were talking deeply and meaningfully all of a sudden, so why not? "Did someone hurt you? I can't think of why else someone would choose to come here."

The large man in front of her was silent for a moment, and Sophie realised he looked tired and sad. He sighed and then answered.

"In a way, Sophie, yes, I guess I did. I have no wish to rake up the past, and sometimes things are best left buried." He looked over the edge of the boat. "Or perhaps, in this case, drowned. Maybe that's why I like this *pukur*? I feel safe here, just like the creatures down there feel safe where no one can see them. The pool *hides* life and keeps it secret from any who don't know there's anything to find. No one would guess to look here."

He looked down at his hands. "No one has ever come looking for me here. Not in fifteen years. Or however long I've been here. I forget."

"Until Aunty Hannah did just that and brought me."

"Indeed."

Sophie felt her cheeks flush. The odour was stronger now.

"I guess I wrecked things for you. Spoiled your secret place."

He put down his things and took Sophie's hands in his. "No lass," he said, looking deep into her eyes. He had a way sometimes of looking at you so intensely it was as though he knew all your deepest thoughts. "You didn't wreck anything. The *pukur* may keep the fish safe and secure, but if nothing changes, the water becomes stagnant and poisonous. Life *has* to change, or it becomes death. You've reminded me of that. You've brought a little part of me back to life. You've made me have to think about someone else again. I didn't think I could do that. I didn't think I wanted to."

"But you *do* care about others, Uncle Joshua. I don't believe you ever stopped doing that. I see it in your classes – how you act with the kids. You try to be gruff, but they love being with you. They see you care. Even I can see it…some of the time anyway." Sophie laughed.

"Oi," Uncle Joshua responded with a mock frown and letting go of her hands to wag a finger, "don't tempt me to start being nastier, young lady."

She threw up her hands.

"I won't."

Silence settled between them, and her uncle began rowing again to place them more centrally in the pool.

"*Didi* told me what you did for her over the years. How you cared for her."

He said nothing but rowed twice more before putting down the oars again.

"Oh…that. It would appear I have a little-realised soft spot for young ladies in distress. I thought she was a one-off and my knight-in-shining-armour days were over. But then you came along, and I guess I'm here again. Only this time, I think I've bitten off more than I can chew. I don't think I'm doing a very good job of it. I am a better employer than I am an uncle."

"You paint yourself as this mean old man who hates people, but really you're not, Uncle Joshua. I don't know why you try to pretend you are."

Joshua looked back at her and peered over his spectacles. "Because I am a mean old man, Sophie Shepherd, and don't you forget it! I don't pretend to be anything. Just because I don't beat my students like other teachers in some schools do, and just because I haven't thrown out two miserable, wretched girls when they were forced into my hands doesn't mean that I actually *like* either of you." He was raising his voice now. "I do the best I can and try to be honourable towards everyone – but only for as long as they don't cross me. *That's* why I don't like being around people. Someone always tries to get one over you, do better or...or...choose someone better looking or...anything really. Or even cause a damned fool argument – just like your father did!"

They both sat in shocked silence for a few seconds, neither able to believe he had just mentioned Sophie's dad and had done so in anger.

"Can we drop this blasted subject now?" Joshua said, eventually. "It's probably time we headed back anyway. *Didi* will have got lunch sorted by now."

They came back into the *bari*, meeting *Didi* on her way out with a bucket of washed clothes she was going to peg out on the washing line in the vain hope they might dry in the fog. Sophie ran up to her room, her head buzzing with thoughts.

Uncle Joshua had a big fall out with my dad, she thought to herself, *but why?* What could pull two brothers away from each other? Why didn't I ever hear mention of my uncle from either Mum or Dad? And what is that awful smell?

Sophie came out of her room. It wasn't a strong smell, but it wasn't pleasant either, and it seemed to have followed her from the *pukur*.

"Uncle Joshua," she shouted from the top of the stairs, "The fish smell awful. Take them outside."

There was a scuffle and then the sound of footsteps.

"What?" Joshua appeared at the bottom of the stairs and looked up with a puzzled expression. "What are you on about? We didn't do any fishing!"

"Well, the smell must be coming in from somewhere. It's in my room." She sniffed. "It's *here* too."

"Sophie, there's no smell. I never bring fish home anyway because I don't want every cat and rodent in the area coming into our house." Joshua replied. "I always give them to *Didi*, who waits near the *pukur* to collect them, and she goes off to skin and prepare them. Sometimes I'll do it if I have time and the sun is not too hot – but always outside. And there is no fish anyway. Did you tread in something?"

Sophie thought for a moment, then said, "Of course not! Well, if it's not fish, then it must be you or something. I can *definitely* smell something rotten."

Uncle Joshua gave a grin.

"Why does it have to be me?" he scoffed. "Might be your own personal body odour problem, young lady. I believe it's a problem that teenagers are known for."

Sophie stuck out her tongue at him and then said, "Ha ha. Thanks. *My* personal odour is very nice, thank you very much. But this? This is…."

She gave a little choke, went limp and collapsed onto the concrete landing. Her head and torso flopped over the top, and her unconscious body began to roll down the steps.

Joshua leapt up the stairs in an instant with a cry and caught her by the time she'd rolled down to the middle. He picked up her limp body, which was now writhing convulsively.

"Good God, what's happening?" He shouted to the open front doorway.

"*Didi, esho!* Come here quickly!"

He looked down anxiously at Sophie, who now seemed so small, so helpless and carried her to the front room. He laid her on the sofa.

Didi came into the house in a rush. She knew when she heard this voice that Joshua Dada was upset. It didn't happen often.

"What is wrong, *Dada?*" she said, then stopped in horror when she saw Sophie prostrate and shaking violently.

"She's having some sort of seizure." Joshua cried. "Get a doctor. We need help urgently!"

CHAPTER NINETEEN - ASHROY

She died the next day, they said; the strange little *bideshi* girl. The Teacher's daughter, they said. You know the one. It had not been quick, apparently. She had been in agony for hours before it all became too much for her skinny little body to cope with and she stopped trying to remain here. She obviously had never eaten well. She always looked ill – not enough fat on her. They never fed her rice. Everyone knew that. It was inevitable this would happen.

On the other hand, some were of the opinion she had been possessed by a demon. After all, hadn't she shown such violent tendencies when she tried to kill that innocent girl in her class? And there were rumours she walked alone to many well-known places where spirits live. Didn't she like to go into the forest and spend time with the albino witch? Didn't she conjure the witch with a single spell to beat an innocent boy and humiliate him in public? If you walk with the devil, he will claim you as his own one day and carry you off to his world.

This was nonsense, said others. It was her uncle who did it. She was a wayward girl who had rebelled against his iron rule. Hadn't they all heard the arguments coming from their corner of the village? None of their children would be so poorly behaved as to speak to their fathers like that. So, like the colonial man that he is, no matter what he might claim or how many ways he has helped the community – he had 'dealt' with her just like the British masters of the past. Some said he had taken her out to the *pukur* he loved so much and drowned her, but her body wouldn't sink, and so he brought her home secretly to make it look like she died accidentally. Others said he beat her for disobedience (and she was so *very* disobedient, wasn't she?) until her head exploded and her brains leaked out. The ambulance car was all a show. He had paid *ghush* to the driver to keep his mouth shut and tell no one the girl was dead before she left the house. Some even wondered if he had actually been the one responsible for her parents' deaths – although they were at a loss for how he could have done that from so far away. Still, *bideshis* have their magic and their technology, and he is undoubtedly a very clever man.

But many believed there was nothing wrong with a good beating and, perhaps, if her uncle had not been so lenient and just given her a good thrashing right from the start, then she might still be alive and a perfectly decent person. A girl must know her place; then she will be happy in life. Instead, they insisted, she had met her end by her own hands. She had been dancing outrageously to pornographic Western music and fallen down concrete steps. She had still been wriggling her body to the music as she fell, so she bashed her head many times, and that is why she died.

Some said yes, she died by her own misadventure, but it was not dancing. She had gone swimming in the *pukur* naked, and a snake had bitten her. Her *bideshi* blood was not strong enough to survive the toxin, and she died crying to Allah for forgiveness. He was merciful and took her soul to him.

No, no, no! She was not aware of proper ways and what you could eat and what you could not, poor girl. She had been seen drinking milk and eating pineapple. Everyone knew that these things together made poison in your stomach and would kill you!

Whichever way, though, all agreed that her mother was to blame. The poor child had no idea of the wrongs she was committing. Her mother should have taught her to obey her male guardians, not listen to sensual music, keep away from snakes and never, ever eat pineapple when drinking milk. This was basic parenting!

All agreed that her death was long and painful, and no child should ever meet their end that way. It was a tragedy, and they would all say their prayers for her soul.

"You look as rough as I feel."

Joshua looked up from the floor he'd been staring at morosely for the last two hours and rubbed his tired eyes. Then he looked in the direction of the voice.

It took him a while to wake himself out of his stupor. The last few hours had left him dazed and terribly distraught. Nothing he could do would eradicate the image in his mind of Sophie collapsing at the top of the stairs and rolling down them. It replayed like slow-motion video and each time got progressively worse. The few times he could shake the image were replaced with snapshots of the hours in the ambulance looking at her limp body, holding her hand and speaking quietly to her that it was going to be okay.

The ambulance had, in truth, been little more than a glorified people carrier with the back modified to allow a basic version of a stretcher. He and *Didi* had been cramped and uncomfortable, but neither deviated from their concern for Sophie. He had scowled at *Didi* and mildly rebuked her every time she burst into tears, but the truth was he had been so close to doing the same himself repeatedly. He had not slept since then and kept vigil by her bed. *Didi* had slept out in the corridor on the benches where at least fifty others were doing their same, keeping watch over their loved ones.

Now he looked over in the direction of the bed and saw two tearful but happy eyes looking back at him. He got up and rushed over.

"Oh, Sophie, it *is* good to see you awake," he said, taking her hand, "you've had us both really worried."

Before Sophie could respond, the door burst open and *Didi* stared open-mouthed for half a second before rushing over and giving her a big squeeze. She babbled incoherently in Bangla and Sophie laughed at her dynamism.

When *Didi* finally let go and stepped back, she had tears in her eyes, but her smile could not have been wider.

"How are you feeling?" Joshua asked.

"Lousy," Sophie replied, "but mostly confused. Why am I lying in a hospital bed?"

Joshua took a deep breath.

"You died from too much dancing and milk and pineapple poisoning."

"What?"

"According to the village. You're the talk of it. I'll take a little vindictive delight from seeing their faces when we go back, I'll admit."

"Did you say milk and pineapple poisoning?"

"Yes. Don't worry about it. Just an old superstitious belief. Sophie – what can you remember about what happened?"

His niece shuffled herself upwards in the bed, wincing as she did so.

"I don't remember anything. I think...I think I remember standing outside my room and was going to shout to you, or I did shout...or something. Then...nothing else. What is going on? And why do I feel like I've been punched all over my body?"

Didi stroked her cheek and began to cry again. It was clearly going to be Uncle Joshua who would be giving answers coherently.

"You will have to wait until the doctor comes to see you," he began, "but, from what I understand, I think most of the pain you feel is from collapsing onto the concrete landing and then bouncing down a few steps before I could catch you. I *think* the doctor said you've had a seizure as a result of a head injury. It's probably something that wasn't or couldn't have been seen after the accident last year. Apparently, it's rare but does happen."

Sophie rubbed the side of her head. It hurt – not just the side itself, as though badly bruised, but inside too. Her uncle's words swam around confusingly in her mind, and she felt like bursting into tears. She held back, fearing that *Didi* might flood the room with her tears if she did.

"Does this mean there's something wrong with my head and I'm going to die?" she said after a few seconds. "I've heard about people doing stuff like this with brain tumours. Is that what I've got, Uncle Joshua?"

Despite her efforts, she felt a tear roll down her cheek.

"No, no, child," Uncle Joshua responded, squeezing her hand. "No, forgive me, I'm crap at explaining things. It might be best to wait until the doctor comes and he can answer all your questions. I'm just an English and History teacher; I don't know all this medical mumbo jumbo! But I'm pretty certain that this is a one-off. Though, we will have to keep an eye on you to be sure."

"Okay. Okay, thank you."

He saw her look up at him, her eyes glistening and evident relief showing in them and Joshua felt his heart would break. What this child had been through over the last year simply didn't bear thinking about, and he felt incredibly inadequate. He'd never been a parent himself, and he really didn't know how to look after a teenager – especially one who had had such a rum deal given to her. He was, in many ways, the worst person to be given the task. As he had so many times, he gave silent thanks that *Didi* was here and she could work her magic on the girl. He felt like he was swimming against the current and simply drowning.

He almost said aloud, 'Oh, thank God for that!' when someone knocked briefly on the door to the private hospital room and entered, saving him from his momentary self-pity. He certainly breathed a loud sigh of relief when he realised it was Dr Roy, the consultant who had been dealing with Sophie since they arrived a few hours earlier.

The doctor, who was relatively young, beamed enthusiastically at Sophie and told her, in no uncertain terms, that she was a very lucky lady that she had such a good father (missing completely both uncle and niece flush with embarrassment) and that his quick actions had ensured no permanent damage and very likely a good prognosis.

Dr Roy was certainly talkative and gave very little opportunity for anyone to speak, but he was informative and encouraging, and no one seemed to mind. Sophie had had a complex seizure, almost certainly as a result of the accident last year. Such delayed seizures didn't happen often and probably wouldn't again, but she would need to go on anti-epileptic medication to make sure and have regular checks.

What had triggered this seizure now? Unclear, but lack of sleep is often a symptom. At this, the young patient had admitted that she rarely slept well. Nightmares occurred every single night, often multiple times and she hated sleeping. It would take sheer exhaustion to finally put her to sleep for the remainder of the night. She got enough hours to survive, but nights were not a good time for her.

This seemed to explain a lot to the ever-smiley Dr Roy, who said she needed to work through her sleep issues and get some proper rest. To her uncle, he made it clear she needed some proper rest and suggested he took her for a holiday. Her uncle said he had thought of just the place and would make the arrangements.

After that, all that was left was a few tests just to make sure there was nothing else to worry about with Sophie's health and then she could be discharged. This was a warning, Dr Roy had said; she needed to look after herself. If she did so, then he was sure all would be well.

The journey to the *Sundarbans* reminded Sophie of her first day in the country. The car journey from the hospital to Jessore was long, but it was also beautiful. Miles and miles of fields, now often covered in the misty *kuwasha*, but still always green and luscious. It was just like that first car trip with her aunt. Even leaving the posh, semi-clean, air-controlled hospital resulted in the same effect as leaving the airport – the hot air hit her hard. She couldn't believe that in wintertime Bangladesh could still feel hot.

Uncle Joshua had often spoken of how beautiful the *Sundarbans* were and how peaceful. Sophie was glad that he was splashing out (using some savings, he told her) to give the three of them a week-long boat trip in the region. She couldn't picture what it would be like there, but she knew it would be good if her uncle loved the place so much.

From Jessore, they took a train to Kulna, which led them to the edge of the Sundarbans, the most southern region of the west side of Bangladesh. This region was shared with India and was, apparently, the largest mangrove forest region in the world, but exactly what that meant, Sophie wasn't sure. The journey to discovering that, though, was exciting. After getting off the train at Khulna, the three of them were greeted by a representative from the boat company Uncle Joshua had hired for the week. The man beckoned them all to follow him, and they walked for about ten minutes through busy, noisy side alleys and small roads in the busy city until they reached the main river edge. Finally, they all clambered on board a small motorboat which looked to Sophie as about as likely to stay afloat as she could fly. Yet somehow the boat steered its way through a busy waterway with countless boats and ships of all sizes moving up and down. She was told to rest herself on some blankets, and she did so, lazily allowing her hands to drape over the edge and into the water to feel the ripples rush over her fingers as they moved.

Sophie was tired and drained. Her head hurt and body ached, yet she still enjoyed the first opportunity to be on the water in this country where rivers were the veins and arteries. They were going to the boat where they would stay for a week, her uncle had said. That was a bigger boat than this one transporting them – which was little more than a three-man fishing boat with a motor – and could sleep around twenty or thirty guests, taking them into the heart of the *Sundarbans* themselves.

The *Sundarbans*, Uncle Joshua had assured Sophie, was one of the most peaceful places on earth.

"Even more peaceful than your beloved *Pukur*?" she'd asked playfully. He had shot her a half-accusing, half-serious look and then answered, "Oh yes, undoubtedly more peaceful. If I lived here, I would buy a boat, just like the one we're going to, and live on it all year around."

He gave a big sigh and added, "Of course, we live in the real world, and even here in Bangladesh, I still have to earn at least a little token of an income to justify my visa every time it has to be renewed. So, regrettably, teaching in the north will still have to be my main occupation rather than watching tigers and swimming with crocodiles."

Sophie sat bolt upright, flinging her hands out of the water.

"Did you say crocodiles?" she spat. "There are crocodiles here?"

"Oh yes," her uncle said, oblivious to her panic and not noticing her look at her fingers as though checking they were still all there and not nibbled as a light snack, "indeed where we're going is the origin of a common Bangla expression, 'crocodile in the river, tiger on the bank!'"

"What does that mean?"

"Effectively, 'out of the frying pan and into the fire.' Its meaning is rather more real and to the point than ours, I think. Ah! We're here – look, Sophie!"

She looked to where he pointed further down the river which had now expanded to such considerable size that she could barely make out the buildings and boats on the edge of the far side. She could see one medium-sized boat which looked capable of holding twenty people. It did not, however, look like a luxury ship to enjoy staying on. She sighed. By now, she should know better than to put up hopes of anything clean, new and expensive-looking in Bangladesh.

The boat moored up alongside the larger vessel and a plank of wood was thrown across to act as a gangplank between the two. Sophie was helped off first, holding the outstretched hand of one of the Bangladeshis on the other boat. Uncle Joshua went second, eschewing any proffered help. *Didi* came last, to Sophie's dismay, as she was sure the men had dictated the order according to status – the white people go first – rather than 'ladies first,' which she considered more polite. Her uncle didn't seem to pay any heed, though and strolled off into the ship. Sophie and *Didi* followed on behind.

There were three layers to the boat, Sophie quickly found out as they were taken on a tour around. There was a bottom layer in the depths of the hull where the engine crew worked, and there was a kitchen for preparing their meals. The first deck was sleeping quarters, arranged in two rows with a corridor between them. The top deck consisted of observation platforms, front and back, Captain's cabin for steering the boat and a lounge/eating area with tables and chairs. It was actually more impressive than the rusty, paint-peeling appearance, first seen as they approached, had suggested. Nothing felt new, but it seemed clean and the staff pleasant enough. The top deck, for sure, was the closest thing to luxury that she had seen in Bangladesh.

The engines started, grumbling deep in the ship's bowels and they set off further downstream while *Didi* and Sophie sat on one of the leather seats around the side of the lounge, gazing out of the windows at the view. Uncle Joshua toddled off – remarkably cheerfully, almost with an actual spring in his step – to find some *cha*.

After just a few minutes, the number of boats on the river reduced, as did the number of buildings on the banks. As the ship gained speed, the sense of being alone on the waters increased. The number of trees and foliage on the banks replaced all sense of human habitation or work and Sophie felt such serenity that she felt as though she was floating. Her body literally felt lighter.

Uncle Joshua came back with three cups of *cha*. Sophie supped hers, staring out over the waters. She noticed that something would appear briefly at the surface every few seconds and then dip down again.

"Uncle Joshua – what is it that keeps dipping up and down in the water? Is it a fish?"

"It's a dolphin," said a voice from behind her. Startled, Sophie turned to look at who had just spoken so close to her. Sat just behind her was a young twentyish Bangladeshi man with long wavy black hair. He was, she couldn't help notice, incredibly handsome.

"These waters are home to many species found only in the *Sundarbans*," he continued as though oblivious to Sophie's shock even though he had smiled when she jumped, "and freshwater dolphins are known only around these mangrove forests and a few major rivers such as India's Ganges."

"Erm...right..." said Sophie, desperately trying to make her head work again and her heart stop pounding, "thanks for that."

The man smiled again. He had a gorgeous smile – nearly as amazing as *Didi's*, Sophie thought.

"Allow me to introduce myself, "he said, holding out his hand to Sophie to shake. "I am Aatiq. I am the owner of this boat company." He moved on to shake Joshua's hand and then *Didi's*. He gave an extra-large smile when he took her hand. "And I will be your guide during your stay with us. If you have any questions, then please do ask me and I'll endeavour to answer as best I can."

Joshua grumped a vague hello at Aatiq and carried on sipping his *cha*. Although it was doubtful the young man would have seen, Sophie knew her uncle well enough to know he was not impressed with the man. Certainly, Aatiq seemed very confident of himself. His accent was astonishingly British, and she had never seen a Bangladeshi man with long hair before. She didn't think it was allowed.

"Did you say you own this boat company?" she asked. "You seem a bit young to have your own business?"

Aatiq flashed another heart-stopping smile at her. He clearly didn't feel offended that this thirteen-year-old had doubted his credentials.

"Indeed, indeed," he said, gesticulating with his hands, "I am very young, it is true. I am lucky that my parents set up this business along with many others and they gifted me this particular one when I returned home after I completed my degree."

"Wow," said Sophie, "nice parents! So, how big is the company?"

"Yes, my parents are very wonderful, it is true. We have four boats on the *Sundarbans* and three more on the east side of the country in the *Bandarbans*. Have you ever been there?"

"No," said Joshua, his interest now piqued, "but I've always wanted to go. I made it to Chittagong once, but never as far as Rangamati or *Bandarban.*"

"Oh, you should go," Aatiq beamed, "it is a beautiful part of the country."

"I have no idea where any of these places are," Sophie admitted, sadly, "but I know here is beautiful. I didn't know Bangladesh could be so amazing!"

"It is for sure," Aatiq nodded, "which is why I came back to this country. I studied in the UK," he held his hand to his chest, "but I was drawn back to this golden land."

Joshua rolled his eyes, and Sophie grinned.

"Don't you find it nerve-racking to be in charge?" she asked.

"No, no. I have grown up in the business for so long, and I know how it works. And most of the crew here and our employees generally have been with us for many years. They really know how to do the work themselves. I am here to make sure guests – like your dear selves – have the most relaxing and wonderful time. I am the only one who knows Western ways, so I am best suited to this task."

"Do you get many British people here?" Sophie was quite astonished at the thought. She'd never known anyone come to Bangladesh from her country.

"Occasionally," Aatiq admitted, "though they tend to be NGO workers – Non-Governmental-Organisation workers – who are living here to do charity work. They come here for a break sometimes. But we do get a lot of British Bangladeshis here. There are many British people whose parents came from here originally. They are used to British ways but still visit relatives in Bangladesh regularly."

"Oh, I see," said Sophie. "I didn't know that. I've never really thought about where British Asians come from. I always thought they were just Indian background."

"Oh no, not at all!" Aatiq laughed. "In fact, did you know that most 'Indian' restaurants are actually Bangladeshi?"

"What? Really? Then why do they call themselves Indian then?"

Aatiq smiled broadly and wagged his finger. "That is a very, very good question! This is partly because many of the owners came to the UK many decades ago when Pakistan had only just separated from India. But mostly because British people fell in love with Indian food when they had the colonial empire, but modern-day people have no idea where Bangladesh is and not much idea where Pakistan is either! So, the restaurants keep their 'Indian' names rather than lose business. People still like to think of their empire days."

"It feels like that's wrong somehow," Sophie replied.

Aatiq spread his hands far apart. "Ah well, that's a discussion for another day. We have plenty of time. But now, I've intruded on your time enough and shall leave you in peace!"

The young man waved goodbye to the three of them and moved on. Sophie leaned over to *Didi*.

"Oh my god, *Didi* – how dreamy?!"

Didi grinned back at her. "Yes, he is," she laughed.

"God above," Uncle Joshua rolled his eyes again, "save me from easily impressionable women!"

He got up and walked off. Sophie and *Didi* looked at each other and burst into laughter.

The days spent on the boat were perhaps the happiest she'd ever know, Sophie thought later when the holiday was all over. She had witnessed stunning sunsets over the river as they passed by equally stunning forests. She saw deer feeding on the riverbanks and watched dolphins come up for air not far from where the boat moored each night. The mornings arrived with a gentle mist which made the calmness of the environment as serene as it was eerie. For the first time in this country, Sophie felt genuinely alone and away from humanity. There were no signs of human life on the muddy banks and no other boat on the waterways, interweaving between the foliage. When they passed close to forests, she could see snakes lazily draped along overhanging branches and sounds of distant movement within the dense greenery, but no other sign of life.

Her cabin down below was tiny, but her bed was literally under the window that had no glass. She could stare through her curtains out onto the waters at night and was awake with the rising of the sun to see the most marvellous dawns which rivalled the sunsets. Even her nightmares had calmed to merely fitful dreams which woke her constantly but left her with no sense of fear.

The food on board was tasty, and she had sampled a wide range of meat, vegetables and, most of all, fish. Even though it had all been curry, Sophie wondered how each meal felt completely new to her. Best of all, it was always Aatiq who served them food.

She admitted she had a huge crush on the young man. He oozed charm but wasn't creepy with it. He was genuine and friendly and – what was really, *really* important – he treated Sophie as an equal, without condescension or disrespect. He didn't show the slightest dislike of her company, and in the evenings they would spend many moments together standing out on the observation platforms drinking *cha* or water and talking about everything in the universe – or so it seemed to Sophie.

Aatiq had studied Anthropology at Cambridge after having an English-medium school education in Dhaka. His parents had not come from a wealthy background but were both educated and made good choices in business which had seen them flourish. For himself, he didn't care about money but valued independence and the opportunity to explore what it meant to be human. He didn't mind running this business as he got to spend so much time in nature, but his aim was to save enough money that he could stop working one day and travel the world, living frugally with nothing but a backpack and see all the different cultures he could. He had studied anthropology to understand more about what it meant to be human and this, for him, was all that was important; to be and to understand being. Finding peace within being, he had said, was your *ashroy* – your sanctuary, your safe haven. Sophie thought to herself that perhaps she had already found her *ashroy*. She couldn't imagine finding the peace she knew in Bangladesh anywhere in England.

Sophie felt as though she was entering a whole different world being with him in this place. The highlight, though, had been an early morning trek through the forest on their last day.

They had gone out in a smaller boat, moored to the side. This enabled them to move stealthily through smaller rivers. Sophie watched mudskippers leaping up the banks and saw freshly-made pawprints from tigers that had come to drink water at first light. She was scared at the thought of walking through a land where tigers lived and elated at the same time. They moored to a bamboo landing strip after about twenty minutes and got out. With an armed guard in front and one behind, Sophie, Joshua, *Didi*, Aatiq and two or three crew members from the boat walked in single file through the trees. The forest was almost deathly quiet, only their footsteps making any noise. Sophie tried not to shrink with terror when she saw snakes coiled loosely around branches not far from her head, but everyone else seemed oblivious to them, so she assumed they must be harmless despite their size.

After a while, they reached a sandy clearing which they walked across. She said to Aatiq that she hoped the guards were good shots, for if a tiger were to come out into this clearing, one of them would surely make a good meal. The guard behind her said in Bangla with a big grin that the guns were not for the tigers but for humans – it was better to shoot a person than let them suffer the mauling of a *bagh!* Sophie had no idea if he was joking or not but walked a little faster to keep near to Aatiq and the others just in case.

In the end, virtually disappointingly, Sophie never got to see a tiger, shy as they are. She did briefly hear the call of one in the distance and was surprised by the almost effeminate cough. She had expected a deep 'manly' roar. Her disappointment was soon forgotten when they reached the beach, however.

As she looked at the huge expanse of water, with waves sloshing hard onto the soft, clay-like silt sand, Aatiq told her she was looking out onto the Bay of Bengal, the way into Bangladesh by sea. Sophie was so used to the farmers' flat fields that filled this country that she hadn't even considered that it was anything other than landlocked. So to see an ocean before her was mesmerising.

With hardly any time to process this, *Didi* had called her over. The woman had wasted no time before getting into the water and lathering herself with the mud.

"Try it, Sophie!" she had told the girl. "This mud is famous for being good for the skin."

Sophie had followed her friend's lead and thrown herself into the sea. They were both wearing *shalwa kameezes*, and despite being *sheetkal* season, it was much warmer in the *Sundarbans* than at home. Both water and mud felt smooth and invitingly warm to the touch. Even Uncle Joshua had taken off his shoes and socks, rolled up his trouser legs and was paddling.

When both girls had spent quite some time lathering each other in the mud, including their faces, Joshua called to them both and pointed out into the waters. Their boat had come around the long way and was now anchored offshore a little distance. The smaller boat had come round too and was now on the shore where Joshua, Aatiq and the other men were now getting on board.

"You can either join us now or swim," Joshua had shouted to them. Both girls looked at each other, looked at the ship in the distance and called back to him that they would indeed swim.

Sophie felt so alive as she splashed through the waters, slowly nearing their ship. She was no strong swimmer and was badly out of practice having not swum for well over a year or longer, but the men rowed back to the ship slowly, staying near to both girls in case of trouble.

As they pulled up near to the hands reaching down, ready to grab them, she heard Joshua shout, "Is that a crocodile?"

Sophie screamed and immediately started splashing about, her head going under, saltwater filling her mouth. She threw herself towards the boat and, as hands helped lift her up towards the short ladder overhanging the side, she realised the men were all laughing, and she had been tricked. There were no crocodiles on this side of the forests. It was saltwater here and not freshwater.

"Uncle Joshua," she panted as she stood dripping on the deck, "I hate you." Everyone laughed, including Sophie.

Saying goodbye to Aatiq and the other crew members had been one of the saddest things Sophie had ever done. She desperately wanted to stay and hated the thought that she would never see her older friend again. He had made them all promise that they would all come to visit again and use his company when they did. Sophie felt instinctively though that she was the only one of the three who meant it.

As they took the small boat back from the ship to the Khulna port where they would catch a train home, Sophie sat in silence, mulling over all that had happened over the last week.

"Uncle Joshua."

Joshua turned towards her. "Yes, Sophie?"

"I think I really like being here."

"The *Sundarbans?* I'm glad so. I do too."

"No. Well…yes, of course. But I meant – in Bangladesh. I really like living here."

Her uncle turned more fully towards her, intrigued.

"Really?"

"Yes. I think I've realised just how special this country is. There's so much more to learn about being here that I don't know."

He smiled kindly at her. "Well, I'm glad you've found it so, Sophie. I, too, have always felt like that about Bangladesh. I've been here for longer than you've been alive and, I have to say, I'm still learning new things and still finding there are places I don't know. It's a magical place. No wonder the English called India the jewel in the crown and no wonder Bengal was such a prized part of it. I'm glad you have found this too."

"I have," Sophie agreed. She paused and then added, "Do you think it is possible to postpone going back to England? Could I maybe stay until the summer at least?"

Uncle Joshua beamed gently at her.

"I would like that very much indeed, Sophie. Very much indeed."

CHAPTER TWENTY - REBEL

It is fair to say that residents of the village were rather shocked by the apparent resurrection of the strange *bideshi* girl. By this time, however, rumours and stories had become embedded into the fabric of 'what is known' and were never going to be easily erased. But how to deal with the very obvious and undeniable fact that Sophie Shepherd was most certainly alive and well?

The answer was simple. Joshua dada was an even greater man than had been thought. He had used his great learning to use and brought his niece back to life. He was now on a par, for many, with the great faith healers in the more remote villages – some of whom were also known to have raised the dead. The only thing that saved Joshua from an embarrassing long line of would-be patients at his door was the assertion that he had used *bideshi* magic rather than *deshi* and, of course, this would be very dangerous – perhaps fatal – to *deshi* people.

Nevertheless, the odd one or two did try their luck with him, only to see themselves turfed away by an angry, red-faced and clearly completely *pagla* white man ranting in a barely comprehensible mix of Bangla and English. With curses such as 'blithering idiots' and 'for the love of God how can people be so imbecilic' those foolhardy enough to try soon passed the word around that the wrath of the white man is at least equal to that of the faith healers; and no one tempted the wrath of the *kobiraj*. Thus, was the status of Joshua and his young ward elevated even further; hence too, villagers further afield became even more scared of white strangers.

But talk soon passed to other things, as it does. Idle gossip is remarkably energetic and likes to move on to something exciting after a while. In this case – for once, not unlike the English – it was the weather.

When February came, the sun found its strength again and quickly tore through the *kuwasha* until it gave up entirely and returned to its proper place of barely perceptible mist over the fields just for a few minutes as the day dawned. Such a sight was reserved only for those who took night buses and trains, to peer at wearily through sleep-deprived eyes for no one can ever rest properly on any public transport.

For this brief time, the sun is no longer 'the enemy' but enjoys a triumphant, joyful return. It won't last long. Come March, it will burn too fiercely, and people will again run from its rays, a victim of its own success. But in February, everyone loves the sun.

It took less than two weeks from returning to the village for Sophie to tell her uncle that she hated him again. Cross words between them had started almost immediately, dismissed at the time as just tiredness after travelling most of the day from the *Sundarbans*. But as time went on, Sophie became cockier, more arrogant in her responses to her uncle and Joshua became less tolerant of some of her habits, such as leaving the toilet seat up and not lining up her sandals neatly on the porch when she came home. A fight was brewing and, as with most of their tussles, it started over something trivial – at least from her point of view anyway.

For Uncle Joshua, it was on coming into the front room to find not just coats and tops discarded by Sophie on every seat, but a pair of her knickers on his desk seat. *Didi* was taking a day off, so this couldn't be blamed on her sorting out washing and he merely badly timing his return from the *pukur*. This was Sophie's littering, and he hit the roof.

For Sophie, she had started by bringing down her washing to be helpful, knowing *Didi* was away and the washing needed sorting. She had promptly realised she'd left a 500 *taka* note in one of her pockets and knew it wouldn't survive a washing particularly well. She dumped the clothes on the sofa and flung ones without pockets out of the way. *Taka* located, she ran upstairs to her room to put it safely away in her money box – and promptly forgot all about the clothes downstairs.

It is an eerie quality of children that they often have a premonitory sense when it comes to trouble. Sophie had, suddenly, and with great horror, realised what she had forgotten literally one second before she heard Uncle Joshua open the front door. She was on her feet and just about to open her bedroom door as her uncle roared at her, saying that she better bloody well get down here this instant and clear this goddamn mess up, for the love of God, for so help him, he would indeed lose it.

So, it was a rather indignant Sophie who rushed down the stairs, complaining she was already coming to do it and that she was just trying to help out.

"Oh, so throwing your dirty underwear around is helping then," Uncle Joshua had responded. "Well, forgive me for not realising it then. Why don't we just invite all our neighbours round to throw their smellies around my room too? Just clear this damned mess up and next time, don't forget what you are doing."

The accusation of forgetting maddened the girl and she denied the claim (which was a lie), insisting she was already coming down to do it (which was true) and therefore convincing herself that he had no right to falsely accuse her that way. He was not, after all, the only one whose house this was.

That was enough for her guardian. With face purple with rage, he dragged her by her arm up the stairs, reminding her that she was a guest in this house and she bloody-well better not forget it, and throwing her into her bedroom before shutting – and then locking – the door. About time you learn that freedom in this house is earned and not free, he bellowed as she responded with her fists on the other side of the door.

And with that, he came downstairs again, saw that there were still most of the clothes lying around and figured he'd go back to the tranquillity of the *pukur*. He did so, hesitating briefly on shutting the front door, quashing the deep sense of unease and the voices in his head saying he was definitely in the wrong on this one.

"Rubbish!" he snorted at himself and pounded off to the pool.

Sophie sat on her bed, alternating between silently fuming and screaming to herself while kicking and hitting her mattress. Her uncle could be an absolute idiot sometimes. He really could. She spent some time thinking similar thoughts until she suddenly remembered that Adhora was supposed to be coming round very soon.

She looked out of her window, overlooking the outside balcony at the back of the *bari*. There were stairs leading down from it to the ground, which Didi sometimes used for taking out washing to hang at the back. It was also where the *murgha wallah* would come with his chickens to slit their throats and let the bodies flap around frantically for a few minutes. *Didi* would then pluck the feathers and take the carcasses inside.

Sometimes, Adhora would take a different pathway to the village, leading her along the back and past this part of the house. With luck, Sophie could call her attention and get her to come up the back stairs.

She waited for about half an hour – of course! Bangladeshis are never on time, she had learned – and, on seeing her friend walk by, she hollered her name as loudly as possible and beckoned her over.

Adhora took notice of the first shout and came up the back steps. "What are you doing, Sophie?" she asked through the netting of the barred windows.

"My idiot of an uncle has locked me into my room," Sophie replied, scowling as she noticed Adhora grin a little and suppress a giggle, "and I need your help to get me out. I think he locked the front door but try this back one here."

Adhora went to the back door. Like all the outer doors, it was made of metal, with metal bars and mosquito netting. She could tell immediately that it was bolted and padlocked on the inside. She turned and shook her head at Sophie.

"Damn," Sophie huffed. She thought for a minute and then bent down to peer at her keyhole. Yes! The key was still in the lock. She stood up and looked out onto the balcony. There were a few sheets of newspaper on the ground that *Didi* used to peel potatoes over. She had an idea based on something she read in a spy book as a kid and never had a legitimate excuse to try out. Now she had good reason.

"Adhora, pass me a sheet of paper," she said, pointing to the floor and moving the sliding panel which held the mosquito netting in place in her window. Her friend grabbed a sheet, rolled it up and slid it through the gap and between the metal bars.

Sophie grabbed it and, unrolling it, slid it under the door so half stuck out her side and half the other. Then she grabbed a pencil, ran to her lock and tried to push it through. Too thick. Damn.

She ran to her *alna* and threw a top off one of the wire coat hangers. She straightened the hook as best she could and ran back to the lock. This would fit. She placed the wire into the lock and tried to see what angle the key was at. It was slightly twisted so that a straight push wouldn't get it out. She carefully poked at the teeth with the wire until the key turned enough to be straight on with the keyhole. And then she held her breath and pushed.

She heard the clink of metal hitting a solid floor and shouted a triumphant "Yes!" at Adhora, who promptly gave a little jump of excitement even though she was still at a loss to figure out what Sophie was doing.

Sophie got on her hands and knees. The last two hurdles: did the key bounce off the paper? If not, will the key fit through the gap between the door and the floor? She slowly pulled her side of the paper back in. No sign of the key as she pulled in most of the paper. Then, just as the last sliver of paper cleared the door, she saw a few millimetres of the key's handle. It must have bounced off the paper on falling, but a part of it had fallen back, allowing the paper to drag it in. Just.

She sighed with relief, carefully grabbed at the key with her fingernails to make sure she didn't shoot it back under the door by mistake and, once she had it securely in her hand, hastened to unlock her door.

Sophie was out in a flash, unlocked the padlock to the back door and let Adhora in. Both girls hugged with joy over their little triumph.

"Right," said Sophie, "let's show Uncle Joshua what happens when he messes with us! Adhora, is there somewhere private we can go where we can't be seen easily? Someone's home or a storehouse or something?"

Adhora thought for a moment, then said, "There's my uncle's shed? It is quite big and he stores machinery in it which he doesn't use at this time of the year, so we could go there?"

"Right. Perfect – give me a minute, and we'll go."

Sophie grabbed her rucksack and then put a handful of clothes and some boxes from her desk into it before zipping up the bag and putting it around her shoulders.

"Let's go," she said, her face grim with determination. She picked up the newspaper and hid it under her bed. She then locked her bedroom door as she left.

"What are you doing?" Adhora asked.

"I'm leaving a shock for my uncle. When he comes back and opens this, he's going to find me gone and will be completely confused about how I got out. I wish I could see his face when it happens."

Adhora giggled.

"Sophie, you are naughty!"

"Yep. Come on, let's go."

They left through the back door, Sophie locking the door with the padlock on the outside this time. Her uncle would never notice that. They shot off out of the village using the same back pathway Adhora had used to make sure they didn't bump into Uncle Joshua or anyone else they knew between the *bari* and the *pukur.*

It took the two girls around half an hour to get to Adhora's uncle's shed. It was another part of the area Sophie hadn't been to yet, and it was relatively isolated. Her uncle's *bari* was opposite the shed, which was unlocked, and the home looked deserted. A dirt road lay between them, stretching out in both directions towards forests.

Entering the shed, Sophie saw a tractor and some metalworking machines taking up around two-thirds of the room. Nearest them, as they sneaked in through the large metal front gates, were some wooden packing boxes. Some were stacked high, but in one place the boxes were just over waist height. They climbed over these and had an ideal area to hide on the other side. The high roof had several barred windows cut into it, so the light inside was surprisingly plentiful – at least for as long as the sun was out, full and bright.

"What are we doing?" Adhora asked as they sat on the floor, sprinkled with straw. A cool breeze wafted over them from a hole in the brick all near them. A metal sheet was hanging on the outside, acting as a cover, and it flapped as the wind blew. The hole was about a foot and a half square, and grooves in the floor leading from it suggested it was some kind of sluice gate to let liquids – perhaps water used to clean machinery – drain out of the shed to the outside.

"This," Sophie replied as she pulled out one of her boxes from her bag and opened it to reveal lipsticks and other make-up items. Adhora gasped.

"No, Sophie," she pleaded, "we should not do this. If my father finds out, he will kill me. No make-up."

"Yes, make-up. Don't worry; I have some wipes here too. We can clean up before we leave and no one will ever know. We've been promising to dress up forever, and it's about time we did it. I've brought some skirts too."

This was too much for her friend, who now audibly squealed with panic. Sophie held her hand and calmed her down.

"Look," she said, "you're my best friend, Adhora, and I want to do this with you. I'm going to tell you something I've not told anyone before – not even *Didi*. Do you know what's special about today?"

"No. What?"

Sophie paused and took a deep breath. Even before she spoke, she could feel tears welling.

"Today is one year since the car accident. One year since my mum and dad died."

"Oh, Sophie." Her friend gripped her hand tightly.

"I didn't even get to bury them, Adhora. I was in a coma for weeks afterwards. I refused to visit the graveyard initially when my aunt asked me because I was still so numb. I couldn't have survived it. But Adhora, it is time for me to move on. I'm growing up, and I live, for now, in a completely different place; I have a different life. I'm not a little girl any longer. And nor are you. So. It's time we started finding out how beautiful we can be. There's no harm in it, and it's *my* day, and this is what I want to do."

Adhora looked at her with wet eyes and nodded her head in reluctant agreement. Sophie wiped the tears from her face, and both girls hugged. Then she picked up some lipstick and opened it.

"Here goes," she said, half to herself, and moved towards Adhora.

Joshua put down his fishing rod. He wasn't even trying to fish, he admitted to himself; there was no point doing this any longer.

He was still fuming at how Sophie had spoken to him, but now he was fuming much more at himself. He should not have locked her up. Such draconian measures were the kind of things his own parents would have done to him or his brother when they were kids, and the thought of being like them was loathsome to him.

Joshua had always prided himself on how he treated his students with respect. Yes, they had to follow his rules and, yes, he would bellow fiercely if needed when students got out of hand. But most of that was an act – a little psychological drama designed to quickly snap them back into place. Most of the time, he spoke to students as equals with dry humour and kept his lessons moving at a swift pace to avoid boredom as much as possible. As a result, he almost never had to resort to any kind of punishment, even with some of the most irksome kids he was given at times.

So why did Sophie get under his skin so much? He knew the answer deep down: she was so very like her mother. The thought was painful to him, and he tried to wipe the image of her from his mind. Even after all these years apart, he still missed Elizabeth. Barely a thought went to his brother – though he was, of course, sad that Stephen had died and sadder that there had been no one to tell him of their deaths – but it was Elizabeth who remained in his mind, and he saw her in Sophie every day.

Buried deep inside him, Joshua knew he had regrets about how things had finished, how he'd ended up taking the mad offer of working in a foreign country with little or no resources. He'd given up his comfortable head of department job at a fairly affluent British school and jumped ship, all because of a fight involving the three of them. He'd gone to escape as much as he'd gone to help. Or had he? Such thoughts just confused him and got him cross.

"Sod it," he said out loud to no one in particular, "let's go for a walk, you old fool. A bit of exercise might shake all this nonsense off rather than contemplating with the fish – who aren't coming out to play anyway."

He put away his fishing rod and tackle and carried his fishing box back to the *bari*. He dropped it into the porchway but didn't bother to unlock the front door. No one would steal it. He hesitated, wondering if he should go in and unlock her door, but then decided that he still wasn't ready to face his niece yet. He'd go for a walk around the area and come back refreshed. He wouldn't be long, and she'd be safe. Yes. That would be absolutely fine.

The girls had at least an hour of half-muffled laughter as they covered each other in make-up and tried on different combinations of their clothes and those Sophie and brought. They were both in *shalwa kameezes* and had tried mixing these with the skimpy tops and skirts from Sophie's bag. Adhora, it had turned out, looked like a supermodel in a skirt. Sophie did not look as good, but a skirt over some *kameeze* pants had worked, albeit that colour-matching would have to be improved next time.

They had plastered eye-liner and lipstick on one another multiple times and there now lay a small pile of tissue wipes used up and clearing one set of colours off to apply another. With neither girl having tried this before, their attempts were heavy-handed, but it was fun trying, nonetheless.

The fun ended abruptly, though when they heard the sound of men's voices outside, not far from the front gate.

"Oh my god, Sophie!" Adhora cried. "Someone is outside."

"Dammit," Sophie replied, grabbing instinctively at her things and beginning to stuff them into her bag.

"Quick, go over to the gate and see who it is. I'll get this stuff put away."

Adhora nimbly but nervously leapt over the boxes and tiptoed to the gate. She peered through the gaps to glimpse who was outside without being seen. Her eyes widened, and she ran, full speed, back to the boxes and threw herself over them, banging one of them with her leg in the process. The box moved and scraped against another, emitting a loud screech that could easily be heard.

"Oh no. Oh no," Adhora wailed. "It's my uncle, and he's talking to my father. This is awful."

"Shut up!" Sophie hissed, clearing the last of the things into her bag and zipping up. She looked at Adhora. She still had make-up all over her face, and Sophie guessed her own face was similarly covered. There was no time to worry about that now. They had to get out without being seen, or this would turn out pretty bad. She looked at the hole in the wall and pushed on the flap. It opened quite far out.

"I've got an idea," she said.

"Oh no, no," Adhora replied, seeing exactly what she had in mind, "it will never work, Sophie. It's too small for us."

"No, it's not. It's perfect. Trust me, Adhora – this is going to work."

CHAPTER TWENTY-ONE – CAUGHT

The hole was, in theory, big enough for either of them to squeeze through, but only just. It was rough brickwork, however, and the metal flap was heavy and had sharp edges. There was no choice, though.

The voices were getting louder, and that undoubtedly meant at least one member of Adhora's family was likely to enter the shed at any moment. For that reason, Sophie told her to go first.

Adhora got on her knees and pushed her way through. Sophie was dismayed to see that there were no gaps around her body which meant she only just fitted. Adhora was the thinnest of the two of them.

"*Acha, acha, thik achey bhai….*"

She turned to see the hand of one of the men come round the side of the gate as he was saying goodbye to the other. There was no time to worry if she would fit now. Adhora was through to the other side, and Sophie thrust her bag through the gap and followed headfirst.

Most of her went through without an issue, though the bricks scratched her arms as she went. But her hips held tight. She twisted and turned desperately and heard the ripping of clothing, but she managed to pull herself out of the hole by turning like a corkscrew. She had no idea if the man had come in and seen her doing this, but the metal flap clattered loudly as she pulled her feet out and stood up. There was no time to lose – they had to get away from here quickly.

She clutched at Adhora's hand. "Come on; we need to go." She started to pull in the direction of the nearest path away from the back of the shed.

"Adhora? What in the name of Allah…?"

Sophie's heart sank at the sound of the voice behind them. She knew that voice. It was Adhora's father. Both girls turned to face him.

"Yes, Baba," said Adhora meekly. Her father stomped over to them.

"What is going on here? Why are you two skulking around here, and…is that…is that make-up on your face?"

Sophie gulped. They'd had no time to deal with any of the make-up on their faces. She'd hoped they would get away first and wipe it all off as they went home. Just as bad, she realised she had stuffed their *ornas* into her bag rather than try to put the scarves on around their shoulders while scrabbling out of the shed. Despite wearing long-sleeved *kameezes,* she knew that they were both, effectively, naked as far as Adhora's conservative father was concerned.

"You are a mess, daughter," he said, voice beginning to rise with anger. "What is the meaning to all this?"

"Please, Mr Haque...it's my fault," Sophie started to say, hoping to take some of the flack from her friend.

"It is damned right it is your fault," he spat angrily at her, wagging his finger. "I have no illusions about that. But I have brought my daughter up properly, and she knows better than to behave like this regardless of the temptations of a very, very bad girl like you." He turned back to Adhora. "You know what this looks like, huh? You know how my clients will see this? They will laugh and say I have a whore for a daughter. I will lose business and be a laughing stock. You have brought shame on your family."

Adhora stood, head down, eyes firmly fixed on the ground, looking utterly ashamed. Sophie felt wretched. It was all her fault, and there was nothing she could do.

"Is something going on here?"

Sophie's hopes dropped further. Of all the coincidences, all the people who could have suddenly turned up in this place for no good reason, why did it have to be him? Why not *Didi* or even *Mashima?* They would have helped. But no, standing behind Mr Haque, inexplicably *not* at the *pukur* where he could always be found, was Uncle Joshua.

If he was surprised to see Sophie there, he didn't show it. He did make eye contact with her, his piercing eyes holding her firm until he looked at Adhora's father and gave him the attention.

"What's going on here, Hasan?"

"I could ask you the same thing! Do you have no control at all over your girl?"

Joshua held up his hands as if to suggest Hasan should calm down. He glanced briefly at Sophie and said, "I don't have as much as I thought, that's for sure. But I am at a loss to understand what has been going on. Can you please explain this to me?"

"What happened is that I find these two skulking out of my brother's shed after no doubt getting up to bad business, on their hands and knees no less, and covered in ridiculous make-up and barely dressed!"

"I see."

"Tell me, Joshua – is this how young ladies behave in your country? Is it? It is not how they behave in *this* country, I tell you." Hasan puffed out his chest. "We have *honour* here, I tell you."

"Yes, yes Hasan, I understand. You're telling me. I think perhaps I should take Sophie home and get to the bottom of this." He glanced at her again. "There's several questions I'd like her to answer, frankly."

Joshua's response seemed to annoy Hasan all the more. He turned back to the girls. Despite both girls clearly chastened and scared by the turn of events, he was spoiling for a fight. Sophie's lack of knowledge was never more inadequate at this point. Whereas Adhora had her head bowed in meek submission and avoided eye contact with either adult, Sophie was looking at him to indicate just how seriously she took his words rather than look away disinterested.

"Do you think this is funny?" he shouted at her.

"No Mr Haque. No, honestly…"

He cut her off with a wave of his hand and then grabbed Adhora by the arm, pulling her close to him.

"You think this is acceptable behaviour? You think shaming me in front of everyone is how you show me you are growing up?" Adhora shook her head dumbly.

"It was my fault, Mr Haque." Sophie blurted out. "Please don't blame Adhora; she tried to tell me we shouldn't do it. I didn't listen." He looked Sophie in the eyes and stared at her. She looked to Joshua, her eyes begging him for help. He just looked back at her sadly. There was nothing he could do, and she knew it. This was her doing.

"This is what you get for hanging around with a *bideshi* girl," Hasan shouted at Adhora. "This is why I was not comfortable with letting you be friends with her. You promised me you would be good. I *knew* she would have a bad influence on you."

He stepped back from Adhora, shot a glance at Sophie and then wagged his finger at his daughter.

"You are a wicked and evil girl. You are not a good Muslim."

Even Sophie knew that this was a stinging remark – a total rebuke, effectively in public. Adhora's tears began to fall to the ground she was staring at, and her shoulders began to shake from the urge to sob she was so desperately trying to keep inside.

"Hasan, I think everyone needs to calm down. I don't think any damage has been done, really. Sophie, where are your *ornas*?"

Sophie hastily opened her bag and retrieved their scarves. She got tissues out too and, handing some to Adhora, began to wipe her face.

"There, see?" said Uncle Joshua, "no harm done."

Hasan whirled round at him.

"You bloody English think you can still come here and do what you like as if you still ruled here."

"Now steady on, old chap."

"I will *not* steady on. I will not permit my daughter to have anything more to do with your whore."

"I said that's enough," snapped Joshua. His commanding voice silenced even Adhora's father. "I mean it, Hasan – you will not carry on in this vein. They've been silly, and Sophie will be punished, I assure you, but I will not allow you to speak of her in this way. We have our honour too, and you are trampling on it."

Hasan opened his mouth to speak, but Joshua shut him up with a raised finger.

"And don't interrupt me. I know you are upset, but you have no right to overreact like this. You have no idea what this poor girl has gone through over this last year, and she's doing her best to learn a life that is utterly alien to anything she knew beforehand. She meant no bad…" he glanced at her again, "…mostly, and she certainly would not have wished for her best friend to get into such trouble."

"I'm really, really sorry, Mr Haque," Sophie pleaded. "I really wasn't thinking. Please don't stop Adhora and me from being friends. I promise nothing like this will happen again."

Hasan grabbed Adhora's hand tightly and started to walk away, dragging her with him.

"You're damned right nothing like this will happen again. You will not see her outside of school again, and tomorrow I will write to the headmaster to demand you are not allowed to sit with her in classes any longer."

He added a parting shot to Joshua.

"I've never approved of your meddling in this area. You with your 'I know better than you' British attitudes. Thought my house would perish in flooding and told me I was putting my family in danger – ha! We're still waiting for that, aren't we, hey? Three years on! My house still stands proud. My house! You keep away from us, you bloody foreigners. You know nothing."

Joshua and Sophie watched the two of them walk off along the track; Joshua quiet, Sophie now openly weeping. Joshua turned to her. She didn't look at him, but there was kindness in his eyes.

"Well," he said gently, "I think he was a little bit upset, but I'm not sure."

Sophie laughed but, in doing so, cried all the harder.

"I've made a horrible, horrible mess of things, haven't I?"

Her uncle smiled, reached out and stroked her arm.

"Bangladeshis are prone to a little…*beshi abheg* – too much emotion – sometimes. I've seen men verbally humiliated by their wives standing on the opposite side of the road, laying into them for some affrontery or another. I've seen *ayahs* scold their mistresses who have accused them of stealing in full view of others because they've lost their temper, sometimes after years of abuse. I've seen brothers try to kill one another because one accuses the other of swindling them out of money. But eventually, the wife cooks for the husband again; the *ayah* carries on working for the mistress, and the brothers drink *cha* together at the *dokans*. Things usually work out. Give it time."

Sophie sniffed. "Do you really think so? Do you think Adhora's father will forgive me?"

Joshua looked over at the two figures now just dimly visible in the distance.

"Well, let's see. For now, let's just go home and see what *Didi* has left for us to eat."

"Okay."

"And on the way, you can tell me just *how* you got out of your room."

"I'm sorry that I did. I feel so wretched."

"Yes, I'm sorry that you did too. But...I'm more sorry that I did it at all. I shouldn't have. Please forgive me."

Sophie burst into tears afresh. It was the first time she could ever recall any adult ever saying sorry to her and asking *her* forgiveness, and that it should come from Uncle Joshua of all people when she was so clearly the one who had screwed things up completely was all the more astounding. In any other circumstance, she would have been beaming with joy, but right now, she felt nothing but dejected. She had lost her best friend, it was entirely her fault, and there was nothing she could do about it.

CHAPTER TWENTY-TWO – GRIEF

They said very little to each other for the rest of the day. Sophie was still too upset over losing Adhora, so Uncle Joshua gave her some space. They warmed up the leftovers which *Didi* had prepared and went to bed early that evening.

That night, Sophie dreamt of Adhora. She dreamed she had wandered into the *pukur* area in the middle of the night in search of her friend who was calling to her softly from the distance and sobbing. *I'm here*, she wanted to cry out to her, but the words wouldn't come out. She looked into the waters, as she had in so many dreams before, and searched for her friend. She could hear Adhora yet, at the same time, not hear her at all. And then a cold, white arm reached up from the depths and grabbed her hair, pulling her towards the pool. *You kill everything you touch*, a different voice shrieked at her, *you should go back where you came from, rakkosh.*

Whether or not Sophie screamed herself awake or merely screamed in her dream and awoke, she had no idea. She lay in her bed, sweating and panting hard – almost routine for her now – listening in the dark to see if she disturbed her uncle. She was fairly certain that on many occasions he had indeed been woken up by her cries and had crept to her door to listen in on the other side before leaving just as quietly once sure she was okay, bare feet occasionally quietly shuffling on the concrete floor. She had even taken to breathing a little heavier as if to simulate mild snoring just to reassure him so he could go back to bed sooner. She wondered if he was outside her room now, listening in as she was listening out, both concerned about the other, both not wanting to disturb.

In the morning, the sun shone brightly, and Joshua decided that, as it was the weekend and he hadn't managed a 'satisfactory' time at the *pukur* the previous day, he'd try again. He'd woken Sophie up and told her she was coming too. There was no fight from her; she nodded assent.

When she came downstairs, *Didi* was busy preparing their *nasta* and lunch to take to the *pukur* with breakfast already laid out on the dining table.

If Uncle Joshua had told her about the exploits of the day before (and Sophie was pretty sure he would have done), *Didi* betrayed no sign of it. She greeted Sophie with her usual cheeriness and a hug and went back to her work, gently humming and smiling to herself.

They both went out to the *pukur* in silence. It was one of those lazy mornings where the sun was shining, but not too much, and no one seemed particularly anxious to get started with the day's chores. The odd sound of a cow complaining about something or other, the occasional distant laughter from little children being bathed outside their homes under the water splashing down from the *nolkups*. Sophie followed her uncle through the gates to the *pukur* and along to where the boat was moored.

It was odd that the *pukur* never frightened Sophie in real life even though it featured almost permanently in her dreams. She was wary, perhaps, not too keen to peer over the edge as she inevitably did in dreamland – improbably too, seeing as the banks were too angled in the real *pukur* and to look on hands and knees into the waters would certainly mean toppling over. The *pukur* did mystify her, though, and she understood, though not entirely felt, the peace her uncle found through being here.

They got into the boat, and her uncle pushed off and rowed them to the centre as he'd done before. Then he put down the oars and looked at her.

"Well," he began, "of all the stupid, pig-headed and ignorant people in all the world...."

"I know I'm a disappointment to you, Uncle Joshua," she interrupted, "and I know I have shown you no gratitude for taking me in, nor in any way made you proud that I am your niece. I'm sorry I've made such a mess of things, and I understand now why you would want to send me away."

Uncle Joshua stared at her for a moment with what Sophie interpreted to be dismay. Then, she saw a slight twitch of a smile.

"I was talking about Adhora's father, Hasan, not you, you goose," he said calmly.

Sophie didn't know what to say. She sat there, open-mouthed.

"Hasan Haque is a silly and arrogant man, and I've said it for years," He continued. "He never takes advice; thinks he knows it all and just won't entertain the idea that I might know a thing or two *simply* because I'm a *bideshi*. My mere presence here, he's convinced, puts the whole nation in jeopardy."

Sophie laughed gently. "Joshua Shepherd," she said jokingly, "destroyer of nations."

Her uncle chuckled at this and shrugged his shoulders.

"Yes, well…you seem to be doing a better job at wrecking things than anyone. Only it's your own happiness you seem determined to spoil."

Sophie sighed.

"Yes, I know. And I think I know why too."

"Go on. You have my attention."

She looked half-absent-mindedly over the *pukur*.

"Guilt," she said.

"Guilt? Guilt for what?"

"Guilt that I survived and they didn't. Guilt that I basically begged my mum to let us go on the picnic. If I hadn't, then Dad would probably have given in to her and given up the idea."

She looked back at her uncle, tears streaming.

"I killed them, Uncle Joshua. It was my fault they died."

"Oh child," he replied softly, "have you really kept this inside you for all this time?"

"I try to bury it for so much of the time, I really do. I try and I try. But I knew the year anniversary of the crash was coming up and it weighed more and more each day on my mind as the date approached. In the end, I didn't know what I was doing or what I was saying. I was even mean to *Didi* sometimes – not that she'd ever show it – and I just got angrier and angrier with you. And I'm really sorry. I'm such a stupid mess."

She sat sobbing, and Joshua looked at her, not saying a word, just letting her cry. He didn't have any words for her; he knew that. These were her demons she was battling, and she had to battle them on her own.

"Sophie," he said after several minutes had passed, "I don't have any great pearls of wisdom, and you know already that I'm not exactly any good at any of this emotional stuff. I don't do gush. But I do know that you are not responsible for what happened with your parents. They were your parents for a reason – to be the responsible ones – and to love you with all their hearts which I'm absolutely certain they did. I know you won't exactly take this in, but...you didn't kill them – a young man driving recklessly did. And he's already paid for that himself if you see things in those terms. Nothing I can say is going to help you with coming to terms with this, not yet, not while you still grieve. But I know that I came to Bangladesh with sorrows and issues of my own, and a combination of time and being in this most marvellous of countries helped me find my own peace. Sometimes it isn't about trying to be happy; sometimes it is just about being content with who you are even when circumstances aren't great. Does this make sense?"

Sophie sniffed, wiped her cheeks and nodded.

"I also know that my home is as much your home now and I promise I will try to get used to that. I certainly won't try to force you to remain in the house again. It was stupid of me to do so and quite wrong. You have a home here until you're ready to go back to England – and there's no rush. Battle your demons, then leave them here when you leave."

"Okay."

"Good. Let's do some fishing."

He unpacked the bag and Sophie got out the *tiffins* full of *nasta*. As her uncle set up his fishing rod and prepared to cast off, Sophie looked around the waters.

She suddenly realised, in one corner, which she must have walked past a hundred times, there was a large dark circle with vertical lines running down it, buried into the bank and half-covered with reeds.

"Uncle Joshua?"

"Uh-huh?"

"What's that big hole thing I can see in the corner there? I've never noticed it before."

Joshua looked where she was pointing.

"Oh, that? Well, actually, it's one of my little inspirations."

"Really?"

"Yes. Although, truth be told, it turned out to be one of those youthful ideas foreigners get when they first come to places like this. They think they can see all the problems and know all the solutions. But, most of the time, they're wrong."

"And what was your idea?" she asked. "What actually is it? I can't see clearly – it's too far away, and everything is overgrown."

"Well, it's a sluice gate of sorts. It is a tunnel connected straight to the *Satya* River. I'm quite embarrassed about it, really and it probably did nothing to help Hasan's impression of me all those years ago."

"What's it for? What do you mean by sluice gate?"

"Basically, it allows water from the river to flow into the *pukur*. I realised that one of the reasons our particular part of the village doesn't flood during the rainy season is because we're a little higher than the areas on either side of the river. That makes sense if you think about it – rain waters will tend to drain into rivers because they're lower."

"So, you thought you could use the *pukur* as a kind of overflow pipe?"

"Ah, well," her uncle scratched his beard, and he frowned quizzically, "not entirely, but it did get seen as that – which is probably why I was able to secure funding for it and persuade several day labourers to spend months digging the trench, laying in the concrete to make the tunnel and then recover it all. I certainly was very worried about the *Satya* flooding in those days, and it still makes me nervous now."

"Why? I know it rains during monsoon, but it is so hot that waters dry really quickly."

"Yes, they do – except when they don't. The Bengal area is a harsh and unforgiving land for poor people, and its history is rife with terrible so-called natural disasters. At times the rain can be so bad that whole rivers have completely changed their course and, in doing so, have changed history for the country. We go from droughts to floods in the blink of an eye. One moment the crops are dying from lack of water because the rains haven't come; the next, the crops are being ruined by floods. Either way, people starve and, if governments don't do their job properly, famine ensues."

"Really? That's awful! Why don't people prepare better for floods and droughts, though?"

"They do – in the hill places and areas where flooding happens every year, shelters and flood defences are in place. But flooding is unpredictable.

The *Satya* once had a terrible flood – the best part of a century ago – which is why I know it *could* do again. Most years though, it floods a little, sometimes a lot; but never catastrophically."

Uncle Joshua pointed over towards the school.

"You know the school playing field? I've seen that filled to the brim with water from the floods. We even started fishing there to catch as many fish as we could before the waters receded, and they would be trapped in the field and die."

He shuffled his feet and looked embarrassed.

"Which brings me to why I really had the sluice gate done. This *pukur* gets pretty low. You can see right now that it is a good three feet lower than the bank, yes? Do you remember when you first came here? It was near the very top."

"Yes," said Sophie, "I do recall. I hadn't thought about how much it has changed, but you're right; we're much lower."

"Which is why we're fishing in the boat in the centre, which is deepest. You won't get any fish at the edges until the rains return in April. So…the sluice gate is used to top up the *pukur* if it gets too low and also to replenish fish stocks."

Sophie laughed.

"Wait, you're telling me you had them build the tunnel so you wouldn't run out of fish? Uncle Joshua, that's probably the baddest thing I've known you do!"

Her uncle chuckled.

"Honestly, it was not the original intention. I really did think it could help with overflow and, perhaps it does! We opened the gates a couple of times over the last ten years or so, but…yeah…really, I just get my fish topped up."

He shrugged and went back to his fishing. Sophie carried on looking out over the *pukur*. They were silent for about ten minutes and then Sophie spoke again.

"What am I going to do about Adhora? Do you think if I apologised to Mr Haque, he would be calmer now and would let us see each other again?"

"I really don't know Sophie but, I'm sorry to say, I doubt it. He's a stubborn man and very, very proud. When he makes a decision, he tends to stick to it. To his credit, this makes him very honourable, and he is good to his employees, gives generously to the community and keeps his word – something that people often don't do in these parts. But I suspect you're going to have to wait quite a while before you can see her again. You'll have school breaks and lunches – they can't stop you talking then and I'll make sure the headmaster doesn't try."

"Thank you. I'm sorry I'm such a bother."

"You're not, Sophie. We've both had steep learning curves. I like kids in the classroom, but I like my space too. I always did, really. So it was a total shock when your aunt dropped you on me, but it wasn't your fault, and I'm afraid I very much took it out on you."

"It's okay. I don't think I exactly helped either – and it wasn't fair on either of us. But, you know, you're okay, Uncle Joshua – except when annoyed admittedly – but otherwise, you're pretty cool in your own way."

Uncle Joshua chuckled again.

"Damned by faint praise – ha! – I'll take it anyway!"

They both laughed at this.

"What you do need to do though Sophie," he continued, "is embrace the culture more. You need to be here in Bangladesh a lot longer than the few months you have been before you can start to judge. And frankly, the longer you stay here, the less you can work this place out. Which is just as well because judging is never a good idea anyway."

"Don't you find that maddening, though?"

"A little, sometimes. But mostly, no. It's refreshing, and it keeps you humble. This country is a world of contradictions: It's thousands of years old yet was only born in 1971; it has droughts, yet it has floods; it is a rich and fertile green land, yet it is ravaged by poverty; the people are deeply religious, yet it is secular; there are many problems, but there is a great culture and spiritual understanding too. You can spend your life trying to work out the country and the people and, in the end, you still won't work it out."

"How can I fit in then if I can't work the place out?"

"Good questions – I'll tell you when I find out for myself!"

They both laughed again. Sophie liked it when Uncle Joshua laughed. He made a deep sound out of his belly, and it made her smile.

"More seriously, Sophie, learn from *Didi* and *Mashima*. I know you learned a lot of the language from Adhora – which is excellent, very important for understanding the culture because language changes how you think – but you need to learn from Bangladeshis themselves. Both of those ladies are...a little different...but that's no bad thing – and another contradiction of this place: everything is the same, and everything is different. No one person is the perfect example of 'how to be Bangladeshi' – not even Hasan, for all he might think otherwise."

Sophie thought about this. She had spent so much of her first few months just desperately wanting to get back to England and to her aunt – who she still couldn't believe had treated her like this – and she'd paid no thought to try to learn about this country. Now she felt more settled. Indeed, she was torn about leaving one day now that Uncle Joshua had sorted all the paperwork. The urge to go back to her aunt, who, presumably, would still choose her useless husband over her niece, was lessening day by day. It would really hurt to leave *Didi* and Adhora. She didn't even think she'd be glad to leave Uncle Joshua either. Would learning about the culture now be too little, too late? Would it make it worse when she came to leave?

On the other hand, Uncle Joshua doing the paperwork meant that Sophie was now legally entitled to *stay* in Bangladesh. He'd made no recent mention of when she would leave, and Sophie guessed it would not be until August at least. That's more than six months left. It would pay well to learn more about the culture and not get into quite so much trouble.

She decided at that moment that she would take Uncle Joshua's advice and get *Didi* to take her to *Mashima's bari* this afternoon. Then she would ask for help to better understand Bangla culture. Sophie felt certain that *Mashima* would be delighted to tell her just how she should behave. She also wondered if the old woman could have some influence over Adhora's father. If she could be persuaded to speak to him...? It was worth a try.

"Esho."

Sophie wasn't sure if she really believed in magic, but if there was any proof of its existence, it was *Mashima*. *Didi* and Sophie had reached *Mashima's* veranda, and the doors to the rooms were shut. She was sure they had been silent as they'd approached, and yet the old woman had told them to come in as soon as they'd slipped off their sandals and were about to knock.

She had suggested going to *Didi* as soon as she'd returned home from the *pukur* with Uncle Joshua. Amazingly, he'd caught a fish and so was positively jovial. *Didi* had said that should be okay and she would take Sophie over there after clearing up lunch things, which she did. During their walk, Sophie had told her of her plan and, to an extent, how wretched she was feeling without Adhora.

When they entered *Mashima's* room, they saw that three cups were laid out and the *cha* was ready to serve. Sophie had absolutely no idea how her wise old friend did it. It wasn't like *Mashima* never went out or anything. The woman seemed to turn up at the oddest places – and always just when needed. It was an uncanny ability.

"Hello, *Mashima*," she said as brightly as she could.

"Ah, hello, Sophie," *Mashima* replied, "I hear you are the new supermodel for the village."

Sophie's heart sank. *Mashima* knew. Of course, she did. *Mashima* always knew.

"You've heard then," she responded as she sat down on the floor and watched *Mashima* pour out the *cha*. The woman nodded.

"Who hasn't? Hasan *bhai* has not been singing your praises for sure."

"Does everyone hate me now?" Sophie could feel tears welling up.

"Oh – pfft!" *Mashima* waved her hand dismissively, "it's already old news and been nothing more than humorous. Girls and boys have got up to much worse, believe me."

Sophie smiled at this. She thought how much she appreciated *Mashima's* no-nonsense way of talking. Now that she was quite fluent in Bangla, Sophie found it easier to talk to her elderly friend and the two of them, along with *Didi*, used what they called 'Banglish' to speak freely. Every sentence was a mix of both languages and Sophie could never recall afterwards which parts had been more English and which more Bangla.

"I don't know how to 'be' here," Sophie said. "I don't like the way girls have to be under boys here. Boys get away with anything. Girls just have to look at someone wrongly and can be in trouble. That's not how I was brought up. In England, we're taught males and females are equal."

Mashima grunted and nodded her head.

"Yes, yes," she said as she finished pouring and offered plates of *nasta* to both girls. "I know what it is like in your country. It is different here but not different too. There are different ways to be equal. Even Bangladeshis forget this too sometimes."

"Can you teach me about the ways here and help me understand how to be more like a Bangladeshi. I want Mr Haque to see that I can be trusted with Adhora and persuade him to let us be friends again."

"I can teach you what I know about how people think here, yes. But you should be ready to wait a long time before you can see Adhora again. Hasan *bhai* has a head full of concrete – just like your uncle! They should knock their heads together!"

Didi giggled at this and put her hand to her mouth as if to stop herself from doing something naughty. Sophie smiled at her then continued to talk to *Mashima*.

"I find it really hard to accept women being weak in this society," she said.

"What! I don't know *any* weak woman. Who are these weak women of whom you speak child?"

"Well, okay, maybe not weak – but you know what I mean?"

"No, I do not. Tell me!"

"I just mean the way women are expected to get married and serve their husbands all their lives, and daughters have to do everything their fathers tell them."

"No, no, no, no," *Mashima* said, shaking her head vehemently. "This is not how it is. You are still thinking like a westerner. Too much 'me me me.' You don't think like an Asian. You need to understand."

"I want to. Tell me."

And so *Mashima* did. They spoke for the rest of the afternoon together – *Didi* mostly listening and helping to explain words which Sophie didn't quite understand – until the sunlight began to fade a little and *Didi* said they needed to get home so she could finish the cooking for their dinner that night.

Mashima did more than explain to Sophie how to 'think like an Asian.' She told her much of her own life story in doing so.

Westerners say, 'I think; therefore I am,' she said, and the famous expression revealed much about how white people, who live in colder places, think. Everyone thinks as an individual, the solitary hunter, getting what they can to survive alone. But almost every 'warm' country – where people have darker skins and live in warmer climes – the expression was more 'I am because you are.' This, she said, changes everything.

Bangladeshis are communal people; farmers, village dwellers. They depend on each other for support and help in desperate times. It was never about trying to push for riches and fame – these are western ideals and were slowly encroaching here, causing tensions and arguments as they did. No wonder so many were suspicious of anything the white man brings.

"We are a nation born out of suffering and learned from the beginning to need each other," *Mashima* had said to her. By 'born' she had meant the birth of modern Bangladesh in 1971. When *Mashima* was a little girl, the country she knew was the newly formed Pakistan. But Pakistan meant two things – two huge countries separated by the head of India, to which they had been a part, somehow considered to be one because of their Muslim populations. But the two peoples were nothing like each other, she said.

Things had come to a head when East Pakistan fought for independence in 1971. *Mashima* was a young woman then, living contentedly in her small village. Being an albino had meant that marriage was never likely. It might have been different if she had been raised in a city like Dhaka, but in the villages, people would have been too superstitious about taking her on. But this suited her. She was the brightest student in school and had a sharp mind even then. She liked her own company and didn't need anyone else – least of all a man child to have to marry and fuss over.

"And then the war came to our community," she added, "and all former life came to an end."

She watched, helpless, as soldiers came into her village and set fire to everything they could not loot. She watched her father and uncles and brothers shot dead and heard the wails from the women young enough to be dragged into the bushes and 'used' one by one by the men with guns in their hands. The women who were not then tortured, stabbed and murdered chose to join their husbands, brothers and sons by throwing themselves into the fires raging from every home. The prettiest suffered the worst. They would often be taken away to the cantonments – where the soldiers lived – tied to posts and left except when the men wanted to make use of them. Shot if they became too ill and worn.

She had been left because their soldiers had been scared of her. Not certain if she was *bhut* or *rakkosh,* they had left her, not wanting to bring the attention of their deeds to the spirits and demons in the area. Sometimes, superstition can be helpful. It saved *Mashima's* life.

For months she wandered from place to place, clothes torn, desperate for food, often rejected and made to leave. *Mashima* learned her independence not from choice but out of necessity. Like many women, she took up arms and joined the *mukti bahini* – the freedom fighters who struck against the Pak armies for as long as they could. As the year came close to an end, it had felt like this could not go on much longer. The Pak army was better resourced, financed by West Pakistan where the battles were not taking place. East Pakistan – Bangladesh, as it had declared itself – was decimated.

And then the Indian army joined in, and suddenly Pakistan found itself dwarfed by its giant parent with more money, weapons and troops. The government swiftly caved in, and it was all over in two weeks.

By then, *Mashima* had learned all she needed to about life, how to survive in the wild, and, most importantly, what people are really like. She'd seen the most inconceivable evil of brother turn against brother, Muslim against Muslim. She'd also seen the most incredible bravery from men, women and children. There were no weak people to be found in this country, she said with pride. Those of us who survived are the strongest in the world.

But strength didn't mean standing alone. Standing alone means death. Strength is found in unity. When you all work together, then you are strong, she said. There are good marriages and bad marriages in Bangladesh, just as in any other part of the world, but never think that marrying is a weakness.

Sophie did her best to take this in. She was horrified by the details of the war she'd known nothing about. She was astonished by *Mashima's* bravery and inner strength. Most of all, she came away with at least an inkling that there wasn't just one way to look at things, to look at people, other cultures. She would never have thought of the idea that working to serve your community could be a strength. Suddenly her English lifestyle seemed so empty and cold. She wondered, why were they always told to pursue money and possessions? Who said that these things would bring happiness? Most of her friends seemed pretty miserable for most of the time. Looking back, she found it hard to think when she'd seen any Bangladeshi – even those who were clearly very poor in outer-lying villages – look remotely sad. Angry, yes; grief over death, yes. But discontent with life? Never.

For the first time in her life, Sophie realised that the peace from the *pukur* wasn't just there. It was all over the land, and it was well earned by the people who lived in it.

CHAPTER TWENTY-THREE — Birthday

By the time February ended, the sun was back with such a vengeance that people hardly realised they'd ever missed it during *sheetkal* time. By March, the yellow orb was scorching everything, and everyone thought of it, again, as the enemy. For the Shepherd household (as Sophie increasingly thought of as her home), the lovely 'perfect British summer' was over, and now both Sophie and Uncle Joshua made slow dashes – for there was no other way to move but slowly in this heat – from home to school to minimise the time spent directly in the heat.

Sophie was given very little opportunity to see Adhora and the pain never left either of them. They had been separated from each other in classes according to Hasan Haque's demands, but Uncle Joshua had stepped in to make sure no teachers interfered during the breaktimes. As a result, the girls got barely fifteen minutes together each day, at most, when they had been used to spend as much of the day together as possible. Weekends were the worst for with Uncle Joshua spending most of his time either reading in his study or at the *pukur;* Sophie only had *Didi* to talk to or, when she had time to take her, *Mashima* as well.

For most of the time, this was okay. Sophie was satisfied with her own company, and she would often go for walks around the permitted boundaries of the village and surrounding fields. The rule was, essentially, if she remained in sight of the home or workplace of someone known to her family, then she was okay. She always covered up and knew enough about the ways of the community to stay safe – and she had enough Bangla to ward off any stranger who took too keen an interest in her.

But she never stopped aching for her friend or blaming herself for being so selfish and behaving so recklessly. Adhora's mother picked up Adhora from school every day and took her home. Adhora wasn't even allowed to look at her as she left to say goodbye. It broke Sophie's heart.

One Saturday morning, mid-March, Sophie returned home from one of her walks only to find Uncle Joshua standing on the doorstep brandishing an umbrella and his fishing bag, evidently waiting for her arrival.

"Come on," he said, "I have an errand for us to do."

"Does it have to be now?" Sophie complained, "I've only just come home, and I'm hot."

She reached for the front door handle. Her uncle dived at her hand and pulled her away.

"No!" he said, surprising Sophie with the urgency, "I need your help right now. Come one!"

She sighed and, knowing that she could do nothing about it, resignedly followed Uncle Joshua out and into the *began* area behind the *pukur*.

"What are we doing here?" she asked as he put down the box and opened it to reveal empty jars.

"We," he said, staring up into a tree, "are going to collect bait for fishing with."

"Seriously. You've taken me away from home for this? That's not funny, Uncle Joshua."

"Trust me, this will be educational," he dismissed her complaint and picked up the umbrella to open it. At that point, Sophie could see that it was not a standard umbrella. Where there should have been a handle, there was a straight and pointed stick. It looked more like a weapon.

"I literally have no idea what you're doing," Sophie said, arms crossed.

"This, my cynical young ward, is my secret tool for getting ant eggs. They make excellent bait!"

"Ants eggs? I don't much fancy the idea of that, Uncle." Sophie involuntarily took a step back.

"Don't worry," he laughed, "I'll do the collecting. All I need you to do is open the jars, help me funnel them in and then get the lids on. It's easy, trust me!"

Sophie was less than convinced.

"Watch," he said, opening a jar and putting it at the base of the tree and then picking up the umbrella again. He held it so the stick pointed upwards, and the open canvas was in his hands like a bowl. "So, you see the nest up there just over that branch? I simply poke the stick into it...like this... and there you go!"

Sophie squealed as a shower of ants came down and landed in the umbrella bowl.

"You see?" her uncle said triumphantly, "help me funnel them in. Quickly. The ants don't matter so much, but it's the eggs we need." He curved the fabric inwards to make a slide and tipped it towards the jar. Sophie, tentatively, helped to fold the canvas inwards. She watched as large ants and white eggs tumbled into the jar. She didn't like Bangladeshi ants – they were several times larger than British ants and bit with a nasty venom that felt very much like a bee sting. It didn't happen often, but she always knew when one had bitten her. It was excruciating.

They finished funnelling the ants and eggs into the jar, then Uncle Joshua closed the lid and held the jar up for Sophie to see.

"There you go!" he said proudly. "Piece of cake."

"Okay," Sophie conceded, "that didn't seem so bad."

"Good. Two more jars to fill. Next one!"

He began the process again as Sophie picked up another jar from his bag, took off the lid and laid it on the ground while he poked at the nest. Another flurry, and they held each side of the umbrella to slide the scurrying insects, eggs and larvae into the jar. She scooped the lid on top and grinned as she held it up for her uncle to see.

"Excellent!" he said, delighted. "One more."

She reached for the bag to get the last jar as her uncle began to poke again. Then she heard an almost cartoon-like twang followed by "Son of a...for the love of bloody god...."

She turned to see that the noise she had heard was that of the spring mechanism to the umbrella breaking and the bowl deflating, just as a shower of ants rained down. Uncle Joshua, who'd been standing directly beneath, was now dancing around shaking his coat and simultaneously trying to brush ants from his hair.

Sophie did her best not to giggle as he cursed and flung his arms around. He soon had his coat off and stood, bent over, vigorously shaking his white hair.

"Are you okay, Uncle Joshua?" she asked after a while, hoping he couldn't hear the smirking in her voice.

"Umm…" he said, standing up, "I think so, yes. I think we might leave it there, Sophie. We've got enough, I think." He kicked the umbrella. "I think I need a new one. Clearly, that one is too old for the job now. Oh well."

"Did any of the ants bite you?" she asked as he collected jars back into his bag. He looked at her uncertainly.

"I think I may have received one or two, yes. I shall check more carefully in the privacy of my bathroom later. For now, we'd better get back. You go ahead, my girl. Don't wait for me."

Sophie set off without complaint. She was sweating from the sun, even under the tree's shade, and was looking forward to a nice glass of water from the fridge when she got in. She reached home, kicked off her sandals in the porch area and then entered the front room.

She almost screamed as she stepped through the door and was greeted with shouts of "Happy birthday!" from within.

The front room was filled with people. *Didi* was there, holding a cake, and so was *Mashima,* who, clearly out of her comfort zone, skulked at the back near the doorway, half hiding behind it. Several of Sophie's classmates stood there too, along with many neighbours, people from *Didi's* village and a couple of Sophie's favourite teachers.

Her uncle shuffled in behind her and chuckled at her reaction. "Happy birthday, *amar maye,*" he said, giving her a quick but loving sideways hug.

On the wall hung a huge banner. It had been handmade – clearly decorated by several different hands – and it said:

HAPY BIRTH DAY SOPIE

Sophie had not even thought about it being her birthday. The thought had not even crossed her mind. Last year, she had been in hospital, still in a coma, and her thirteenth had passed by without any recognition. Whilst she had been in Bangladesh, she had very little concept of dates and times. Just the seasons seemed to matter. She knew it was March – her birthday month – but only vaguely. She laughed at the surprise of everyone being there but also that she hadn't even thought once about becoming fourteen.

Uncle Joshua whispered into her ear. "Sorry about the spelling on the banner. I didn't know they were going to do that until this morning while you were out and they put it up. *Didi* wrote it – don't let on, she'll be devastated."

"It doesn't matter," Sophie replied, "I think it's wonderful."

"Perhaps, but still not a great advert for my teaching abilities, I think!"

She grinned at him then asked, "Is this why you took me to get ant eggs? To keep me out of the *bari* while they finished getting ready?"

He looked at her with mock surprise. "I don't know what you're talking about," he winked.

The party was genuinely delightful for Sophie. Everyone made a fuss of her. Cake was cut, and *Didi*, as was the tradition, fed her the first mouthful. *Nasta* and refreshing cold fizzy lemonade were served, and Sophie was given gifts by everyone, which she opened later after everyone had gone. The gifts were cheap and, by Western standards, pretty awful – mugs, pens, sweets and *khatas*, all of which you could buy from the nearest *dokan* for very little *taka*. But for Sophie, they were the best gifts ever. She knew how poor some of her class friends were, and she was grateful for their efforts.

After a couple of hours, the guests started leaving. *Mashima*, despite keeping well out of the way, was the last to go. She hugged Sophie just as she left and looked deep into her eyes.

"You are growing," she said, almost as if criticising. Sophie was now an inch or so taller than her. "You won't be a child much longer. Don't forget that."

"I won't, *Mashima*, I promise you. I'll be okay with your help and kindness."

"Ha!" cried the old woman as she turned to leave. "Kindness! Ha!"

Sophie shut the door as she left and leaned against it. A sudden wave of sadness hit her in the empty room. She helped *Didi* clear things up and then went quietly to her room. She sat on her bed and heard a tap on her window.

"*Sophie!*" a voice whispered.

She jumped to her feet and rushed to her window.

"Adhora? Is that you?" she whispered back.

"Yes. Shush! I had to see you on your birthday. I've managed to get away from everyone, but I only have a few minutes."

"Oh, thank you so much! I'm really happy to see you." Sophie had moved the mosquito screen over so that she could reach her fingers out between the window bars. Adhora did the same, and the two clasped hands.

"I wanted to give you this," Adhora said, passing an envelope to her. "It isn't much, but it was all I could do. Happy birthday my lovely Sophie. I've got to go."

"Already? Really?"

"Yes, yes. I must. If they see me up here on your veranda, I think my father might actually explode and fly to the moon!"

The two of them giggled, and Adhora broke away from their grasping hands. Sophie closed the screen again before too many mosquitoes could get in and looked out as Adhora quickly descended the steps and ran off.

Sophie looked at the envelope in her hand and tore it open. Inside was a birthday card, beautifully handmade and filled with folded pieces of paper. In the card was a message from Adhora:

My dearest, darling Sophie,

Happy birthday to the best friend a girl could ever hope for. Don't blame yourself for what happened – but I miss you every day. I know we don't get to see each other outside of school, and I don't think Baba is likely to change his mind any time soon. So – I've written you little notes so that on weekends you can open one each day to have a few words of love from me. There's enough to keep you going until summer, and then I shall write you some more, inshallah. It's better than nothing, and at least then you might not forget me, which would be the worst thing EVER. Read them to remember me. Your ever-loving and faithful best friend.

Sophie cried and laughed at the same time as she read the card and looked at all the folded pieces. It must have taken Adhora hours of work, and she would have had to be very sneaky to keep them all hidden from her family and *ayah*. Sophie was impressed! But she was also very, very grateful.

"I won't forget you, I promise," she said quietly. "Best friends forever."

Coming downstairs again, Sophie found Uncle Joshua in his study. He was frowning at the newspaper, but he looked up and smiled kindly at her.

"Did you enjoy your party?" he asked, inviting her to sit down.

"Yes, I did. Very much. Thank you for arranging it," she replied, sitting on one of the chairs.

"*Bapre!* No, don't thank me for that. It was *Didi's* doing, of course. I just gave my consent."

"Well, thank you all the same. Are any of the ant bites still hurting?"

Uncle Joshua winced a little. "There are *one or two* which are slightly uncomfortable," he admitted, "but let's not talk about that."

Sophie smiled and agreed, then asked him what he was frowning about when she came in.

"Oh," he said, picking up the paper and turning it around for Sophie to see. There was a picture of a tiger behind cage bars. "Remember that tiger that was caught several months ago? You remember you felt quite sorry for it? Well, you'll be pleased to learn the little devil has managed to escape from the zoo where it was sent."

"Oh cool!" said Sophie, "I hated the idea of the poor creature locked up like that. Wild animals should be wild."

"Well, that may be so, Sophie, but that zoo is not too far from us. Which means, however unlikely it is, that you need to be careful when going out alone until they catch this creature again."

"You think it will come here?" Sophie gasped.

"I don't, no. This area is too flat, too open. She'll want much more forest land than we have, I would think. But…" he leaned forward and stared at Sophie directly, "…I don't want to take any risks. They'll catch it soon enough. But don't stray far, Sophie. So far, she's only got a taste for goat meat. I'm not keen for her to savour white girl flesh, if it's all the same to you."

"Okay, I'll be careful, Uncle Joshua. The tiger is a she?"

"I don't know, actually but, I'm assuming she is."

"Why?"

He looked at her with a smirk.

"Well, she keeps outwitting the men. Must be a woman!"

CHAPTER TWENTY-FOUR - TIGER

The *bagh* was the talk of the area. Whereas the news last year had been interesting but nothing more – for the tiger was very far from these parts – now no one could think of anything else. Only *Mashima* seemed completely at ease.

"*Ore!*" she would say, shaking her head. "A tiger has got to eat like anyone else. If he needs to eat me, then he will eat me. After all, if I will eat a chicken because I am hungry, then why shouldn't I accept that something might eat me one day too?"

Most villagers, however, didn't take the same view and were keen that none of their families got eaten. Even more importantly – for some of the men, anyway – the goats and cows needed to be safe. After all, you can easily get another wife and make more children. Such men would get a scolding – especially from their mothers – for saying such things, but there was a degree of truthfulness and honesty to their words. Either way, people were worried, and men typically found lounging and gossiping outside *dokans* drinking *cha* and eating fried *nasta* would now be found sharpening sticks to use as weapons and preparing bows and arrows or guns if they had them.

The children at the school, of course, were giddy with both excitement and fear. The younger ones were most excitable, having little concept of the danger a tiger could pose. The older ones split firmly down the middle; the girls were terrified, and the boys were full of bravado, fighting tigers heroically in the playground or dying trying.

Sophie, however, was rather indifferent and really couldn't see what the fuss was all about. It had been nearly two months since the newspapers had announced the beast's escape, and even though reported sightings were all over the *bibhag* – which made this the fastest, physics-defying tiger ever – strangely, no one had claimed to see it in their *upazila*. It would also be the fattest tiger ever, too as claims of goats being snatched in the night and eaten abounded despite the fact a tiger could survive for a week on just one goat if it were large enough. All this told her that everyone was making a rather big fuss over nothing. Even so, she only took walks now with *Didi* when she had the time and didn't stray too far from home.

Her greater concern, though, was for the great cat itself. It turned out that Uncle Joshua was annoyingly correct: the tiger was a female. He had delighted in this once it was revealed by the press and would make some joke or comment almost every day about the deviousness of women. Still, he had a point – the cat had avoided capture, and men were the ones attempting it. Sophie worried that as time went on, the animal might be killed rather than caught. It upset her greatly to think of this. For some reason, she felt a great affinity with her and desperately hoped she would be caught humanely.

The only thing she had in her favour was that tigers were an endangered species. Sophie had done her research in the school library, and from what she could tell, there were less than five hundred tigers left in the country. Even Sophie knew this was a pitifully small number and she hoped that those in charge of trying to capture her would bear this in mind. But what about locals, though? She saw those men sharpening their sticks and cleaning their rifles; these sights made her most afraid. Deep within her, she was rooting for the animal.

One day, Sophie came home from school to find her uncle had beaten her home – which was unusual as he usually worked for another hour at school before returning.

"Have a seat, Sophie," he said, a serious look on his face. She felt the blood drain from her face. *What have I done wrong?* she wondered, wracking her mind for anything she could have done by accident. She sat down

Uncle Joshua looked intently at her.

"We need to go to Dhaka," he said.

"Why?"

"Because it is the only place we can get official passport-type photos done. We need them to complete your paperwork for going home."

But this is home, Sophie thought but just said, "Oh, okay. Sure."

Uncle Joshua continued looking at her.

"You're okay about this, Sophie?"

"Yes, yes. Of course," she lied, now feeling the blood rushing back to her cheeks too much. "Honestly. Yes. I guess there's still lots of preparation you have to do for it all so I can go back in the summer."

Her uncle looked relieved and turned slightly away as if starting to get on with whatever the next thing was he had to do.

"Yes, indeed. June isn't far away. When school ends near the end of the month, there will be nothing to keep you here. So you might as well go in July and get away before the summer gets ridiculously hot again. I'll get us train tickets, and we can go down at the weekend. *Inshallah,* we won't miss a day of school."

"Great," said Sophie, "is that everything?"

"Yes, of course. Why? Anything else we need to talk about?"

"No," she said, standing and started walking towards the stairs, "nothing at all."

Sophie ran up to her room, shut the door and sat on her bed. For a long while, she just stared at the wall, unable to think or feel anything; she just felt numb. There was nothing she could do, really. She had no right to stay in Bangladesh, and it didn't make any sense to try. Uncle Joshua wouldn't want to 'bring her up,' and there was no way she could do things alone here. But, at least in the UK she would get an education paid for. And she could probably be fostered by another family if Aunty Hannah wouldn't take her back. That wouldn't be so bad, would it? And it would only be for a couple of years. Then, once she was sixteen, she could get a job and a place of her own and live alone and....

She had to stop herself. Sophie gave herself a shake. "Get a grip, girl," she said, mimicking Uncle Joshua's voice. "You're British. Stiff upper lip and all that!"

But in her heart, she felt caught in a deep hole with no chance of getting out.

Excitement reached fever pitch, though, when the 'tiger catcher' came to school and gave a talk to all the students. They all gathered together in the Assembly Room where they started the week each Sunday, singing the National Anthem (usually pretty badly – the melody was so complex that not even the teachers could agree on how it was supposed to go) and would then have some moralistic story presented by staff who begrudgingly took it in turns each week to attempt presenting something which the six-year-olds and sixteen-year-olds would find relevant; equally inevitably, they always failed.

Uncle Joshua also had to do this occasionally though the discomfort on his face perhaps made sure his name occurred less often on the rota. When he had to do an assembly, he always made sure he spent most of the time making the kids laugh or amaze them with something visual and then finish with something vaguely moralistic like 'don't go running off' and leave it at that.

But when the tiger-catcher came, the usually bored faces were all attention. Everyone had questions they wanted to ask.

His name was Puli. He was Indian rather than Bangladeshi, and he reminded Sophie – quite painfully, as she missed him so much – of Aatiq. He was tall, thin, quite good-looking, and she guessed he was in his late thirties. He had the looks of a young man but the confidence of one older. While she was as interested as everyone else to hear what Puli would tell them about the tiger, her mind would drift off to think of the *Sundarbans*, boats and the handsome Aatiq.

Puli – his hair was long but not as long as Aatiq's, Sophie noticed – started off with lots of pictures on boards showing tigers at various angles. She noticed that his Bangla sounded somehow smoother or more cultured than what she was used to and wondered if they spoke it differently in India. He explained that despite the headmaster's introduction as 'The Tiger Catcher,' he was an environmentalist who specialised in the Royal Bengal tiger, found predominantly in the *Sundarbans* region, which spanned both Bangladesh and India. Although he was in the area as part of a team hoping to 'rescue' the tiger, he was not a specialist in catching the animals.

"And there are two good reasons for this," he said. "Firstly, we try to allow tigers the freedom to be themselves without getting involved – these wonderful animals are so very fragile with so few left in the world. We try to avoid disrupting them. Secondly, there's no likely danger of the tiger coming to your area. I doubt very much you have anything to worry about. Tigers are shy creatures and do their best to keep away from humans."

This was met with a mixture of relief and disappointment among all the eighty or so children sitting on the concrete floor, largely depending on their sex. It didn't stop the barrage of questions, though – how large are tigers? How much do they eat? How long does it take to eat a human? How do you kill a tiger? Can you outrun a tiger? What should you do if you meet one in the wild? What do they do at night time? Do they hate the rain like dogs do?

Puli did his best to answer as many as he could: they don't eat as much as you might think – a goat could last them days; he had no idea how long it would take to eat a human and hoped he'd never find out (this brought an eruption of laughter from all); you try not to kill tigers if you can but if you had to then with a gun and, most importantly, quickly (more laughter); you couldn't outrun a tiger for long – every muscle in their body is built for speed – but most likely you'd never need to because tigers stalk their prey, so the chances are you wouldn't see one until it was too late (immediate gasps and a wince from Puli realising this wasn't a sensible thing to say); in the wild, if you see one, hope that it is asleep and move away very, very quietly – they have incredible hearing; at night time they hunt – their eyes are just as good as their ears and they are experts at stalking, so don't go out at night!; and no, they don't dislike rain – living in the *Sundarbans*, tigers are expert swimmers and don't mind rain at all, although they probably wouldn't choose to hunt during a torrential downpour.

Sophie raised her hand to ask a question. When Puli saw her, he looked slightly startled. She knew full well he wasn't expecting to see a white girl and she smiled to herself that she had attracted his attention. He nodded to her to ask her question.

She took a deep breath and, feeling suddenly very nervous, hoped she got her Bangla right.

"Is it true that you can scare a tiger away by running at it and shouting loudly?" There were titters around the room, but Sophie hoped they were because even her classmates found it funny to hear her speak Bangla rather than her accidentally saying something silly. She was still wincing inside from asking *Didi* the other day for a kiss instead of a spoon by mixing up two similar-sounding words, *chumu* and *chamoch*.

"Oh wow! Excellent Bengali," Puli said in flawless English. To Sophie's annoyance, he continued in English. "Yes, you are right; tigers can be startled and will run away at the first sign of confrontation with men. But, if they think you are weak, then you have just run up to them and said 'eat me!'" Again, huge laughs. "But if you had to try this – and I don't recommend it at all, and I certainly wouldn't try it! – then, don't forget to stare at their eyes to intimidate them. Never look at the ground. Never show weakness or…they will *pounce!*"

At this, he leapt at one of the smaller girls on the front row. She screamed, and everyone, including the girl, laughed hysterically.

Whether or not Puli put minds at rest at the school wasn't easy to ascertain. But the children did go back to their *baris* and excitedly told their parents at least some versions of what he had said, so some of it trickled upwards to the parents and then on to relatives. One way or another, the excitement about the tiger abated. With assurances that it wouldn't bother coming to their region, men stopped sharpening weapons and cleaning guns. Life returned at least partly to normal.

Only during the night did they remain on high alert, and even that calmed a little after one of the local elders found himself on the end of a rifle held by one overzealous and nervous young man after appearing out of some trees. The youth had his gun confiscated with a cuff around the ears and, the next night, the local elders had banned the carrying of guns. No one wanted to be mistaken for a tiger.

Sophie, though never forgot the beast. Her dreams now often featured the animal. They were always hunting her but, when caught and trapped in a cage, Sophie would always come to look through the bars and see her own eyes, her own face, staring back. Confused, she would look at her hands to see if she was still herself and see paws and striped fur instead of human limbs. She would realise anew, no matter how many times the dream returned, that it was actually Sophie who had been trapped, and the tiger was still at large. But no one would listen, and no one seemed to care.

CHAPTER TWENTY-FIVE – GOING HOME

If you want to be rich
There you'll have to cheat
"Live honestly and help others"
That's what they profess
If you live honestly,
You'll never get rich.
Don't just listen to my words
Look at the rich and you'll see…

– Nochiketa

Sophie looked up from the book she had been reading and surveyed the scene before her, momentarily unnerved by a sense of dèjá vu. She'd seen this all before, so clearly, so exactly the same. The only difference this time was how hot and sweaty everything and everyone was because it was June now instead of December. But the carnage, the chaos, the noises and the mayhem – and any other adjective you might choose to describe the last day of term – was the same as it always was at Christmas time.

Ruefully, Sophie thought that there was perhaps one other difference: Adhora was not by her side, and they were not preparing an outrageous performance on the stage together. Adhora was there in the Assembly Room, of course, along with most of the school, getting into costumes and finding swords, boxes, banners and many other bits and pieces needed to turn that small stage into a palace, a classroom, a jungle or whatever else was necessary for all their performances.

The ban against the two girls was still firmly in place – the headmaster never slipping in enforcing Adhora's father's wishes to the letter – even after it was announced that Sophie was leaving as soon as term finished. The girls were still not even allowed to sit near each other in class and could do little other than give each other a sheepish smile as they moved from classroom to classroom.

They caught little snatches of time together at break time, but Adhora always seemed so busy with other friends and, in particular, Mahfuza had made intimations of friendship towards the girl. Sophie knew this was simply to exact revenge against her; Mahfuza had no real interest in Adhora at all, but she was still powerful and well-connected, and Adhora couldn't say no. Sophie hated it, but there was nothing either of them could do. She didn't blame Adhora, especially as Sophie would soon be gone and all protection for her friend would then be over. She knew Adhora needed to 'be in with the cool kids' if her life wasn't going to be hell next year.

She moved through the crowded room and couldn't help but tearfully reminisce about how wonderful it had all seemed last Christmas. It was almost like a repeat performance with everyone excitedly practising their lines and their moves. Sophie had opted out of performing this time, and as she was leaving, no teacher made a fuss about this. So, Sophie was able to watch and help others get dressed or practise their lines with the scripts and so on. She was glad she didn't have to prepare anything herself, but it did make her feel left out on the fringes of school life.

After the concert tonight, they would all receive their reports and find out just how they did in the exams taken just a month before. Sophie was nervous about this. Her mid-year report last November hadn't been brilliant, but everyone admitted that she'd done well considering she'd lost six months of lessons last year *and* changed both schools and curriculums. Nevertheless, she hated getting less than an A in any subject.

She'd managed a few A grades – English, of course, plus maths and science, which had been very similar to what she learned in England – and a handful of B grades which she would live with. History, though, which she prided herself on, had come out as a C, and she hadn't forgiven herself about that. She wanted to scrub out the shame she felt about the grade even though most of the test had been about Bangladesh history, and no one had expected her to do well in this anyway. She had worked hard on her Bangla history and made sure she knew her dates and names. The *Mughal* Empire had been her favourite, and it *had* come up in the test. She only hoped it had been enough.

Earlier that day, she had been given a special leaving party at school. The whole school had gathered in the Assembly Room (before rehearsals had begun for the evening and the room was cluttered with clothes and props). Sophie had sat on a chair at the front of the whole school and, class by class, they had come up to present her with homemade cards saying goodbye and wishing her well for the future. 'Don't forget us!' many of the cards had said, and these messages had left her both happy and desperately sad. They had brought in *nasta* and cake for everyone to share, and Sophie felt for much of the time as if she was watching this all take place from a distance. At times she wondered if the whole day wasn't just one of her dreams and wouldn't have been surprised if she'd suddenly found herself at the *pukur* again or in a cage screaming silently.

But no cage or pool appeared and the day moved on far too speedily for her liking. Sophie and her uncle would be taking the night train down to Dhaka soon after the school concert was over, and there was nothing she could do now to end it.

Uncle Joshua, who also hadn't seemed quite himself for several days now, had decided they would spend two days down in Dhaka before he took her to the airport. *Didi*, he had decided, would not be coming with them. She was already half-sobbing all the time in the kitchen when preparing meals, and every time she looked at Sophie, she became teary-eyed.

"I'm not going to cope with Dhaka if we have that melodramatic woman weeping hysterically all the time," he'd said, more aggressively than usual, "she'll drive me mad!"

The time for the concert came. The crowd gathered. Those who knew Sophie and knew she was going made a point of chatting to her and wishing her well. She looked around the marquee, marvelling again at how swiftly Bangladeshis put these things up and made them look so beautiful and thought how she wouldn't see another school concert or go to a wedding or enjoy any of the many festivals she'd experienced while living here. She'd made numerous promises that she would return, come back to visit everyone, but despite Uncle Joshua going to great lengths to make sure she knew she was always very welcome to visit, Sophie knew they both knew she wouldn't come back. No matter how important Bangladesh had proven to be, life in England would soon take over again and eventually, she'd only think of the place as a strange and distant memory. She knew how these things worked.

The performances came and went in a blur. Sophie sat with *Didi* and Uncle Joshua at the back, enjoying the show, but, in truth, she barely registered who was on stage until the call came for all the students to gather on stage for the awarding of their reports and certificates.

Sophie found herself on stage, lined up in a row with her class. By pure coincidence, she ended up next to Adhora. Neither girl dared to look at the other, aware that Adhora's parents were in the audience, but, standing near the back and so at least half-hidden, they snatched at each other's hands and entwined fingers for as long as they could. This, Sophie knew, was their goodbye to one another. Silent, wordless, but perfectly communicated, their bond was still there, which was enough for them both.

Envelopes were handed out one by one as names were called, and each student came to shake hands with the headmaster and receive their report. He barely looked at Sophie as he handed her the envelope and shook her hand, but Sophie didn't care. Her attention was entirely on the report.

As soon as the kids were all allowed to shuffle off the stage after joyful applause from the audience, Sophie tore into her envelope and opened the report. A few seconds silence and then a *"Yes!"* shouted under her breath: she got her A – all of them, in fact, were A grades. The universe was back on track again after all.

Standing on the railway station two hours later was something of an anti-climax. Uncle Joshua stood comfortably at ease while Sophie was more wary. Despite the late hour of the evening, the local station still had hundreds of *deshis* milling around and many who passed by noticed the pair of them. Some of the men would walk by and then return to stand directly in front of them, staring, saying nothing. Her uncle seemed oblivious, but Sophie hated it – especially when some of them looked not at her face but about a foot lower; or when a crowd of men, women and children would build up. They would all stand there, staring and saying nothing.

When the crowds built up, eventually either Uncle Joshua would awake from his thoughts and mutter something quietly in Bangla at them to shoo them all away. This was only partially successful at best. More often, it was the station master with his *lathi* raised in hand who would come, shouting obscenities at the crowd – mainly directed at the women and children – and see to it that they all ran off and left these *boro loks* alone; at least for a few minutes anyway. And so the cycle continued for the two hours they waited for their train. It was running late, which was no surprise.

"I've waited six hours for a train before today," Uncle Joshua told her, chuckling as he reminisced. "I hope that doesn't happen again tonight. Two to three hours is normal. Once, the train came, and they had completely forgotten to add the first-class carriage, and I was squeezed between a mullah and a woman carrying a goat in a carriage so full that even the aisle was filled with people standing. Happy days…"

Rather than dwell on the awful prospect of waiting many more hours to then stand in a cramped carriage, Sophie let herself think back over saying goodbye to *Didi*. It had been one of the most painful moments of her life.

When they had come home from the school concert, Uncle Joshua had asked for a cup of *cha* before they left for the station. *Didi* had gone to the kitchen and Sophie had followed her in. *Didi* wouldn't speak, wouldn't talk to her, and, worst of all, wouldn't smile. It seemed so wrong for her not to have a smile on her face, those perfect white teeth shining out with radiant joy.

Didi had made the drinks in silence, and when they were done, Sophie couldn't bear it any longer. Stepping up close behind her, she said, "*Didi* – please…."

Her friend spun around to face her, burst into tears and hugged Sophie tightly, wailing as she did so. As if crying was contagious, Sophie too burst into tears and hugged *Didi* back, her whole body flooding with pent-up emotion she hadn't realised until then had been there all along. The girls hugged and hugged without saying a word, just holding each other and caressing their hair.

Uncle Joshua, eventually, popped his head into the kitchen, wondering where his drink was. His face dropped at the spectacle and then, after a moment of indecision, crept into the room, past the girls and grabbed all three mugs of *cha* quietly. He left the room and placed them on the dining table, taking his own to his chair so he could read the paper one last time before they left.

Sophie caressed *Didi's* head again and whispered, "I promise I will come back and see you again. It's not forever *Didi*. We'll see each other again."

She hated herself as she said it. She had no idea if it was true or not. She had no idea what her future held for her and if returning would ever be possible. *Didi* released her grip, pulled away, nodded – but without looking at Sophie – and turned back to the stove to tidy up. Her face seemed to say, *I know you will not, but I accept your attempt to say it will be so.*

When Sophie and Uncle Joshua came to leave, they took the long path to the main road and *Didi* walked with them. They found a *vangari* and loaded themselves onto the back. *Didi* remained behind. She gave Sophie one last sad smile and hugged her briefly again.

"Be good," *Didi* said, brushing Sophie's cheek with the back of her hand.

"I will never forget you," Sophie said in return. "You were my friend when I had no one, and you saved me. I love you and will always have you in my heart."

They touched foreheads together, then the *vangari* set off, pulling them apart. The twenty minutes or so it took to get to the station were largely spent in silence. The crickets were chirruping loudly, and fireflies danced in the fields as they sped past. With her feet dangling over the back, Sophie looked out on the village as it receded into the distance in the blackness of the night.

Overhead, miles away, odd flashes told her that a storm was coming. It was silent and mysterious now, but she knew these storms would creep up in this way until they let loose all the crashes and flashes of hell itself. She hoped she would be on the train by then. She was in no mood to be soaked, no matter how refreshing the rain might be.

In the end, the train wasn't six hours late, and they did indeed beat the storm, nor was any carriage missing. Sophie and her uncle bundled themselves into the correct carriage and a two-berth first-class cabin. The train itself looked as if it were sixty years old. Although it was pulled by a diesel engine, it had all the feeling of a steam train rumbling into the station. It was dirty and smelly, but at least the cabin was just for them, and they could lock the door.

Tired, they both decided to sleep. Uncle Joshua took the lower bunk and Sophie climbed up to the top. From there, she was able to peek over the curtains to look out of the window. She could see nothing for most of the time, but whenever they pulled into a station, she was able to see the people who milled around there. Each time, it was just like their own station – many dozens of people, carrying cases, clothes, selling food or holding drinks, shouting and gossiping as though it were the middle of the day. It amazed her that Bangladesh never slept. And with that thought, Sophie fell fast asleep herself.

The journey to Dhaka was a good ten hours or more of travelling, so when Sophie woke up in the morning, they had not arrived. Once Uncle Joshua had woken up, Sophie climbed down and used the lower bunk as their seat. Sophie got to look out of the window and catch her last glimpses of the country. Uncle Joshua left the cabin to try and find *cha* and something to eat for breakfast.

Breakfast secured – fried chicken wings and some kind of patty that neither could identify as potato or fish or anything else – they supped their *cha*, ate what they could and read books. Occasionally they chatted. Mostly, Sophie watched the world go by the window.

If Bangladesh had always seemed busy to Sophie for the last few months, it turned up the action when they arrived at Dhaka. She had forgotten just how crazy the city was. The station platform heaved with bodies. Uncle Joshua took both of their suitcases and shoved his way through the crowd to give Sophie a chance of not being squashed behind him. She kept close and pushed her elbows out to keep those around her at bay a little.

They finally made it out of the station, where a new crowd of men gathered around them – offering taxis, CNG baby taxis or *rickshaws*. Sophie let her uncle do the talking and bartering but discovered he played the part of 'grumpy *bideshi*' far more vigorously here than at home. Flurries of conversation with lots of fingers sticking up in the air to represent fees, followed by angry shakes of head and Uncle Joshua dismissively marching off to the next would-be chauffeur. Eventually, they found a man who was brought down to a price Uncle Joshua would accept.

Joining the traffic on the main roads brought Sophie back to all those months ago when she arrived in the country. She felt sick to her stomach remembering that time, all the more so knowing that she was now going straight back to the people who had brought her here. Aunty Hannah would be there at the airport at the other end, Uncle Joshua had told her, and would take her home.

Home. Sophie couldn't even begin to think of what that meant any longer. She felt like a weed that had been snatched and pulled up, roots tearing away in the process. She felt the pain physically in her scars which ached with heat.

It took around an hour for the traffic to slowly shuffle along and for them to reach their destination – a cheap little guest house in what Uncle Joshua assured her was the 'posh' part of the city: Gulshan. All Sophie could see was road after road crammed with dirty skyscrapers or construction sites building new ones.

They booked into the guest house – two reasonably clean rooms, though Sophie could imagine *Didi* tutting and rolling her eyes if she were there. They dumped their suitcases, and Uncle Joshua insisted they go straight out.

"Time to get you adapting to western life again," he said. "I'm going to take you to my club!"

Sophie found it hard to imagine her uncle belonging to a club. She immediately pictured him wearing a tuxedo and smoking a cigar while guffawing outrageously with similarly attired men, and the image made her giggle. She had no idea what a club in Dhaka would look like, but it was something new, and she was up for the adventure. They set off to flag down a *rickshaw*.

When they finally reached the club, down some small and unimpressive dump of a road, Sophie didn't know what to make of it from the outside. It seemed rather small and plain, if she was honest. However, that impression changed when she and her uncle got through the little security booth after the guard had checked her bag and Uncle Joshua had her signed in; then, they stepped into the courtyard of the building itself.

"Wow!" Said Sophie, and Uncle Joshua laughed.

"Welcome to my humble club," he said with mock grandeur. "I call it my little bit of heaven. They do the finest steaks here. You can't beat 'em!"

You couldn't see from the road, over the security fencing, just how long and deep the club was, but the ground sprawled on for some time housing tennis courts, a large gym, a *huge* swimming pool (so Sophie thought), two poolside bars (one at each end), a games area complete with pool table, darts area and a big flat-screen TV permanently tuned to a sports channel – and the main building which housed another, larger, bar, a downstairs area with tables and sofas and a larger upper area which was the main restaurant area.

Sophie guessed that, had she come here when she first arrived in Bangladesh last year, she would have found it less impressive. It wasn't *that* big and certainly wasn't shiny and new. But after nearly a year in a village with barely functioning electricity and almost no Western influence at all, this place was a dream oasis. The pool even looked *weird* to Sophie – it was blue and clear rather than off–green and sludgy as the *pukur* looked pretty much all year.

"I think I'm going to like it here," she said to her uncle. He looked at her and put his hand gently on her shoulder.

"I'm sure you will," he said kindly. "Come on, I'll buy you a drink and then we can have some lunch."

They sat at one of the poolside bars, and Sophie giggled at feeling so grown up. She drank a coke while Uncle Joshua had a beer, both straight from the fridge. The air was warm, and no one was in the pool at the time. It looked so inviting, and Sophie wished she had a swimming costume she could wear. Pop music played gently out of speakers overhead, and she could see waiters carrying drinks to various people around the club. There were perhaps twenty people around, Sophie thought, and the place felt deserted; it also felt white. The staff were *deshis,* but all the guests here were white, just like the pair of them. It was very, very strange, Sophie thought.

While her uncle trotted off to find some menus, Sophie rummaged through her bag and pulled out her book in readiness to read it a little while they waited for their dinner. Joshua returned with two cards, one of which he handed to her. He spied the book.

"Good God girl," he laughed, "are you still reading *Wuthering Heights* after all this time?"

Sophie laughed.

"Yes, it did take me a while to get back to reading it, I'll be honest. I'm nearly done now. Just a few more pages to read."

"And? What do you think of it now? Still enjoying the 'solitude' you were so keen on all those months ago?"

Sophie screwed up her face a little and said, "Not so much, I'll confess. I've got so used to people *always* being around in Bangladesh that I think I find those bleak, desolate moors a bit too much now. That said, despite how bad he is, I *do* find Heathcliff a bit of a dish."

Her uncle threw his head back and roared with laughter, causing a couple of people to look up from their drinks and stare at them. Sophie didn't care; she loved to see her uncle laugh. He did it so rarely, but he did seem to more often these days.

"Yes," he laughed, "you're not the first woman to think that. Emily Brontë absolutely nailed it when she created the first 'antihero.' Bad guys have been charming ladies ever since!"

Sophie laughed and looked through the menu to order lunch. She giggled to see British food listed. *Deshi* food was in a separate list at the back; otherwise, it was pies, steaks, chips, pasta and pizzas all the way. The experience was surreal, but Sophie realised how much she had missed this kind of food.

She ordered a pizza while Uncle Joshua ordered a steak, then he bought more drinks – another coke for Sophie and a glass of red wine for himself to go with the steak.

Twenty minutes later, the food arrived, and they moved to one of the dining tables inside the main building. Sophie shivered as she stepped through the air-conditioning, her feet slipping on marble floors. It was all so shiny and luxurious.

"Why have you not brought me here *before?*" she jokingly complained at him. "This is incredible – and look at the food!"

Her pizza sizzled away, and the aroma of cheese made her melt inside. It was divine.

Her uncle laughed. "Well, I do come here once or twice a year – mainly just to keep my membership up-to-date. It's not entirely my kind of scene, if I'm honest. I don't like cities and Dhaka is, let's face it, the *worst* city in the world. The pollution, the noise, the traffic jams. God! And the heat! It must be at least five-ten degrees hotter here than up in the north. It's unbearable."

"This is true," Sophie admitted, "but even so – this!" She held her hands out to display the club.

"It's new for you," he laughed, "but I've been coming here for twelve years at least. I'll admit, I do like to get the occasional steak or shepherd's pie here but…," at this, he patted his stomach, "…you have to be careful not to do it too often, or you could get fat."

Sophie looked at his round belly and giggled. Then she picked up her knife and fork (which in itself was strange after a year of eating with her right hand) and started on her pizza. The taste was every bit as good as the smell had promised and she soon devoured the whole plate.

Once Uncle Joshua had finished too, he took himself off to the toilets and left Sophie sitting quietly at the table. She started to read *Wuthering Heights* but soon became aware of some women talking at a table to the side of her. She kept her reading pose but listened in on their conversation.

There were four of them, and they all had very British accents. One of them, tall, thin and looking to be in her mid-fifties, was regaling the others with a tale.

"…and honestly, I can't tell you how much I despair of her sometimes…."

"Oh, I know what you mean, darling," said one of the others, "mine is forever shirking responsibilities. I don't know why we bother employing them sometimes. You'd think they'd be grateful, really, wouldn't you?"

"Oh completely, Sylvia, I completely agree. I guess we only take them on because this country is so ridiculously dusty and dirty all the time. It's a permanent battle to keep our apartment clean."

A third woman now entered the conversation. "I just wish they weren't all so lazy, though, you know? My maid is always pretending to be sick – at least once a week. I'm very close to sacking her."

"You should be careful, Margaret," the first one replied, "there's a good chance she's stolen something of yours and is selling it when she is supposedly 'ill'!"

"Oh, do you think so, Barbara?" Margaret now said worriedly.

"I do Margaret, I do! These maids, they're all thieves, you know. I have to keep all my money and jewellery locked up and hidden in one of our cupboards. They're absolutely atrocious. You can't trust a single one."

Sophie could feel her cheeks getting hot. She was trying not to look at the women to see who they were, but she knew full well they were talking down about their *ayahs* – people like *Didi*.

"I still can't get mine to cook properly," bemoaned the one called Sylvia. "I'm not joking when I say her bread dough is the worst in the world. Flat as a pancake out of the oven – every time! The trouble is, these *deshis* don't know what bread is supposed to be like, so they get it so wrong *all* the time. It's impossible to teach them."

Uncle Joshua rejoined the table. He was about to say something to Sophie then stopped. He could see she was fuming. She discreetly pointed with her finger towards the women, and he turned to look. It took only a minute or two of listening while finishing the last sips of his wine to appreciate why she was so upset.

The women continued to share stories of how their *ayahs*, cleaners, drivers or landlords had been stupid, ignorant, untrustworthy, or a host of crimes and misdemeanours.

"Come on," he nodded at Sophie, "let's go upstairs to the bar there. There's a nice view of the area."

They went up a flight of stairs leading to another bar and a rooftop dining area. There were around a dozen people in there already, but there were plenty of tables to spare. They got drinks and sat down. Sophie stared at the view. They were high enough to see over the club walls and see far down two roads. The shape of the buildings was somehow more beautiful from this angle.

"Why were those women so mean, Uncle Joshua?" Sophie asked, trying to calm herself.

"In what way did you think they were mean, Sophie?"

"They were talking about Bangladeshis who work for them – people like *Didi* – and accusing them of being stupid and liars and thieves and things. I felt like they were saying it about *Didi*. I had to stop myself from shouting at them."

"Yes, I could see you were holding it in, which is why I suggested we move," Uncle Joshua said, laughing.

"Didn't you feel angry too?"

Her uncle sighed. "I think I used to in the early days. It is easy to feel outrage when you are learning about a people and marvelling at them. We can easily hold new cultures up as holy and perfect just as we can condemn those we don't like as wrong and bad."

"So, you think what they were saying was okay?" Sophie crossed her arms in a huff.

"No, no! Don't get me wrong, Sophie. Their words were unjust, but – well, life isn't black and white."

"You still sound like you're justifying what they said."

"I'm not. But these women are typical of ex-pats – especially British ones. It is very likely they have come because their husbands work here for international firms or NGOs – Non-Governmental Organisations – like charities. There's *a lot* of those in Bangladesh, and rightly so. After the 1971 war, there was a lot of devastation and this country has had to build itself up from scratch. It's done remarkably – but not without a great deal of help. These women are not unlike a grown-up version of how you felt last year: they don't want to be here. And they live in Dhaka *all* the time. They don't know the villages or anything about the culture or history. They're here because they go where their husbands go. Some of them will be gone in six months to another country. Others will suffer living here for years until they can persuade their husbands to retire. I'm not excusing them, but I can imagine their frustration, and I pity them a little."

"Yeah," scoffed Sophie, "it must be hard relaxing here by the pool all the time."

"Be fair," said Uncle Joshua, "we both know Dhaka is pretty awful. They still have to live – and some will work too – in the city, coping with the noise and traffic and dust all the time as well as the heat. We have fields and trees and the beauty and peace of the *pukur* plus the love and gentleness of the villagers – it's easy for us to love the place. Just remember how angry you were to be here. They feel something of that all the time."

Sophie sat thinking for a moment, then said, "Okay, I can accept that to a point. But calling people who work for them those horrible things – that's not fair."

"Again, things aren't always black and white. The fact is, all maids and cleaners are poor – otherwise, they wouldn't do those jobs – and pretty much all westerners here are rich. Even you and I – yes, I know for you we live very frugally, but compared to *deshis*, we have a huge concrete house and live very well indeed. It must be very difficult to come from a home where you have several children to feed and very little money and come to work where you see expensive items and bundles of *taka* sitting around. Sooner or later, people can be tempted."

"But *Didi* doesn't...."

"And nor do most *ayahs*. Bangladeshis have great pride. I remember once seeing a little girl selling nuts to passengers on a train. She was dirty, shoeless and clearly painfully poor. I didn't want nuts, but I tried to offer her money, and she leapt away from me with obvious great offence. I had to buy nuts or give nothing at all. She had her pride. But not everyone has such high morals. We are very, very lucky to have *Didi*. She is very precious indeed."

"I know," Sophie said, feeling sad again. "I will miss her very much."

"So you should," Uncle Joshua smiled. "The fact is, just like in England or anywhere else in the world, you get good people, and you get bad. And sometimes good people do bad things, and bad people are capable of good. It's all very grey, and that is something not everyone can easily see. If all your friends are telling you every day that these people are bad, you end up believing them. It doesn't matter if you have any actual evidence or not. But look at the papers, and you will find plenty."

"Do you not fancy this expat life? How come you didn't teach in a school in Dhaka?"

Uncle Joshua laughed.

"Well, I have had a few offers over the years. But why would I give up my life in our village?"

Sophie picked up his wine glass and shook it.

"For wine and steak?" she said.

Her uncle laughed again.

"Yes, that *is* a temptation! But in the end – no. For all I'm telling you to be reasonable about those elderly miscreants downstairs, if I came here too often, I don't think I'd just lose my rag: I'd commit murder!"

They both laughed at this.

"I can picture you doing it too," Sophie joked.

"You better believe it," her uncle replied with a wink.

They sat for several minutes then, just watching the world go by as they drank their drinks. They saw people come in and leave the club; sometimes, someone would come out in swimwear and splash in the pool. Outside the club, beyond the high walls, they could see Dhaka life continuing. Sometimes traffic suddenly flooding and blocking the roads; other times the cars dissipating and then people would appear again. *Rickshaw wallahs* waiting for rides from the club, chatting to each other; small children picking through litter dumped in piles in the streets, searching for salvageable plastics; maids and garment factory workers going about their business. There was so much life, Sophie realised, even in this city of concrete, metal and noise. There were real people here too.

And with that, Sophie had an epiphany moment. What did she have in common with those women downstairs? What was she really missing about life in England? Where did she really think her heart belonged? She had nothing to lose, so she might as well say it.

"Uncle Joshua, can I ask…"

"Sophie, I wanted to say…."

"Sorry…go on…."

"No, no…you first!"

She smiled. Her moment of dreaded revelation, and they'd managed to talk over each other. That seemed so appropriate for the relationship they'd always had together – a string of misfires. She tried again.

"I wanted to ask…would it be really, really bad if I *didn't* leave Bangladesh? Would that be awful?"

She expected him to be cross or at least an oh-for-heaven's-sake kind of comment. Instead, he smiled.

"Sophie, I was literally just going to say to you – you don't have to go back home if you don't want to."

"Really?"

"Really?"

"Because I think I know now for certain – England isn't my home. I know mum and dad are buried there, somewhere; I don't actually know where and I know I do need to see them one day, but I have nothing there to call home, and I've stopped wanting to be there. I like it here. Well…" she wafted her hands around the club, "…not here, here but Bangladesh."

"I understand you."

"But I didn't want to say because you've spent all that money on a plane ticket and, and, I know you find it hard having me under foot."

Uncle Joshua tilted his head, and his eyes shone with kindness.

"I have been reluctant to say anything because you're so young and I felt a teenage girl needs to be with friends of her own age and culture. But I've known for some time I would rather you stay. I know a hundred times over that *Didi* would!"

Sophie laughed and started crying.

"How silly – I'm so happy I don't know why I'm crying!" she said through the tears. "So, can I stay? Is it too late?"

He reached forward and grasped her hands on the table.

"I will cancel the ticket when we get back to the guest house," he said. "Then I will phone your aunt. I'm pretty certain she's not going to make a big fuss."

"Thank you. Thank you so much."

"And then I will get us a train ticket to go home. We could be back in the village by tomorrow evening."

Sophie now openly wept and stood to her feet. She stepped around the table and hugged Uncle Joshua around the neck tightly. For a moment, his arms blustered around confusedly, and then they settled lightly around his niece. He closed his eyes and smiled.

"We'll review this," he said to her gently. "When and if you feel you want to go back, then we'll make sure you do. I won't keep you against your wishes. Whenever you want to go, you can."

"Okay," she snuffled, "but I won't be wanting to. Just don't lock me in my room again."

They both laughed, and Sophie sat down again.

"I'll try not to," Uncle Joshua promised, "but no promises."

Again, for a short while, they were silent, both wrapped up in their own thoughts. Sophie looked out onto the streets again. The sun was beginning to go down, and there was the rumble of thunder in the distance. It would rain soon, she thought. Now there was something different in all that she could see before her. The people, the buildings, the busyness – she felt like she owned this now. That she was part of it, not just observing it. Tomorrow, they would take a train back to the village and the *bari*, and she could finally think of *Didi* and Joshua as her real family.

Sophie was finally going home.

CHAPTER TWENTY-SIX – ONDHOKAR

Today the wind and sky are whispering
Arises the new word among the forest flowers
Would that I could today express my heart!

– Kazi Nazrul Islam

Sophie was excited to the point of unbearableness – or at least to the limit of what her uncle could bear – for most of the train journey home. This was exacerbated by the fact that with having little time to book a ticket before travelling, they were now sharing a four-berth first-class cabin with a Bangladeshi family of four who had the luggage of a family twice the size. Joshua – not a small man by anyone's definition – felt distinctly cramped, so a giddy and talkative niece was not helpful.

When Sophie wasn't chattering to Uncle Joshua about what she was going to do when she got home, and how she was going to move things around in her room and make it more her own, and how she'd learn some Bangla cooking off *Didi*, and how she would learn more from *Mashima* about her life because it was ever so interesting and did you know she saw her family killed in the war, and how she couldn't wait to see the headmaster's face and Mahfuza's too, and a hundred other things, she spent time looking out of the window watching all the fields and villages and stations go by over the course of twelve hours as though she'd never seen them before.

Occasionally she would take notice of the little boy and girl sat opposite her and she would brave a little conversation with them in Bangla. When she first did this, she impressed their mother – a plump, older woman in an expensive *sari* – and she told her husband all about this remarkable *bideshi* girl, even though he was sat right by his wife and heard Sophie for himself. He didn't try to engage with her, respecting her as an unmarried woman, but instead engaged with Uncle Joshua, who was polite but, Sophie could tell, really didn't want to chatter in Bangla.

They had stayed at the club until the evening to have dinner the night before, and Sophie chose to eat fish and chips, symbolically like a last supper before casting aside all Englishness for what would, presumably, be many months to come. She secretly had a plan to persuade Uncle Joshua to let them come down more regularly and perhaps even to bring *Didi* too. The meal had been even more delicious than her pizza, and she laughed to think that a food which was so commonly British she now craved as a delicacy. She liked curry more, though, so didn't regret at all not returning to England to have British food – but a regular trip to the club certainly wouldn't go amiss. She wondered how hard it would be to get *Didi* to make potatoes chips from time to time.

Sophie was thankful that this carriage had air-conditioning, unlike the night train they had taken down two nights before. You could almost forget that the heat was oppressive, although this came at a cost – leaving the cabin to go to the toilet was like walking into a sauna.

The toilets were even hotter and were foul. Little more than a hole in the train, the stench was worse than any public toilet Sophie had gone to in Britain, and she had to take a deep breath and hold her nose when she stepped in each time. If she went *quickly*, she could just about manage to do everything she needed to in one breath. However, when she didn't quite manage it and was forced to take a gulp of air, she always regretted it and felt like retching.

When back in the carriage and while Uncle Joshua was talking to the father or out procuring food, she would often gaze out of the window and fantasize about seeing *Didi* again and the look the woman would have when seeing Sophie again for the first time. She grinned from ear to ear just imagining how her friend would look.

A more difficult thing to imagine was how Adhora would react. Would she be pleased? Would her father relent and allow them to see each other again? Perhaps school might start letting them sit together again? Or would Adhora be upset and stop seeing Sophie even during breaktimes? It made Sophie feel sick just to think of it.

As the train continued its journey relentlessly away from Dhaka, Sophie noticed a change in the stations. It was subtle, but the further away they got, the more obviously 'poor' the stations grew. Station buildings became less impressive and, apart from one or two clearly 'major' stations, shrunk in size. The people moving around the platforms seemed to age and decline in social status. Within a few hours, it was rare to see a woman dressed in a beautiful *sari* with fine jewellery and more common to see one in a dirty and coarse *shalwa kameeze*. Men, who usually wore western-style shirts and trousers (and sometimes full suits) gradually gave way to jeans and T-shirts and finally to *lunghis*, often without any shirt at all. The further they went, the more beggars she saw and the more homeless people were sleeping on the platforms.

Sophie wondered why she had never really noticed the differences before. She knew, of course, that there was a lot of poverty, but she'd never really paid attention to the gradation. Was she just growing up or had her attitudes changed now she saw this country as 'home'?

The train finally pulled into their station, and by now, the sun was going down, and it was rapidly growing dark. Uncle Joshua carried their two bags out of the train, so Sophie didn't have to manage hers while taking the rather large step down to the platform. She was grateful for the thought, her excitableness having given way to fatigue. She just wanted to sleep.

As they walked along the platform, her uncle called over two *kulis* to take the bags. Sophie wanted to stop him.

"Uncle Joshua, I can take my bag – it isn't too heavy, honestly."

"No, no child, these chaps will take them much more easily than we can," he replied without turning to look as he strode on. Sophie looked at both men, who looked at least in their sixties. They were nothing but skin and bones, wearing *lunghi*, dirty T-shirts and worn sandals. She felt she was at least as strong as either of them, and her uncle most certainly was.

"But don't you have to pay them *taka*?"

"Yes, of course! But it isn't very much," he turned to look at her. "You don't begrudge them that, surely?"

"No! I just feel like we're using them as slaves or animals to do our heavy lifting when we could do it ourselves."

They had to go over a footbridge to get to the other side of the station, and Sophie privately admitted she wouldn't have enjoyed lugging her case up and down the uneven and often wobbly steps. But, for all their frailty, the *kulis* carried the cases on their heads as though they were paper and rushed on ahead. By the time Sophie and Uncle Joshua had reached the other side, the men had secured them a waiting *vangari* ride.

As they walked through the station room to get to the front entrance where *rickshaws* and *vangaris* awaited, Sophie was struck by the mass of bodies. A huge crowd bustled noisily around the ticketing office, and she thought just how different this was to England, where everyone would line up and await their turn quietly and politely. Others were sat down on benches or squatted where they could find a place. And at least twenty people – men, women and children – were lying on *kombols* on the ground, seemingly asleep and oblivious to the noise all around. It was impossible for Sophie to tell if they were beggars or just passengers awaiting their train, and it made her sad to think that she couldn't tell one from the other. In Dhaka, distinguishing rich from poor was relatively easy. Here, you had to discern poor from poorer.

They got on the *vangari* and set off for the village, continuing their conversation as they did so in the coolness of the evening.

"I know it is hard to get used to it," said Uncle Joshua, "but I learned long ago that it is more important to use these people than do the 'British' thing and pinch pennies to do menial tasks ourselves."

"But isn't that very 'colonial'?"

"Yes, it does feel like it, doesn't it? But let me tell you a story to explain my take on it."

"Okay," Sophie said, giving him the thumbs up, "shoot."

"What? Never mind. Soon after I arrived here to take up my post at the school, I came with several bags. Again, two *kulis* came, and I reluctantly let them help because there was no way I could manage them on my own. But one chap carried two cases – one on his head and one in his hand.

I tried to help him with the one in his hand as we went up the steps of the bridge, but he absolutely refused. In fact, he looked horrified that I'd tried to help at all. Quite ashamed, actually."

'In my country,' I told him, 'we try to help our fellow men no matter what their profession.' I thought if I could explain my motivation, it might help him understand my good intentions.

'No, no,' he replied to me, almost as if explaining to a child which, in a way, I guess I was – culturally. 'In my country,' he countered, 'you are *boro lok*. You are above me. You are always above me. So if you take the bag to help me, then you are putting yourself below me.'

'That's okay in my country,' I told him. 'In my religion, being the servant to all is considered an honourable and exemplary way of being. Our God is sometimes called the 'Servant King' and modelled self-sacrifice this way.'

Yes, I know, I'm not religious, I know, I know – but people here *are* and even back then, I knew it was important to try and meet them where they are. Besides, it is true. Whether we follow the Christian faith or not, our whole culture is centred around hundreds of years of its teachings and practice. Anyway, he floored me with what he said next.

"Dada – that may be fine for your country and your people. But here, if you put yourself lower than me, *I am still lower than you.*"

Sophie watched her uncle use his hands to demonstrate his meaning. With one hand held flat up high to represent the *kuli* and the other held higher to represent her uncle, he lowered the highest hand below the lower to indicate putting himself below the *kuli*. In his final words, he took the *'kuli'* hand and placed that lower still below the other hand, and Sophie could see it was now very low indeed. She got the point.

"Oh, I see," she said, "so by putting yourself below him, he was still lower than you, and so you'd put him in the gutter basically."

Uncle Joshua gave her the thumbs up. "You've got it," he said.

"But then, how do you help anyone?"

"Maddening, isn't it? I've spent years here, Sophie and I'm still trying to work that one out. It is an incredibly delicate balance. I've only been able to work out two rules for trying to do anything."

"What are they? I'd better learn!"

He looked at her with a wry smile.

"You won't like them," he said, grinning.

"Try me."

"Rule one: just do it anyway. Rule two: ask forgiveness afterwards."

Sophie laughed at this. She wasn't entirely sure if her uncle was joking, but she could see the logic to this idea, perverse though it seemed to her 'Britishness.' She realised that now she would learn a lot more about the differences between the two cultures. She felt like Bangladesh was, in many ways, holding up a mirror to her and enabling her to see her own culture for the very first time.

They let the *vangari wallah* cycle right up to the *bari*, and Uncle Joshua slipped him more *taka* than agreed to say thank you. He again took both bags and signalled Sophie to notice a light on in the house, which could mean only one thing.

"I think you'd better go ahead," he said, "and best you have your hands free."

Sophie trotted to the door and opened it.

"Hello?" she said tentatively as she stepped into the front room. She instantly heard something from the kitchen clatter. Then a head popped through the doorway on the other side. Momentarily frowning, then a gasp of astonishment followed by a scream, *Didi* ran to Sophie and threw her arms around her, squeezing her painfully hard.

"*Bapre bap*! Oh, Sophie! Oh, *Dada*!" she told off Uncle Joshua with stern looks. "You brought her back! Is she staying? Is she staying forever?"

"Well, I'm not sure forever, *Didi*," he laughed, "but she's definitely not going back to Britain. She's going to live with us here."

Didi screamed again and jumped up and down, still holding Sophie. Uncle Joshua looked at both girls and had to admit he couldn't tell which one was beaming more broadly nor which one was happier. He wasn't even sure if it wasn't a competition between the three of them and decided that he needed a cup of *cha* to calm things down before they got silly. He desperately hoped that *Didi* had been here preparing a nice cuppa for him.

Sophie finished her evening with a brief walk around the *pukur* to stretch her legs. The *ondhokar* – the darkness of twilight – was surprisingly fresh. Usually, it was oppressive with heat and humidity. But tonight, it was welcoming her back with a cool breeze. The *ondhokar* kept her hidden from sight, so she didn't have to worry about the neighbours noticing her as she walked. She could see them, though, in their *baris* made of brick, concrete or clay, cooking, cleaning, washing or even, in some cases, watching a small black and white TV set.

If she was a *Bangalee,* she thought, she should be standing and staring, watching anything and anyone catching her attention without shame or embarrassment. But she wasn't quite there yet and kept moving instead. She walked twice around the pool, in the end, enjoying the freshness.

She was about to step into her house when a sudden gust of wind from behind nearly blew her so hard she had to grasp at the bars and netting of the front porch as she neared the door. She turned around to see what was going on. Such a wind would have been common in England, perhaps in Springtime, but not here in this hot, humid country where barely a breeze was ever felt. It was such a strange night.

She looked around her. All the trees were swaying wildly, and, for once, the animals and insects were completely quiet. There was something now quite ominous about the silence, something not quite right. In the distance, despite the *ondhokar,* she could see even darker clouds from behind the *lichee bagan* trees. They weren't just dark, they were almost blacker than black, and they crossed the whole horizon as far as Sophie could see.

That's quite a storm cloud brewing there, she thought. I wonder if it will make it this far? She knew that if the storm didn't change direction, they would get a superb lightning show – this storm was going to be impressive.

She remembered all too well the storms from last year that came during her first few days in the village. Only this time, there would be no *Mashima* making scary appearances at the window. Or if she did, Sophie wouldn't be half so frightened. She was glad to see it coming, and it explained the unusual coolness of the night – they so needed cooling down, and the wind was most definitely welcome.

"Come storm," she said into the wind, "you're more than welcome here."

And, as if in response, the black clouds gave a low, growling rumble in the distance.

CHAPTER TWENTY-SEVEN – THE BREAKING OF CHAINS

In great vacant skies
You play with pleasure, engrossed
Breaking and making incessantly, moment by moment.

– Kazi Nasrul Islam

English storms are just like the English themselves: full of bluster but ultimately lazy. Storms of the Indian subcontinent, by comparison, are mighty and powerful: these storms have been to the gym. Bangladesh storms will think nothing of drowning everything and breaking trees – not your ordinary branches from oaks, mind you, or picking off trees that are weak and infirm from the roots, as you might expect in the West. No, no – Bengali storms will take on even the mighty banyan trees and win; if they desire to do so.

When the storm comes, if it does so during the day, the whole sky becomes black and day becomes night. For hours beforehand you may see the heavens lit up by great flashes obscured by the clouds – which themselves look like the tableaus of ancient gods forging away much like the *dokaners* in repair shops in every village, celestial torches firing for mysterious purposes. But the silence of these heavenly flashes is ominous and foreboding. *'Run,'* it seems to say, like a predator creeping up to you and deciding to use you for sport. You can feel the power just waiting, waiting, waiting for the right moment; there is no rush, and there will be no doubt when it comes.

And when the rains do come – not in dribs and drabs – but suddenly, without warning, the ground is a river within seconds. After a few minutes, the waters have eaten almost every patch of ground which has not had the foresight to be raised higher than the rest. If the rain is heavy enough – and it surely will be – and if the rain goes on throughout the night, the waters will rise to dangerous levels. In many areas, where floods come frequently, the locals have small boats in their homes and will exchange their bicycles for boats to get around without a second thought. Many an adult will have fond childhood memories of paddling to school in a raft or small boat for a few weeks at a time each year.

But fun turns to fear when the storms decide to stay and pound a village or town until it gives up and washes away completely. Then the laughter and excitement stop. Then it is no longer a case of repairing roofs or clearing away trees when the water levels abate. Then the dangers become all too real and often too late for anyone to do anything about it. It turns on you without warning, without reason. The weather brings life, and the weather takes life away.

That night the sky erupted with flames. Sophie awoke to the sound of a thousand missiles pelting the metal roof. The lightning fired so often that she didn't need to turn a light on to see where she was going when she got out of bed. This was just as well, for the power had gone out completely, and there was no electricity at all.

She left her room and padded down the stairs to check the downstairs rooms, as was the drill she remembered well from last year. Check that all shutters are properly closed, check for leaks, check the rain isn't blowing in under any of the external doors. Then lay down towels anywhere rain has got in and put out buckets underneath any leaks from the roof.

So far, it was all okay. One shutter had been slightly left open, and there was a small leak down the wall, but the pool of water was minimal. It would dry by the morning once the storm stopped. Sophie took herself back to bed.

In the morning, she awoke and realised it was still raining hard, though the thunder and lightning seemed to have stopped. She got up and padded down to the front room again. As soon as she stepped through the doorway, she realised her feet were wet. The entire floor was covered in enough water that as she moved, she could see ripples move in different directions, snaking across the tiles.

"Uncle Joshua," she shouted, "you'd better come and see this!"

"I already have," he called from behind her, carrying an armful of towels from the back storeroom. "Here, grab this towel and tuck it under the front door. The rain's coming in from there."

"What about the water in here?" she asked as she waded across. "Will towels soak it up?"

"No, there's too much." She noticed he had rolled his trouser legs up and giggled at the sight. Her uncle looked more like an old man on an English beach than a cool teacher living in Bangladesh. "We'll let *Didi* deal with this best when she gets here. Probably a mop and bucket are needed for this. She's late, though. I suspect the rain is making it difficult for her to get here."

As he spoke, there was a noise from upstairs and the telltale sound of the veranda door being unlocked. After a few seconds, the soft padding of bare feet confirmed *Didi* had arrived. She came down the stairs, and both Joshua and Sophie laughed at her.

Didi was soaked from head to foot, her *shalwa kameeze* clinging to her body, and she left a trail of water behind her.

"Not funny," she laughed, wagging a finger at the pair of them. "It very wet."

"Yes," Joshua acknowledged, grinning and pointing at the sodden floor, "we have noticed that. I was going to ask you to mop this up, *Didi*, but I think you need to go change into dry clothes."

He turned to Sophie. "Sophie, have you got a large-size *shalwa kameeze* set? I think *Didi* could fit into one of your larger, baggier ones. You two are the same height."

"I'm pretty certain I've got a perfect set on my *alna*," Sophie nodded. "Come on, *Didi*, let's sort you out!"

The two girls headed back up the stairs, giggling as they went. Joshua smiled but then turned back to the floor and slowly waded over to one of the windows. He looked outside, noticing the amount of water now covering the gardens and fields. He frowned. A lot of water had fallen, and the rain needed to pass soon before this became a problem.

But the rains didn't stop. In fact, they got worse, and, throughout the day, the thunder and lightning came and went with apparent gay abandon, as did the men coming to see Joshua.

Sophie remained in the *bari*, having no wish to get soaked, but she noticed that as *Didi* busied around the place doing her work, she wasn't smiling and increasingly looked worried.

"What's wrong *Didi*?" Sophie would ask.

"Oh…nothing," *Didi* would inevitably reply, but she would then look out of the window and frown again. Whenever men came to the door asking to see Joshua dada, Sophie would notice that *Didi* would hang around close to the doorway, pretending to sweep some part of the floor but, obviously to Sophie, actually trying to listen in.

When Sophie saw the men themselves as she trotted in and out of rooms, she noticed their expressions were similar to *Didi's*. Joshua himself looked grim while he talked to them in hushed tones. She knew something was going on, but what, she couldn't tell.

Then came the moment a man came to the door and this time wanted *Didi*, not Joshua. It was the same young man, Maruf, from *Didi's* village who had helped Sophie to harvest the field. He looked worried.

Joshua noticed he was here and came into the room to join the conversation. Sophie hung back. They spoke too quietly and quickly for her to work out what they were talking about. Eventually, though, *Didi* turned to Joshua, her eyes pleading. He asked her some questions, to which both she and Maruf nodded, apparently to reassure some worries Joshua had, and then he said to her, "Okay. Go. Be safe. *Khoda hafez.*"

Didi ran to collect her sandals from the upstairs veranda where she'd left them that morning and ran out of the house with Maruf.

"What's going on, Uncle?" Sophie asked Uncle Joshua.

"The storms," he said, "they're bad. The outer villages are suffering quite a lot of damage."

"Is everyone alright? What about *Mashima*? Do we need to find her and make sure she's safe?"

Uncle Joshua held up his hands at Sophie.

"No, no. Sophie, you need to stay here. I'm sure *Mashima* is okay, and I'm reasonably confident *Didi* is in safe hands. Maruf will look after her.

They all know how to deal with storm damage – far better than I do and *much* better than you. So stay here and stay safe. I'm hoping I won't be needed."

Sophie was alarmed by this. "Why would you be needed?" she asked.

"Sometimes it can get bad enough that *dokans* start to collapse. The ones which are just made of tin and bamboo, anyway. Then it's a case of manpower." He held up his arms. "These are the only things I have of use at times like this!"

"So, what can we do from here?"

Uncle Joshua took a deep breath and tucked in his shirt.

"We do what we Brits always do best," he said, moving to the kitchen. "We make a cup of tea and wait it out."

The sun went down at six – not that much of it had been seen at all during the day – and it was once the sky was completely dark with night rather than the storm that another knock on the door came. This time a man from the village came who Joshua obviously knew, and the tone of his voice was urgent. Gone were the hushed tones. He was all but shouting. Joshua looked grave but nodded at the man and started putting on a rain mac. The rain was still gushing down.

"Uncle Joshua, you're not going out in this, surely," blurted Sophie, very alarmed.

He turned to her, and Sophie saw the seriousness in his face.

"It's now a case of the whole village working together," he said. "I have to go. The *Satya* has flooded, and if it breaks the flood defences we have in place along the banks, then we're all in trouble."

"Okay, then I'm coming too."

"No, you are not, young lady," he replied angrily. "I need you here. I need you safe. I need to know exactly where you are, or I won't be any help to people who need us."

"I'm not staying here on my own when I could help too."

"And do what Sophie? Look at you? What use would you be? I have the muscle and bulk of a man in his forties and the advantage of height for holding things and pushing up roofs that are collapsing. There's nothing you can do. Stay here."

Sophie, hurt by his stinging rebuke, clenched her fists and moved to grab her coat from the coat rack near the door.

"I'm better than nothing, and I'm *a lot* stronger than you give me credit for. So I'm coming to help. I'm not sitting here while *Didi* and *Mashima* and everyone we love is in danger."

Uncle Joshua held up his finger at her.

"Enough, Sophie. You'll be more trouble than good. You're staying here, and that's the end of it."

He opened the door and moved outside with the man. Sophie grabbed her coat and started putting it on as she headed to the porch. Too late, she saw that her uncle had stepped outside, closed the metal door to the porch and was snapping shut the padlock on the outside.

"No! No, Uncle Joshua!" she cried, running to the door and banging on the metal bars.

Joshua held his hand up near her face and rested it on the door.

"I'm so sorry."

"You promised you wouldn't do this, Uncle Joshua."

"I know. I'm sorry. I'm so sorry. I'll make this up to you. But, right now, I need you here where you're safe."

"Don't do this. Please," Sophie begged, tears streaming down her face.

"I'm sorry."

He moved off with the man and didn't look back as Sophie banged hard on the door with her fists.

"Come back! Come Back! Don't do this," she shouted after him, her anger rising. "I hate you, Uncle Joshua. I hate you," she shouted one last time as he vanished into the storm.

Sophie sat herself down, fuming as the lightning crackled outside. Just *who* did he think he was? It wasn't fair, and it wasn't right.

"Just because of a bloody storm," she said out loud, walking over to looking out of the window and watching the lightning. As if in reply, a crash of thunder shocked Sophie backwards; she tripped and fell, landing on the wet tiles. That was a big crash and, for all she wanted to slap him hard,

Uncle Joshua was still out in it. Her annoyance was beginning to turn into fear for him. Why did he have to go out in the rain anyway?

An hour later and there was no change in the ferocity of the storm. Sophie had gone to her room and didn't hear the hammering on the porch door. In the end, it was the small but familiar sound of "Sophie!" that drew her attention. She sat, puzzled, straining to hear against the noise of the storm until she thought she heard banging again and the soft but pleading sound "Sophie!" It was Adhora's voice.

She shot out of her room and down the stairs to open the front door. She saw a wet, shivering and terrified Adhora on the veranda porch on the other side of the metal door, locked by her uncle.

"Adhora, what are you doing here? You must be soaked to the bone!" Sophie said, wishing she could get her inside to dry her.

"Oh, Sophie *bon,* please, please help!" she cried. "The river has flooded and has covered all the fields."

"I know," said Sophie. "Have the defences held? Is everyone alright?"

"No, *Bon*! All the fields have gone. It has surrounded our house, and my family is trapped inside, cut off from the village. I was away from home, and only when I tried to come back home now, I realised there was no way to get there. They are completely surrounded by the *Satya nodi.* Oh, they are going to die, I know it. Please! Tell me what to do. I'm so scared."

CHAPTER TWENTY-EIGHT - THE FLOOD

Sophie stood silently in disbelief.

"What?" she said dumbly. "Who's going to die?" She was shouting, struggling to be heard over the sound of the storm.

"The river has flooded its banks," whimpered Adhora.

"I know," Sophie said, trying to sound calm, to calm Adhora down too, "but why will it hurt them? I don't understand. You guys are in a *paka bari*. Concrete won't wash away."

"Because when rivers flood, they are very powerful. The *Satya* has already knocked down every tree in the fields surrounding our house, and it is still rising. Oh, your uncle was *right*. *Baba* should never have built there. It was too close to the river."

"So what's happening now? Why haven't they left?" Sophie was looking at the door and already trying to figure out how she could get out this time. Uncle Joshua had padlocked this door, and the back gate was padlocked too. There was no chance of her pulling the same stunt as last time.

"They can't! They are trapped by the waters. All around them is now the river, and it is moving so fast and hard. Baba might make it to land if Allah willed, but Ma and Tahira would never survive. They are not strong enough." Adhora was so wet from the rain it was difficult to tell, but it looked like tears were streaming down her cheeks. She rested her head on the metal bars of the door. "Oh, please help, Sophie. Please."

"Okay, Adhora, I will. Just as soon as I figure out how to get out of this place."

Sophie pulled helplessly at the bars, just to see if anything would give at all, but she knew that this would be hopeless. A metal door that could be wrenched open so easily wouldn't be any good as a barrier to protect the house from thieves. She knew the back gate leading to the stairs would be just as impossible. *Didi* took the keys with her when she left earlier. There was no way through any of the windows, which was a shame because even with the upstairs windows, it would have been impossible. Around the outside was a ledge about two feet wide, which workmen used whenever roof repairs were needed. But every window had metal bars cemented into the walls. With both doors locked, it was impossible.

"I really don't think I can get out," she said apologetically.

"Then my family are already dead." Adhora collapsed to the floor in a heap of sobs. Guilt ran through Sophie. There *must* be something she could do? It was crazy that this house had only two doors, and they were both padlocked.

Except. There was another door.

"Oh my god," Sophie said excitedly, "Adhora, meet me round the back veranda. I think I know how to get out of here."

Adhora didn't need telling twice. She shot around the house, getting drenched again, but her fear and worry meant she barely noticed. She bounded up the metal stairs to the veranda outside Sophie's back gate.

Sophie ran upstairs, having grabbed her sandals and her coat from the porch, and ran straight to the room at the end of the inside veranda which led to the back of the house and Uncle Joshua's bedroom. She had rarely gone in his room, respecting his privacy. Occasionally, when he was out, she might stand in the doorway chatting to *Didi* while her friend tidied the room; otherwise, she kept well away. She had completely forgotten about a door on the back wall, which led to nowhere.

She ran into the room and straight to this door now. In the semi-darkness, she tried the handle, but the door didn't budge. Like the inner front door downstairs and the bedroom doors, this was a thick wooden door that was locked with a key. Sophie felt under the handle to see if there was a key still in the lock. To her relief, there was. She turned it, felt the lock click and then tried the door again. It opened.

Rain immediately pelted her, and she was glad she was wearing her raincoat. But, more worryingly, the water was now soaking not just her but several of Uncle Joshua's books which were lying nearby on the floor in a pile before she could step out and struggle against the wind to shut the door firmly.

The books will dry eventually, thought Sophie, now beginning to clock up the number of misdemeanours that her uncle would undoubtedly hold against her when this was all over. She, however, would not dry so quickly, and already she began to feel cold and tired. She had only been outside a handful of seconds.

Sophie realised she was standing on a small balcony with railings all around, and a single bamboo chair was placed just to the left. This seemed to be another private place Uncle Joshua liked going to, and she could imagine him sitting, looking over fields while sipping *cha* and reading a book.

She looked over the veranda railings. The ledge looked much thinner than she had remembered. She peered around the corner and could see Adhora standing by the back door.

"Adhora!" she shouted out to get the girl's attention, "I'm out! I'll climb over the railings. I can walk around the ledge and get to you."

"But, Sophie," Adhora protested, "The ledge is only this big." She held her hands out about a foot wide. "It is wet, and it is dark, and it is raining hard. The ledge will be very slippy, and you have nothing to hold on to."

"I've got a good sense of balance," Sophie retorted, "and, besides, I can't think of anything else. It's all we've got."

Adhora looked down, sad for a moment and then looked at Sophie and nodded.

"Ok, Sophie, but be careful." And then, in typical Bengali fashion, added, "But please hurry!"

"This is not going to be as easy as I thought," Sophie said aloud to no one in particular. She swung her legs over the railings and used them to hang on to for as long as she could before she had manoeuvred too far away to hold them any longer. She turned the corner and hoped she would be able to see well enough to keep track of where the ledge was. *Don't look down*, she thought. It was only four or five metres long, but it might as well have been fifty in the dark and torrential rain. Sophie gave a little gulp and suddenly became very afraid. If she lost her balance, she would plunge onto the concrete path below in the dark, and it would be unlikely Adhora would find her uncle or anyone else to help. Not if things were as bad as Adhora said they were.

She began her first steps. With determination now, Sophie took another step. So far so good. A few more. She wavered a little, but otherwise, it was ok. There was just room for her foot to go sideways. The hardest part was getting her inner right leg from behind to step in front. It kept scraping against the wall, each time pushing her body out a little and causing her to wobble a bit.

She was quickly halfway there and beginning to get the hang of things when a very large and unexpected gust of wind blew from a completely different direction for a second, blowing her one way before then returning instantly but strongly back to where it had been coming from. The result was that Sophie countered her balance too much *twice*, and suddenly she was teetering on the edge. Adhora, watching every step, screamed – which didn't help Sophie's concentration as she tried to right her balance before she fell.

She threw her full body weight against the wall, winding herself but, somehow, managing not to fall. She half-crouched for a moment, catching her breath and then continued along the ledge. Slower, she thought, don't get cocky. Step after step, she took, almost within reach of the railing on the veranda where Adhora stood, biting her fingers in fear. I'm there, Sophie thought and grabbed at the railings with both hands.

"Yes, you did it, Sophie!" Adhora beamed.

"I told you I could," replied Sophie, bringing her left foot onto the ledge at the bottom of the railings. She just started to lift her right foot to swing her leg over the railing and to safety when her left, which had been barely on the ledge at all, slipped, and Sophie fell downwards.

Adhora stepped back and screamed again as Sophie now hung with both hands from the wet railings, desperately gripping with equally wet hands.

"For God's sake Adhora, stop screaming and help me up. I can't grip for long," she barked at Adhora, and the girl stopped screaming; she started sobbing instead. She did, however, immediately come over to the railing and grab Sophie by the arms and begin pulling. *Adhora is bloody useless in an emergency*, Sophie thought, *but at least you can order her around and she does it.* The two girls heaved and strained and, between them, managed to get Sophie back over the railings and to relative safety.

They both lay on the veranda for a moment, catching their breath.

"I'm *never* doing that again."

"I never want you to do that again. It was a stupid idea, Sophie. You could have been killed."

"Yes, well," said Sophie, picking herself up and uselessly brushing the dirt off her sodden raincoat, "if we don't get to your home, someone *is* going to die, so we'd better hurry. Come on."

They ran down the steps and around to the front of the house.

"Where do we go, Adhora?" Sophie asked, half-shouting over the noise of the downpour.

"I don't know."

"What?"

Adhora shrugged. Sophie sighed. She loved her friend; she was loyal, kind, and always did what she said she would, but she was useless at making decisions.

"Right," Sophie said, "let's head towards the school and see if we can cut through the fields towards the river and your house. I'll see how bad it is and figure something out."

She was lying. She had no clue what to do, but at least she could see the *Satya* for herself and work out if Adhora's family really were in danger. Bangladeshis sometimes would be more melodramatic; she knew this. Every time anyone had a slight cold, they always claimed they 'had a fever' and somehow, without the use of a thermometer, knew their temperature was 'nearly 104'. They were stock phrases but those that said them believed them implicitly. Maybe the river wasn't too bad, and it was just their house would get a little flooded for a day or so?

They ran as fast as they could around the boundaries of the *pukur* and over to the school. They slowed down as they approached the building.

"Oh my God," said Sophie surveying the playing field. It had gone completely. Where the school grounds had previously stretched out, bounded by trees and then several fields, the railway line and finally the *Satya*, with Adhora's *bari* in the field on the other side, now there was nothing but water stretching into the wet gloom. Most of the trees were gone, and the few remaining tree trunks were submerged in water. The branches waved like drowning hands, begging for someone to save them.

Adhora started crying again.

"You see Sophie? It's all gone."

Sophie momentarily considered wading into the water. She quickly dismissed the idea. The playground and fields would probably be quite shallow, but there would be no way to know when they reached the *Satya*, and the muddy ground would probably make walking impossible anyway. They needed a boat.

"I have an idea," she said, turning around and heading in the opposite direction. "There's a boat on the *pukur* – come on, we can drag it over to the school and row to your house."

They ran to the *pukur*, went in through the gates and moved carefully around the bank to where the boat was moored. Sophie was grateful that this side of the village area was raised up, but even so, pools of water were everywhere, and the brick paths underneath were mossy and very slippy.

She had never seen the *pukur* so full – it wouldn't be long before the pool would overflow itself. For now, there were just a couple of feet at most to go. At least this would make dragging the boat up the bank easier.

They ran to the jetty where the boat was moored, and Sophie grabbed at the rope to pull the hull closer. She held on to one side of the bow and called Adhora to grab the other. Together they pulled hard to get the bow onto the bank.

"Bloody hell, that's heavy!" Sophie exclaimed as they stopped heaving and the boat slipped back the few inches they had managed to move it. They tried again, but it was clearly going to be hopeless. The boat was far heavier than Sophie had even begun to imagine it would be. Even if they could get it over the bank, the chances of them carrying it to the playground were slim.

She slumped on the jetty, defeated. Desperately trying not to cry, she looked at Adhora and shrugged resignedly.

"I don't know what to do," she admitted.

Adhora reached over and held her hand. She was holding back her sobs but smiling at Sophie.

"It's okay. You tried. Thank you for trying."

Now Sophie burst into tears and hugged her friend. She felt utterly wretched and useless. Uncle Joshua had been right. She couldn't even look after Adhora and give her a dry place to rest until the morning came and, hopefully, the storm ended. They were trapped out of the house. Sophie could risk walking back along the ledge to her uncle's back door, but it was far too risky to let Adhora try it. If she slipped and fell to the concrete below, Sophie would never forgive herself. She couldn't leave her mourning friend though, either. So now they were both homeless, and just as Uncle Joshua had predicted, were two girls who needed rescuing.

I can't believe how heavy this boat is, she thought to herself. Perhaps if they waited until the *pukur* flooded, they could try rowing from here? But that was unlikely as the waters would probably flow back to the *Satya* through the sluice gate.

Sophie sat up with a start.

"Wait. There's one more idea we haven't tried."

"What is it, Sophie?"

"Get in the boat, Adhora!"

"What?" Adhora looked uncertainly at the boat, which already had quite a lot of water in it.

"Just get in. Trust me."

"But Sophie…I can't swim. What if the boat sinks?"

For the love of God, Sophie thought, *now she tells me*. For a brief second, Sophie wondered if she should admit to Adhora that she couldn't swim either and, in fact, was rather afraid of water. She decided that admission would do nothing for her friend's confidence.

"Don't worry. I'll make sure you stay safe. Just *how* did you expect us to get to your family Adhora when they're surrounded by water?"

"I don't know. I didn't think that far. None of us can swim except Baba, and he isn't very good."

This just gets better and better, thought Sophie.

"Just get in the boat, Adhora. We'll sort it out."

They both got in, and Sophie reached under the seats to find the oars. She also found a plastic box which she assumed Uncle Joshua had left from the last time he came fishing.

"Take this and start scooping out water," she said, handing the box to Adhora. Then Sophie untied the rope holding them to the jetty and hooked the oars into the rowlocks. She began moving the boat. Luckily, the oars were quite light, and she could move them easily. The water, however, was hard to push through. Still, she managed it, and soon they were at the sluice gate.

"Wait, Sophie," Adhora said, eyes wide with alarm, "you're not thinking of going through that, are you?"

"It's the only way. I can't think of anything else."

"But it will be full to the top with water. We'll drown. And…it's underground…for a very long way."

"I know, I know, but we have no other choice. If the water gets too full, then we'll just have to come back the way we came."

"But it will be dark and…underground. What if we get stuck? They'll never find us…."

"Please shut up, Adhora," Sophie snapped. She was terrified herself of being underground for so long in the dark, and she hadn't even considered what might happen if they got stuck.

She grabbed at the gate and pulled hard. The gate was tangled in weeds, but at least it wasn't locked, which Sophie had feared might be the case. It gave way a few inches, and each tug pulled it open a little more. Eventually, she was able to pull hard and open it fully. It was the first thing that had gone their way, and it filled her with hope.

"Here goes nothing," she said as she looked into the tunnel. It was half-full of water, and the remaining space was just enough for the two of them and the boat – as long as they both crouched down. The girls were both small, which was a blessing. Uncle Joshua could never have done this with his huge frame.

Sophie put the oars back in the boat – there was no room for them. Instead, the pair of them used their hands above their heads to push the boat along.

"There's metal handles to grab," Sophie said when she realised. A small metal loop would jut out every couple of metres, and it gave good purchase for a really good heave.

"*Alhamdulillah*," Adhora cried. Incredibly, the plan was working.

They moved like this for ten minutes, creeping forward in the pitch black. Sophie breathed hard, doing her best to control her rising panic while monotonously, rhythmically pulling and pushing with her hands. This was worse than any nightmare she'd ever had. But it wasn't dissimilar to the many she'd had about being dragged down into the *pukur*. In a way, the familiarity of this scene allowed her to control her fear. She knew this game. And besides, she realised at this point that she *trusted* the *pukur*. Instinctively she felt that any waters coming in or out were part of that pool and, no matter how scary the depths of the waters there might be, the *pukur* would look after her. It was stupid to think so, she knew this, but she felt it, nonetheless.

Her thoughts distracted her for a while until she realised she was crouching far lower than she had been, and her head was beginning to touch the top of the tunnel.

"Adhora, are you okay?" she asked in the darkness.

"Yes, I think so."

"I think the waters are rising."

"Yes, I noticed that too."

Sophie reached forward in the gloom and found her friend. She held one of her hands as they stopped pushing.

"I think we both need to lie down in the boat and push from there. There's just room for us to lie down together under the seats."

"Okay, Sophie."

Sophie's heart warmed to the sound of her friend's voice. She could hear her trembling and knew she was even more scared than Sophie was. And yet, Adhora trusted Sophie, and that trust and loyalty overcame the fear. Sophie just hoped she wouldn't let this dear girl down.

As they fumbled around moving their bodies to slide partially under the seats, Sophie thought, this family better bloody well be there and not be rescued already when we get to the *bari*. She laughed to herself.

"What?" said Adhora.

"Oh…nothing. It doesn't matter. Come on. Let's get pushing."

The progress was much slower now. The girls had to stretch their arms up awkwardly, and they got tired easily. The sides of the boat often scraped against what remained of the tunnel above the surface, and Sophie noted it happened more frequently as time went on. The water was still rising, and soon they would be stuck. She tried not to think of it.

Doggedly they continued, and Sophie could hear Adhora's panicky breathing. She hoped Adhora couldn't hear her own. But it was Adhora who heard the sound of running water first and pointed it out to Sophie.

Sophie raised herself onto one elbow and peered over the rim of the boat. In the darkness, there was a vague and slightly less dark spot appearing.

"We're near the end, Adhora! I think I can see the end of the tunnel," Sophie shouted gleefully. Her heart raced. They were nearly free.

They pushed harder, adrenaline giving them strength despite their weariness. Eventually, the boat halted suddenly, and they heard the clunk of the bow hitting metal bars. Sophie looked up and realised she could see the bars dimly, black against lighter blackness. Having been in such complete darkness, it was almost like daylight to her, especially with the lightning flashing in the distance. The thunder still rumbled, but it sounded distant. The storm was finally beginning to move on. Thank God, she thought, hope springing up from nowhere.

She tried to push the gate open, but it wouldn't budge. She couldn't give a decent push from inside the boat and knew she would have to go into the water.

"Adhora," she cried to her friend, "we need to push the boat back. I have to get out to try and kick this gate open."

Adhora didn't attempt to persuade her not to try. On the contrary, she followed Sophie's every instruction. The pair now started to push the boat backwards until there was room for Sophie to fit between the boat and the gate. She slid herself over the edge and into the water. There was barely room, and briefly, she went under completely and had to claw her way past the boat before she could come up for air. The water was surprisingly and horribly, cold and it made Sophie gasp when she came up.

Now it was her turn to be scared. It was okay sitting in the tunnel, but she knew she'd never survive if she didn't get back into the boat before they entered the river. She had minimal swimming skills – barely able to float in swimming lessons back in her junior school days. Sophie had never had any interest in water sports, and she regretted it now. She could hear how fast the *Satya* was moving. It sounded more like a huge, rushing waterfall than a river. But there was no turning back now.

She kicked at the gate with one leg and then the other repeatedly. The gate squeaked and groaned, but it did give way. Thank heavens this side wasn't locked either! She kicked again and again until just as the gate reached the halfway point, the river caught hold and wrenched it back the rest of the way with a crunch.

Sophie knew this was the greatest moment of danger. She shouted to Adhora to start pushing on the ceiling again, and as Adhora did so, Sophie clung to the bow. Slowly, they inched out, and Sophie swung a leg up over the edge as she felt the current taking hold like a brick wall wrapped in a wet blanket pushing against her body, trying to make her release her grip and be carried away.

She threw herself into the boat just as the current caught hold completely and shot the craft away from the tunnel, spinning them in doing so. Both girls screamed as the boat tipped over to the side, nearly going all the way, Sophie throwing her body to the other side to keep them from capsizing. They rocked from side to side as the boat spun round and round.

Sophie knew they had to take control and get rowing across the river to stand any chance of getting to Adhora's house. If the river took them past the house, they would never be able to row against the current to get back.

"Grab the oars, Adhora," she screamed, "we've got to row – fast!"

They took an oar each, fixed them in the rowlocks and heaved with all their strength. The boat instantly steadied and stopped spinning, and Sophie was able to gain some sense of direction. Fortuitously the action of the river had taken them across much of it as well as downstream. She looked out to see if there was any landmark left she could recognise, but it was too dark, and nothing looked the same.

She was reminded of school maths lessons back in England where they would have to calculate the angle of steering a boat to counteract the current in order to end up straight on the other side. She remembered how the teacher had carefully explained how you had to row against the current if you wanted to stay straight – which was counterintuitive to most kids, but Sophie understood the idea. Now she recalled this idea and knew that the best they could do was do the same and hope they could get out and find Adhora's house once they reached the drowned fields.

She shouted instructions to Adhora, and between them, they heaved the oars to work against the pull of the river as well as across it. Sometimes they lost it, and the river turned them back to face downstream, but they kept working the oars to pull them back, Sophie using every memory she had of how Uncle Joshua steered this boat to remember which oar to drag in the water and which to lift to correct.

After what felt like an eternity, Sophie realised her oar was hitting reeds and mud, and she knew they must now be rowing across the fields on the other side of the river. The current was slower here, but they were exhausted. She started to look anxiously to see if there was any sign of Adhora's house.

"Look," said Adhora, pointing a little further downstream, "that light. I think it is coming from my house!"

Sophie turned to look. She hadn't seen it before but seemingly hovering several feet above the water was a small, flickering light. Someone had lit some kind of torch. There was no other house in the middle of the fields at this side of the river, so it must be them surely? Even if it wasn't Adhora's place, it was someone – and they had no better option than head for it.

Still rowing against the current, but not at quite so steep an angle, they kept rowing across, and gradually the light drew closer. Before long, they could see it was coming from the roof of a building. By some miracle, Sophie could gradually make out, they had indeed made it to Adhora's home.

It was the most bizarre thing for Sophie to row through the gates of the walls surrounding the home and sail up to the doorway. She could see that the waters were at least three feet up the entrance. She could also see people on the flat roof. It was an oil lamp that had been lit.

"*Baba! Amma!*" Adhora cried out. A head appeared over the side. It was Adhora's mother.

"Adhora? Is that you? *Alhamdulilah!* You're alive and safe!"

Mr Haque then peered over with lamp in hand. He looked completely confused and then ecstatically happy.

"Allah be praised!" he said excitedly. "How did you get here?"

"We got a boat, Baba," Adhora responded as if this answered everything. Sophie realised this reunion could last a long time, and they needed to get moving. It was still raining, though not as much as it had been, and the boat had a lot of water sloshing around inside again. Both Adhora and herself were soaked to the skin too and utterly exhausted. They had to find shelter soon.

"We have a boat, Mr Haque," she shouted, "and we can probably just about fit you all in. But where do we go? It will have to be downstream. Do you know if there is anywhere which might be above the flood level?"

"Wait. We'll come down. I think I know."

The girls waited for Adhora's parents and her baby sister to go down their stairs and wade through the water to their front door. The girls busied themselves using the plastic box and their hands to get water out of the boat. Sophie was unsure of trying to squeeze five of them into a boat which was only made for two. Three men could just about squeeze in; she hoped two small girls, a woman, one man and a small child would manage.

The family came out of the doors, and Adhora's father helped his wife and Tahira into the boat before getting in himself. They rocked worryingly as everyone adjusted themselves. Sophie tucked into the bow and looked over the edge. The boat was so loaded down now that there were only a couple of inches of the rim above the water level. She told Adhora to keep hold of the plastic box and start scooping water if any came over the side.

"Where do we go, Mr Haque?" she asked.

"My brother's home," he replied. "It isn't far, and their land is probably the highest around here. So they should be fine if the storm hasn't damaged their home."

"Okay. Can you row? You're the only one in the right position, and I think I'm too tired anyway. My whole body is aching."

He looked at her and smiled kindly.

"Of course, I will. You are a good girl. I will never forget your bravery, Sophie." He turned to look at Adhora. "You are a good girl too. I am very, very proud of you, my girl." Adhora beamed at him despite feeling so tired. He turned back to Sophie and said, "Please forgive me for my terrible behaviour to you."

"If you row us to safety, I'll consider all forgiven," she grinned back at him. He nodded, took up the oars and began to row.

After the drama of making it across the river, Adhora's father's rowing was much more controlled. He took them across the flooded fields where the current was slower for much of the journey and only entered the slipstream of the *Satya* itself for the latter part. The river jerked them along, and Adhora's mother and sister screamed at the motion, but after a few seconds, Mr Haque had it under control. *What a difference the strength of an adult man makes*, Sophie thought. It would have been a begrudging thought after all her efforts that he was better than she, but she was very grateful under the circumstances. After that, she never wanted to row a boat again.

She saw lights and then felt the oars and the bottom of the boat catching on the ground, which was rising underneath them. The boat slid to a halt, and both Mr Haque and Sophie got out and pushed the boat as high up on land as they could manage before helping everyone else off.

Not more than a hundred metres away, Sophie could see the glow of lights from Adhora's uncle's *bari*. Opposite was the shed where their friendship had been forced apart through Sophie's stupidity, and she thought it ironic that they should all end up back here now all these months later.

Exhausted, they dragged their feet along the lane towards the house. It was still raining, but the storm had passed. Hasan shouted to his brother as they walked, and after a few seconds, a man stepped out onto his veranda to look at them. Excited chatter followed, calls inside, women coming out and exclaiming as they ran to the bedraggled group, put *kombols* around Adhora's mother and sister, and helped them into the house. Finally, they all got inside, and Sophie felt deliriously happy. They were safe, they had rescued Adhora's family, and Sophie was largely responsible for that. She felt sure she had done good, and Uncle Joshua would be pleased. She was also sure that she had just won back permission to be Adhora's friend. This in itself was worth all the work and the danger.

It would be all for nothing, though; the thought suddenly came to her if she lost Uncle Joshua's boat. She realised she hadn't attempted to tie it to anything and didn't trust that the river wouldn't rise further and carry it away. She rose quickly and stepped outside onto the veranda.

"Sophie, where are you going?" Adhora came out after her.

"I'm just going to tie up the boat," she shouted back as she headed into the rain again, "Uncle Joshua will kill me if anything happens to it."

Adhora stepped out into the rain too. "Wait, I'll come with you," she shouted.

"No need. Wait there! I'll be just two minutes."

Sophie ran down to where they left the boat. She waded back into the water and grabbed the rope from the bow area, then looked around for somewhere to tie it. A little further away was a thin tree, and she got back onto the dry land and heaved at the boat to pull it near enough to wrap the rope around the trunk.

Job done, she trotted up the nearest path back to the home, which brought her up to the back of the shed. It was here she had been caught by Mr Haque and Adhora's uncle. She walked along the side back to the front of the shed and saw that Adhora had taken her literally and hadn't moved an inch from the few feet in front of her uncle's *bari*. She was about to shout to her and say that when she said 'wait for me' she didn't literally mean 'stay right where you are' when Sophie herself froze in her steps.

She could see that Adhora was standing rigid. Terrified. Legs trembling, clearly deliberately *not* looking at something, breathing shallowly and fast. Sophie turned to look in the direction Adhora's head was turned against as though by not looking she could will it to go away.

There, a few metres away, half out of the bushes, shone the eyes of a tiger, and they were focused entirely on Adhora.

CHAPTER TWENTY-NINE — BAGH!

Sophie looked at Adhora again. Her friend still hadn't moved, and it was probably the best thing at that moment. Sophie tried to recall what Puli, the tiger catcher, had said all those weeks ago. Don't run. That was it. Once you run, you become the prey, even if you hadn't been until then. Adhora stood, wide-eyed and staring at the ground. From the glare of the house light, Sophie could see that the beast was being cautious – it knew such close proximity to humans was a danger – and yet, very clearly stalking Adhora. Sophie side-shuffled slowly, but as quickly as she dared, towards the shed doors hoping she wouldn't be seen. She could feel her heart beating wildly, and her mouth was dry.

Her first instinct was to run into the shed and bolt the thick doors for safety, but there were two problems with this idea. Firstly, the bolt was on the outside rather than in. She couldn't be sure she could keep that door closed if the tiger pursued and tried to prise the metal doors apart with its claws. The second was that doing so would leave Adhora stranded. Even if, somehow, she could signal Adhora to run to the shed, it would still leave the family exposed. If anyone came out to look for them – as they were sure to do soon anyway – then they would be potential prey. She could barely breathe, but she knew she had to get Adhora back into the house and warn everyone. But she had to distract the tiger for this to work.

And after that – where would Sophie go for safety?

Never mind, she'd work that out.

What if Adhora doesn't make it back in or can't shut the door in time? Sophie thought, panic rising in her throat so much she couldn't swallow. The baby's in there—the whole family.

Whether it was courage or just dumb pride, Sophie wasn't sure but was damned if she was going to let the family she had just managed to save be eaten by a cat! That just was not an option. She could feel her stubbornness kicking in and her fear subsiding. What was she going to do? There had to be something.

All she could think was to sacrifice herself. Try to make the tiger chase her and give Adhora time to escape. She knew that even if somehow the adults came out fast and chased the tiger away or killed it, whatever it would have done to Sophie by then would be too much. But she had no choice.

For a fraction of a second, she allowed herself the thought of how much she loved Adhora and how sorry she was that she was so bloody thoughtless when they were last here. How much precious time they had wasted all for the sake of dressing up in a shed. Even if they hadn't tried to escape, maybe her uncle wouldn't have come in or seen them behind the boxes or....

And that was it—the plan. Sophie knew what to do, even though she also knew there were a dozen things that could go wrong. But this was the plan, and there was no other.

It was now or never – no time to see if this could work. One way or another, this tiger was going to attack one of them. If it was Adhora, then her friend was dead. But if Sophie could draw the tiger's attention to her, she might just have a chance to live.

Might.

She ran towards the metal door, fear and excitement rushing to her head and banged on it with her fists as hard as she could. Again, remembering Puli's advice as best she could, she charged at the cat.

"Look at me, you big cowardly *bagh!*" she screamed at the creature. For a moment, the tiger was startled by her approach, as though it hadn't even noticed her before. It took a step backwards, and for a brief moment, Sophie thought the technique might scare it away. But the beast stopped, and she could tell it was sizing her up as a potential enemy.

"Get away from her, beast!" she yelled and then decided this was enough. She couldn't get too far from the shed. She turned and ran back as fast as she could with a last defiant: *"Esho biral! Ekhane esho!"*

The first three flaws in her plan were now apparent. She could not afford to look behind her to see if the tiger was chasing her. She couldn't check either that Adhora was taking advantage of her distraction and moving to safety. Worst of all, she couldn't check that if her friend *had* started moving that the tiger hadn't returned to her original target and was now pouncing on Adhora. As she reached the doors, she heard the sound of feet padding and a deep growl. One way or another, the tiger was chasing. There was no time to find out who.

For one moment, Sophie thought, *What if this is the last time anyone would see her alive again?* This was followed by; *this is a ridiculous way to go.*

Too late now. She flung open the metal doors and threw herself into the shed.

"*Dada, dada.* Come quickly!" *Didi* rushed over to Joshua, who was busy helping five other men to prop up a *dokan*. The bamboo supports had given way as the ground they were screwed into had turned to mud and washed away. Inside were hundreds of vegetables and fruits that would be destroyed if they did not keep the roof up over the produce. Joshua knew the *dokan* had to be saved. Tomorrow would be hard enough without villagers starving too. So much food had already been lost in the storm, they couldn't afford to let any more go.

"What is it, *Didi*?" he shouted impatiently. "We're a bit busy here at the moment?"

"Oh, *Dada.* Terrible news. Sophie gone!"

"What? What do you mean? She can't be. I locked the front gate. She can't get out of the *bari.*"

"Masud *bhai* came to me before and said he see girl that look like Sophie on *pukur* in boat with other girl."

"What rubbish! That Masud should stop smoking his *ganja* and try helping the village instead of going around telling stories." Another bamboo pole gave way, and suddenly the whole tin roof shifted, causing everyone to lose balance and nearly lose their grip. There was a lot of shouting, a lot of commands in Bangla – push this way, no push that way, take my weight, take my weight – and a lot more swearing from Joshua in English. He had landed hard on his knee, still pushing the pole he was gripping and keeping his side of the roof up, but he was struggling to get back on both feet. *Didi* helped him up. She was trembling from the cold. She had spent hours in the rain helping to rescue precious items from her village while the men did their best to prevent the storm from washing away their homes.

"That what I think too, *Dada,* so I went to house and check. Sophie not there! I check everywhere. She gone."

Joshua stared at her, dumbstruck for a moment.

"Blast that child," he said eventually. "Why can she never just do what she's bloody well told. Where the hell is she?" He looked at *Didi.* Bless her, the poor girl was out of her wits with worry and shivering. She should be inside, assuming her home was still standing.

"*Didi,* can you get a group of men together to go looking for her? I'll come looking as soon as we've secured this blasted *dokan.*" He felt ashamed to be asking her at all, but his niece had to be found.

"Yes, *Dada.* Of course, I will. I go now."

The flaws in her plan rushed to Sophie's mind. It had been four months or more since she had been in this shed. What if Adhora's uncle had changed everything around? She was completely in the dark and had no time to check where things were. She was about to throw herself behind boxes she hoped were still there and still where she remembered them being.

And then there was the issue of the hatch. What if Adhora's uncle had done what Sophie had heard he'd promised to do months ago and nailed shut the metal flap she and Adhora had broken through that fateful day, the last day they had been allowed to be friends? If he had, then she would be facing the most horrible and painful death any second now. She was relying on the Bengali sense of timekeeping and guessing that he might not have remembered to do the work or not yet found time for it.

She had no time to find out but launched herself into the darkness where she hoped a space would be. At the same time, she heard the sound of a thud against metal and the angry growl of a tiger. That answered her first set of questions: the tiger had followed her. Her heart raced even more. *This is it,* she thought. *This is where I live or die.*

She landed on hard ground, one leg grazing painfully against wood which she guessed were the stacked wooden boxes that hadn't been moved from before. She heard a crunch and felt one of the boxes push against her leg. Something large and heavy had just crashed into them. Sophie couldn't help but cry out in panic, and she scrambled to find the metal flap in the wall.

Her hands outstretched before her made contact with the sheet just before her head did. The sheet gave way.

"Yes!" She cried and thrust herself through the flap – arms, head, body – silently thanking Adhora's uncle for saving her life, even albeit inadvertently. Then, as she twisted her body to pull her legs out, she heard the sound of wood creaking and guessed the tiger was climbing the boxes.

Sophie pulled her feet out from under the sheet quickly, but as she did so, a huge paw shot out and slashed at the ground where legs had just been. She swore and scrabbled backwards. The paw continued to reach out through the hole, but it was clear there was no way the whole body would follow.

"Yes!" Sophie cried again, thrusting her fist in the air. Then she realised: this would have all been for nothing if the tiger turned around and came back out of the shed doors.

She scrambled to her feet, slipping in the mud but doing her best to race around to the front of the shed. Sophie desperately hoped that the tiger was still investigating the flap to see if she was still there. It was the time she would need to get the doors both closed and bolted. She knew she would not be able to hold them against the full weight and fury of the monster. She got to the front and did not even look to see where the creature was but rushed to push the door.

Something flashed in front of her, startling Sophie and making her panic. Then she realised that something had thrust itself against the door and not out of it. There stood Adhora, seemingly in her right mind now and no longer frozen in fear. She hadn't run inside as Sophie had intended she would. She'd stayed for her friend.

As both girls heaved against the metal door, they heard the menacing and angry growl from the beast within and could tell it was now coming back to the only source of light. The doors shut, and Adhora flung the huge bolt across both and into the rings on the other side just as the doors bulged violently, sending both girls crashing into a pool on the floor.

Sophie looked up to see if this was the end and grabbed her best friend's hand. If the bolt didn't hold or hadn't gone in properly, then they were both dead. But hold it did, and they heard violent crashes and bangs from inside as that magnificent devil flayed around the shed, angry at being imprisoned once again. After a few minutes, the barn went silent as the animal either came to terms with the futility of trying or was staking out other possible exits. Both girls knew there were none.

The girls still lay in the mud holding hands, panting hard, completely beyond exhausted but exhilarated. People started rushing out of the house, having heard the commotion and started chattering away at Adhora, but Sophie didn't concentrate on hearing what they said. Instead, she lay back in the mud and grinned.

The storm was over, and they had won.

She padded over to him as softly as she ever did. She knelt at his side and touched his arm gently as he crouched by the side of the road, head in his hands.

"What news?" he asked quietly.

"They have found her," she caressed his arm.

There was a pause. He wiped his eyes and looked up at her.

"And...?

"She's safe. She's alive."

She smiled that gorgeous bright white smile at him, and he looked at her tenderly. Then, he reached out and stroked her cheek.

"Take me to her *Didi*. Take me now."

"Sophie *meye*, I am so sorry."

Adhora's father looked so shaken his face was pale, and he clung to his daughter every bit as much as she was clinging to him. "You have saved my life, my wife's and both of my children. You are, from now on, like my own daughter!"

He looked down at Adhora, curled up next to him on the sofa, for a moment too.

"You too, Adhora. You showed more bravery than I ever imagined you could." Adhora grinned back at him, and Sophie could see just how proud her father had just made her. Then, he turned back to Sophie and her uncle.

"It must be the influence of this remarkable *bideshi* friend of yours."

Now it was Sophie's turn to grin. She turned to her uncle, who had his arm around her in a comforting embrace. She had never appreciated how soft and warm he felt, like a big pillow.

"Dada, I am so sorry, my brother. You were right. I never dreamed the river could flood so badly. Please forgive me."

Joshua waved a hand both to silence him and to tell him words were not needed.

"Forget it *bhai*. I am sorry that I failed to talk to you properly. I was so ignorant you were bound not to listen to me. I wouldn't have listened to me either!"

He looked at Adhora's mother coming out with her sleeping child. "Our pig-headedness nearly cost the lives of those more sensible than we." Hasan grunted his agreement and held out his hand towards Joshua, who reciprocated and shook it firmly.

"One thing I ask of you," said Joshua, "in return."

"Anything, my friend. Anything."

"I think there are two girls here who have shown just what true friendship is, defying both their guardians in order to remain loyal to each other and ultimately to save lives."

Adhora and Sophie both looked up in eager anticipation of what Sophie's uncle was about to say.

"I think it's about time we gave in and let them be friends again. Don't you?"

For a moment, Hasan said nothing and the girls held their breath. Then he smiled and said, "I would not have it any other way. Sophie is welcome in our home – our *new* home, of course – any time she wants. Our home will be her home. We are family now."

The girls looked at each other, grinning from ear to ear and then Sophie launched herself at Adhora over Mr Haque's lap and clasped her in her arms. They giggled like the schoolgirls they still were at heart.

"Just one thing," Hasan Haque said suddenly in a voice that made them stop and look at him anxiously.

"Yes, Baba?" asked Adhora.

"No more *dushto*…okay?"

Sophie grinned again. "I promise you, Dada, no more *dushto.*"

"Oh, don't promise more than you can keep," said her uncle. "I have a feeling that your mischievous days are far from over, Sophie Shepherd."

Sophie grinned at him again and then yawned. Suddenly, she was feeling incredibly tired. The rains had stopped, but she was still soaking despite the towel around her. Even the summer evening heat, which had returned after the end of the storm, was having no effect.

"I think we need to get you two to bed," said Joshua. "You both look utterly shattered."

Hasan took Adhora off along with the rest of his bedraggled family. They were going to stay the night at his brother's and then, tomorrow, would start the process of seeing exactly how bad the damage had been. Salvaging and re-building would have to wait until another day.

Outside stood an ever-increasingly large body of men, many armed with guns or their sharpened lathis, ostensibly guarding the shed but really coming to try and gawp at the tiger by clambering on the roof to look in through the windows and to be able to say they were there when it came to recounting tales in the villages later.

Uncle Joshua carried Sophie home in his arms. She was so tired that she couldn't keep her eyes open. *Didi* was waiting for them at the *bari* when they got back, and she helped to get Sophie into bed once Joshua laid her down. She got her out of her clothes, dried her down with a fresh towel and dressed her in clean pyjamas. When she was tucked up in bed, Sophie's uncle came back into the room, sat on the edge of the bed and held her hand.

Sleepily, Sophie said, "I'm sorry I disobeyed you and got out of the house. I couldn't not help Adhora."

"It's okay, pet. Don't worry," whispered her uncle as he stroked her hair. "You did well tonight, and I'm very, very proud of you."

Sophie smiled with her eyes closed and snuggled her head down into her pillow. She gave one last yawn and then fell soundly asleep, still holding her uncle's hand.

And Sophie, for the first time in well over a year, had a good night's sleep with no nightmares whatsoever.

EPILOGUE

Take this offering of my song
My heart is quivering like this lamp's flame
You, O Beautiful, are worshipped
in songs, in songs.

– Kazi Nasrul Islam

The next day it was almost as if the storm had never been. The hot Bengali sun had risen again, as it had for thousands of years, and dried the whole area. Most things were dry by the late morning, and people busied around as they usually did throughout the day. The only difference was that instead of setting up the *dokans* or transporting goods back and forth, now men, women and children were building, building anything that the storm had damaged and replacing anything it had destroyed. The work would take days, but it would happen.

The river was still swollen and flowing fast but abated a little day by day. Adhora's house had suffered considerable damage, but at least it was still standing. Ten houses on the outskirts of the village had been destroyed – caught completely by the flood – and many others had lost roofs because of the storm. There were five deaths recorded in the early days, most tragically of all, though others were missing. Periodically, high-pitched wailing sounded in the area as another body was found and returned to a family.

Sophie missed all of the rebuilding. She slept through the whole day but woke briefly in the evening. By that point, a fever had come to her, and she could only just eat some soup and a little bread. She slept well, though, and the next day the fever came down, and she was well enough to sit up in bed and start eating properly. It was the third day when she was strong enough to leave the house, and it was a Friday. It was time to go back to the *pukur*

— this time in glorious sunshine rather than the torrential and deadly rain. She did so but limped all the way. Her body was still full of aches and pains, and she had bruises all over. But, with her uncle's help, she made it to the jetty where he liked to fish. He set up his rods, and Sophie sat quietly by his side.

"You know, I never thought I would like it here. I've spent so long desperately wishing I was back in England," Sophie said thoughtfully. Joshua nodded and gave a little grunt as he threw out the line. "But now I can't help but wonder what I saw in the place," she added.

"The west has a lot to offer, you know," Joshua replied, looking at Sophie. "There's no shame in being English, you know, Sophie. Don't think that I don't miss old Blighty in some ways. There are many things I wish I had from there that I can't get here. You, at least, will get a chance to go back there one day. I'm too old now to bother."

He looked around and signalled all around with his hand. "This is my home," he said. "I don't have any other, and I don't want any other."

Sophie looked around the *pukur*. It was so peaceful today, as if the events of the other night had never happened. The sun was out, the birds were singing, the village was humming in the background with a thousand jobs being done by hand. The *pukur's* waters were still and calm apart from the occasional ripple from a fish snacking on a mosquito, and the odd splash from the banks as a snake slithered into the water for a swim.

"Hmm. I'm beginning to think the same thing. What else could you want that you don't get here?"

They were both silent for a while, sitting watching the waters. Nothing stirred, and the rod remained motionless. Even the fish, it seemed, did not want to cause a stir, not even for a tasty morsel. Six months ago, Sophie had been dying of boredom doing this with her uncle. Where was the adventure in fishing? But now, she'd had her fill of adventure and had an inkling that this was not so unusual for the Bengalis here. So for now, just for now, peace and quiet were enough.

Eventually, one of them had to break the silence.

"Marshmallows."

"What?"

"Marshmallows."

"What about them?"

"That's what I would want," said Uncle Joshua with a sheepish grin. "That's what I miss from England. A big bag of marshmallows to toast on an open fire during December when it gets a little chillier."

Sophie laughed. Even now, her uncle surprised her. Just when you were used to his serious, gruff nature, he would come out with these bizarre, funny and very *human* comments. Deep down, she thought, there is a sense of humour in him forever trying to break out.

Uncle Joshua grinned back at her and then turned back to his rod, serious face back on but with an uncontrollable smirk that Sophie could see clearly. Instinctively, she linked her arm through his and leaned her cheek on his shoulder. She could feel him tense for a moment, turn his head to look at her for just a second, then turn back and relax. It seemed she surprised him as much as he surprised her.

"What happened to the *bagh*?" she said without moving from his arm.

"Don't worry. The authorities were contacted, and they came by morning time with all the right paraphernalia. You know, I think you've ended up saving that tiger's life too. If she had killed someone, that would have been the end. You're a bit of a legend now, by the way. *Everyone* knows you caught a tiger 'with your bare hands!'"

Sophie laughed.

"They'll have me walking on water next," she giggled.

"Well, between Adhora and Hasan regaling everyone with the tale of what you two did, I suspect that trick is already a 'known fact'."

She grinned and then added, "I'm glad she's safe anyway."

"Who? Adhora or the tiger?"

"Ha! Both, I guess, though I meant the tiger really. She was only doing what nature has compelled her to do. I think she was actually quite scared with all the flooding."

"Yes," Uncle Joshua nodded, "I think the theory is that she ended up here because she was carried down the river by the flooding and only got to dry land near Hasan's brother's place. It's a miracle no one from that family was eaten earlier. God knows when the tiger arrived."

"We've all been very lucky, I think. Or blessed by God. Even the tiger."

Uncle Joshua grunted.

"You're right, but that animal better not escape again. Or better still, they need to return her to the *Sundarbans* where she belongs."

Sophie nodded and then snuggled into his arm again. He felt comfortable, and for a long while, she said nothing at all.

"You never mention my mum," she said, serious for a moment. She felt his body tense again but decided to push further. "You've talked about my dad, and I know you two didn't get on. But never Mum. Why?"

Joshua was silent for a moment; then, he took in a deep breath.

"You know I knew Elizabeth before your dad did? I introduced them."

He pulled at a piece of grass by his side and threw it into the water. "I've spent years thinking what an idiot I was. At the time, I was quite certain my brother didn't deserve her."

Sophie knew better than to push things further than that. If Uncle Joshua opened up about something, that would swiftly turn to anger, and she didn't want to spoil the moment. But she knew enough for now. At the very least, Uncle Joshua had had feelings for her mum, and he'd fallen out with her dad over the matter, long before they were married presumably. Maybe that was why Uncle Joshua had come to Bangladesh? He had left round about when they would have got engaged, she reckoned. He certainly hadn't been there while Sophie had been growing up, which made her certain he had gone by then.

She sat there quietly, not expecting another word from him, but suddenly, he put down his rod, turned his body and grabbed her by the arms.

"Sophie," he said, looking slightly misty-eyed, "I've always thought their marriage was a mistake, and I've blamed my brother for years for 'ruining' Elizabeth's life."

Sophie went to say something, but he carried on without pause.

"But you coming here has made me think again. Made me wonder if I was not too harsh on him – on them both, really. How can he have got it so wrong if the result was, well…you? You remind me so much of your mother, do you know that?"

Sophie shook her head. She could feel tears welling up in her eyes as he spoke.

"Well, you do. Maybe that's why I was so harsh on you to begin with. I wanted to keep you at a distance. I was shocked at how much pain I felt and annoyed with myself that I could still have such a weakness. I've given my whole life to helping this community, and I did not expect to have such a distraction."

"Is that what I am?" asked Sophie trying to blink tears away.

"To begin with, maybe, but you are so much your mother and… Uncle Joshua looked down for a moment, "and quite a bit your dad too. So you have an unfortunate share of the same Shepherd genes as I have."

Sophie laughed.

"Yes, I know what you mean."

"What I'm trying to say, Sophie," Uncle looked straight into her eyes, "is that I've come to love you very much. I've never had a wife, a family, so I don't know how to be a parent. I'm sorry I'm pretty rubbish at it. But I am glad you came into our lives. Into *my* life. I will miss you when you go home to England. You will undoubtedly do that one day – you have to. You can't stay here forever. You need your own culture. But for now, I am very, very glad you are here with me, with *Didi*. You are a blessing, believe it or not."

Sophie said nothing for a moment. She knew, at that moment, that this was her *home* now. England held nothing there that she wanted. She wanted to be here. Not just for Adhora and *Didi* and *Mashima*. Not even for Uncle Joshua himself, realising too just how much affection she had for him. But for Bangladesh itself. *Ami Bangalee,* she thought to herself, getting a feel for the words. They were coming true.

She linked arms with him again as he went back to his rod.

"I don't need my own culture. Not today," she said. "I think we can go a few years before we need to worry about that. Besides, when I want to think of my own cold, isolated English ways, I'll always have *Wuthering Heights* to read."

"Yes," Uncle Joshua agreed with a laugh, without looking up from his rod. "I think we can. If for no other reason than I swear it will take you years to finish that book again."

Silence fell again. The water was peaceful. The village was calm.

"Right then!" Sophie sat up with a determined look on her face. "If I'm going to be here a bit longer, I think it's about time I did the dutiful *meye* thing and learned how to do this fishing lark. You've hogged this *pukur* far too long."

Uncle Joshua laughed. "I thought you hated fishing?"

"I've changed," said Sophie, a twinkle in her eye. "It doesn't seem such a bad thing now."

I've changed, she thought to herself, *I'm not the same person I was. I've got rid of some of my demons, and for the first time in my life, I feel like I could get rid of them all one day.*

She looked over the *pukur*. If this quiet village pool had not been here, some people would not be alive now. Sophie herself might have been physically, but she wouldn't have been so inside. The place that had been so full of fear and danger for her had come to represent everything here that had given life back to her. She was not the same Sophie Shepherd who stepped off that plane nearly a year ago. She had changed.

And the change was for the better.

She floats over the lake, her bare feet just dipping into the cool refreshing waters from time to time. She approaches the bank and can see a figure standing on it. The figure is all in white and seems to be glowing. Is this an angel? She hears a distant sound and looks in the direction it came from. Standing on the opposite bank is a dark, shadowy figure. She can feel the malevolence, the anger and the blame emanating from the darkness, but somehow she knows it cannot get to her. It cannot get to the other side of the lake. It no longer belongs to these waters.

But she does. It does not know how to cross to the other side. She does. It can no longer harm her and, even if it could, she knows the strange figure in white will keep her safe.

She turns back to the figure who is very close now. She can see her face, smiling. She knows this face. She knows it well. She reaches the bank and runs to this woman in white. They hold each other, and she is filled with joy. Out of the corner of her eye, she sees the darkness move away and leave, vanishing into nothing. It will not come again. She looks into the eyes of the woman she knows. So beautiful, so perfect. She mouths words silently, knowing in this place she cannot speak. I'm sorry, she tries to say. I'm sorry you died. I'm sorry I made it happen. The woman says nothing but looks at her and smiles. Warmth floods them both. Then the woman releases her hold, turns around and slowly walks away. She does not try to chase after this beautiful, magnificent woman of light. She does not need to. The smile told her everything and gave her everything. The smile will see her through any darkness. She knows she is loved. She knows she is forgiven.

And that is enough for now.

Light, O my light, the world-filling light, eye-kissing light,
   heart-ripening light!

Ah, how the light dances, my love, at the centre of my life;

it strikes the chords of my desire, my love;

the sky opens and the rivers run wild, as laughter covers the whole earth.

Butterflies spread their wings on an ocean of light,

lilies and jasmines rise up on the crest of a wave of light.

The light breaks into glittering gold on every cloud,

and spreads a profusion of jewels, my love.

Mirth spreads from leaf to leaf and endless is the gladness, my love.

The river of heaven has burst its banks and a flooded abroad with joy.

— *Gitanjali,* Rabindranath Tagore

GLOSSARY

Acha/Thik achey	Okay, no problem
Alhamdulilah	Praise God; used by Muslims
Alna	Clothes rail
Alta	Red dye used to paint hands and feet
Amar	My; mine
Ami	I, me
Amma	Muslim word for mother
Apa	Older sister, also used as an honorific term for any older woman
Asalaam alaiakum	Traditional greeting by Muslims
Ashroy	Shelter, safety
Ayah	Housemaids, cleaners and child carers, common in middle- and upper-class homes
Azaan	The Islamic call to prayer played from all mosques
Bagan	Garden
Bagh	Tiger
Bangalee	Bengali; roughly equivalent to Bangladeshi but includes people from West Bengal in India too
Bapre bap!	Expression suggesting wonder or exasperation
Bari	House
Baul	Bauls are spiritual singers with both religious ideology and singing tradition
Bazaar	Market
Beshi abheg	Literally 'too much emotion'
Beton	Wages
Bhai	Brother, a term of respect given to adult men
Bhut	Ghost
Bibhag	Division. Bangladesh is split into eight divisions.
Bideshi	Foreigner; someone not from Bangladesh
Biral	Cat
Bon	Sister, little sister
Boro Din	Literally 'Big Day' – Christmas

Boro lok	Literally 'big person' – important person or dignitary
Bosho	Please sit down
Boti	A sharp metal blade on a stand that sits on the floor. Food is sliced by pushing the food towards the blade, and the stand is usually held in place by the foot.
Cha	Tea, usually milky, thick and very sweet.
Chador	Thick blanket worn like a scarf during winter months
Chagol	Goat
Chamoch	Spoon
Chawallah	Seller of cha, usually in the streets
Chula	Cooking stove made in the ground from mud and using straw as fuel for heat.
Chumu	Kiss
Chuti	Time off, holiday, vacation
Daal	Soup-like food made from chickpeas
Dada	Usually means 'older brother' but occasionally 'grandfather.' Both often used as honorific terms
Dak nam	Nickname or familial name for everyday use
Dawat	Dinner invitation
Deshi	From Bangladesh
Dhak	Large double-ended drum played by striking bamboo sticks at each end
Dhol	Long double-ended drums worn with a strap
Dhonnobad	Thank you
Dhorni lok	Rich person
Didi	Sister; an honorific term for any older woman
Din	Day
Dokan	Shop
Dotara	Literally 'two strings,' a stringed instrument used commonly with folk music
Dudher Machi	Milk Flies – an expression similar to 'fair-weather friends,' meaning people who appear when someone is prospering.
Dushto	Naughty, naughtiness
Ekhane	Here
Ektara	Literally 'one string,' a one-stringed instrument played by picking the string and squeezing the sides to alter pitch.

Esho	Command to come given to a young or inferior person
Gamcha	Towel or piece of cloth
Gaye holud	Literally 'yellow body.' A traditional form of pre-marriage party where guests feed the bride-to-be and smear each other in yellow turmeric paste.
Ghorar dim	Horse's egg – an expression roughly the same as 'fool's gold'
Ghush	Bribe
Gourib	Poor
It khana	Brick-making factories
Jari	Songs from the Islamic tradition
Jubok/jubokra	Young males, roughly aged 12 -25; plural jubokra
Kao	Drink; an instruction to drink given to younger or inferior persons
Khal	Stream
Khata	Books to write in – usually in the form of exercise books for students
Khoda Hefez	God be with you
Kirton	Call and response song from Hindu tradition
Kobiraj	Folk doctor
Kombol	Blanket
Kuli	Porter
Kuwasha	Fog
Laal cha	Literally 'red tea' – cha without milk which has a sweet and bitter taste
Lagbe	Needed. E.g., 'cha lagbe' = I need tea
Lichee bagan	Garden area of trees giving lychee fruit
Lok	Person
Lunghi	Wraparound cloth worn by men either working in the fields or rickshaws) or relaxing at home
Maf korun	Please forgive me
Mali	Narrow muddy walkway separating one paddy field from another
Mangsho	Meat
Mashi	Maternal aunt

Mashima	Aunty, mother's sister – 'ma' is added as a term of respect for any older woman. Used by non-Muslim Bangladeshis
Mathi	Field
Meye	Girl, daughter; an honorific term for a girl who you consider to be family
Mishti	Sweet food, pudding
Moyna	Myna bird
Mughlai	A range of spicy food blended from styles of Persia and India
Mukti bahini	Freedom fighters from the Independence War of 1971
Murgha wallah	Street seller of chicken meat
Muri	Puffed rice, often mixed with various spices for a snack or added to laal cha
Napit	Barber
Nasta	Snacks, usually fried
Nodi/ nodina	River
Nolkup	Deep water well operated by pumping a handle to bring up water
Nomoshka	Non-Muslim greeting; the equivalent of 'Hello.'
Ondhokar	Darkness
Ore!	Expressive statement of disbelief.
Orna	Long scarf made of thin material, worn by women around the neck or over the head, primarily to show modesty but also has a range of uses such as to dry hands or tie up keys, money, etc.
Oshikkhito	Uneducated person
Pagol/pagla	Mad; pagla is used for males
Paka bari	Buildings made from concrete
Poisha	Smaller currency than taka. Very rarely used
Pukur	Pond or pool
Punjabi	Longer kameeze-like dress for men which reaches to the knees or lower
Rakkosh	Mythical monster
Rickshaw	Three-wheeled bicycle with seats at the back. The most common form of transport in Bangladesh, particularly in Dhaka

Rickshaw wallah	Owner and pedaller of a rickshaw
Sari	Woman's formal dress made from one long drape wrapped around the waist with one end draped over the shoulder
Shalwa kameeze	Loose and baggy shirt and trouser combination worn by unmarried girls and working women made of pyjama material
Sheetkal	Winter season
Shetu	Small bridges, usually for roads going over rivers and streams
Shonggi	Companion, someone who helps
Shukor bacha	Insult; literally 'child of a pig'
Shukto	Popular vegetable dish in Bangladesh
Sundarbans	The world's largest mangrove forest area shared between India and Bangladesh, on Bangladesh's southwest coast
Taka	The main currency of Bangladesh
Tiffin	Metal containers that stack on top of each other, commonly used for snacks and lunches
Upozila	The smaller districts of zilas. There are 493 in Bangladesh
Vangari	Three-wheeled bicycle with a large flat wooden back end, used for transporting large goods or several people at a time
Wallah	General word for someone in charge of something such as a stall, rickshaw, vangari or similar
Zila	The name for major sections, rather like counties. There are six-four zilas in Bangladesh

ACKNOWLEDGEMENTS

This novel has taken many years to write and it is hard to remember just how many have come and gone who have been a part of its making. There are so many that I can't name you all, but there are a few I must give mention to here.

Thank you to Grace Priyana Pahan for her advice about fishing in the 'real pukur' along with anecdotes which inspired some elements of the story, and to Holly Roy who gave me important advice concerning medical procedures when dealing with head injuries. Any errors resulting are entirely due to my own misunderstanding.

Thank you too to the staff and students at LAMB English Medium School who put up with my own 'Uncle Joshua' moments and allowed me many happy years of teaching there. It is because of you, and everyone at our little NGO tucked away in rural Bangladesh, that I wanted to write this story. It's meant to be a tribute; I hope you found it so.

I've had several people read parts of this novel over the years and give their advice – you were all so helpful and I couldn't have done it without you. Two people especially must be mentioned for trudging through the whole thing: Muna Hoque and Nicholas Graham. You both gave me good advice and generous encouragement in equal measure.

Finally, I must thank everyone at Histria Books for taking a chance on this unusual story. Dr. Kurt Brackob, Sheila Grimes, Dana Ungureanu, Silvio Sequera, and Diana Livesay have all contributed to getting my manuscript into print, putting up with my rookie errors and constant demands along the way. I'm glad we've worked together on this – thank you for making this book become a physical reality.

And finally, finally, I must thank Vikki, Sam, and Jess for putting up with me right from the beginning when I announced I was going to become a writer and have handled me when I've had deadlines to meet and became useless for anything else so many times now I think we've all lost count (and, perhaps, hope). I guess, for now, I'm still not going to get a real job. Ah well.

ABOUT THE AUTHOR

D.K. Powell is a freelance writer, educationalist and social activist living in the UK but working around the world. He is the author of the acclaimed *Sonali* (2016), the bestselling *The Old Man on the Beach and other stories* and the highly popular *Try not to Laugh*, a study and revision guide for students. He has written several educational courses on psychology, sociology, and related subjects and has contributed chapters to numerous educational and academic books. His articles are regularly published in major publications all over the world.

D.K. Powell was born in Wigan in 1971, trained as a teacher in Cambridge in the 1990s, where he met his wife, and they moved to Cumbria in 2000, where they raised their two children. In 2005 his family's love affair with Bangladesh began, with several visits occurring until they moved out there in 2008 to work for an international medical NGO. He worked as an educational consultant, training teachers and providing O Level education at the NGO school. While living in Bangladesh, he began writing commercially and turned full-time as a freelance writer in 2013. He returned with his family to Cumbria, UK, in 2014 but continues to make regular visits to Bangladesh and other parts of Asia.

D.K. Powell writes and speaks on social and cultural issues internationally and writes as a journalist and reviewer for national newspapers. His TEDx talk on '*Why we need to embrace the Global Village*' has been watched over 40,000 times, and he is in demand as a guest speaker. He continues to give training and advice to education providers throughout Asia and can be contacted for speaking engagements or consultancy advice at dkpowell.contact@gmail.com.

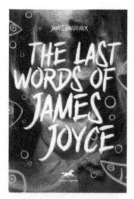

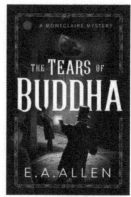
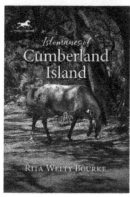